Charles Egan was born in Nottingham, England, of Irish parents.

When he was five, the family returned to Ireland as his father had been appointed Resident Medical Superintendent of St. Lukes, a psychiatric hospital in Clonmel, in County Tipperary.

Every summer they visited his father's family's farm, outside Kiltimagh in County Mayo for a month, where his grandmother and uncles spent many evenings talking about family and local history.

The family subsequently moved to County Wicklow, where Charles Egan initially attended the De La Salle Brother's school in Wicklow town. He then went to the Jesuit's Clongowes Wood College (James Joyce's alma mater), and subsequently studied Commerce in University College Dublin, graduating in 1973.

After an initial career in the private sector, including Marubeni Dublin, (where he met his wife, Carmel), he joined the Industrial Development Authority (IDA) in Dublin. After a few years, the desire to be his own boss led him to resign and set up his own business, which has now been running for over 30 years.

Apart from business, his main interests are history, film and worldwide travel. Find out more at www.thekillingsnows.com.

Also by the author

The Exile Breed
Cold is the Dawn

The Killing Snows

CHARLES EGAN

SilverWood

First published in 2008 by Discovered Authors
Re-published in 2010 by CallioCrest
Third edition (revised) published in 2012 by the author using
SilverWood Books Empowered Publishing®
14 Small Street, Bristol BS1 1DE
www.silverwoodbooks.co.uk

ISBN 978-1-78132-057-0 (paperback)
ISBN 978-1-78132-058-7 (ebook)

British Library Cataloguing in Publication Data
A CIP catalogue record for this book is available from the British Library

Set in Sabon by SilverWood Books
Printed on responsibly sourced paper

"Good God, what a frightful thing this is, happening to such a people, to such a country, all Christendom looking on."

The Telegraph or Connaught Ranger
County Mayo, August 1846

For Carmel

without whose encouragement and hard work
this book would not have been written

Preface

This book is fiction. The story that inspired it was not.

In 1990, I came into possession of two documents which were fascinating, and in their own way, quite savage.

My father had been brought up on a small farm in County Mayo in the West of Ireland. Following the death of one of his brothers, he gave us a box of documents which, by their dates, had been stored for over a hundred years. They included a lease, a number of letters and two payrolls from the 1840s.

It was with a sense of shock that I realised what they really were. These were the documentary evidence of the Great Irish Famine in East Mayo. They were also the confirmation of the stories I had learnt as a child as to how my family survived the Famine.

The two payrolls were the most horrific. They detailed the wages for gangs of men, women and children working on two roads in east Mayo in the winter of 1846. The desperately low rates of pay proved that this was Famine Relief. Local research filled in more of the story, a brutal one of hunger, fever and death.

The Irish Famine had started with the partial failure of the potato crop in the autumn of 1845. In 1846 the potato failed again, and this time the failure was nearly total. The Workhouses could not cope, and so the enormous Famine Relief schemes were started, and kept running through the coldest and worst winter of the past 300 years. Hundreds of thousands of starving people were employed on roadworks, building and repairing roads all across Ireland.

Hunger killed thousands of them. The murderous blizzard of December 1846 killed many thousands more, and brought the Works to a halt all across the country. But they opened again in January 1847, and the arctic cold went on. By the time the soup kitchens took over in March the Works were employing three quarters of a million survivors, mostly in the West of Ireland, all trying desperately to feed their families on pitifully low wages. Then, as the winter receded, a vicious fever epidemic killed hundreds of thousands of people right across Ireland. 1846 was shocking, but Black '47 would never be forgotten.

But the research also confirmed an old family tradition which I had never believed. This was the story of utterly impossible love set against the terror of the times. So in the end 'The Killing Snows' is much more than historical fiction. It is an attempt to understand how such a love could have happened and how the impossible became true.

Finally, a note about italic use in this book. Where the reader sees dialogue in italics, the character is speaking in Irish. In County Mayo in the 1840s few could speak English, and even those that could often spoke Irish out of preference.

Charles Egan

Luke's Family

Luke Ryan
Michael, his father
Eleanor, his mother
Pat, his younger brother

Murty Ryan, Luke's uncle
Aileen, Murty's wife
Danny, their eldest son
Nessa, their daughter
Murtybeg, their youngest son
Brigid, Nessa's daughter

Sabina McKinnon, Luke's aunt
Ian McKinnon, Sabina's husband

All characters, except for a few historical persons, are fictitious.

In County Mayo, the county towns of Castlebar, Claremorris, Westport and Ballina are real, but the East Mayo towns of Kilduff, Knockanure and Brockagh are fictitious, as are the settlements and mountains around them.

Prologue

In November, the first snows came to County Mayo.

The wind came from the east and north east, bringing bitter cold and blizzards from Siberia. Some nights it snowed, but the next day the people would still tramp through it, rags wrapped around their feet. Some days too, the snow was blown on a violent gale that brought to mind the Big Wind of 1839. Now he saw the full cruelty of the piecework system. The work rate slowed, the wages dropped.

Every morning, he rode out to the Relief Works with a feeling of dread. He rode past skeletal figures struggling against the wind, out along to where the roads were being built. They ignored him, it was as if he did not even exist, but he was used to this by now. Whether he wanted it or not, his duty was to supervise the Works, and theirs was to work.

By the winter of 1846, the Workhouses across Mayo were full, tens of thousands still clamouring for admission. Road-building was the Government's answer, the last and only chance for hungry people to earn their few pennies for corn. Here in the mountains he was the supervisor, the one who forced them to work or die. They despised him, and he felt he could not blame them. How could it have come to this?

For stone they collected rocks from the fields around, but this ran out. There were many places where rock showed through the surface. With an eye well used to this, he had small quarries started beside the roads. They were tiny compared to anything he had ever seen in England, but even so, as they deepened, the people fought for the right to work in them. They were the only places where they could work out of reach of the freezing winds.

But still they came.

Every evening, as he rode back to his lodgings, he would think of her. When he arrived, she would be with her mother, cooking. Hard gritty corn, cabbage or turnips, rarely meat. He would sit with her father at the table, sometimes talking about the Works, more often silent. Always she would serve the food, leaning across him as he sat, her breast touching his shoulder or her knee touching his leg. For fear of what her father might say, he tried not to look at her, but it was impossible. Whenever their glances met, she smiled at him.

Already he knew what her father thought. He saw him as a Government man, an outsider. Even though the two men worked together, and worked

11

well, the older man would always treat him with suspicion.

As the cold intensified on the roads, the people stuffed hay inside the saturated rags around their feet, but their toes and shins were bare; blue and purple and black with cold. Few had jackets, and very few had coats. The women tied their shawls around the children's bodies as they worked. They brought blankets too and wrapped them around their freezing bodies. Many days it snowed or sleeted without cease, and the heavy wool only absorbed the bitter cold water faster. The children were the first to die, but age no longer mattered now. Every day, there were deaths on the Works.

Sometimes the wind would shift to the south, the temperature would rise and his spirits with it. But always it shifted back again, and the Siberian cold returned. By December, people spoke of the worst winter in memory; no, more than that, the worst that Mayo had ever seen. Blizzards for days on end, lakes frozen over, drifts higher than a man, men and animals dead from the never-ending cold.

And the Works went on.

As the people died, and the numbers dropped, he would accompany the priest around the parish, or ride around on his own, to recruit more workers. Some days he had to fight his way through gales and drifts to pay the dying, or the families of those who had already died. But still he signed up more for the Works. He kept hoping, desperately hoping, for an easing in the weather.

But the cold continued, the Works went on, and the people died.

He kept thinking of her, he could not stop. It was more than attraction, much more. The horror of the days was bringing him close to the edge. Sometimes he felt a fear of the mountain. Many days he could not even look at it. He did not know why this should be, but often he felt himself slipping towards the void, and only the thought of her would bring him back. It was not just that he wanted her; it was that he needed her, more perhaps than he had ever needed anyone. Only the evenings in the house, the warmth of the fire, the warmth of her presence, gave him the strength to wake in the mornings and ride back to the Works.

He was caught. During the blizzards, all human feeling in him screamed to stop the Works, but if he did the roads would never be built, and he knew what Morton would think of that. Worse, he would not be able to pay them, not even the basic wage. Nothing.

So the Works went on.

Every two hours he called a halt. They built fires sheltered from the freezing winds; shivering in the quarries, behind hummocks, behind the walls of abandoned cabins and houses, anywhere they could get in from the cold. This caused fighting, as everyone tried to get closest to the fires, so he began to stagger the breaks, allowing only twenty off work at a time. At first the people carried their own turf slung over their backs in rough-made carriers of blankets and rags, but many families had little enough turf for the freezing winter, and they began to steal it from ricks belonging to families living in cabins near the Works. This caused more fighting, and he tried to have it stopped, but it was impossible.

He tried to use dead wood from the woods nearby, but this was wet or frozen through. He had rough shelters built beside the fires, trying to dry the wood, and sometimes he succeeded. But no matter what was done, it could not keep the cold away. As he rode down the lines of workers, all he could see were hammers, pickaxes and shovels grasped in rag-wrapped hands, lifting and swinging slowly. Rags on hands! He had never seen that on the railways. There were many things here that he had never seen. Driving sleet and snow for weeks at a time. Bitter winds screaming down from the mountains.

Dead men. Dead women and children.

But still they came.

When he was not thinking of her, he was thinking of a time before the blight and hunger. Carrigard – a different world then. Only twenty miles away, but it might as well have been a thousand. The farm and the house, his father and brother planting and reaping, his mother baking brown bread and cooking potatoes. Family and friends.

And the love of another woman then.

Was that so important now? He no longer knew.

He thought too of the years he had worked on the English railways – another world again. The gang, the comradeship, everyone talking and laughing long into the night. It was hard work building railways, but he had been earning more money then than he could ever have earned in Mayo. Far more.

But he had left it all, and for what? For this? No, not this.

He had returned from England to farm again in Mayo. Even then there had been hunger, but not like this. When he had returned, he could not have known that this would happen, no-one could.

But it had happened, and he knew that he would never again be certain of anything, not even of life itself.

Chapter One

He had come home in April, because his father had ordered him home.

Luke's father, Michael Ryan, was perhaps the toughest man that Luke had ever known. Michael had expected total obedience from him, not only through the years of his childhood, but also through all the years he had spent working in England.

Michael was a tenant farmer – a smallholder – in Carrigard, a small estate of twenty farms outside the village of Kilduff in the east of County Mayo. The estate was owned by the Burke family, who were based in County Galway. Michael's lease was tiny – eight Irish acres, or fourteen acres in English statute measure. But it was the largest farm in Carrigard, and Michael was a man to respect, accustomed to responsibility from a young age.

Michael had been only fifteen when he took over the running of the farm, after his own father had been imprisoned. Luke was curious about this, but he could get no information on it. He knew that it related to the Rebellion of 1798, but he had no idea how. He never dared to ask Michael about it, and anyone else he asked refused to talk of '98.

Whatever the cause, Luke's grandfather had spent ten years in Claremorris Gaol. He spent all those years breaking stones, and in the end the stones broke him. When the old man was released in 1808, he was no longer a man to respect. He had a son well used to authority, running the farm alone and commanding the respect of everyone in the family, including his own mother. But Michael had to yield authority to the older man, and bitterness ensued. Michael knew how to farm, but reckoned his father knew nothing.

It was then that Michael had conceived the idea of the quarry. He wrote to the landlord in Galway suggesting that they bid on a maintenance contract for the roads around Carrigard. The contract had been for five pounds a year, and was in the name of the landlord and nominally in the name of Michael's father. The quarry was located on the edge of the farm. It had given Michael the chance of running the farm on his own again, and it gave his father – Luke's grandfather – the chance to do the only thing he knew how.

Breaking stones.

For fourteen years Michael waited. But the old man hung on and did not die until the fever epidemic which came with the famine of 1822. Michael's mother was already ill and died a few weeks later. The next year, when he had paid off the back-rent, he travelled to County Galway to meet the landlord and his agent. He negotiated a twenty-one year lease, which was rare in Mayo. Now the law was on his side. If the rent was paid, he could not be evicted. As soon as he returned to Carrigard, he started to build a solid stone house beside the mud cabin that the family and cattle had lived in for generations. He left the old cabin to the cattle and, in a year of brutally hard labour, he worked the farm, quarried rock, broke stones, repaired roads, and built his house. He was forty years old and a free man at last.

In 1824, he married Eleanor O'Kelly, his younger brother's sister-in-law. Of their children that lived beyond a year, Luke was born in 1825, Pat in 1828 and Alicia in 1836.

By 1846, Luke was working as a navvy building railways in England, Pat was helping his father to work the farm and quarry in Mayo, and Alicia was dead.

Luke was at breakfast in his lodgings in Dover when Michael's letter arrived. He glanced through it, before reading it again more slowly. Then he folded it and stuffed it into his pocket.

'What does he have to say?' Danny asked.

'Nothing much,' Luke said. He stood up to leave the table.

'You've left half your breakfast,' Danny said.

'You can have it.'

When the men were finished eating, they walked out along the railway to the cutting. It was raining. Luke and Danny joined the other men, hacking away the sides with their picks, while the others shovelled the clay and shale towards the wagons.

Danny was Luke's cousin. He had been working on the railways in England since the age of twelve and had developed a quick witted toughness since then. Unlike most of the gang he, like Luke, could read and write, and he could calculate faster than almost anyone.

After two hours, Matt McGlinn brought their tea bucket to the shack. When he came back, Luke and Danny scooped up mugs of tea and stood by one of the wagons. The rain had stopped.

'Aren't you going to tell us?' Danny asked.

'I told you,' Luke said, 'it's nothing.'

'I thought someone was dead, from the way it took you.'

'No-one's dead.'

Owen Corrigan was leaning on his shovel, staring at the ground. 'It's the hunger, isn't it?'

'Perhaps it is,' Luke said.

'Of course it is,' McGlinn said. 'It's in every letter we're getting from

Ireland, nothing but hunger and more hunger and send us more money. You'd never know how bad it is, they make it worse in the telling.'

Luke said nothing more. They finished their tea and went back to work. Corrigan's question had surprised him. Michael's letter had not even mentioned hunger, and that was odd. McGlinn was right. Everyone else wrote telling of hunger in Mayo, but Michael never did.

It was getting dark when Farrelly called a halt, and they walked back along the track towards their lodgings. Luke went upstairs and flung himself on his bunk. He stared again at Michael's letter.

For six years he had been with the gang. There were twenty of them, all Mayo men, working under Farrelly as their own elected gang-master. They had built railways all the way up and across England, from the western end of the Great Western Railway snaking towards Exeter, up to the Lancaster & Carlisle approaching the Scottish border and down again to the eastern terminus of the South Eastern at Dover.

Farrelly ruled absolutely. He was tough, a man to respect and totally honest. He never took a skim from the gang's earnings but ensured that most of their wages, after board and lodgings, were saved or remitted home to Mayo.

Luke had every intention of continuing working in England. But then Michael's letter had arrived. 'Come now, or come never.'

He knew his father well enough to know what that meant.

The door opened, and Danny came in. 'What in hell's biting you?' he asked.

'Nothing. I was just tired.'

'The devil, you were. Luke Ryan tired this early. You expect me to believe that?'

'Why can't I be tired?'

'Because I'm not letting you. Come on down, and join the rest of us.'

'But I don't want to.'

Danny sat on the bunk across from him. 'Look, don't let the hunger worry you. All you have to do is work hard and send them money. They'll be happy enough.'

'I suppose you're right.'

'I am right. You know I'm right. Now come on down.'

'Not now. I'll come later.'

'Have it your own way,' Danny said. He went out and closed the door.

Luke lay back again watching the flickering light of the fire on the ceiling. Yes, it was odd about the letter, but he reckoned if the family was really hungry Michael would have said it. Or would he? With his father it was impossible to tell. Still, he was sending enough money home. Even if the price of corn had gone up, there would be enough to feed them all. But if they were

17

depending on his wages, what would happen when he went home?

Go home? Six years he had been waiting to go home. Waiting to see family and old friends. Waiting to farm again in Mayo. Now at last he was going home, but he no longer wanted it. Why not? Why should he think like this? He did not know.

A few nights later, Farrelly called the gang together. They gathered in the bunk room, sitting on bunks or leaning against the wall. Danny was lying on his bunk in the corner.

'I wanted to tell ye,' Farrelly said, 'I met one of Brassey's fellows today. They're looking for men up in Yorkshire – the Leeds & Thirsk Railway. Brassey's got the contract.'

There was silence around the room.

The men had not worked under Thomas Brassey since 1844. They all knew that Brassey was the largest railway contractor in Britain, but far more important was that he never permitted subcontractors to exploit the gangs. When they were working for Brassey, Farrelly negotiated directly with his managers, bypassing the subcontractors and agreeing a rate for each job based on cubic yards of muck shifted or yards of rail laid.

No subcontractors meant they were free to work as they pleased. There was no base wage, but Farrelly expected long hours of hard labour, and then the men in the gang earned wages that were among the highest on the railways. It was tough work, but the gang were well used to that and even took a certain pride in it. But Brassey was not the contractor for the South Eastern, and for two years they had been working under a subcontractor they despised, at wages that were hardly half of what they had earned before.

At last Bernie Lavan spoke. 'Brassey?'

'None other.'

'He has the contract?'

'He has. Or sure as hell the most of it.'

'Well, that could sort a lot of things out.'

Danny had pulled himself up on the bunk. 'It'll sort things out, right enough. God knows, there's little enough work left around here, and to be working for Brassey again, what more could we ask?'

'That'd be up to Martin,' Lavan said. 'But one thing's for certain, Brassey's the best, and if we don't get the best deal out of his fellows, we're no good at all.'

As the other men walked to their bunks, Danny and Luke stepped outside. It was a clear evening, not yet cold.

'By God,' Danny said, 'wasn't that a surprise. Back up north, and working with the best contractor in England.'

'It'll be great for you all, no doubt,' Luke said.

'For us all?'

'I'm not going.'

'You're not what?'

'I'm going home.'

'Going home. You're going...'

'Home,' Luke said. 'Mayo. Carrigard.'

'But what...? When?'

'Soon. I'll have to wait until Martin gets a few new fellows. After that.'

'You're not coming to Leeds?'

'No. I've had enough.'

'Enough!' Danny said. 'Like hell you have. All these years we've been waiting for another contract with Brassey. Now we can get it, now we can make real money, do it all our own way, and you're going home. What class of eejit are you?'

'No eejit. It's what I want.'

Danny stared at him. 'You're crazy.'

'No, I'm not. Carrigard is our home. You know that as well as I do.'

'It might be your home, but it sure as hell isn't mine. Mayo's finished, it's got no future.'

'It's got my future. Father won't last forever, and I'm to inherit the lease. It's Pat that'll have to work in England. It'll be tougher on him.'

'Then let Pat inherit the bloody lease. It's no damned use to you. Just look at them all. The hunger's back. It's 1840 all over again. They're starving, I tell you.'

'If they were starving, Father would have said so.'

Danny said nothing for a moment. Then he shook his head. 'Look, would you have a little bit of sense. Sure, your family mightn't be starving. And why not? Because you're here, that's the why. Every month you're sending them back money to buy corn. And now you're going home and cutting them off from the very money they need to live. Are you mad?'

'They'll be fine after the harvest. We all will.'

'The harvest? That's what they always say. The harvest, the harvest. Every year, they're there with their empty bellies waiting for the harvest. It'll never change. Never.'

'It's my farm,' Luke said, angry now. 'I'm the one that'll be feeding the family when Father is no longer able for it.'

'Yes, and in another ten years' time you'll have a dozen more mouths to feed and the rent to pay, year in, year out. And when your sons are twelve years old, you'll be sending them off every summer as *spailpíns* working the English harvest. And why? Because the farm can't pay for itself.'

'But it's our land.'

'Our land, bedamned,' Danny said. 'They've all got their heads turned towards the past. Brian Ború, Owen Roe, Wolfe Tone, our glorious history, we've heard it all. Don't make me sick.'

'Yes,' Luke said. 'But Murty...'

'Damn it to hell, don't remind me. My own father, buried in the past. You and me know it, and we know it well. The new schools are coming to Mayo, and they sure as hell won't approve of him. He's no teacher. He's not trained their way – you've said it yourself. They'll close his little school. What'll he do when it's all over? He's too old for work on the rails. He won't be able to feed his family. And he doesn't even know what's going to hit him.'

'Maybe he does.'

'He's a fool if he does,' Danny said, 'and an even worse fool if he doesn't. And you'll be a fool if you go back to Carrigard.'

For a few more moments, Luke said nothing. There were many thoughts racing through his head, but he could not put them in order. 'So I'll be a fool,' he said at length, 'but I'll be worse than a fool if I stay here. If I don't go home, Father will be evicted. They're saying he's too old, and they won't sign another lease unless I sign it too.'

'They're saying what?'

'They'll evict him. I have to sign it with him.'

'But that was signed years ago.'

'No,' Luke said, 'we thought it was signed years ago. It was only that he let on it was signed. They've been running two years without the lease, and Father never told me.'

'Two years? They could have been evicted.'

'Isn't that what I'm telling you?'

'But why?'

'Look, he's sixty three. They won't sign another 21-year lease with a man that old, and I can see why. They know damned well that he won't be able to work the farm and the quarry that long. They reckon they need a younger man...'

'But what about Pat?' Danny asked.

'They say he's too young.'

'But...'

'There's no way around it. They won't take Father on his own, and they won't take Pat. They'll only sign again if I sign it with Father. Otherwise they'll bring in another fellow for the lease, and the three of them will be out on the road – Father, Mother and Pat.'

'So why don't you just go back home, sign the lease, and then come back over to Leeds. There's no reason for you to stay. All Burke wants is for the legal fellows to see you signing it.'

'No,' Luke said, 'they want more than that. They want me back working the quarry too. They reckon Father can't work it. If they hear I'm gone, they'll have another fellow in for the farm – quarry and all.'

For a few moments Danny said nothing, pacing up and down. Luke had never seen him lost for words before. He turned back to Luke. 'Damn it,' he said, 'that's blackmail.'

'No it's not. He's no choice, and neither have I. Can't you see that?'

'But you do have a choice.'

'The hell, I do,' Luke said.

'Yes, you do. You can come to Leeds with us and bring them all over.'

'Bring them over! To Leeds?'

'Where else? You're going to have to pay for them all anyhow, and the farm won't earn enough money for that, good years or bad. You'll earn far more money in Leeds, and even your father will get some class of job around, and your mother can work in the mills.'

'Don't be stupid. That would never work.'

'Yes, it would. It's just that you can't see it.'

'Look,' Luke said, 'I have to go home. You go to Leeds if you like.'

'Damned right, I will,' Danny said. 'There'll be years of work in Leeds, and with Brassey too. A man would be mad to do anything else.'

'And when that finishes, what then?'

'The next contract,' Danny said. 'If Brassey doesn't have contracts in England, he'll have them in France, and if it isn't France it'll be Spain. You'll see.'

'France or Spain? You'd go…?'

'Why not?'

'But you can't keep working like this,' Luke said. 'It'll kill you. You'll be fine till you're forty, then it'll be too much. You'll be back on the roads with not a penny in your pocket.'

'Not me, I won't. That's for the fellows who drink everything they get. We're different, you and me. We're going to save our money.'

'And buy a farm?'

'That isn't the future.'

'So what is the bloody future then?'

'Railways,' Danny replied. 'Railways, but not as a navvy. Look at Brassey. He started off with nothing. What is he now? – one of the richest men in England.'

'So you want to be Tom Brassey!'

'No, I'm not that foolish. But look at all the other contractors around us. Muck-shifters, that's all they are. They can't read, they can't write, they can hardly add or subtract. All they can do is get men to work.'

'Muck-shifting? Is that what you want so? Muck-shifting.'

'Yes,' Danny said, 'muck-shifting. Rock, shale or mud, who cares? But I can do it better than those fools, and so can you. There's a future in contracting on the railways. Deep down you know that, even if you want to deny it. You might never be as rich as Brassey, but by God it's a hundred times better than starving in Carrigard.'

Luke spoke with Corrigan and McGlinn. They had already decided to sign off at the next payday and return to Mayo. He agreed to travel with them. Over the following days, he still worked alongside Danny, but little of importance passed between them.

Two weeks later, they started their journey, travelling by the open wagons of the South Eastern Railway from Ashford up to Reigate Junction and along the tracks of the London & Brighton Railway to the terminus at London Bridge.

They walked across London in driving rain to the terminus of the London & Birmingham Railway at Euston. Corrigan led them to a boarding house he knew on Pentonville Road, where they dried out their clothes as the landlady served them a hot dinner.

'Good food here,' McGlinn said, as he cut into a thick pork chop.

'Didn't I tell you it'd be good?' Corrigan said.

McGlinn elbowed him. 'Yer man's awful quiet.'

'Sure hasn't a man a right to be quiet, if that's what he wants?' Corrigan said.

Luke glanced up from his plate. 'It's nothing. I was only doing a bit of thinking...'

'And sure there's no harm in that, neither,' Corrigan said. 'A man has a right to think.'

'And a right to share his thoughts,' McGlinn said. 'A man has that right too.'

'A man might have rights,' Luke replied 'but that doesn't mean he has to inflict them on his friends.'

'We'll have no more excuses,' McGlinn said. 'Let's hear it.'

'*Arra*, it's nothing,' Luke answered. 'It's just that when I first came over here, I was so frightened of it all.'

'Of course, you were,' Corrigan said. 'Sure you were only a young *gossoon*. We were all frightened when we first came to England.'

'It wasn't just that, though,' Luke said. 'We had to pay the rent, and it couldn't be paid without me going to England, and that was bad enough. But I'd heard so much of England, what a rough, tough place it was meant to be. And when I came over first, I was sick for home. Day and night, I'd be thinking of Mayo. I couldn't wait to work out my time in England, make the money and get home. There were two things that kept me going – the fear that they couldn't keep the farm without my money, and the knowing it'd be mine in the end. My own farm, that's what I wanted, and working in England was the only way to do it. So I just had to put up with it all, and that was an end to it.'

'Wasn't it the same for all of us,' Corrigan said. 'Either we were working to pay the rent or saving to buy our own.'

'Anyhow,' McGlinn interrupted, 'you had your friends over here too. Working with Farrelly, what more could a man have asked than that? If you were working for one of the other gangs, then you'd have cause to be crying at night.'

'I know,' Luke said. 'Ye're right, and there's no doubting we had great times together. But still the one thing I wanted was getting home to Mayo and getting the farm. And then, all of a sudden, a letter comes from Father saying I'm to come home straight away. So in another few days, I'll be seeing them all again, and in a few years the farm'll be mine. And now I just don't want it anymore.'

'Would you listen to him,' McGlinn said. 'Give him what he wants, and he's still miserable.'

'Worse than miserable,' Luke said. 'Mayo frightens me. In fact, it terrifies me.'

They travelled third class on the London & Birmingham line as far as Birmingham city. They saw dozens of navvies in the station, powerful men compared to the small group of haggard families standing at the end of the platform. As Luke walked past the huddled families, he noticed the children were speaking in Irish. He hesitated.

'Come on,' Corrigan said. 'There's nothing we can do.'

In less than an hour, they were headed north again on the Grand Trunk Railway as far as its junction with the Liverpool & Manchester at Newton. This time, McGlinn led them across the tracks to a freight marshalling yard where they jumped a boxcar heading towards Liverpool.

Corrigan was doubtful. 'What if we're caught?'

'We won't be caught.'

As Luke's eyes became accustomed to the darkness inside, he noticed that there were two men sitting in the corner.

'Have you travelled from far?' he asked.

There was no answer. Luke repeated the question.

'*We cannot understand*,' one of the men replied, speaking in Irish.

'*I'm sorry*,' Luke said, switching into Irish. '*If I had known you were Irish speakers, I would not have annoyed you with English.*'

'*That is not a thing to care about,*' the man replied.

'*I was asking how far you had come.*'

'*We have come from Leeds where we have been trying to get work, but they would not take us. They say we are not strong enough to work on the railways.*'

The train rattled as it went over a crossing.

'*You're from the south, I would say,*' Corrigan said.

'*The west side of the county of Cork,*' the second man answered. '*Between Schull and Skibbereen.*'

'*Is that where you are travelling?*'

'*That would be lunacy,*' the first man said. '*They have little food there. It is to Liverpool we are travelling. Perhaps we will work there. Perhaps we will make enough money to get to America.*'

'*Is it so bad in Cork?*' Corrigan asked.

'*Bad enough. The potatoes were good when we harvested them. But then the rot came to Schull, and we lost many of them. The people are hungry now. It is not as bad as 1840 yet, and we pray it will not be.*'

'*It will never be as bad as that again,*' Luke said.

It was dark when they arrived in Liverpool. They walked across the tracks towards a side entrance to the station. Suddenly McGlinn grabbed Luke's collar. 'Run, Luke, run.'

Four policemen were rushing towards them. Luke ran. One caught him by his belt, but he broke free and kept running. He followed McGlinn and Corrigan, crossing tracks, platforms and access roads; weaving in and out between engines, wagons, carriages, carts and horses. One of their pursuers slipped on horse manure, the others hesitated and were cut off by a slow moving cart. They continued the chase, but Luke and McGlinn and Corrigan outran them. They raced up a stairway and stopped, leaning on a wall under a gas lamp, gasping for breath.

'You're a damned fool,' Corrigan said to McGlinn. 'I knew we shouldn't have listened to you.' But McGlinn only laughed.

'Where are the other fellows gone?' Luke asked.

'Over there,' McGlinn replied, pointing down between the tracks. The two men were lying face down on the ground. As Luke watched, they had their wrists trussed up behind them. Then they were stood up and dragged off.

'I wonder where they're taking them,' he asked.

'The Workhouse,' McGlinn said. 'If they're lucky.'

'And if they're not?'

'The boat back to Cork.'

They went to Buckley's boarding house at the bottom of Scotland Road. During the night it turned wet, and Luke lay awake on his bunk listening to the drumming of the rain on the windows.

The next morning, they left early. It was only now that he saw the poverty around him. The boarding house stood in stark contrast to the rest of Scotland Road. Again he saw the miserable people with shrunken faces, some begging in the rain, others just standing at street corners. He could see through filthy courtyards and down stairways into rooms and cellars crowded with people.

They walked to the George's Dock and paid their passage on a steamship for Dublin. As they waited by a shed on the pier, they saw a cattle ship tying up on the other side of the dock. The hold was open to the weather, the cattle steaming from the rain. As the drovers started driving the cattle off, Luke saw hundreds of people disembarking from the hold alongside them.

'They're travelling with the cattle!' he said.

'Isn't it the cheapest way over,' Corrigan replied. 'Thruppence a man, why wouldn't they? There's not many can pay two shillings for their passage, you know.'

Luke walked to the end of the pier and watched as the stream of cattle and humanity flowed along the docks.

A young woman walked past him in the crowd. Her face was thin, but it carried its own gaunt beauty. She wore a patched shawl, washed out to a dull grey colour. Her hair showed wet and lank beneath it. Her shift hung loose from her shoulders, torn in places and shredded at the hems. She had bare feet, and her ankles and shins were streaked with manure from the cattle. She saw him staring and stared back with a look of contempt and defiance. Startled at the aggression in her eyes, he turned away. When he looked again, she was gone.

He returned to Corrigan and McGlinn. An hour later, their own ship slipped its moorings and set sail from Liverpool.

Chapter Two

The Liverpool Mail, April 1846:

As to famine in Ireland, in what year since the traces of history can be relied upon, was there not more or less famine in some part or parts of that apparently doomed island? Where there are from two to three millions of beggars, the want of employment and the prevalence of abject poverty, of disease and other evils, must be perennial and co-existent. There is always famine, because there is nowhere where beggars are not in multitudes; in rags, inured to filth, lazy, insolent, professional and incapable of improvement.

They docked at Dublin. Six days of hard walking lay ahead of them.

In the city, there were hundreds of ragged people walking towards the docks. One family stopped them, asking for directions and questioning them about England and the railways. Luke knew they had no prospect of work on the rails.

On the west of the city, they met families making for the Workhouses – the North Dublin Union or the South Dublin Union. Luke wondered if either still had the space for them.

Lucan, Leixlip and Maynooth. In the small towns, there were beggars everywhere. Every day on the roads, they met groups of silent people walking towards Dublin.

Kilcock, Enfield and Kinnegad. They questioned more people. Some were young men going to spend the summer working on the English harvest, as they always did. But most told a different story, one of hunger, fever and despair.

Mullingar, Edgeworthstown and Longford. More beggars, crowds of them outside the Midlands Workhouses. More ragged families trudging across the bridge on the Shannon.

Termonbarry, Strokestown and Tulsk. West of the Shannon the solidly built houses of the midlands gave way to smaller thatched cottages and mud cabins. The fields were smaller and stonier. There were fewer hedges and no fences; only blackthorns and rough-built stone walls along the sides of the fields. The roads were deeply rutted after the winter.

Bellanagare, Frenchpark and Ballaghaderreen. On their last night on the road they slept in a barn just outside Knockanure. They were worn out, and it was well past dawn when the farmer roused them. They went through the town and past the Workhouse. A crowd of hundreds of thin and ragged people stood in line along the outside wall.

They walked on towards Carrigard.

Two hours later, they arrived. He shook hands with Corrigan and McGlinn. They left him and walked on to Kilduff.

He stood at the gate to observe the house. The gable that had collapsed in the 1839 storm had been rebuilt with carved lintels over the windows. The walls had been freshly whitewashed. The thatch on the roof had gone, replaced by regular rows of grey-black slate.

The door was half open. Silently he stepped inside.

His mother was sweeping the floor with a rush broom, her back to the door. So much had changed, but she had not. She was dressed better than he remembered though. Her long black skirt hung straight, with no rips or patches. A grey jumper clung tight into her back, the folded black triangle of her shawl hanging down over it, loosely tied around her neck. Over both hung her long hair, black as he had always remembered it.

'God with you, Mother.'

She spun around. The broom clattered on the floor. For a few seconds, she stared at him in fright. Slowly she began to recognise his features. 'Luke?' she whispered. 'Luke? Oh, my God...LUKE.'

She ran over and hugged him, her head into his chest. She had started to cry. 'Luke. My son, my son...'

'It's fine,' he said, not knowing what else to say. He had not expected this. He waited for her to finish, but the sobbing went on. He put his arms around her. 'Don't be vexing yourself. You'll be fine, I tell you.'

Suddenly she pushed back from him, rubbing her eyes. She pulled his head down and kissed him on the cheek. 'You're a right fathead, do you know that?'

'Oh, I know it well enough,' Luke said.

'You put the heart crosswise in me. All these years, and you just walk in on me like that. You could have been the death of me.'

'I'm sorry.'

'And so you should be. Why didn't you tell us you were coming today? I wasn't expecting you.'

Within minutes, he was sitting at the table, trying to answer his mother's questions through mouthfuls of buttermilk and oatmeal porridge.

The table was solid smooth-planed timber, four inches thick he reckoned.

The earthen floor was gone, replaced by flagstones, squared off with mortar between. They had been scrubbed and brushed clean. The stone walls were scrubbed too. A ceiling made of long wooden planks covered the entire room, with no sign of staining from smoke.

At the gable end, where there had been a hole to let the smoke out, there was now a well-constructed chimney over a large, wide hearth, pots on a ledge down one side, two more hanging on small cranes over the fire, bubbling. On one side of the hearth, there was a creel of turf, a stack of logs just beside it. Against the back wall, there was a butter churn he had not seen before, a spinning wheel beside it.

'*God knows, you've become a powerful man,*' she said to him. '*Those English fellows know how to work men, didn't I tell you so?*'

'*Oh, it wasn't the English.*'

'*It must have been tough on you all the same.*'

'*It surely was. Farrelly would never let up. He had us working day and night.*'

'*Yes,*' she said, '*but it was best you were with Farrelly. He's a man you can trust, and we knew he would take care of you. You were only a child. Fourteen years old, and to have the whole family depending on you. It wasn't fair.*'

'*But it had to be done, Mother. Wasn't that the way of it?*'

She shook her head. '*Maybe it was, but I couldn't stop worrying. Lying awake every night I was, thinking of you over there in England. Hard work expected of you, and money expected of you every week.*'

'*But wasn't it hard for ye here too?*'

She flinched, as if the question had not been expected. '*Yes, it was hard. That first year you left was desperate. God, we were hungry. Never enough to eat and the rent to pay. There were times I cursed Michael in my heart for the promises he made. The rent, the back rent and interest too. No one else around was able to do that, and they weren't evicted. But it was his pride, his cursed pride, that made him do it. It was fine for him, wasn't it? But it was you that had to do the paying, taking a man's work on a boy's shoulders. Oh God, how I've missed you.*'

She reached across the table, putting her hand on his arm. '*You're not to go away again.*'

He gulped down his porridge. '*No, Mother,*' he said. '*But tell me about the farm. How is it going?*'

'*It's safe now you're home. Now you're the one that will be the farmer.*'

'*Yes,*' he said, '*and nearly wasn't, from what I hear. Two years without the lease. You'd think he would have told me before.*'

'*I don't know about that. Maybe he didn't want worrying you.*'

Or maybe he was too damned proud, he was thinking. Too proud to admit he was getting old, and they wouldn't give him the lease.

To hell with that. There were other matters to think about. What future had Mayo if the potato had failed again?

But everything here seemed so normal; far, far better than when he had left. Yes, his mother was a few years older than she had been in 1840, but even that was difficult to detect. She most certainly was not hungry.

It made no sense.

'*What about the hunger?*' he asked.

She looked up, startled. '*Who told you about that?*'

'*No one. Couldn't I see it with my own eyes, and I crossing the country?*'

'*Yes…I expect you could. Well, we're doing well enough.*'

'*No hunger?*'

'*No hunger.*'

'*And Murty?*'

'*Murty and Aileen too. And why wouldn't they? Don't they get the money from Danny?*'

'*And everyone else?*'

She looked away, avoiding his glance. '*Oh, I don't know. Sure we'll talk about it all some other time.*'

Some time later, Michael and Pat entered. Michael sat on the bench by the door and started unlacing his boots.

He had certainly changed. It was almost as if he had gotten smaller. He had aged too. He still had the powerful arms and chest of a man of half his age. But his hair was grey now, cropped close, but thinner and showing bald on the crown. The face was older too – still tough, but more wrinkled and weather-beaten. But his eyes had not changed; they still reflected a hard life and the hardness to deal with it.

'We've got a visitor,' Eleanor said, speaking in English now.

'Who's that?' Michael said, peering into the room. He kicked off his boots and strode over towards the stranger. 'Who in hell…?'

'It's your son,' Eleanor said.

His eyes lit up. He grasped Luke by the arms. 'Well, by God…So you're home.'

'Yes, Father.'

'You got my letter, then.'

'I did.'

'You took long enough in the coming.'

'I'd to stay another few weeks. We had to wait out to the end of the work before we were paid.'

The men sat, and Eleanor started to ladle out cabbage.

'You've changed a lot,' Michael said. 'I didn't know you.'

'What did you expect?' Eleanor asked. 'Wasn't he only a scrap of a lad when he left?'

'It's not just that he's taller, he's full of muscle too.'

'That's what hard work does,' Eleanor said, as she placed the pot of corn on the table.

'Harder than here?' Michael asked.

'A lot,' Luke said. 'And longer working too.'

'You'll be well able for the quarry so.'

'Ah now, would you leave the poor fellow alone,' Eleanor said, 'He's only just home.'

Michael scooped corn from the pot and ladled it on to Luke's plate. 'And what of Danny?' he asked. 'Going to Leeds, I hear.'

'For a few years anyhow,' Luke answered, chewing on the corn. It had the toughness and feel of gravel.

'Will he come home then?' asked Eleanor.

'I don't know, Mother.' The corn tore at his throat as he swallowed.

'I think you do,' Michael said. 'You just don't want to tell us. Isn't that it?'

'Maybe it is.' He took another forkful of corn. This time he chewed it more carefully.

'You'll tell us later, so' Michael said. 'We'll be seeing Murty and Aileen this evening, you'll tell us then.'

'Yes, Father.'

That afternoon, he walked the farm with his father.

'You'll find a lot of changes,' Michael said.

'I know,' Luke said. 'I saw the slate. It's well set.'

'Isn't it. And the first slate roof in Carrigard.'

They walked across the yard. There was a new paddock with a horse Luke had not seen before. They climbed over the fence and walked up to it. It was frightened of Luke and reared up, but Michael calmed it. 'Easy there. Easy, easy.'

He held the horse's head back. Luke pushed up the horse's lips, looking close at the teeth. Then he lifted one of the front legs, looking to the fetlock.

'You'll not find lameness there,' Michael said. 'I know how to buy horses.'

They climbed back over the fence and stood leaning against it.

'I'd say there's not many around here have horses,' Luke said.

'Horses, is it? It isn't horses they'd be worrying about now. Sheehys have gone, you know. Byrnes too.'

'I know. I'd heard.'

'Murtaghs and Tolans, all gone.'

'Tolans? I hadn't heard that.'

'Last week only. What chance had they? Nine children, all under twelve. They had no sons to be working on railways, I tell you.'

'Where did they go?'

'Liverpool they were making for, but whether they'll get there or not, God only knows.'

Luke thought of the pitiful families he had seen on the road. He would not have known them anyhow. Hunger changed the look of people.

'It'll be hard on them,' he said.

'It will,' Michael said. 'And on everyone else too. It's been tough, these past months, and it's going to get tougher. We'd heard stories from England of potatoes rotting in the ground, but we had them all saved, we thought it had missed us. And then, in a few days there before Christmas, we lost the half of them. If it wasn't for the amount I'd planted and the corn we were buying in, we'd have been like Tolans and the rest of them, off on the road to England.'

He followed his father through the fields – meadow, corn and potatoes. They stopped by the potato field.

'You've enough planted right enough,' Luke said.

'What did you think? There's enough to make sure we won't run low.'

'Unless the rot gets worse.'

'*Arra*, no. It can't rot them all.'

They crossed the meadow down to the quarry. Luke whistled when he saw the piles of rocks and stones that had been broken from rocks. 'Would you have call for all this?'

'By God, we would. I never told you – we're repairing more roads than we used to. Got Sheehy's contract when they left. Worth twelve pounds a year now. Half to Burke and half to us.'

'Six pounds. That'd damned near pay the rent on its own.'

'It would. And your mother wants me to get more contracts around. She's hoping to keep Pat here working the quarry.'

'You reckon we could get more?'

'She thinks we could, though I think she's only trying to believe it herself. She doesn't want Pat going away on the railways.'

'Working the quarry on his own would be tough enough with that number of contracts.'

'That's true,' Michael said, 'but it's not just that. It's all she hears about the fighting, the drinking, the women...'

'God, Farrelly would never allow that sort of nonsense.'

'Tell that to your mother.'

They scrambled down into the quarry. Luke walked around, examining each pile of stone and gravel. 'So what are Pat's plans now? Will he stay?'

'I'm sending him on the harvest to England. When he's home again in September, then we'll decide.'

They climbed out again and walked back towards the house.

'Why didn't you tell me earlier, Father?'

'About what?'

'About the lease. You could have told me two years back.'

'Why should I? It didn't matter to you. I didn't want you home then. I do now.'

'But you could have been evicted.'

'That wasn't your concern,' Michael said.

'But it was.'

'You stayed in England because that was what I wanted. And you came home, because I ordered you home. That is all for you to know.'

'No, it is not…'

'You will not defy me, Luke. Not now. Not ever.'

Luke said nothing for a few moments. 'Damn it to hell,' he said at last, 'let's not argue about it. We've got the lease to be signed, and the sooner we get that done the better.'

They walked back to the house.

'Where's Pat, Mother?'

'Over milking.'

He walked across to the shed. It was dark inside, and he could barely make out his brother's form against that of the cow. He breathed in the familiar stench of cow manure together with the mustiness of the shed and the warm smell of milk. Pat was working fast, milk from the cow's teats splashing into the pail.

Luke walked up behind him. 'You were a bit quiet there earlier.'

His brother turned around, startled. 'Damn it, don't come up on me like that.' He turned back to the cow. 'I'm sorry. I didn't mean to be so quiet. Of course I'm happy to see you home, we all are. It's just…'

'Yes,' Luke said. 'It's the farm, isn't it?'

'Of course it's the farm. What else could it be?'

'But that's the way it was always going to be.'

'I know it was,' Pat said. 'And I know you've been sending all the money back all this time. You've paid the rent every year. It's your farm.'

'But you were half hoping I'd stay away, were you?'

'Half hoping is right. Half of me wanted you home, and the other half wanted the farm.'

'That's a fair way of putting it,' Luke said.

Pat finished the milking and washed the cow's udders. He picked up the pail. 'Hold on there, I'll just drop this over to Mother.'

When he returned, they both followed the cow and calf back towards the field. Then they leant on the gate, watching the sun go down over the side of the Mountain.

'What's this about you working the quarry after?' Luke asked.

'Who was telling you that?'

'Father said it to me.'

'Yes, well, it's what Mother wants, but I doubt a man can make a living out of it. And even if he did, there wouldn't be much of a living out of the farm without the quarry, and you wouldn't want that, would you?'

'I suppose not,' Luke said. 'Though there's other farms around here empty, from what I hear.'

'Would you want that? Rent a farm where a man's been forced out by hunger.'

'Maybe not.'

'Or evicted?'

'I would not.'

'No, you wouldn't,' Pat said, 'so I reckon it's going to be the railways for me. And Murtybeg, he'll go too, though Aileen is terrified of that.'

'Why should she be terrified?'

'Oh, I don't know, it's just Aileen, you know what she's like. She can't take in that Danny is gone. She'd never face up to losing both her sons.'

'But they'll need the money.'

'They will, but she doesn't see it that way. She thinks Danny's money is enough, and Murtybeg should stay teaching in the school with Murty.'

Luke ran the calf out of the ditch. 'When would ye go though?'

'Oh, I don't know. It won't be for a few years yet.'

'So what about this year. Father was saying how you'll be going on the harvest in England for the summer.'

'I will.'

'Murtybeg won't be going with you, will he?'

'Oh, he'll go right enough. We're going over in a couple of days, the both of us.'

'Why so quick?'

'Why not? Now that you're home, we wouldn't have the money for corn if I didn't go. I'll have to work the summer in England and come back in September. You should have a good crop of potatoes by then.'

'I hope to God we do,' Luke said. 'But what about Murtybeg then? Will he come back in September?'

'He's only going on the promise he'll come back with me. Aileen insisted on it. But I reckon he won't.'

'Why wouldn't he?'

'He thinks there's nothing to come back to, that's why he wouldn't. Murty's school is near finished. There's hardly anyone coming now, and even if the potato crop is a good one the Government schools will close him when they come. No, Murty doesn't stand a chance. Not a chance in hell. So I reckon Murtybeg will stay in England, promise or no promise.'

'I see,' Luke said. 'So Nessy will have to teach the school instead of him.'

'Well...no.'

'No?'

'Not while she's waiting for her baby, she won't.'

'Her what?'

'You heard.'

'But...is she to be married?'

'There's not a hope of that, I'm afraid.'

'Then who...?'

'Jimmy Corrigan's the father, if that's what you're asking. But don't say I told you.'

They walked back along the bramble lane towards the house. Luke picked up a stick and slashed at the heads of the ragwort on the ditch. Murtybeg leaving? Nessy expecting? What more could go wrong? He thought again of the road from Dublin. Hungry beggars and families in rags. Could it happen here? Had it already begun?

'There's something else I don't understand,' he said to Pat.

'What's that?'

'The hunger. They're all very quiet about it. Just how bad is it?'

'Well, you've heard about Sheehys leaving.'

'Yes, Father told me about that. Murtaghs and Tolans and the rest of them.'

'And many more. But I'll tell you this, it's nothing like the Mountain. There's fever up there, hunger too. And bad and all as it is, it'd be worse if it wasn't for the corn lines.'

'Corn lines!' Luke exclaimed. 'Just like 1840.'

'Aye, and longer too.'

He thought of the Soup Kitchens then. The long lines of hungry people. The look in his father's eyes.

'But Father – he wouldn't take charity.'

'He had to,' Pat said. 'Or should I say, Mother had to.'

'He wouldn't stand in line?'

'Of course not. You know Father – it's not a man's place to be shamed.'

'Too damned proud, eh?'

'Maybe. But it changed after the first few weeks. They started a paying line, and then Mother and Aileen had to pay for their corn. And you know why? Because Father and Murty wouldn't let us be fed for free, and that was an end to it.'

'I see,' Luke said.

'Yes,' Pat said, 'that's the way it was. But it was still your money and Danny's that was doing the paying, and they knew it. Everyone did. One way or another, there was no pride in it.'

Luke stopped in the dark, watching a half moon coming up over the Mountain. 'Ye all look well fed.'

'We are, though like I say, there's many enough around here that are hungry. And from all we hear, it's desperate out the west of the county. Worse even than the Mountain. They keep passing along the road, poor devils, scarce able to walk. They can't make it out through Westport, they don't have the price of the ticket. Their only chance is the cattle boat from Dublin. If they get that far.'

Luke saw a figure approaching in the shadows. 'Who's that, do you think?'

Pat looked up. 'You don't know him!'

'I do not.'

'Tis Murtybeg, that's who it is, you eejit.'

Murtybeg strode up to Luke. 'Don't mind to his teasing now. I'd not have known you either.'

'But God, you've got tall,' Luke said. 'You must have put on a good two foot in height since I saw you last.'

'Sure, I had to, didn't I. I couldn't stay a little runt for ever. But come on now – they're all waiting for you back at the house. We all came down visiting just to see you, and there you were – gone. We thought something'd happened to the pair of you, you were taking so long.'

They walked back through the dark lane.

'Pat tells me ye're both going away to the harvest,' Luke said.

'We are.'

'Ye're going early.'

'No reason not to. There's not much happening at the school. No one's got the cash to pay. And they can't pay any other way neither – the potatoes are gone, and the corn's all for rent.'

'But you'll be back in the autumn, will you?'

'I don't know,' Murtybeg said. 'We'll see.'

They went into the house. Murty rose from the table and grasped Luke's hand. 'By God, so this is the great fellow back from England. Making more money than a poor Mayo schoolmaster could ever do, yourself and Danny.

35

You'll have to tell us all how you do it.'

Murty was Luke's uncle and Danny's father. He was a softer man than Michael. During the 1798 Rebellion, he had only been four years old, but the horror of those August days had remained with him, recurring in nightmares.

Unlike Michael, Murty had never lived with his father again. His mother had ambitions for him. In 1806, Murty had been sent to stay with a cousin of the family, a priest in Tuam, and for seven years he studied at the diocesan school there. He spent another ten years travelling around Galway and Mayo, carrying his blackboard on his back and picking up odd jobs teaching in towns and remote villages.

In 1823, he returned and started his own school in Carrigard. Some saw him as a spoilt priest and refused to send their children. Many more could not afford schooling for their family. But for most families, the school was seen as the only way out of poverty, and within a few years Murty was teaching over a hundred boys and just about a dozen girls. There were no other teachers in Carrigard School. Instead Murty used the brighter pupils from the senior classes to help him teach the juniors and infants.

Michael was not too proud to learn from his younger brother, and during the early years he had spent many evenings with him, studying arithmetic, reading and writing in the guttering light from the rushes.

A few months after Murty returned to Carrigard, he had married Aileen O'Kelly. Three of their children survived to 1846. Nessa was born in 1824, Danny in 1826 and Murtybeg in 1827.

Aileen came across from where she had been sitting beside the fire. She held her hand out shyly. 'Luke,' she whispered. She had the same face and figure as her sister, Eleanor. But the eyes showed it all, a frightened look, hunted even. He wondered what had caused that.

Nessa had certainly changed. Her face was thinner, but she was more feminine and alluring than he remembered. He could see too that she was carrying a child.

They sat at the table as Eleanor served out hot punch made from rough distilled *poitín* spirit. They questioned him about England and about the Carrigard and Kilduff men working with Farrelly's gang.

'Tell me,' asked Murty at last, 'what's Danny going to do?'

'Yes,' Nessa said. 'Tell us about Danny. When will he come home?'

'Oh, I don't know that,' Luke said.

'Of course you do,' Nessa said. 'You'll have a view surely?'

He hesitated, looking from one face to another. 'I do,' he said. 'I can tell you what I think, though it might not be what ye want to hear. I'd thought he might come home, but that was before he decided to go to Leeds. But he won't now.'

'But why not?' Nessa asked. 'Why wouldn't he?'

'He reckons he's nothing to come home to.'

'Nothing to come home to,' Murty exclaimed. 'We thought he'd save up and buy himself a farm. Isn't that the thing to do? Or teach even.'

'Not for Danny. He favours the railways.'

'But the railways will kill him. He can't work like that for the rest of his life.'

'I don't think he's thinking of swinging a pick for the rest of his life. But he'll still stay with the rails.'

'But what else could he do?' Nessa asked. 'Some kind of clerking?'

'Something like that, Nessy. But if he does, I think it'll be on his own account.'

'I don't understand…'

'He'll work for himself, Danny will.'

'With men working for him?'

'I think so.'

'But that's only your view.'

'It is. My view, nothing more.'

Murty tamped down the tobacco in his pipe. 'You heard about Pat and Murtybeg going on the harvest in England?'

'I did,' Luke said.

'There's a gang of them going – the Roughneens, Michael Jordan, Fergus Brennan, Bernie McDonnell and half a dozen more.'

'They're going early enough from what I hear,' Luke said.

'They are, but at least they won't be staying,' Murty said. 'Four months on the harvest, and they'll be home again.'

'*They promised they would,*' Aileen said.

'*They did,*' Eleanor said, patting her sister on the arm. '*They promised they'd be home in September. Now you're not to be worrying about it.*'

Murtybeg stared into his *poitín,* saying nothing.

For a few minutes, Luke said little either. He was feeling an attraction to Nessa. The man who won her would be a lucky man, though many might be put off by the thought of another man's child. Still, she was a striking woman, there was no doubt of that. He tried to put it out of his mind. She was his cousin, his first cousin at that. That could never be.

It was late when the others stood to go. Luke went out with them. It was a brilliant night with stars.

Murty stayed back as the others walked on. He took Luke by the arm. 'What you were saying about Danny, it took Aileen quite by surprise.'

'So it would seem.'

'You know, she still keeps his bed in the outshot. Makes sure it's warm every night and lets no one sleep in it. It's as if she's expecting him to walk in the door every day, though she knows he's in England.'

'I didn't know,' Luke said. 'I should have kept my bloody mouth shut.'

'Oh, it's as well for us to know. But still it'll upset her dreadfully if he stays away. And she's enough troubles already.'

'Troubles. Like what?'

'All sorts of things, you know Aileen. The linen price is down – she reckons we'll have to give it up. The school – she keeps worrying about that, reckons we'll have to close. But Nessy is the real worry. Nessy's in trouble.'

'I know.'

'You noticed, did you? Aileen's known it for months. I was wondering what was biting her. They only told me lately, the pair of them. Soon everyone will know, and there'll be all hell to pay then.'

'So what about the father?' Luke asked, feigning ignorance.

'Jimmy Corrigan, God damn him.'

'Owen's nephew?'

'That's right. His father's dead, and his mother doesn't want to know. I'd have a word with Owen about it, but I don't think that's going to do much good.'

'Damn it, I'll have a word with Jimmy myself.'

'If you can find him. We can't.'

He was breaking stones with his father and brother. Michael handed him a pick. Luke raised it, struck hard at the loose rock, swung out and brought it down again. He continued in a regular rhythm, soon joined by both Pat and Michael working alongside him, keeping up, blow for blow. Michael had always been proud of his powerful build, and Luke was too intelligent to try to work faster than his father, though he knew he could. Even so it astonished him how strong his father still was, more so than Pat, who was already sweating heavily and working slower.

Some time later, they all stopped and sat on the edge of the rock, Pat gasping hard.

'So this is the way you'd work in England, is it?' asked Michael.

'Well, perhaps,' Luke said, 'but not quite. They've different ways of doing it over there.'

'Like how?'

'Using spikes. It's much faster. Do it in one go. Bring the whole lift down.'

'The what?'

'The lift. The whole ledge of rock, with everything under it.'

He jumped up and strode up to the shelf of rock they had been working on, studying it closely. His father followed, curious.

'I'm not sure if the rock is the same,' Luke said. 'But look here. See this line running along the rock here. This is what we'd call a 'line of weakness.' If the rock acts the same as I've seen it, all we'd have to do is start driving heavy spikes in along the line until we split it from top to bottom.'

'Top to bottom?'

'You don't have to drive it all the way. After a while, the rock does the job on its own. It just comes down.'

Michael shook his head in disbelief.

An hour later, Luke took some of his own money from the house and rode into Kilduff, but he could not find the heavy spikes he wanted. He rode to Knockanure, and it was late afternoon before he returned. Pat and Michael stopped to watch as he carried the heavy spikes over.

He walked along the line of the rock. 'We'll try the first one here. Pat, you hold it.'

His father handed him a heavy sledge-hammer as Pat held the spike over the crack. Luke smashed the hammer down onto the spike which vibrated violently.

Pat whipped his hands back. 'Damn it, that hurt.'

'What did you expect and you holding it so tight? Here, hold it again, only grasp it gentle this time.'

After a few minutes, when the spike had entered the rock deeply enough to stand on its own, he started with a second spike.

'This time, I'll use the hammer,' Pat said.

'Fair enough.'

Some time later, they had six spikes hammered into the fault in the rock. 'I hope this works,' Michael said, 'because if it doesn't, we'll never get them things back out.'

'Of course it'll work,' Luke said. 'Now what we're going to do is this. We'll take the sledgehammer in turns, a dozen blows on each spike, and we keep doing that until it goes.'

They worked on, passing the sledgehammer between them. Suddenly, silently, the split in the rock started to widen. Michael looked on in amazement.

Luke, who had been last with the sledgehammer, handed it to Pat. 'Here, we'll give you the chance. Last spike on the left, just belt it a few times. And stand on this side of it.'

'Do you think I'm a complete *amadán*?' Pat asked.

'I don't know, maybe you are. Go on.'

Pat did as he was told. There was a roar as hundreds of tons of rock teetered out and collapsed.

*

Next morning, Pat and Luke filled the cart with stone and gravel and led it out into the Kilduff road. They stopped close to the entrance to the well and started to fill potholes and ruts. There was a group of emaciated women at the well, whispering among themselves.

He tried not to think about them, but from time to time they passed close to him, going to and from the well. Sometimes he recognised women he knew and spoke to them, but very few had much to say. On one occasion he saw a very old woman struggling from the well with a bucket that was too heavy for her. He went to help her, but she shook her head.

As he worked, he saw a young woman coming towards them. At first he did not know who she was, but as she came closer he recognised her as one of the Cunnanes who lived a little further out towards the Mountain. The eldest perhaps. Kitty? Kitty Cunnane? Yes.

She wore a patched grey shawl, and the hair that showed beneath it was straggled. Her dress was hardly a dress; more of a shift, patched and stitched many times. It was torn and muddy at the hem; more mud on her shins showing over bare feet. Her appearance would not have surprised him since her family was a large one with little enough for clothes.

But what was it about her? He had not seen her for years. She was no longer a girl. He reckoned she would have been some years older than him. But it was more than maturity, more than the lack of familiarity. It was the look in her eyes, the way she walked, and even the way she wore what she wore. Where her shift was torn in the centre, it had not been stitched. Through it he could see the round brownness of her breasts, and the material had been rucked in under them to emphasise them more. She walked erect, head back, breasts forward, her hips moving from side to side, swinging the shift over her bare shins.

As she crossed the road, he turned to greet her.

'Kitty Cunnane, if I'm not mistaken...'

'Excusing me, Mr. Ryan, we'll have none of that. Mrs. Brennan, if you please.'

He made a mock bow and opened the gate to the well. 'Yes, Mrs. Brennan...'

He stood with Pat, watching her walking down the narrow gravel track to the well. 'Mrs. Brennan?' he asked. 'Who's Mr. Brennan then?'

'Fergus,' Pat replied. 'Surely you remember Fergus Brennan.'

'Of course.'

'They were married last year.'

'By God, wasn't he the fast mover?'

'Wasn't he ever. We were all surprised. From all the talk we heard from the lads in England, we thought he'd be bringing back an English wifeen.'

'Aye. We'd all heard stories about that.'

She filled her pail with water. She took off her shawl, twisted and knotted it, and wrapped it around the top of her head, almost like a crown. Then, with a quick swing of her arms, she hefted the heavy pail and stood it on her head. None of the other women spoke.

She started walking back the track towards the gate, holding her left arm akimbo, her right arm angled up balancing the pail, her hips swaying ever so little. Then she brought both arms down to her sides, still balancing the pail on her head. She kept walking, eyes forward.

As she came to the gate, he went to open it.

'I'll be thanking you not to be so forward, Mr. Ryan.'

'I never said a word.'

'You didn't have to.'

She side stepped him, and in one quick movement she swung the pail from her head and walked off. He watched until Pat interrupted him. 'Are you there? Are you with us at all?'

'Oh, yes,' Luke answered. 'Only watching.'

'Just like all the fellows. Takes a lot of watching, our Kitty. Did you see how she knew you?'

'She was only guessing. I was with you, wasn't I?'

'Perhaps. Still, she must have known you were home. She's a sharp one, she is. She was the one got Nessy into trouble, you know. Best of friends, the pair of them. Out with the lads all the time. But Kitty's got Fergus now, and Nessy's got no one, only the baby coming.'

When they had spread the third cartload of stone and gravel, they led the horse and cart back to the barn. Two young men approached them.

'*We have nowhere to sleep,*' one of them said.

'*Ye may sleep on the hay,*' Pat replied without hesitation.

'*That God may bless you.*'

'*Have ye come from far?*' Luke asked.

'*Mulranny,*' one of them replied. '*There's little enough potatoes there. We had to leave, or the rest would go hungry.*'

'*Where will ye go?*'

'*Liverpool. America perhaps.*'

Pat let the two men into the shed. Then he unhitched the cart and led the horse to the paddock.

'You didn't invite them into the house,' Luke said.

'Into the house! They might have fever.'

'They'll be cold in the barn tonight.'

'What are you saying? That we should give them a blanket?'

'Well, perhaps…'

'And get fever ourselves?'

'They don't have fever.'

'How do you know? And anyhow, they're crawling with lice. Look, we've done what we can, now let them be.'

He lay awake in bed that night. There were images he could not get out of his mind. The quiet, haggard women at the well. The ragged appearance of the two lean men begging for shelter. He thought of Pat's comments about fever and lice and remembered the pitiful families on the road and in the long lines outside the Workhouses in the towns.

But there were other images too. Tight breasts. Tight hips. A torn shift swinging over bare ankles. Why should it matter? And at a time like this too. But it did.

'I didn't think that business of the spikes was going to work,' Michael said to Luke as they walked to the quarry. Pat was still cleaning out the cowshed.

'To tell you the truth, I wasn't sure either. The rock's a little different here.'

'Aye, but it worked. Saved us a lot of hard labour too. I never thought we could do it so fast.'

'It's fast alright,' Luke said. 'The lads on the railways though, they had faster ways of doing it.'

'Faster!'

'Faster, but bloody dangerous. What they'd do was to dig in under the lift when the fellows on top were trying to split the rock.'

'I don't understand.'

'They'd put a gang of lads down below working their way in underneath with their picks. That way the rock would collapse faster when there's nothing beneath to hold it.'

'And what about the men down under?'

'They'd run like hell as soon as it started coming down.'

Michael looked at him in disbelief. 'That's mad. Pure madness.'

'It is. Still, there were lads that would do it. The Donegal fellows – they'd do anything for money.'

'And you lot? What would ye do?'

'Oh, Farrelly would never let us work like that. Dig in a little – fine – but not all the way until it was ready to go. Danny and me, we once saw two fellows killed right beside us. Donegal lads of course. After that, we never wanted to do it neither, money or no money.'

When they arrived at the quarry, they started smashing rock. Luke watched his father as he did. There were questions in his mind, questions he hardly dared ask. Michael was still as he always remembered him – tough and stubborn. But what had made him that way? Michael had supported his own father's family from a young age, but what was so different about that, he himself had done the same. Hard work perhaps? No different than the railways.

It all came back to 1798. He had never lived through a rebellion. Michael had, but would never talk about it. Luke wanted to know more about the Rebellion, and it was not just curiosity. He felt he would never understand his father, far less Mayo, until he understood what had happened in 1798.

After ten minutes, they stopped, both leaning on their sledgehammers, gasping. 'There's something I'd like to ask you, Father,' Luke said.

'What's that?'

'The Rebellion.'

His father looked at him, eyes narrowing. 'The Rebellion, is it?'

'Yes. I'd like to know more about it.'

'The devil, you would,' Michael replied. He hefted the heavy sledgehammer over his shoulder and brought it smashing down on a rock between them. Luke jumped back as the rock shattered.

Pat arrived. They worked the rest of the morning smashing rock into smaller rocks and then smashing those into stones. Pat and Luke spent most of the afternoon shovelling shale and stone on to the riddlers to separate out the finer shale and gravel.

Michael worked alone on the other side of the quarry, breaking stone and thinking.

1798:

Baile na Mhuice he called it. Pig Town. Ballinamuck.

For days desperate men had been passing the house in Carrigard, most travelling at night, alone or in pairs. Now one had come in, begging for refuge. A local man.

Michael's father looked at the man in horror.

'*So it's all over?*' he asked.

'*Aye, it's all finished.*'

Murty, still the baby at four years, cowered behind his mother, staring at the monster. The gash across the man's forehead had turned to a black scab, and where it crossed his left eye the eyelids were closed and oozing pus. Two fingers on his right hand were short blackened stumps, his clothes were tattered, and the stench was sickening.

'*And the French? What about the French?*'

'*They gave up. Humbert surrendered to Cornwallis without even fighting. They just went over to the Redcoats and left us to be slaughtered.*'

'*Paudeen Brennan?*' Michael's mother asked suddenly. '*Where's Paudeen?*'

'*Dead. Skewered on a bayonet. I saw it myself.*'

'*And Mikey Lavan?*'

'*Dead too.*'

'*And Bernie O'Kelly?*'

'*I last saw him with the Knockanure men in the bog. They were cornered by the Cork Militia, and butchered like pigs.*'

'And you?' Michael whispered in English.

'I ran,' the rebel replied. 'I cursed Humbert, I cursed Ballinamuck, and I ran and ran.'

Over the next few days, they heard stories of rebels being shot on sight or hung before sullen crowds of silent people. By the time the militias reached Kilduff, it seemed their fury was spent, but an unnatural quiet came over the town and the area around.

Now the Ryans were in danger. They had agreed to shelter the rebel and had hidden him above the cattle, hoping no one else knew of it.

After a few days, Michael's mother sent him to Kilduff to find the rebel's wife and tell her that her husband lived. All the rebels' houses were being searched, and it was far too dangerous for the man to return to his family.

Afterwards Michael returned to the potato digging with his father. He had not mentioned anything about calling into the rebel's house. It hardly seemed important. When they came in for their midday meal, the rebel's wife was with him in the kitchen.

'Where the devil did she come from?' Michael's father shouted.

'She only came to see her man,' his mother replied. 'It's a natural thing to do.'

'It's also a bloody dangerous thing to do. She might have been seen.'

They sat and ate in silence.

Michael was the first to leave the table. He opened the door. The house was surrounded by militia men. An officer sat impassively on a horse.

'Search it.'

The soldiers dragged Michael's father into the haggard. The rebel ran up the ladder to the loft above the cattle, trying to escape through the tiny window though there would have been no way through the ring of soldiers. He was dragged down, kicking and screaming. The officer never dismounted, nor said a word. His face was expressionless, bored even.

The two men had their hands tied behind their backs. The rebel's feet were tied too. His woman was screaming, Michael's mother holding her back, her own face white with shock. His father was grasped by both elbows and pulled out onto the road. The rebel was dragged under a tree in the haggard, a rope was thrown over one of the branches and fixed around his neck.

'Finish the business,' the officer shouted at a corporal, as he wheeled his horse away. Another length of rope was looped around Michael's father's waist, and he staggered as he was jerked along by the soldiers following the horse. Michael ran after them. A militia man stopped him, a gun pointed at Michael's stomach.

'Where are you going with him?' Michael shouted.

The man stared at him, uncomprehending. Michael realised he did not understand English.

'*Where are you going with him?*' he asked again, in Irish now.

'*Clár Chlainne Mhuiris,*' the man replied. Claremorris.

'*Will they hang him also?*'

'*If they didn't hang him now, he won't hang later. But he'll rest a while in the gaol.*'

Michael ran back to the haggard. The women were being held back by two of the remaining soldiers as the noose was tightened around the rebel's neck, and he was pulled high. His face turned purple, his tongue protruding, a dark patch spreading down his trousers.

The rebel's wife broke free, running forward. One of the militia men swung around and smashed the stock of his gun into her mouth. She fell to the ground, bleeding through her broken teeth, screaming and screaming and screaming and screaming.

Chapter Three

Telegraph or Connaught Ranger, April 1846:
Provisions have been landed at Westport from war steamers.
This supply has not, however, contributed to increase the quantity of provisions in the country, for at the very time the Indian meal was landing, several vessels were receiving on board, for export, cargoes of Irish oats and meal. This, we submit, is a strange process for providing food for the starving Mayonians.

There was a letter waiting. Luke glanced at the Leeds postmark. That was quick, he thought. He sat on his bed in the outshot, reading the letter.

Mr. Luke Ryan	Price's Lodging House
Carrigard	Bramhope
Kilduff	Yorkshire
Co. Mayo	

Dear Luke,

I have not written to you since arriving a few days back, so I thought I might write now and tell you about the railway here. We are working in Bramhope, a small village convenient to Leeds. There are hundreds of other Irishmen here, so we have no need being lonely. We are all happy to be working under Brassey again. Our own contract, so we are free to do as we please. With Martin that means working 14 hours a day.

There's few enough of the other Irish gangs that would be up to that kind of work. I do not know what has been happening in Cork and Kerry and even the far ends of Mayo, but as far as working goes, they are a miserable lot. Many of them get better when they are here long enough and have enough food inside them, though God knows it takes time.

There is talk here of starting a second gang, and we might try to get some of our own fellows who have been working on the harvest, since they will be better fed after a few months in England.

But what about you? There is good money to be made in this country, and there will be for some time yet. Would you not come back over?

Daniel

England? Could he never get away from it? Six years ago he had thought he would be there for six months, a year at the outside. Before that he had never thought he would go there at all.

1839 had been a year of disaster. The hurricane on Little Christmas had devastated Mayo. Michael's house had been destroyed, and the family lived in the old cabin with the cattle for six months, while Michael, Luke and Pat rebuilt the house. It was then too that Alicia had died. In August, the final disaster arrived.

The potato failed.

As the food slowly ran out, Luke had felt the gnawing pain of hunger for the first time. Both families, Michael's and Murty's, joined the long queues for the Soup Kitchen in Kilduff. Luke never forgot the gaunt figures carrying their bowls, shuffling forward towards the giant pots. But most of all he never forgot the look in his father's eyes, the look of humiliation and broken pride.

The early harvest in 1840 was a good one. They had survived the hunger, but they had not paid the rent for many months. They were in breach of their contract and could be evicted.

Their landlord, Dominick Burke, was not the evicting kind. He was seen as being a fair landlord, which was perhaps the main reason that the Ryans held a twenty-one year lease. But they knew that Burke might be close to bankruptcy himself, and events could force his hand. Already there were stories of many evictions in the west of the county.

So when Burke's agent appeared in Carrigard trying to collect the little rent he could, Michael had guaranteed him not only that he would pay the rent from now, but also that he would pay every penny of the back-rent, with interest, and within one year. When the agent questioned how this could be done, Michael replied that Luke was going to go to England to work on the railways and would send his wages home to pay his father's rent. It was the first that Luke had heard about it.

When he had first arrived on the Great Western Railway, even his years of working in the farm and the quarry had not prepared him for the shock of what was expected of him at Box Tunnel. If this was because hard work was expected of any man in building England's railways, it was also because he worked on Martin Farrelly's gang.

But the impossible had been done. After a year working on the cuttings, embankments and tunnels of the Great Western Railway, Luke's wages had paid off all the back-rent on the farm, with interest, and the lease was secure again. He was fifteen years old.

But that was then. What now?

'So what does he have to say?' Eleanor asked.

'Not much, Mother. Just telling what Leeds is like, and how hard Farrelly is working them.'

'Nothing else?'

'He says Farrelly might be starting a second gang in the autumn.

'Where would he get the fellows for that?'

'He reckons on waiting until after the harvest and getting some of the Mayo lads in England before they come home.'

Eleanor looked at him in alarm. 'From Bromwich?'

'Perhaps. Who knows?'

She came across to the outshot and stood beside him, staring at the letter. She shook her head. 'Whatever you do, don't mention that to your Aunt Aileen.'

'No, Mother.'

He stood and took a stool by the fire, staring into the flames. The letter had disturbed him too. 'Would you not come back over?' Not an order. Only a suggestion, but a very strong one. He lay in bed that night, unable to sleep.

Before his father's letter had arrived, he had reckoned another three years on the railways would give him enough to buy a farm freehold. But now there would be no second farm, and he had to stay and help his father, though he no longer knew if that was what he wanted. Pat was the lucky one, though he did not know it yet.

The next morning, Pat and Murtybeg left Mayo for England. It was a Fair day, and the harvest gang had arranged to meet in Kilduff.

It was still dark when Murtybeg arrived down at Michael's house with his family. Aileen was there already. She was crying.

'You'll be back in the autumn,' she said, hugging Murtybeg.

'I will, of course. We both will.'

Eleanor packed a brown loaf and a clay jar of butter into Pat's pack.

'I'll just go down with you,' Luke said.

Aileen hugged her son again, and then they were on the road towards Kilduff.

'Where are ye all meeting?' Luke asked.

'McKinnon's,' Pat answered. 'We'll need a good hot whiskey inside ourselves before we move on.'

They walked past men and women driving cattle and sheep towards the Fair, others driving donkeys and carts carrying trays of eggs and barrels of butter. Even in the early light, Luke could see that many people were thin from months of hunger.

They made their way to McKinnon's bar and past the donkeys and horses tied to the rail outside.

The bar was owned by Michael's sister Sabina and her husband, Ian McKinnon.

Sabina had been born at the wrong time. In 1799, her father was only beginning his sentence in Claremorris. For three years her mother struggled to rear her, before Michael decided she would have to be fostered. She had been sent to a sister of her mother, who lived with her husband high up the Mountain.

Her foster-parents were childless, and they looked after her as they would any child of their own. But they too were poor, and when her foster father died, her foster mother moved in with another sister, and Sabina had to leave the Mountain. She worked as a barmaid in Kilduff and learned to speak English. Over the years, she gave up any hope of marriage. Then one night in 1838, a Scottish surveyor walked into the bar and changed her life forever.

Within weeks an attraction developed between them, and in 1839 McKinnon had approached Michael who, as Sabina's eldest male relative, accepted his proposal of marriage on her behalf. They were married in the summer, and Sabina continued to run the bar while McKinnon found occasional work as a roads surveyor either with the County Council in Castlebar, or later with the new Poor Law Union in Knockanure. They lived on her wages, and after five years they had saved enough from his commissions to buy the bar.

Luke pushed his way through to the bar, Pat and Murtybeg following. The bar at least had not changed – the same rough sawdust sprinkled on the floors, the same grubby walls, the same tobacco-stained ceiling, the same smell of tobacco, beer, whiskey, burning turf and unwashed bodies.

Sabina looked up for the next order, staring at him, not recognising him. Then she saw Pat and looked back to Luke. Her eyes lit up. 'Luke?'

She leaned across the bar and grabbed him to kiss him on the cheek. 'We'd heard you were home.' She flicked a wet cloth at Pat. 'Isn't it time you brought him down to see us, you eejit.'

'Oh, he hasn't had a chance yet,' Pat said. 'No time for idle chatter, Father says.'

She came out from the bar and hugged Luke. 'It's great to have you home again. You're to stay this time, do you hear me? Leave the travelling to the young lads now, and take care of your mother.'

'I will,' Luke said. 'You needn't be fretting about that.'

'And what about Danny? Did you not bring him with you?'

'Oh no. Danny's gone to Leeds. Hadn't you heard?'

'I'd heard right enough, but I didn't believe it. What would he be wanting to go to Leeds for? Shouldn't he be coming home now? Find a nice girl and take care of his mother.'

'Aye, he should,' Luke said.

She returned to the bar and poured out three whiskies. 'Here you are, lads. Get yourselves around that.'

A barman walked down from the far end of the bar and started to draw beer from the keg beside Sabina.

'See who's here, Ian,' Sabina said.

McKinnon turned around. 'Pat and Murteen, is it? Off to the harvest?'

'We are,' Murtybeg said.

'Do you not see who's with them?' Sabina asked. McKinnon stared at Luke. 'Who's that?'

'It's Luke, you *amadán*. Luke.'

'What! Luke? By God, so it is.'

Luke had known McKinnon even before Sabina had. He had been twelve years old in 1838 when McKinnon had first arrived in Kilduff and introduced him to a wider world, far beyond Irish farms and even English railways.

They had first met when the Scot was measuring out one of the Ryan fields for the Ordnance Survey. Luke had been intrigued to discover that McKinnon had fought in the Napoleonic Wars right up to the Battle of Waterloo. He extracted a promise from McKinnon to tell him of all the battles he had fought in Spain and France. McKinnon had kept his promise, and for as long as he was working around Carrigard, Luke followed him everywhere. He was entranced by the many names of battles and places which were far outside his experience.

Busaco, Torres Vedres, Santarem and Almeida.

He would make McKinnon write down the names on a scrap of paper and pronounce each; repeating them himself until he was happy he knew them.

Almarez and Salamanca. Ciudad Rodrigo and Badajoz.

At night he would still think about them, puzzled by the odd sounds of them.

Vittoria and Pamplona. Roncesvalles and San Sebastian. Bayonne and Toulouse.

Luke had been intrigued by the romance of them, but McKinnon had never forgotten the horror of them. He remembered the thousands who had died of fever in those places. He could still smell the stench of the camps – human excrement and horse manure everywhere. He could see the fever tents in rows, the fever sheds made out of rough branches, the lines of fevered men lying in the open. The shrunken faces of men he had known for years. The desperate, hollow eyes. The wasted corpses piled high like turf ricks, waiting for mass graves as the rats gnawed at them.

They died in battle too. Men shot or bayoneted or knifed in close combat. Artillerymen torn asunder by precision bombardment from the French guns. More bodies to be flung into the ever-lengthening trenches. More sackfuls of men's guts, limbs and carcasses to be slopped on top. More rats.

But he told Luke none of this. At times he talked of the brutality of war and fever and killing, but in 1838 Luke was too young to understand and more interested in fighting than dying.

McKinnon had told him too that he had been present at the battle of Waterloo, where he was one of the very few who had broken Napoleon's last attack. But this was all he would say about it. Luke was wildly curious about Waterloo, but no matter how much he begged him, McKinnon said nothing more. He had promised to tell him of Spain and France. But Waterloo was in Belgium, and that had not been part of the bargain.

McKinnon shook his hand. 'By God, you're most welcome. Now you just wait there a moment...'

'I'm not going nowhere.'

McKinnon brought the full mugs of beer to the other end of the bar. He came back carrying empty mugs and started drawing more beer. 'Yes,' he said, 'we'd heard you were home. I couldn't believe it when they told me. Couldn't understand it either. You were making good money, from all accounts. Why would you come back to this?'

'Father's orders,' Luke replied.

McKinnon shook his head. 'Michael ordered you home, did he? Now why the devil would he do that?'

'It's all to do with the lease,' Luke answered. 'They reckoned he was too old. They won't sign us for another twenty-one years unless I sign it too.'

'Couldn't Pat here sign it?'

'Too young. They won't take him.'

'But will Burke hold to the twenty-one years?' Sabina asked.

'Seems like he will.'

'There's few enough leases like that around here.'

'You won't find twenty-one year leases up at *Gort na Móna,*' McKinnon said. 'Clanowen won't have any truck with leases.'

'That bastard,' Sabina whispered. She turned to serve a drover at the other end of the bar.

'We're busy this morning,' McKinnon said. 'Eddie Roughneen and the others are in the back room there, waiting for Pat and Murteen. Why don't you go and see them all. We'll talk to you after though; you can tell us all about it.'

They struggled through the hard-packed mass of dealers and farmers to the back room. There were a dozen men or so, some with wives or mothers. Many of the men were too lean. Luke wondered how easy they would find it to cross Ireland and work on the harvest when they arrived in England. He knew some of them, but there were more he didn't recognise. In the corner, he saw Fergus Brennan, Kitty sitting alongside him. Their glances met, but she quickly looked away.

When Pat and Murtybeg had left with the other harvesters, Luke returned to the bar.

'You're busy enough this morning.'

'Oh, don't let that fool you' Sabina said. 'It's the drovers and the dealers; they're the ones with the money. There's few enough of our own fellows here now. Once today is over, you won't see a sinner here from one end of the week to the other.'

'Is it that bad?'

'How would it not be? Sure no one has any money, and any they have they're spending on corn. I don't know what we'd do if it wasn't for Ian, surveying roads whenever they ask him. There's little enough of that work around either, but it's enough to keep us in corn, and I suppose we should be thankful for that.'

'Thankful is right,' McKinnon said. 'And I'll tell you this. It's bad here, but it's not the worst.'

'So I've heard. Pat was telling me it's worse further west.'

'By God it is, you've no idea. I was out that way last week. Mulranny up to Belmullet and back by Bellacorick. Erris is in a terrible way. They're all leaving, anyone who can walk.'

'And all heading to England, from what I can see.'

'England, America, it doesn't matter. Anywhere but Mayo.'

'Enough of that talk,' Sabina said. 'Tell us about England. Six years away, you didn't come back to be talking about hunger.'

For a long time they talked of railways and the men in Farrelly's gang. But Luke kept bringing the conversation back to Mayo and hunger. He knew enough of railways. He had left all that behind. What worried him now was what lay ahead.

'Well, I don't know about the pair of you,' Sabina said at length, 'but I've got work to do, so I'll leave you to it.' She refilled their glasses and went back behind the bar.

'I can understand your concern,' McKinnon said to him. 'There's hunger coming, and it may well get worse across the summer if the harvest isn't a damned good one.'

'It's not just that, though,' Luke said. 'I'm getting to think like the English, that's what it is. Mayo scares the hell out of them, they reckon it's the poorest place on God's earth and we're all wild men. If you said to any of them lads they should come to Mayo, they'd run a mile. Danny too. He reckons there's no future in Mayo.'

'But you don't think that way, surely?'

'I didn't. I'd always looked forward to the day I'd come home. But then father's letter arrived, and I can tell you, it gave me one hell of a shock. It was only then it hit me, I'd no wish to come back at all. Danny told me I was a fool, and I'm inclined to think he was right.'

'So what will you do then? Go back on the railways?'

'I don't know that I can. The lease has me trapped. I can't have them all thrown out on the road. So I'll have to wait around a while, at least till Pat is old enough. By that time I might think better about it, and a few good harvests will see us right. But I don't know, I just don't know.'

Owen Corrigan came in. 'Well, Luke, settling back?'

'Pretty well. What about you?'

'Well enough. I've found a farm – nearly got it bought.'

'Which one is that?'

'The widow Malley's.'

'Over by *Árd na gCaiseal*?'

'That's the one.'

'She's selling?'

'She is. She's got the freehold. Mick Malley bought it from Clanowen twenty years back.'

'Why would she want selling it?' Sabina asked. 'Isn't young Tommy well able to farm?'

'That's as may be,' Corrigan replied 'but she's six other children apart from Tommy, and the farm sure as hell won't support them all. They need the money.'

'For corn?' Luke asked.

'For that and for travelling. They're leaving, the whole family, heading to Liverpool.'

Corrigan and Luke left together. They walked through the stink of animal dung. The street was covered in it, the walls were streaked with it. Most of the farmers had left town, and only a few drovers were driving the remaining cattle and sheep away. Luke thought of the cattle being driven off the boat in Liverpool. He thought of the famished people coming off with the cattle and the look of contempt in a young woman's eyes.

'You heard about Nessa?' Corrigan asked.

'Yes, I'd heard.'

'Look, I'm sorry.'

'There's no need,' Luke said. 'Jimmy's not your son, is he?'

'He's not. But it's just I feel bad about it.'

'Where is he now, do you know?'

'God only knows,' Corrigan said. 'The story was he'd gone to England.'

'Can we catch him there?'

'I doubt it. And even if you did, what good would it do?'

'We might get him to pay,' Luke said

'I don't think you'd get him to pay much. But he's still my nephew. There's no one else to take the blame apart from me.'

'There's not. But still...'

'Look, would you ever have a word with Murty? Nessa too. Ten pounds might help. What do you think?'

'I'll say it to them,' Luke said.

He told his father of Corrigan's offer that night.

'Yes,' Michael said, 'that might help. It's not a bad offer, seeing as it's not Owen should be paying it. Will you have a word with Murty?'

'Yes, Father.'

As he walked up to the quarry the next morning, he could already hear the sound of a sledgehammer and the rhythmic pounding of iron on rock. Looking down from the edge he could see his father, stripped to the waist in spite of the cold. Michael still had a powerful chest at the age of sixty three. He glanced up as Luke came towards him, but hardly broke the rhythm. 'Aren't you the great fellow? You go out before me and arrive after me.'

Luke smiled. 'I just went up to Murty and Aileen as you asked me.'

'So what did they have to say?'

'Murty reckoned Owen's offer was fine. They'll take the ten pounds.'

'Well, that's one good thing. But it shouldn't be Owen paying it.'

'I know.'

He took up the second sledgehammer, and they started working together. The rhythm was the same, beating out the smashing tattoo. Luke stopped to remove his shirt.

It began to rain. Both men put their shirts on again and sheltered under a whin bush at the side of the quarry. Its roots disappeared into a crack in the rock; it almost seemed to be growing out of rock.

Michael picked up the coat he had left there, a very old one with string tying it together. 'Did you bring your coat with you?'

'No, Father.'

'God, do you never learn. Sit down here.'

Luke sat alongside Michael, the old coat covering their heads as the rain got heavier. It was dripping off the whin bush, soaking the coat and running down their faces and off the ends of their noses. It was flowing in rivulets down the sides of the rock walls, forming pools of grey slush in the ground of the quarry.

'What else did Murty and Aileen have to say?' Michael asked.

'Aileen said nothing at all.'

'Not a word?'

'Not one word.'

Michael shook his head and hunched over his knees, staring at the ground. Then he picked up a stone and flung it at the handle of one of the sledgehammers thirty feet away. It hit the handle in the centre.

'I'll bet you couldn't do that, young lad.'

Luke picked up a stone and threw. He missed by six inches. Michael laughed. Then he went quiet again. He picked up a twig and started to draw circles in the slush.

'I'm worried about Aileen. Your mother is too.'

'Well, she is her sister.'

'God knows, it was bad enough already. She works all the hours God sent, Aileen does. Weaving and spinning and weaving and spinning, but you know what it's like with the linen market. They're paying them almost nothing.'

'So I've heard.'

'Do you know there's times I haven't seen her for weeks on end. If we go up, she disappears behind the curtain, and she'll only talk to Elly. And sometimes not even to her.'

'I'm sorry. I never knew.'

'She's terrified of Murty losing the school. She reckons the new schools will close him down. What do you think?'

Luke picked up a stone and threw it again at the handle. This time he missed by only three inches. 'I think she's right.'

'Bloody hell,' Michael said.

The rain had softened into a light drizzle. Michael got up, pulling Luke up after him, and they went back to smashing rock. Hours later, they walked back towards the house, their sledgehammers over their shoulders.

'So what do you think of Nessy?' Michael asked. 'How did she seem this morning?'

'She's alright. Like you said, it's Aileen is taking it worse.'

'Aye, Nessy is a strong girl,' his father replied. 'And she'll have to be strong when the secret is out. Once Flynn finds out, there'll be bloody hell to pay.'

'You mean Father Flynn?'

Michael stopped. 'Look, let's get one thing straight. There's many things that damned man might be, but a priest he is not.'

Michael expected to be called to County Galway to renew the lease, but since there were a number of other leases coming up for renewal in Carrigard in 1846 the land agent, Edmond White, came up from Galway city instead. A legal clerk arrived from Castlebar. They visited the Ryan household first – as the largest farm, it was the most important. For both Michael and Luke it was a vital meeting.

White was dressed well, though Luke knew his neatness decried the rough edges of a tough man well able to deal with tenants and collect arrears of rent. He had always been courteous with the Ryans though.

The clerk seemed a more fastidious type, thin in body and thin in face, well used to deferring to his betters. White had never deferred to anyone.

The four men sat around the table. Eleanor continued washing and cleaning, pretending not to be listening.

'I understand you will be extending for twenty-one years,' the clerk said. 'If I could be so bold as to ask, what age are you now, Mr. Ryan?'

'Sixty three.'

'We would presume you wouldn't finish out the twenty-one years yourself.'

'No. We're doing this for my son, Luke, here. He's the one who'll finish out the lease.'

'Either way,' the clerk said, 'we will have continuity. That is most important to Mr. Burke.'

'Yes,' Michael said. 'We had already agreed with Mr. White that the lease was to be extended on the condition Luke signed it with me.'

The clerk glanced to White, who nodded. 'Now, Mr. Ryan, if you'd be so good as to check through this contract. If you wish, I can read it to you.'

'No, there's no need for that,' Michael said. 'Luke, you read it out to us.' He passed the document across the table.

Luke started to read – 'Lease of part of the lands of Carrigard, Second division in the County of Mayo. Dated the twentieth of April 1846, Dominick Anthony Burke to Michael Ryan and his son Luke Ryan, as co-lessee. Yearly rents eight pounds and ten shillings for twenty one years...'

Michael stopped him. 'Eight pounds ten, Mr. White?'

'Yes.'

'It was only seven pounds fifteen.'

'True,' White answered, 'but Mr. Dawson here is of the opinion that the value of money has slipped over the past twenty three years. It's a long time.'

Luke read on. Eleanor had stopped scrubbing and was listening more intently than ever. There were many more clauses: no sub-letting; no cutting of turf for fuel beyond that needed by the Ryans; duty of cleaning and repairing walls, drains and ditches; providing ten days duty labour per year; providing five days with horse and cart; and many other lesser items.

'The duty labour and the horse and cart will be for the quarry?' Michael asked.

'Indeed, Mr. Ryan. Mr. Burke is most anxious to maintain the contract on the upkeep of the roads.'

There was also a condition for building a 'commodious and substantial dwelling house on said premises with stone, lime and sand together.'

Luke stopped. 'What's this? We're supposed to build a new house.'

'I would have thought this house enough,' Michael said.

'Indeed it is, Mr. Ryan,' White said.

'Sorry, my mistake,' Dawson said. 'It's standard on all our contracts. I should have spotted it.' He reached across and took the contract from Luke. Carefully he crossed out the clause and initialled the change.

When all was finished, Michael stood, leaving the contract with Luke. He ordered him to read it closely a second time and then to check the 'fair copy' against the original.

Since witnesses were needed, Michael sent Luke to find two younger men of legal age who were able to sign their names. Then both copies were signed, and one was left with the Ryans.

'It's been a pleasure dealing with you, Mr. Ryan,' White said. 'Mr. Burke was most particular that you, of all people, should sign again.'

'I don't think you'll have any problem getting others to sign here either. There's not enough farms for the men who want them.'

'True. But it's not a matter of wanting. It's a matter of paying the rent.'

When the two men had left, Eleanor came over and hugged her husband. 'Another twenty-one years.'

'Aye,' said Michael. 'All the way to 1867. Did you see that? 1867. I'll be dead and gone by then. It'll be up to Luke to take care of ye.'

'Would you go on out of that,' Eleanor said. 'The Ryans live forever.'

Next day, Michael sent Luke to get Sorcha, while he continued breaking stones. Sorcha was an old woman who lived with her demented husband. Their holding was only half an acre, sublet from Michael with payment through labour. Many years before, her husband had built a tiny mud cabin which was enough to keep out the rain and cold. He had worked the days of labour for the Ryans then, but that was before his mind had gone. Sorcha worked the labour now. Luke had no idea what age she was, but she was a hard worker, reckoned to be able to out-work any man. She had no knowledge whatever of English.

When he arrived, she was feeding her hens with mashed scraps of potato skins. He could see nothing had changed since he had gone to England. The old cabin still had no chimney. Smoke from the fire was coming out through the gap between the door and the rough sawn, bog-oak lintel. The walls had no windows. There was a thatched roof on top, green with moss. The cabin was barely ten feet in length.

As he approached, she looked up at him, almost in alarm.

Her hair was all white now, falling down the full length of her back. Her face was red, puckered with age and decades of Mayo rain and wind. She was a small woman, thinner than before, but still powerful from years of harsh labour. She wore a grey blouse and a stained grey skirt, torn, and frayed.

The sight of her brought back memories. He thought of the years when he was too young to even work on the farm, and Eleanor would bring him down to Sorcha to keep him out of the kitchen while she was cooking. He remembered those days, playing in front of the cabin as she fed her few hens, or sitting beside the fire inside the cabin as she cooked potatoes and cabbage. He could not have been more than three or four, but it was as if she had been part of the family then, a second mother.

'God with you, Sorcha.'
    'God and Mary to you, stranger. Have you come from far?'
    'Only from the last house back. Do you not know me?'
    'Indeed and I don't. Why would I?'
    'It's Luke that I am. Luke.'
    'Luke?' She grasped him by the arm and stared up at his face. 'Oh saints above, I never knew you. You've become a giant of a man.'
    'No giant. But a bit longer than when I left.'
    She hugged him. 'Back from England, are you?
    'I am. And staying too.'
    'Hard work, was it?'
    'Hard is right. But sure that's no harm to any man.'
    'Nor a woman neither. Is that the reason you came?
    'Well, one of them perhaps.'
    'Your father is looking for me?'
    'He is.'
    She bolted the door with her husband inside, and she and Luke walked back the road together. They started working.

Luke was surprised to see that the old woman could still load and offload the cart as fast as he could. They filled it at the quarry, then swung the cart out on the road and filled the ruts on the hill running down to the ford. This marked off the end of the contract that the Ryans and Mr. Burke held with the county.

On the other side, Luke noticed a mixed group of ten or twelve men, women and children breaking stones. The work was proceeding at a grindingly slow pace. They were thin and pale. They all wore the same uniform, patched and faded over many years of use.

'I wonder who they are?' Luke asked.

Sorcha followed his gaze to the other side of the ford. 'Oh, the poor people.'

'But who are they?'

'They'll be the ones from Knockanure. From the new Workhouse. The Union.'

'Yes, I'd heard tell of that. It wasn't there when I left.'

'It was after the last hunger that they started it. For the ones who could not feed themselves. Poor souls.'

He worked on for a while. He was still puzzled. 'Wasn't it Bensons used to have the work on that part over the ford,' he asked.

'It was. But sure the Union is cheaper than Bensons.'

'Cheaper!'

'Of course they are. They don't have to pay their people at all. Food and lodging, that's all they get. How could they not be cheaper?'

That evening, he discussed it with Michael. 'Oh, I know they're cheaper,' Michael said. 'They could undercut any contract of ours.'

'Why don't they?'

'We've got a three year contract. That's why.'

'I didn't know that.'

'Oh yes, and we're not half way run yet. But it's after that that worries me. They've far too many beggars in the Workhouse and not enough work for them. They can underbid us any time they want once our contract is finished.'

When the rest of the family had turned in that night, Michael stayed sitting on one of the stools beside the fire. Idly he watched the dying embers, sometimes drawing lines and circles in the dead ash with the poker. His mind ranged back to other gangs breaking stones on other roads for no pay at all, their feet in chains. The look of joy on his father's face every week when he arrived with the package of smoked bacon, not forgetting the package for the overseer to look the other way.

He wondered if Claremorris Gaol still bid for contracts on the roads, or whether they would have enough prisoners to take contracts as far as Kilduff if they did. He doubted it. If there was to be any competition in stone-breaking it would be from Knockanure, not Claremorris; the Workhouse, not the Prison.

Chapter Four

Telegraph or Connaught Ranger, April 1846:
The wretched inhabitants are now subsisting on half diseased potatoes, and those, I fear, will not long remain. Really it is shocking to see a family of ten or twelve persons sit down, and strive to eat a basket of lumpers, and those half or two thirds rotten.

Luke was walking home from Kilduff when he heard a cart behind. He stood aside to let it pass.

'Snubbing me again?'

'Kitty? For God's sake, I never even saw you.'

'You expect me to believe that? Anyhow, I was going to offer you a ride home, whether you deserve it or not.'

He pulled himself up and sat in beside her. But the seat on the cart was too narrow, and he was pushed tightly in against her, hips and knees touching. She flicked the reins as he eased himself around to look at her.

'You've not changed since I left,' he said. That was untrue. She had changed. Even sitting, she carried herself with a conscious sensuality, though she was very thin. Her face had the same high cheekbones that all the Cunnanes had. Wisps of hair hung loose by her ears. Her eyes were blue – acute and penetrating.

'I can't say the same for you,' she answered him. 'If I hadn't heard you were back, I wouldn't have known you.'

'No?'

'You know, the last time I saw you, you were just a blushing young lad, not able to put two words together. Such a shy gossoon, you were.'

The wheel of the cart dropped into a rut, and they were shaken together. Her thigh was warm against his. He could feel his face turning red. He was becoming aroused. 'So what have you been doing in Kilduff this morning?' he asked.

'Selling eggs and butter, what else would I be doing? Saturday's market day.'

'Of course. I'd forgotten.'

'Forgotten what? Forgotten it's Saturday?'

'No. It's just…'

'Just what?'

'Never mind.'

She flicked her hair back. Again the cart hit a rut. Again his thigh rubbed against hers. He was more aroused now. He looked straight ahead, trying not to catch her glance.

At the side of the road, a family with five ragged children was sitting under the stone wall. The man's head was between his knees. The woman looked up as the cart passed, and caught Luke's eye. He looked away.

'How's Fergus lately?' he asked Kitty.

'He seemed well enough last week.'

'Before that, I meant.'

'Ah, Luke, stop the pretending.'

'Pretending what?'

'Pretending you care. There he is, off to England, and not a thought for the rest of us. What would you make of that?'

'Damned if I know,' he said. 'I'm not his wife.'

She laughed. 'You're not, but you know him well enough. A great fellow with the ladies, my Fergus. Now he's away on the harvest, getting to know wee girls, a long way from his wife and other prying eyes.'

'Well, you shouldn't be laughing. Wouldn't it be an awful lot worse if he wasn't on the harvest, and you'd all go hungry?'

'Standing up for him now, are you?'

'Someone has to.'

And that's a fine way to be, he thought. Defending Fergus from his own wife, even if it is in jest. And Fergus is away for how long? Four months? Five maybe. What am I thinking? Why am I thinking this? He was sweating now and could feel the hotness of her leg through the damp of his trousers. He was more aroused than ever. He tried to think of something to say, but every jerk of the cart distracted him. They had arrived at Carrigard.

'Thanks for the ride.'

'A pleasure,' she said. 'Anytime.'

He jumped out and crossed in front of the donkey, trying to walk sideways to hide his arousal, his face burning.

'You know,' she said, looking him up and down, 'I was wrong. You haven't changed at all.'

Damn her, he thought, as he walked into the cowshed. Damn her, damn her, damn her.

The next Saturday, Michael and Luke were in the quarry. They had been working since dawn. Eleanor had left the house before them to be with Nessa and Aileen as Nessa's time approached. The men had heard that the birth might be difficult, but they left these matters to the women. By midday, it had become warm and dry, far warmer than would be normal for this time of the year. 'It'd be a good day for turf,' Luke said.

Michael stopped for a moment, looking at the blue sky. 'Aye, it would.'

'I might go down to the low bog and start the cutting. I reckon you won't need me here.'

His father only nodded. Luke went back to the house, took out his *sleán* and walked towards the bog. He started digging turf, always watching the road.

Over the next hour many carts passed, but not the one he watched for. He started to feel angry, even though he knew it was stupid. She had not said anything, so why should he expect anything. Yet he wanted to see her cart passing, and he could not admit why. He saw many women going past. Some were on carts, some were carrying sacks. Then he realised that if he could see them, they could see him. He started digging in a different part of the bog where he could not be seen, but he was close enough to a blackthorn hedge to see through it to the road. Time passed. He was disappointed. He reckoned all the other women had passed by. She would not come past now. He felt bitter.

'Still ignoring me.' He spun around, startled.

'Kitty! Where the devil did you come from?'

'I just came over the back way by your uncle's.'

'I thought you'd come by cart.'

'Looking out for me, were you?'

He turned back to his digging. 'Maybe.'

She grasped his *sleán* to stop him. 'Fergus' father came with me, but he took the cart home. That's why you didn't see me.'

'But why did you come this way?'

'I had to see Nessy. Had you forgotten?'

He looked at her, half giddy, half ashamed. She was right. He had forgotten. He could only think about her. Nessa had disappeared from his mind.

'Did you see her? How is she? Will she...'

'I don't know. She's in terrible pain. It isn't right.' Her eyes were wet.

He thought of Kitty so many years ago. How long was it. Yes, he could remember her, but how she had changed. He had never seen her so vulnerable. The same face, perhaps. And the same grey shawl – he was sure of it now. Whatever Fergus was spending on her could not be much.

'She's going to die,' she said. 'She won't live through this. Aileen knows it, your mother knows it, all the women do.' Her lips were quivering.

'Hush there,' he said. 'She'll be fine. She's a strong girl.'

She was crying now. 'Oh God, I'm so lonely.'

'Lonely? You have Fergus, haven't you?'

'Have I? Have I really?'

Abruptly, she threw her arms around him, hugging him close.

'No,' he gasped. But the rest of him would not obey. He was holding her close at the waist. He looked down at her, tears streaming down her cheeks. Then he was kissing her, holding her head up to him, grasping her even tighter.

A full minute later, she pushed him back. 'No. We mustn't. Not now.' She stood back from him, shaking her hair loose, before gathering it under the shawl again. 'Go and see Nessy.' She walked towards the bramble gate.

He stood still, watching her go. How did she learn to move like that? All the walk of a queen, God damn her. It was in the way she moved, cool and erect; the suggestion of more; the promise of what?

Not now?

He returned to the quarry and was surprised to see his father was not there. He walked into the house. Michael was at the table, eating. Luke stayed standing.

'She's getting worse,' his father said.

'I'll just go up to the house so.'

'Would you not eat first?'

'I'll eat after.'

He walked up to Murty's cabin. He heard a scream. He stopped. Then he went on and knocked at the cabin's door. Murty was there. There was another scream from behind the hanging blanket.

'Luke's here,' Murty shouted.

Eleanor came out from behind the blanket.

'How is she?' Luke asked.

'She's very weak.'

Another scream echoed through the cabin. He looked to his mother, questioning. 'I don't know,' she said 'I just don't know.' She went back inside.

He sat at the table. Murty took down a small cup and poured *poitín* into it. His hands were trembling, and some of the *poitín* spilt. He handed it to Luke. As Luke tried to lift the cup, he found his own hands were trembling too. He put the cup back on the rough-cut table and steadied it with both hands, before lifting it to his lips again. For the next hour he sat with Murty. The screams grew weaker and became mingled with a wailing sound. Then the screaming stopped. Eleanor came from behind the blanket, as the wailing grew louder. 'It's a girl,' she said.

Murty looked up. 'And Nessa...?'

She shook her head.

Luke stayed at the table. Murty was silent, taking sips of *poitín*. The midwife had cleaned and dressed Nessa's body. Eleanor had wrapped the tiny infant in a shawl and was rocking it from side to side. Aileen sat at the edge of the bed, staring at the floor. Luke felt he was more in the way than useful. After a while, he left the house. He could hear the sound of heavy pounding from the quarry. His father was working, swinging the sledgehammer with ease. He did not even look up, as Luke arrived.

'Well, is it a boy or a girl?' he asked without pausing.

'A girl.'

'No trouble?'

'Nessa's dead.'

The pounding stopped. Michael stared at him, still holding the hammer. 'What's that you say?'

'She couldn't take it. She died as it was being born.'

Michael dropped the hammer and strode across to the path out of the quarry. Luke ran after him and grasped his arm.

'No, Father. We'd only be in the way.'

'But Murty...'

'We'll see him later.'

'But what...? Surely there's something...'

'Let's keep working. It'll keep our minds off things.'

They worked on, Michael smashing rock as Luke shovelled it away. From time to time, Michael asked a question or made a comment, but Luke said little. They went back into the house.

'It might be time now.'

'Yes, Father.'

They both stripped off and washed the sweat and dirt from their bodies. Michael dressed in his best clothes which he only used for Sundays. Luke did the same and followed his father up to Murty's house.

Nessa's body was lying on the bed. Eleanor was sitting on the other bed, Aileen shivering beside her. A wet-nurse was feeding the baby. '*Siobhán*,' Murty said, as he handed mugs of *poitín* to Luke and Michael.

'Has the priest been?' Michael whispered.

'Father Reilly's coming. We had to send a lad up to *Gort na Móna* to find him. Flynn wouldn't come, the bastard.'

'God damn him to hell.'

Over the next hour, people arrived. Many of the women paid their respects to Aileen, some hugged and kissed her, but she barely acknowledged them. Her eyes were unfocussed.

Kitty came to the door. 'How is she?' she asked Luke. He said nothing.

Then she saw all the other women. The wet-nurse was rocking the baby. She grasped him by the elbows. 'How is she?' she shouted.

'She's dead,' he said.

Father Reilly arrived. 'God bless you all,' he said.

'And you, Father,' Luke replied.

The men stood. The priest came to Murty, taking both his hands.

'I was so sorry to hear of it. This is a terrible day for you.'

'It's good of you to say so, Father,' Murty replied. 'I'm thankful you came.'

'Aye,' Michael said sharply. 'And there's another that should have and didn't.'

The priest shook his head. 'I know,' he whispered. There was a wailing from behind the blanket. The priest spun around, looking to where the cry had come from. 'It's alive?'

'It is,' Luke said.

The four men went behind the blanket. The baby was lying on the end of the bed, but the wailing had stopped.

'*She isn't sucking well,*' the wet nurse said.

'*She'll not live,*' Aileen said, without looking up.

'*We might have little time so,*' the priest said. '*Bring me water.*'

Luke went out to the kitchen, found a cup and a pitcher of water, and brought the full cup back. The priest blessed it.

'So what's the child's name to be?'

No one spoke.

'Whatever you think yourself,' Murty said at length.

'Then let it be Brigid. A saint, and one of our own.'

'Aye,' Murty responded, 'Brigid it is so.'

Aileen said nothing, still staring at the ground.

'And the godfather?'

'Luke,' Murty said, without hesitation. 'Who else would it be?'

Eleanor spoke before Father Reilly could ask the next question.

'*Kitty. You'll be godmother, won't you?*'

Kitty stared at Eleanor; in surprise or shock, Luke could not tell. She glanced back at the baby lying on the bed. Then she stood as if in a trance and walked slowly around the bed without taking her eyes off the child. Very gently she lifted her and brought her over to where the priest was standing, a look in her eyes which Luke had never expected.

The priest held the cup over the baby's forehead.

'*Ego te baptizo Brigid, in nomine Patris, et Filii, et Spiritus sancti.*'

*

Many people attended the wake the next night. Unlike most, it was a morose affair. Murty had bought whiskey, tobacco and a hundred clay pipes, and there was little left by evening. The kitchen was still crowded, but Aileen stayed behind the blanket, greeting no-one.

Eleanor had put the baby on the bed in the outshot. Danny's bed. Luke wondered how Aileen would react. Would she accept that Danny was not coming home, and that the baby, her grandchild, would take his bed. Perhaps.

Kitty arrived. '*God with ye all*,' she said.

'*God and Mary*,' Eleanor answered. She stood. Kitty sat on the bed beside the child. She had the same expression in her eyes that Luke had noticed before. What was it? Love? Yes, surely that, and stronger than would be expected; the love and desire for a child in a young woman who had never had one. He wondered about that and thought of Fergus. But there was more than that in her eyes. Fear? Maybe. He had never expected that. He thought again of what she had said in the bog. Yes, she was lonely, frightened too. Even Kitty, who laughed at everyone and everything, she had her own fears.

The baby was breathing with no sign of distress. Kitty touched the baby's cheeks. Then she lifted her gently, holding her close.

'*She'll live*,' she murmured.

'*She will*,' Eleanor said. '*God is good. The child will live.*'

As they buried Nessa the next day, it rained without stopping. Many more attended than had been at the wake, hundreds standing between the graves, more spilling out onto the road. Aileen knelt in the mud beside the grave, Eleanor holding her by the shoulders. Luke was surprised to see Kitty standing behind them, sheltering the baby under her shawl, swaying from side to side.

As they lowered the rough-built coffin into the ground, the men bowed their heads, and all the women knelt. Father Reilly led a decade of the Rosary. Luke stood at the back, staring at the bare wet feet of the women. Then he stood at the gate, shaking hands with people as they filed past him. He recognised many thin, pinched faces under battered caps or wrapped beneath ragged shawls. More he did not know.

Afterwards he worked a few hours in the quarry. When he came in, he saw Aileen, bent over the table, shaking. Eleanor's arms were around her shoulders. Michael was pacing up and down.

'That priest,' he shouted at Luke. 'That bloody priest. Will we never be rid of him?'

'What happened? What priest?'

'Flynn, the bastard, who did you think? Came up to her in the street in front of all the other women and told her it was the judgement of God. I swear I'll kill him.'

Murty came to the door the next morning. Eleanor was at the table, sorting the good potatoes from the rotten.

'Michael's not here,' she said.

'It's not Michael I'm looking for.'

She waved him to one of the stools beside the fire. He took out two clay pipes, filled both with tobacco and handed one to her.

'It's Aileen,' he said. 'It's not natural.'

'It was a terrible shock.'

'But damn it, Elly, she's lost children before. Both of you have. She was never like this before.'

'But Nessy wasn't a child. Over twenty years you've had her. She becomes part of you.'

'Oh, I know, I know,' he said. He took a twig from beside the fire and put one end in the flames. 'But Aileen...I thought I'd keep her steady. She was in a bad way, but I thought I could handle her. It was only when she met with that bloody priest...'

'I know. Michael was fit to kill him.'

He held the burning twig across for Eleanor to light the tobacco. 'Can you help us?'

'Of course. I'll do what I can.'

'I don't think Aileen can be left alone. I don't know what she might do to herself.'

Eleanor stared at him. 'You don't think...'

'She might, Elly. She just might.'

Eleanor sucked at the pipe. 'I'll go up every day you're at the school, so,' she said. 'Or you bring her down here. We'll get along somehow.'

'Yes, Elly. I knew you would.' He lit his own pipe. 'But there's another thing too. The baby.'

'The baby?' she cried. 'Isn't *Siobhán* feeding her?'

'She is. But it's when *Siobhán* isn't there, that's when we'll have the problem. Aileen won't take any interest in her.'

'No?'

'No. She thinks Brigid is going to die. She reckons that if she learned to love her, then she'd only have her heart broken again, and she couldn't take that a second time so soon.'

Eleanor thought about that. 'I'm sure you're right. She's shook enough as it is. So what about the baby?'

'I just don't know. And it's not that I'm complaining, but I'll not be able for this. I'm not a young man, I'm not supposed to be changing and cleaning babies, and *Siobhán* isn't going to feed her for ever. The child needs a mother.'

'Should we not just wait a few weeks?'

'I can't. Easter's over. I've got to re-open the school, and that's bad enough. What with Nessy dead and Murtybeg gone to England, it's almost impossible as it is. There's no way on earth I can take care of the baby.'

Eleanor drew on her pipe again. 'Maybe we could persuade Aileen. Have a word with her, the two of us. What do you think?'

'I don't think it's going to make any difference,' he said.

Next day, Eleanor took Brigid home. Aileen had told her that she would take the baby back when she felt better, but already Eleanor knew she would not. The irony of it struck her strongly. For years she herself had tried for another child, but had failed. Now she had the daughter she had wanted, but in a way she had never expected.

When the men returned for their midday meal, Michael looked at the baby in astonishment.

'It's that Aileen isn't able for it,' Eleanor whispered. 'We'll just hold on to the little one for a while.'

Some days later, she and Michael took Brigid down to the church. They knocked on the door of the priest's house. The old housekeeper answered it. They asked for Father Reilly. He came to the door.

'I wanted to ask you,' Michael said. 'Have you written Brigid into the church book yet?'

'Not yet,' the priest said. 'I wasn't too sure what to write, so I thought I'd wait. I meant to ask ye about that.'

'Perhaps we'd better do it now.'

They went through the church to the sacristy. Father Reilly took out the registry. He dipped the pen in ink and wrote down 'Brigid Ryan.'

'Godparents, Michael? Luke wasn't it? And Kitty Brennan.'

'That's right,' Michael said.

'And what should I put down for the father?'

'That would be difficult,' Eleanor said. 'We don't know his name.' She was lying, and both men knew it.

'Yes, I can see that's going to be a problem,' the priest said.

'It will,' Eleanor said. 'A dead mother and a father who's run off. We owe the girl more than that.'

'So what can we do then?'

'You could give our names as the parents,' Eleanor said. 'Myself and Michael.'

Michael looked around in surprise. 'He could what?'

'Us, Michael. Me and you.'

'Are you mad? What would people think?'

'Does that worry you?' Eleanor said softly. 'It never did before.'

Michael drew back with a startled look. Silence.

'Well?' Eleanor said.

'But...'

'But what?'

'Father Flynn. What would he do?'

'God only knows,' the priest answered. 'But I think I can deal with that.'

'Well then?' Eleanor said.

Brigid's parents were given as Eleanor and Michael Ryan.

Sometimes Luke would cut home by the rath above the bog. The rath itself was nothing more than a low, circular ridge on top of a knoll. Inside the circle there were small mounds, showing where mud cabins had stood many centuries before. They were overgrown with grass, blackthorn and whins, The ridge carried a crown of taller trees – alder, ash, birch and one single oak. The rath had been refuge for him from the age of five, a place he could always run to and hide. Because of its height, it was also a place from which he could observe the fields and houses near and far; a place where he could see, but not be seen. He began to remember places that he had forgotten in the years on the railways.

Close in, he could see the farms of Carrigard – people working in the fields or walking along the road that ran from Kilduff towards Knockanure. Further out, he could see other farms and clusters of houses with names he had learnt long before the Ordnance Survey came to Mayo. *Gort mór, Abhann an Rí, Lios Cregain, Cnoc rua, Currach an Dúin, Áth na mBó, Craobhaín, Gort na Móna, Árd na gCaiseal, Sliabh Meán* and *Baile a' Cnoic.*

Big Field, King's River, Cregan's Homestead, Red Hill, Fort of the Plain, Ford of the Cows, Little Branch, Field of Turf, Castle Rise, Middle Hill and Hill Village.

At the edge of it all was the Mountain, with the potato fields of *Baile a' Cnoic* pushing higher year by year.

Two Saturday's passed. The first he stayed working the farm with his father. The second it rained without cease. The next Saturday morning, he was down the low bog on his own. It was a warm, cloudless day.

He started to work on the turf, building it up into small ricks, seven sods on each. He worked fast. Even with the early mugginess, it would be a dry day, and there might not be too many more of them. When his shirt became soaked with sweat, he took it off, hung it on a blackthorn branch, and worked on. Even without it, he continued to sweat.

He thought of Nessa. Her death had hit him hard, more so than he had expected. But at the funeral and wake, he could see that it had touched Kitty more. He wondered too about Aileen. She no longer cried, but did not speak either.

As noon approached, he watched all the carts and walking women passing along the road. Long after all the others had passed, he saw a lone cart coming towards him. She waved to him from a distance, before tying the donkey to a blackthorn bush down a boreen on the other side. She came walking down the road towards him, into the field and across to the bog. He took his jacket and waved to her to follow him to the rath.

As before, he grasped her tightly. This time there was no need for words, as they made love with a desperate urgency.

Chapter Five

The Leeds Mercury, April 1846:
The foundation stone of that stupendous work, the Wharf-
dale Viaduct on the Leeds and Thirsk Railway, was laid on
Monday last. The day, though not wearing a very inviting
aspect, was nevertheless favourable for such a ceremony, and
drew together a very numerous concourse of spectators of
both sexes from Leeds and the surrounding districts. The
display and rejoicing on the occasion were quite commensu-
rate with the magnitude and importance of the work, for the
commencement of which the day was specially set apart by
the company, and made a general holiday for the workmen.

When Pat and Murtybeg travelled to England and Castle Bromwich, they
did not deviate from their direct journey. There were hundreds of harvesters
travelling to England, but the flow of shuffling, ragged families was far
greater. All they saw of Dublin was what they could see from walking to the
lodging house, and afterwards to the docks. They travelled steerage on the
slow cattleboat to Liverpool. There were hundreds of harvesters at one end
of the boat, and the Kilduff men joined them, distancing themselves from the
huddled mass of hungry families at the other end.

'They might have fever,' Eddie Roughneen said.

Pat was seasick all the way, and stinking by the time they arrived. In
Liverpool, the docks astonished him, but he did not have time to explore
them, nor did he have the wish to. Liverpool overwhelmed him, not only in
its frenzied activity, but in all its horrifying poverty. He had not expected that
in England. That night, they stayed in Buckley's, and the following morning
they took the train to Birmingham. When they arrived, they walked out to
the farm in a few hours.

Pat soon felt at home in Castle Bromwich. For the first few days, he
felt homesick, but there were many men from Mayo working on the farm
and on all the farms around. There were other Carrigard men close by, and
sometimes they would walk over, sharing whiskey, playing pontoon and
talking long into the night. No one spoke of hunger.

The men were proud of their ability to work hard. Pat could use a sickle or scythe from the age of five, and he found the work to be even easier than he had expected. But the hours were long. It rained less in Castle Bromwich than in Carrigard, but even so it was necessary to use every minute of sunshine in case the weather turned wet later. The weekends were ignored, and the men worked morning, afternoon and evening. Every day, they started mowing just after sunrise, while women and children followed behind the scythe men, stooking the corn.

They were playing cards one night.

'I forgot to tell you, Murteen,' Mikey Jordan said, 'there's a letter there for you. I left it on your bunk.'

Murtybeg left the room. After twenty minutes, Bernie McDonnell looked up from his cards.

'I wonder where Murteen's gone.'

'I'll just go and see,' Pat said. He went to the bunkroom.

Murtybeg was sitting on his bunk, still staring at the letter.

'She's dead,' he whispered.

'What! Who?'

'Nessy. Nessy's dead.'

The weeks following Luke's departure had been busy ones for Danny. He found three other men to join the gang. None of the other men knew them, but they were from East Mayo, and that was good enough.

He and Farrelly concluded the negotiations with one of Brassey's managers, and a few days later the gang left Dover and were back on the rails, headed for the Leeds & Thirsk Railway. At first they stayed in one of the shanty towns along the Leeds & Thirsk, but after a few days tramping around, Danny found a good lodgings in Bramhope at a good rate, and the gang moved in.

On their fourth day working on the cuttings, the first beggars came. They were two men, father and son, Danny guessed, accompanied by a woman carrying a baby. They wore ragged clothes, and they were all lean and wasted. Farrelly started walking across to them, but Danny was there first. The younger of the two men came up to him.

'*Any chance of the start?*' he asked.

'I'm sorry,' Danny said. 'We have no work for you.'

The man looked at him, uncomprehending. Danny knew from the accent that they were not from Mayo. He reckoned them from further south – Clare or Kerry perhaps.

'*It's just how hungry we are. We haven't eaten for three days.*'

'I don't understand you,' Danny said. 'Try one of the other gangs.'

The man stared at him, with a look of absolute hopelessness in his eyes.

Then, without a sound, he turned and walked away, the rest following.

Farrelly came over to Danny. They both watched the family walk into the distance.

'*Since when did you not understand Irish?*' Farrelly asked.

'*Since I saw them coming,*' Danny replied.

That night they argued about it all.

'We just can't take them,' Danny said. 'They're not able to work. We can't be sharing with the likes of them.'

'But they'd strengthen up,' Lavan said. 'A few weeks here, get a bit of beef in their bellies, and...'

'A few weeks,' Danny said. 'A few months more like, and the old man, he'll never work again. He's too old and too far gone.'

'Aren't you being terribly hard?' Farrelly asked.

'No I'm not, Martin. Take on one of those fellows, and you'll have a hundred asking tomorrow.'

'Well, at least it wasn't one of our own,' Lavan said. 'Wherever they were from, it was nowhere near Kilduff.'

Danny thought about that in his bunk that night. Not one of our own? Not yet. But there would come a time when men at home would hear how much Farrelly's gang was earning and where they were working. Hundreds of starving people flooding in from Kilduff, Carrigard and the Mountain. He knew he could resist the pressure, but could the other men refuse men they knew? A second gang might ease the pressure. It was then that he had written to Luke, though already he had known that Luke would not return.

Over the next few weeks they turned away many Irish beggars, but it was always in Danny's mind. Slowly he began to appreciate that the problem might be no problem at all; in fact, it could be an enormous opportunity. It was just he had never thought of it that way. But then a letter arrived from Carrigard.

He opened it, glanced through it, and crumpled it. Nessa was dead.

'I know,' Farrelly said. 'It's in my mother's letter. Bad news travels fast.'

For the next few days, Danny said little to anyone. He was surprised at his own reaction. He never thought of himself as a man who might cry, but many times he came close to it. Even though he and Nessa were so different, they had been very close when they were children. She, along with much of Mayo, had become less and less important over the years, but her death brought it all back to him in a savage way. For days he brooded over it, unable to accept that Nessa was dead.

Then another thought began to settle in his mind. Nessa had not just died, she had been murdered. Murdered by the man who had caused the baby that killed her. She must be avenged.

He wrote two letters. The first was to Carrigard expressing his grief to all the family. It was a difficult letter for him; he felt he did not have the language to express such emotions. The second letter was much simpler. It was to Murtybeg in Castle Bromwich.

Within four days, Murtybeg's reply arrived. Jimmy Corrigan was the man he wanted, but he had left Kilduff and could not be found. Danny swore that he would find him, and that Jimmy would pay the price.

The work went on regardless, and Danny's mind returned to other matters. During the week it was nothing but hard physical labour – smashing rock with sledgehammers; shovelling broken rock and shale onto rail wagons; dragging horses and wagons along the rails to the tipping points for the embankments. But now he knew that he was going to go further in life than that. Much further.

On the weekends, he spent hours calculating amounts to be bid and amounts due on the contracts. Left to himself, the contracts and calculations were stretching Danny's mind, and he was developing his own ideas further. Everyone assumed that any money that a man did not spend during the month would be sent back to Mayo. But there was no reason why this should be so, and while Danny supported his father's family in Carrigard, he was also saving. This was something he had never mentioned to anyone, not even to Luke or to Farrelly. He had opened an account in his own name in a bank in Leeds. His account now held over sixty pounds in sterling. He was determined about starting his own business. And now he was beginning to see how.

From all his experience with accounts and negotiation, he knew the going rates for each cubic yard or ton of 'muck' shifted, and how it varied depending on whether it was mud, clay, shale or rock. He knew that the main contractors added a percentage on top of this, and he could easily calculate their profits. But on looking through the figures, an anomaly struck him. The men in Farrelly's gang were highly paid. Even though they worked very long hours, four and five shillings a day represented something approaching the highest wages in England.

He knew that good workmen on building sites in Ireland would make a third or a quarter of that amount, even in good times. The hours might have been less, but the difference was still substantial. At Irish wages, muck-shifting could be very profitable for a contractor in England.

The famine in Ireland only made it better. Men fleeing hunger would work for very little. He wondered just how low wages could be driven. In the far west, all along the coastlines of Mayo and Galway, there was no money economy at all. Even the rent was paid in labour days or in kind, almost never in cash. Men who rarely saw money, men who were starving, would work for almost nothing. They might not work hard, but they could be paid very little.

Whenever haggard men approached them looking for 'the start' he was tempted to offer them a pittance to see what they would accept. But in the end it was not necessary.

He was working alongside Farrelly. When they paused for the mid-morning break, he noticed a gang of men two hundred yards down the cutting. 'They won't get much on piece rate,' he commented to Farrelly. 'They're working half what we are.'

Farrelly looked down to the cutting. 'They must be only starting.'

'I doubt they'll work much faster,' Danny said. 'They look pretty miserable from here.'

'You've sharp eyesight,' Farrelly said.

Danny stood up and walked down the cutting, dodging between piles of rock and stone. As he came to the gang, a man came across and stopped Danny. He was by no means thin.

'Where are you going?' Danny recognised the Mayo accent. That was a lucky chance.

'I just thought I'd come and say hello to ye all. You're new, aren't you.'

'We might be,' the man replied.

And you're sure as hell not, Danny thought. Too well fed for that. But there was no point in being aggressive if he was looking for information.

'I was just a bit surprised,' he said. 'A man like you, letting them work that slow.'

'They're only starting. That's why.'

'Starting or not, you can't make any money out of that.'

'And that's where you're wrong,' the other man said. 'There's more profit in these fellows than any gang on this railway.'

Danny decided to challenge him; using the other's own boastfulness against him; baiting him.

'That's impossible,' he said.

'Not at tenpence a day, it's not,' the man answered.

'Tenpence a day? No man would work for that.'

'They'll work for what they're given. We pay them, we feed them, and we shelter them. What more can they expect, and they not even able to speak the Queen's English?'

Danny walked back. An Irish speaking gang, with no knowledge of English. He wondered where they had come from. The contractor was from Mayo, but that might not mean anything.

As he worked through the afternoon, he watched the other gang. When he saw them leaving, he stopped working. 'I just want to finish some of the paperwork tonight,' he said to Farrelly. 'I'll see you in a few hours.'

He followed the other gang as they walked back to their lodgings, staying well back so as not to arouse the suspicion of the gangmaster. As he had expected, they walked towards the straggling line of shacks along the railway line. The gangmaster continued towards the village, and Danny walked faster to catch up with the gang.

The shacks were built from discarded sleepers and crates. He could smell the stink of the open sewers behind them, running off from the embankment. In front, children playing alongside pigs and dogs. Ragged women stood at the doors, or sat outside, watching them.

He listened to the accents around him. It was from the West of Ireland, he was sure of that. It might even have been Mayo, but it was different to what his mother had spoken to him as a child. Still there were enough similarities. He walked up to a group of them standing outside, smoking.

'*Mayo, are ye,*' he asked in Irish.

'*What of it if we are?*' one answered. His voice was dull and broken.

'*I just thought ye might be, that's all.*'

'*Are you Mayo yourself,*' one of the other men asked him.

'*I am,*' Danny said.

'*Why didn't you say so,*' another asked him. '*If you're Mayo, you're welcome here.*'

They brought him inside the shack. Two women were cooking inside, one frying kidneys and livers over an open fire in the centre of the shack, the other boiling a pot of chicken necks over another fire below an opening in the low roof. Danny sat with the men, gnawing on a neck. When he had finished, he threw it into a dark corner as the others had done. He could hear rustling and squeaking in the dark. Rats. The pot was passed around again, but this time he refused.

He learned a lot. The men were from the far west of Mayo, down the narrow peninsula of Erris. They had eaten little for weeks. They told a horrifying story of a desperate walk to Westport, abandoning men who dropped along the way. Most had left their families behind, hoping to earn enough in England to send money back for food. What few sheep and cattle they had, they brought to Westport for sale – mutton and beef on the hoof that was needed for their own starving families. There had been no choice, they needed money to get to England, and the only way to get it was by selling their animals. Dublin was too far to walk from Erris, so they had travelled from Westport in a cattleboat to Liverpool where their gangmaster had met them straight off the boat. He had seemed friendly enough at first. He had given them the first full meal they had had in a year and cash in advance to send back to their families. Now they were earning tenpence a day, and half of that was deducted to pay off what they owed to the gangmaster. They were trapped in a system they did not understand, trying to make sense of it in a language they did not understand either.

Danny walked back to his lodgings, thinking it all through. Tenpence a day? That would not last, but as long as it did, the gangmaster was making good money out of them. He had already assessed their rate of work and was doing rapid calculations in his head again. Even with food and lodgings, the results were far better than he had suspected.

Chapter Six

Mayo Constitution, May 1846:
We again reiterate our former statement. There is no 'famine'
in this part of the country.

Luke found a powerful contrast in his meetings with Kitty. He was always saving himself for Saturday morning and the sheer ecstatic release. He found himself more irritable by Wednesday or Thursday from frustration. Then Saturday, and the build-up to the climax of their lovemaking. Afterwards the return of grim reality. Mayo was hungry, and Nessa was dead.

He could see by how lean Kitty was that she had not been eating much over the previous months as the supplies of potatoes ran down. He was relieved though that Fergus was in England now, and sending money home. At least she had food to eat. Little but hard corn perhaps, but they were all eating that.

Nessa was more disturbing though. She was always in their thoughts, Kitty's most of all. It was more than sorrow. It was guilt too.

'I was too wild,' she told him one day.

'Wild?' he asked. 'How do you mean wild?'

'Sure, weren't we all wild. Me, Nessy, Fergus and Jimmy. We thought we knew it all, we did. Laughing and joking all the time, never a bit of respect for anyone. Why should we? All last summer, it seemed wonderful, the long days up the bog, doing whatever we wanted. And you can imagine what that was, can't you? And the dancing too, all over the parish, wherever there was anything on. He was a great dancer, Fergus was, and Jimmy wasn't bad either. And then going home, hugging and kissing and carrying on, Father Flynn chasing us, though he'd never catch us and never got close enough to see who we were. It was great fun, but we never stopped to think, Nessy nor me. If they were wild then, Fergus and Jimmy, they'd be wild forever. Fergus did the right thing, or so I thought. I reckoned marriage would settle him, it's what all women think. Once they get their man, then they try to make him into a different man. But it never works out that way, that's what I didn't know. And Jimmy, he didn't even hang around, he couldn't face it like a man. Strange, isn't it. Fergus didn't have to marry me, there wasn't a little baby to force him to it. But Jimmy, the one who should've done it, he was the one who disappeared, off to Liverpool and God knows where, as fast as his legs could carry him. Nessy and me, we thought we were so smart. But we were the fools, that's all we were, and we never even knew it.'

He thought about that. He had had women on the railways, but they weren't real women like Kitty and Nessy. He couldn't remember the names of half of them. He was lucky then too. Farrelly had warned him often enough about angry fathers, angry brothers and even worse, diseases that would kill a man. But he had missed all of that.

'But why did you marry him?' he asked at last. 'No-one forced you.'

'Maybe because I loved him. Did you ever think of that?'

'And now?'

Abruptly she pulled him off his elbows, and they started all over again.

She was curious. Perhaps this was one of the things that most attracted him to her. Kitty had never left Mayo. She had only ever lived on the Cunnane farm, and the Brennan farm after she married Fergus. But she wanted to see more of the world. She questioned him about the railways. Bath and Bristol and Corsham. Redhill, Ashford and Dover. And the big cities too – Dublin, Liverpool, Birmingham, London, she wanted to know all about them. He knew this was dangerous. If she ever hinted to her in-laws what she knew, they would wonder how she had found out. Perhaps she was too smart for that.

But it brought a deeper dissatisfaction in her, and it unsettled him too. Already he had the urge to leave Mayo, but Kitty's constant probing only intensified it.

He found it incredible too that an older woman, so much more experienced, could love him above anyone else. Slowly he got to know her better. She had a wildness about her, but she was self-willed too, with a strong determination to see things through. How could she be so loving and gentle. Perhaps her strength came from fear. Would he ever know?

One day, they lay together, huddled close to keep out the cold.

'You know,' Luke said, 'in one way we're married already.'

She did not answer.

'If you think about it, we were both god-parents to Brigid. Godmother and godfather. Surely we're married in that way.'

Still she did not reply. He realised she was crying. Her eyes were closed. He shook her by the shoulder. 'What's wrong?'

She opened her eyes. 'Yes,' she said, 'Brigid. So small, so weak, I wanted to take her in my arms. And then to be her godmother. It was only right.'

'Of course, *alanna*. Of course it was.'

She shook her head. 'But I haven't seen her for so long. I want to see her.'

He patted her head and stroked her, running his fingers through her hair. 'But why don't you, my love? Mother would be delighted. She understands.'

'It's not that though.'

'No?'

'It's you.'

'Me?'

'Yes, you. How could I go to your house, meet with your mother and father with you there. They'd know at once. I just couldn't do it.'

'Yes, I suppose you're right. I wouldn't be able to do it either.'

'But we'll have to. We must.'

'But...why?' he asked. 'Why must we?'

'Brigid – she's why. She's all we've left of Nessy. Nothing else.'

'Yes...I know. You were very close to her.'

'Closer than you could ever imagine. I don't think I could ever explain it to you.'

'I understand.'

'No you don't,' she said. 'She was my friend. And I killed her.'

'Killed her! Don't be silly. How can you even think that?'

'It was that Corrigan bastard. If I hadn't encouraged her, she'd be alive today. A real charmer, he was, just like Fergus.'

Her face crumpled again. He pulled her head in against his shoulder.

Afterwards they lay in the hay together, a rough blanket over and under them. He was drowsy, drifting away to sleep. She tickled him under the arm.

'You remember that first morning together?'

'How could I forget!'

'There was something I never told you. Then or since.'

'What was that?' he asked, still only half awake.

'That I'd always loved you. Even years back.'

'*Arra* what? You expect me to believe that?'

'It's true,' she said, her eyes watering.

'True!' Luke exclaimed, awake now. 'If it's true, wouldn't you have waited?'

'Oh, God,' she said, turning her face away, 'how can I ever explain it to you. You were only a lad when you left. You're not much older now.'

'Oh, thanks. Was it young lads you were after then?'

'Not any young lad. I just remembered you as a lad, but I knew you were different. And you had gone away.'

'I had to,' he said. 'You know that as well as I do. We could have lost the farm back then.'

'I know, I know. But whichever...you'd gone away and Fergus was here. And you know Fergus. Always out for a laugh.'

'Yes, yes. I'm mad jealous, but...'

'But still you liked him.'

He thought about that. 'Yes. I suppose I did. Not that I can remember much of him now.'

They fell silent. Then she leant across, kissing him on the lips. 'I want to talk to you.'

'About what?'

'About us. What's going to happen?'

He stared at the branches above him. 'Damned if I know,' he said. 'Fergus will come home, or maybe he won't. Maybe with all the hunger he'll reckon it's better to stay in England and make money for corn. Who knows?'

'Yes,' she said. 'If only he'd stay away. And here we are, hoping for more hunger to keep him working on the railways. Starve and be happy.'

He slapped her. 'Stop that. Stop it now. We'll have no more wishing hunger on anyone. It'll be a good harvest, and that's all about it.'

She stared at him. 'You hit me.'

'I'm sorry. It's just there's enough suffering about without wishing for more.'

'So what then? A good harvest? Then Fergus comes home, and we leave? Is that it?'

He thought about that. He shook his head. 'I don't know, my love. I just don't know.'

Leave Mayo? He wondered if Danny was right. If perhaps he had been right all along.

As they parted, he walked towards the Ryan's bog. Kitty started towards the Knockanure road. But she stopped and turned, watching him in the distance and thinking. Then she took one of the back roads, well behind the bog.

Eleanor had been preparing the feed for the hens. She was startled by a knock at the door.

'Kitty, child.'

'There's no one in, is there?' Kitty asked.

'Only the baby.'

There was a long silence.

'Are you alright?' Eleanor asked in alarm.

'For sure,' Kitty replied. 'Can I come in?'

'Of course you can.'

She entered, cautious.

'The rest – will they be out for long?'

'What's that – out for long? Sure the day's only half gone. No, they won't be back till they know their food is ready for them.'

'It's just that I wouldn't want them knowing I'm here.'

'Why ever not?'

Kitty did not answer. Still she stood, looking to Eleanor and then towards the blanket dividing the cabin.

'Can I see her?'

'Is that what's wrong with you?' Eleanor asked.

'It's just how I'd like to see her.'

'Well, come on then.'

They both stepped behind the blanket. The baby was asleep, but awoke as they approached. She looked at the two women and started to cry. Eleanor took her up, leaning her into her shoulder, and patted her head.

'There, there, little Brigid. There's no need to cry.'

The baby quietened.

'Can I hold her?'

'Of course you can,' Eleanor said, passing her over. The baby had started to cry again, but like Eleanor, Kitty held her into her shoulder, swinging from the hips and crooning. When Brigid had quietened again, she sat on the bed holding the baby in her lap, and for a long time she said nothing at all.

She left well before the men returned for their meal.

When Michael and Luke had eaten and gone again, Eleanor cleared the table and washed the dishes. Then she walked to the cot, took the baby out, and held her on her knee. She smiled, rubbing the baby's lips. For the first time in her life, the baby smiled. Eleanor looked at Brigid, amazed. Then she spoke to her, still smiling and laughing. The baby's smile widened. Eleanor continued playing with the baby, thinking.

A few minutes later, she stood up, holding the baby out from her.

'Come on there, little Brigid. It's time to see your granny. And you're to keep smiling now, do you hear?'

With that she held the child to her bosom, the shawl wrapped around her, and opened the door. As she left, she took the flagon of poitín, and held it with the baby under her shawl. She walked up past the school where she could hear the chanting of children's voices. She went on to the schoolmaster's house and went in without knocking.

Aileen had her back to her. She was hunched over her loom, the shuttle rattling backwards and forwards.

'Look who I've got here, Aileen.'

Aileen turned around, startled. She stared at the baby, a look of fear on her face. 'I can't take it. I won't have it.'

Eleanor hid her own concern and laughed. 'No one's asking you to take her,' she answered. 'She only came up for a visit, didn't you Brigid? Wanted

83

to see your gran, didn't you.' She smiled at the baby, tickling her under the chin. A smile spread across the baby's face.

'She's not mine, I tell you.' The shuttle was rattling again.

'Not yours! Would you listen to her, Brigid. Of course she's not yours. She belongs to all of us. Don't you, little girl?'

The baby smiled again. The rattling continued though.

'And look what Brigid brought along for her Aunty Aileen.'

'You said I was her granny.'

'It doesn't matter to her. You can be the one or the other. She brought you a present anyhow.'

Aileen looked around. She spotted the flagon, and the rattling stopped. *'Wasn't it very good of her,'* she said, still sarcastic.

'Of course it was,' Eleanor said. *'She's a very good baby.'* She took two mugs, pouring a measure of *poitín* into each. *'Here you are. Brigid insists.'*

Aileen looked at the *poitín*. Eleanor held her breath, still trying to hold her smile. Then Aileen grasped the mug and drank. She placed the mug back on the table, gasping from the harshness of the unwatered *poitín*.

'And what about the baby,' she said. *'If she's so smart, why doesn't she have a mug?'*

'She's only being kind,' Eleanor said, *'offering you first.'* She dipped her finger in her own mug and dabbed the strong spirit on the baby's lips. Brigid's face puckered, and she went as if to cry.

'There, there,' Eleanor said. *'Don't cry, alanna.'*

'At least she doesn't think it's mother's milk,' Aileen said.

'No,' Eleanor said. *'And that might be no bad thing either.'*

She laid the baby in Aileen's lap. Brigid looked at Aileen's face and again made as if to cry.

'Stop that now, little Brigid,' Eleanor said. *'That's Aileen. She's a friend.'*

The baby looked from one woman to the another.

'Smile at her, Aileen.'

Aileen looked at the child and tried to smile. Once again, a wide smile spread over the baby's face. Eleanor said nothing. After a few minutes, Aileen hugged the child into her breast.

'I can't keep her. You know that,' she said.

'Of course you can't. Don't I know. But sure we'll take care of the little mite. She'll still come to visit. Won't you, Brigid?'

Aileen nodded. *'Aye, I'd like that.'*

Eleanor found a blanket, folded it three times, and spread it on the table. When the child was asleep, they laid her on the blanket, and Eleanor covered her with her shawl. Then she placed the two mugs beside the baby and filled them again.

An hour later, Murty returned. The two women were giggling. He looked from one to the other.

'God, we're finished now,' he said. 'Taken to the bottle, the pair of them.' He picked up another mug and filled it with *poitín*.

It was late when Eleanor left Murty and Aileen. For the first time in years she was quite intoxicated. She returned home and put Brigid to bed. Luke and Michael both seemed surprised to see her drunk, but said nothing. She took out her pipe and smoked, looking into the turf fire. After a while, she stood.

'The turf's running low,' she said, and walked out to the turf rick.

The night was clear, stars shining, the Milky Way arching overhead.

Then she stopped dead, and stood still. High over the Mountain, the sky was swirling with yellow and green.

Watching the aurora, her mind divided between wonder and terror. She thought of returning to Murty and Aileen, but dismissed the thought. Aileen was too superstitious. She would remember the last time they had seen the aurora and what had followed. That was all a long time ago.

1839:

On Little Christmas, it snowed.

It was cold when Luke and Pat went out for the milking. When they were finished, Eleanor joined them, and they walked down to Kilduff for the first Mass. There were few up so early. Around them, the fields were white, rising up the mountain to a metallic grey sky of heavy cloud. They walked briskly to keep warm, their breath condensing on the cold air.

Far to the west, there was a deepening depression in the ocean. The pressure at its heart had dropped to levels almost unknown in the north-eastern Atlantic. The winds had reached Storm Force. The storm was moving eastwards, pushing a warm front before it.

When they came out of the church, the snow had vanished. It was far too warm for January.

'I've never seen snow go that fast,' Pat said.

'Me neither,' Luke said.

As the depression moved towards the east, the warm air drifted upwards, and was replaced by a cold front carrying torrential rain. The pressure behind had dropped further. The winds in the ocean were at Violent Storm Force.

During the afternoon, there was a strong wind from the west. The temperature dropped again as it started to rain heavily. The family sat inside, listening to the drumming of the rain outside.

'If it goes on like this,' Michael said, 'the hay will be wet through. I've never heard it so heavy.'

As the storm crossed the coast of Ireland, the pressure at its centre had dropped again. Its winds were well over Hurricane Force and still strengthening.

They saw a pool forming inside the door. Luke went out and started shovelling wet clay around the outside of the door as the water still rose. It was no use. The water broke through under the door. Within seconds, half the kitchen was under water. Eleanor sat back by the fire with the rest, watching the water creeping up towards them. The door was rattling on its hinges.

'We've got to save the hay,' shouted Michael. 'The wind will carry it away.'

Luke went to open the door. It slammed back against the wall, rain and hail peppering his face like shot. The wind knocked him backwards. The roof started to rise. 'Shut the door,' Michael screamed. Luke went out, dragging the door shut behind him. Michael and Pat followed, fighting the door open. They were carrying ropes and a ladder. Luke held the door as the ladder was manhandled out. He dragged it shut again, and they made their way towards the haggard, backing into the wind.

Alicia was crying. Eleanor sat by her cot and sang to quieten her. The storm was still coming to its climax. Then Michael returned, dragging Pat with him. Pat's face was contorted with pain.

'What's wrong?' Eleanor screamed.

'His leg.'

Alicia was crying again.

They laid Pat on the bed, and Eleanor rolled up his trouser leg, looking at the deep gash from knee to shin. 'What happened, Michael?'

'The big tree in the haggard – it came down on top of him.'

Eleanor went to the kitchen, poured well water into a pot, and swung it over the fire. 'Where's Luke?'

'He's just getting the cow and calf in. If they're still there.'

There was an abrupt roar. The thatch had started to rise at the gable end of the house. Within seconds the flickering rush lamps were blown out, and the fire scattered across the kitchen.

'Get out, get out,' Michael screamed. 'It's going to come down.'

He grabbed Pat by one arm, pulled it around his shoulders, and dragged him towards the door. Eleanor took up the child, held her tight, and followed Michael. The child was screaming in terror.

'There, there, little Alicia. You'll be alright.'

'The cowshed,' Michael shouted through the roar of the storm. 'Come on. It's our only chance.'

Eleanor gasped as they came out of the shelter of the gable into the storm, and were swept sideways. The rain had stopped, but the wind still screamed through what was left of the trees. She turned her back into the wind, and crouching over the baby, she made a run for the cowshed. Michael dragged her inside.

'Where's Luke, Michael,' she screamed again. 'He's not back – where is he?'

'He'll be back soon, I tell you. Don't worry. You hold onto Alicia, and I'll take care of Pat here.' He laid Pat down on the straw. Just then they heard a crash as the roof of the house came down, bringing one of the gables down with it.

Michael went out again. He came back, pulling Luke in with him. He had been within seconds of entering the house as it collapsed. Eleanor laid the baby on the straw. She ran through the dark cowshed, tripping over straw and manure, and embraced him.

I thought we'd lost you, Luke. I thought you were gone.

The roof on the cowshed held against the storm. For the rest of the night Eleanor lay with her back against a wall, holding Alicia in her arms, rocking her gently. She could hear her cries of terror above the scream of the wind.

It was dawn before the storm subsided to a regular gale. An hour later, Luke and Michael went outside. Three of the house walls still stood. The rainwater had receded and was draining out of the house. In the haggard, much of the hayrick was still trapped under the trees. There was no evidence of either the cow or her calf.

In the wreckage of the house, there was no drinking water. They found some bread which was still dry. The old dresser had fallen on top of it.

Luke took a pail and walked into the wind to the well. When he returned with the water, Eleanor washed out the wound on Pat's leg. It was not a bad gash, though the area around it was bruised.

'You took a while with the water.'

'The well's all flooded with bog water. I had to go up to Sabina's.'

'Is she alright?'

'I don't know. She was asleep beside the fire. I didn't bother waking her.'

'Was there no one else there?'

'Only Ian McKinnon.'

Eleanor raised her eyebrows, but said nothing.

By now Michael had found dry turf and started to kindle a fire. Luke cleared the manure out of the cowshed, and spent the afternoon washing its flagstone floor out with rainwater. Afterwards they found some of their bedding in the house as Eleanor dried out the clothes. All the while, she sang in Irish, quietening the child's crying, calming her terrors.

That night they slept on hay under what was left of their bedding, all huddled together for warmth. The wind had died, and the hail and rain had ceased. Eleanor lay on one side, cuddling Alicia. Over the sleeping bodies, she could see through the open gap between the shed's rough-cut door and the wooden lintel.

Above the ruins of the house, the cloud cover over the Mountain had separated, and Eleanor could see the stars through the flickering curtains of the aurora.

The next day, she started the hard task of cleaning the shed. She knew that it would be months before they would be able to rebuild the house and live in it again. But no matter how much she scrubbed the floor and the walls, the old shed never seemed to be clean.

A week after the storm, the aurora returned. Then Alicia fell ill and refused to eat. Eleanor became apprehensive. The men watched, saying little. Five days later, a rash appeared, covering most of the child's body. Eleanor knew well what she was seeing, and when the child's face became bloated and turned dark, there was no remaining doubt.

Black Fever.

She isolated the child in one corner of the shed, the rest of the family huddling together at the other end. Often she would rise and mop the child's face and body in cooling water. During the day, she tried to feed her, but she knew the baby could no longer eat. A few days later, Alicia's arms and legs started to quiver, and she screamed with pain. Eleanor tried to calm her, but the child was delirious, no longer even aware of her mother. Gangrene appeared, and the shed was filled with the stench of rotting flesh. Eleanor still mopped the child's brow, singing softly.

On the fifteenth day, Eleanor's youngest child was dead. They buried her the same afternoon, outside a church with no roof.

1846:

Eleanor shuddered at the memory. But God had given her another girl and a second chance. She walked back into the house and went behind the curtain. She looked down at the sleeping baby. Then she sat beside her, and leaned down to the baby's ear.

'But there's no need for you to be afraid, little Brigid,' she whispered. 'You're not going to die. You're going to live and show the whole world the kind of girl you are. The kind of woman you'll be. The kind of women we are. They'll never have the beating of us, Brigid. Never.'

Through the summer, Luke's tension increased. He was startled one day when Kitty confessed to meeting his mother and the baby. This only increased the tension.

He loved Kitty, but there was anger there too. He could not understand how she had started meeting with his own mother, even if it was only to see the baby. He was furious too that she had not told him at first. He wondered why she had told him at all.

But her fear softened his anger. She was frightened of losing him, and perhaps more frightened of losing Brigid. At times she asked if she might continue seeing Brigid, even after Fergus returned. He did not reply, he was afraid to say no, because he knew the pain it would cause her. Perhaps he half hoped that Brigid would give them an excuse to meet again when it was all over, though he knew he could not look his mother or father in the eyes if Kitty was in the same room.

And there was Fergus too. She was terrified of what would happen if he found out about them. Luke had found this very hard to believe. He had always thought of Fergus as a roguish character, never as a man of violence. He would console her, assure her that their secret would never come out. He would tell her too that even if Fergus found out he would only be annoyed and that would be the end of it.

'Oh, Luke,' she said one day, 'you don't understand. You really do think he's like that. A gentle, poor soul. You think he'd just understand and do nothing. But I know him better. He'll beat me, I know he will. And as for you...'

'As for me, what?' he asked. But she was crying and could not speak. He held her close into his chest, stroking her long hair.

The summer progressed, a cold and wet one. There were many days on which they were cold in the old rath, huddling close for warmth. It depressed him further. Achingly he wished they could have a house of their own, a house away from prying eyes with a warm fire in the grate. She wished it too.

'Why don't we just go away?' she said one day. 'Get out of here. Make a life of our own somewhere else.'

'It's not possible, my love. You know that.'

'But it is. You could get work on the rails, you're always on about it. The great days you had, the money you made. And I could work too. Work in a mill. I'm good with my hands. We'd make money, buy a house of our own, and be warm at night.'

'It just isn't possible.'

'But why? Why isn't it?'

'You know the reasons as well as I do. Fergus would come after us. You're always telling me about him. He wouldn't stop in Mayo and let us get away with it.'

'But he wouldn't find us,' she answered.

'Maybe not. But there's other things too. I have to stay with the farm.

89

If I left, we'd be breaking the lease, and they'd all be out.'

'So what? Let Pat take it. He'd be well enough able to run it.'

'But he's too young for the lease.'

'How would they know? No one else knows how old he is.'

'But it's my farm. It's my farm, and I want to run it.'

'And it's your excuse too,' she said. 'All the great stories you've told me. All about the railways and England and running away. It was nothing but boasting.'

'Maybe it was what I wanted to believe,' he said. 'And anyhow, how would you leave? You'd have to leave Brigid behind, how could you do that?'

'Don't use Brigid against me,' she whispered. 'You know I love her, but I love you the more. You're the man in my life. I always believed in you, I thought you were the tough one. But it's Danny's the tough one, he's the one who's going to win.'

'Do you want me to be like Danny?'

'No, I don't. I just want you to be yourself. And I want you to be mine.'

He said nothing. She was crying again. He pulled her close in, kissing her forehead, running his fingers through her hair.

He was working with his father in the cowshed. Michael sat down by the cow, as Luke cleared the manure.

'I want you to stop seeing her,' his father said, without warning.

Luke stopped and looked back. Michael started milking the cow, the streams of milk splashing into the pail.

'What, Father?'

'I said you're to give her up. You're not to see her anymore.'

'Who?' His heart was pounding now. He stared open-eyed at the back of his father's head.

'I am your father,' Michael said, ignoring the question. 'You owe me respect. And I will have your respect.'

'Yes, Father, but...'

'You will also respect the men who are away working.'

'But Father...'

'And their women.'

Michael did not face him. The regular splashing continued, like the ticking of a clock.

'But I don't...'

'If you defy me, you will leave this house.'

Luke said nothing.

'And this farm.'

Still he said nothing.

'Do you understand me, Luke?'

He was confused, trying hard to think. Defy his father? Leave Carrigard? Take her away, far from Mayo? Yes, but it would have to be a long way. If his father knew, who else knew? Who had told him? He might defy his father, but he could not defy everyone, break with all the people he had ever known, and expect her to do the same. He had no time to think, and now his future teetered in the balance.

'Yes, Father,' he said at last in a quiet whisper. He leaned on the shovel for support, his eyes screwed shut, his throat choking.

'Good. Now you just tell her. Be gentle with her, but firm. It's over.'

'Yes, Father.'

Michael still had not looked at him. Luke turned away, and went on shovelling manure.

She stared at him, disbelieving. 'But how could he have known? No-one saw us.'

'Someone did.'

'But who?'

'I don't know.'

'Go and ask him. Ask him.'

'I can't. You know that. And even if I did, he'd never tell me. Maybe he saw us himself.'

For a few moments she was silent. Then she turned to face him, eyes blazing. 'God, can you never stand up to him. I used to think you were a tough fellow.'

'You still don't understand. Of course I can stand up to him, but where would that leave us. I'd lose the farm...'

'Didn't you co-sign for it?'

'Yes, but look, it's not just that. If we stay together, you and me, we'll have to leave Mayo.'

'And what of that?' she asked. 'Leave a father who never lets you do anything? And me leave a husband who runs after other women. Yes, let's leave them.'

'And go where?'

'England. Can't you go back to Farrelly?'

'Farrelly! Go back to the gang with another man's wife in tow. They wouldn't even talk to us.'

'Then anywhere, anywhere...'

'Yes,' he said, 'and where?

'America.'

'America?'

'Why not?'

'Why not, indeed,' he answered. 'You know as well as I do it won't work, and it's not a matter of being tough or standing up to anyone. It's Mayo or nothing. There's no other way.'

'So that's the end,' she said.

'It is, *a ghrá.*'

MEXICO. High on the side of a Mexican valley a peon walked across the terrace to his fields. He was frightened. For some days, he had been watching the stalks blackening. Crossing the fields, he noticed again the sickly sweet smell, but it was stronger now. When he reached his own plot, he started to dig. He saw the potatoes, all putrid, every one of them. He ran down to the middle of the plot and dug again at random. The same. Twice more he moved around the plot, digging and scrabbling. He could not find a single potato that was anything but rotten.

He stared across the valley to the light glistening off Smoking Mountain. The Heights of the Sun his grandmother had called it. The Home of the Gods the old priests had called it, in a time beyond remembering.

He fell to his knees and started to pray, but his gods offered no solace, and his fear turned to terror. The gods were dead.

Chapter Seven

Telegraph or Connaught Ranger, July 1846:
Burrishoole Relief Committee. Measures were adopted to select 700 of the most destitute to be employed. This is a task attended with very great difficulty, and will naturally excite much jealousy, as there are, we understand, near 2000 families in abject want, consisting of near 8000 persons. How the committee, or any member of it, can satisfactorily select 700 out of that number, we are at a loss to conjecture.

For weeks Luke said little to anyone, preferring to remain alone with his thoughts. Working with his father was difficult. Michael was not naturally a talkative man, and Kitty remained a block between them. The one thing that was most important was the one they could not talk about. But they ceased to speak of other matters too. As they worked together, the only words that passed between them were mechanical, only what was necessary for the job in hand.

Eleanor had sensed at once that there was something wrong, but for a few days neither Michael nor Luke said anything. When Michael finally told her, she was shocked. Then, more than ever, she wanted to reach out to Luke, but he was withdrawn, and she sensed it would do little good.

Luke felt isolated. It appeared that he had succeeded in hiding any mention of the affair from other family or friends, but at the time he most needed someone to talk to, there was no one there.

So he stayed alone. As so often before, he climbed to the rath in the evenings. Sometimes too he went there on Saturday mornings, hoping to see the familiar cart passing by. He was not sure if he ever saw it. He thought he did once, but it was too far to be certain. As time passed, he found too that he could no longer picture the face of the woman he had loved the most. Her shawl, her long flowing hair, these he could never forget, but her features had disappeared. There was nothing there.

What he felt was not pain as he understood it. It was nothing, a deep, empty nothingness. Kitty had not died, he could not grieve for her. She had disappeared; become nothing. Sometimes he would sit on the edge of the rath, staring at the long panorama of mountains all the way from Croagh

Patrick, across the Mountain to Nephin, and on to the Ox Mountains on the borders of County Sligo.

He would ponder this nothingness, but was unable to come to grips with it because it was nothing. He wished it was a solid problem, something he could work on and repair. Sometimes, when he felt like this, he would go to the quarry with his sledgehammer and smash rock for hours on end. Sometimes too Michael, hearing the smashing sound, would walk past the edge of the quarry to watch him working. He knew what Luke was doing. In his life too, he had known the meaning of unphysical pain, the numbness of nothingness. Within himself he wanted to reach out, but Michael was a tough man, and did not have the language to express such feelings. In the end, he found the one means of expression open to him. He fetched his own sledgehammer and joined Luke in the quarry, father and son breaking rock side by side in the companionship of heavy labour.

From the house Eleanor could hear the loud pounding, day after day. The heavy beating of hammer on stone told of a pain that would not go away. When she could take the noise no longer, she sat at the table, not working, only thinking. Luke and Kitty?

All across the summer she had suspected that there was someone. She could have asked him, but had decided to wait until he mentioned it to her. She had thought of many girls, but she had never thought of Kitty, in spite of meeting her every week. Or perhaps, she reflected, she might not have wanted to think it.

Looking back on it all, it was so obvious. She had not been surprised that Kitty would have wanted to see the child. Brigid was Nessa's daughter, and Nessa had been Kitty's best friend. And over the months she had been meeting Kitty, the story of Jimmy Corrigan had come out, as well as Kitty's guilt for having encouraged Nessa. Eleanor had accepted all these things, and with it she had accepted the need for secrecy. Kitty had told her that this was because she felt ridiculous being seen to love another woman's baby, and Eleanor had believed her.

The smashing of the hammer went on, echoing through her head.

'Luke. Oh my God, where did we ever get you from? So different, aren't you? I wonder do you know it? I think you do. I was so proud when you lived. Yes, when you lived, not just when you were born. My first living child and a son for Michael. That was so important to him, his first son and now his eldest son. Did I say that right? Oh God, I said I'd stop thinking about this, but I can't. Yes, his first living son. It would surprise you, wouldn't it? There was another before you, another son called Luke. Your brother. I never told you that. Perhaps I never will. My first born. Can you understand it? All a mother's love and all a father's pride. So helpless though. How he sucked! But it was not to be. Six months he lived. And then? *He died. His face black, trying so hard to breathe. All the pain, the terrible pain and the terror. But still he died, just the same way as Alicia did later. Maybe that's why you're different though. There's two Lukes in you. Yes, that's why I named you Luke again, after your baby brother you never knew. Your father told me that I was half mad when my baby died. When you came, I just knew my baby had come back to me. The same life, only a different body. Your father told the priest, and he told me I was mad. But he christened you Luke anyway, I would have it no other way. He said you had a different soul, but for me that only made two souls. Two in one. Why not? God has three. Now I shouldn't have thought that, should I? It must be a sin. Maybe I am mad. Stop it now. I promised Michael I wouldn't think of these things. And I swore I wouldn't think in Irish. But I can't stop thinking, can I?* Fine, I'll think in English today. That way I'll only be breaking one promise. Yes, Luke, you're two in one. That's why you're different. But how, you might ask, how are you different? It's your curiosity, isn't it? Twice as much as anyone else. No, ten times. Always asking me questions, do you remember? What's this? Who's that? When was the other? And why, why, why – always why? You could never stop it, could you? Always coming back from Murty's classes asking me questions. You thought that grown-ups had all the answers. You never noticed that I couldn't answer you. We never had schools on the Mountain. But every time I learnt a little from your questions, and the next time I could try an answer, just to keep you talking. How much I learnt from your questions. But it's not just the curiosity. No, it's what the curiosity does to you. All this talk of battles and wars and foreign places that you got from Ian. I hope to God there isn't a war, you'd fight in it, wouldn't you? But even if there isn't a war, what about all these places nobody else talks about. Places I'd never heard of. England, I'd heard of that. America too. France from the time they came to Mayo. But Spain? Or Waterloo? I hadn't heard of them anyway. So where did you get it all from? It wasn't my family, that's for sure and certain. No curiosity there, they knew no world beyond the Mountain and Mayo. They'd heard of Castlebar and Westport. England too, but America was beyond them. And your father's family, what about them? Your father, a good man, tough with it. Told stories about running the farm and paying the rent and selling the cattle after the Rebellion. Yes, a strong man, even as a lad, but he never had your curiosity, and his world never went beyond Mayo. Maybe your grandfather. He could read. And he knew so much once, what he didn't forget in the gaol. He was just like Murty before that, that's what the old people thought, they all said Murty takes after him. Maybe he does. And Murty is curious too. That's what makes him a teacher – a real teacher. But he never went out of Ireland either. That's his world, for all his talk of everywhere else. And no-one before him went either. *You see, my son, you're going to travel the world, and I know it. You mightn't know it, and your father surely doesn't. He thinks you're going to take over the farm. You might think you will too, but I know better, and I'll never tell you. You see, it's Pat who'll be the farmer. He'll be a big strong fellow, and he's got a softer heart. Yes, it's your brother will be the farmer. But you? You won't stay. No – you'll leave us, Luke. You'll leave us all, and you'll travel the endless roads.'*

McKinnon saw a letter on the table in the hallway. He picked it up, puzzled. 'Who's it from?' he shouted at Sabina in the bar.

She came back, drying a mug. 'Now you don't think I'd open your post on you. Nor be able to read much of it if I did.'

McKinnon slit the letter open, Sabina peering over his shoulder.

'So who is it?' she asked.

'Andrew Irvine.'

'Who?'

'Just a fellow I worked with on the Survey back in '38. I told you about him. Scottish fellow.'

'The one who stayed on in Castlebar.'

'That's right,' he said. 'It seems they want me over there.'

'In Castlebar? For what?'

'To help the Unions with the Relief Works.'

'But you do that already.'

'That's right. But they're talking of full time working.'

'Full time?'

'Yes, and not just here. All around the county, wherever they need me. I'm not surprised, I'd heard they were short of qualified men, and there's damned few surveyors in Mayo. I'd been half thinking of writing to them anyhow.'

'You didn't tell me that,' Sabina said.

'I hadn't decided.'

'What will you do? Will you go?'

'I'll have to. It's good money, and even if we don't need it, your family might. And they really do need surveyors in Castlebar. There's not enough for all the Works they're planning, and there's people starving. There are many might not make the harvest. How else will they earn money unless at building roads, and how else will the Government pay them except making them work, and the Workhouses can't take a fraction of them. I can't possibly refuse.'

'What should I do? Go with you?'

'I think it's better not,' McKinnon replied. 'You might as well stay and run the bar. Not that it'll bring in much over the next few months. But we must keep going.'

'I know. But still…'

'I wouldn't worry, my love. It's not long to the harvest. I'll be back soon enough.'

McKinnon rode out to Carrigard and told them about the letter.

'Well,' Luke asked, 'are you going to take it?'

'Of course, but it's not that I came down for. They're starting with Relief Works.'

'Yes,' said Michael, 'but through the Union. And who wants that?'

'You're missing the point,' McKinnon said. 'Sure, it's through the Union, but they're only doing the organising. Can't you see, it's Outdoor Relief, of a sort anyhow. They still won't feed the people without work, but they're not insisting that they go into the Workhouse either. There'll be no need to break up families. They can stay in their own houses. And there's more good news. It seems one of the new schemes won't be too far away – just a mile down the road towards Knockanure. They've started already.'

'What!' Luke gasped. 'When?'

'This morning.'

'Wasn't the Union working on that part already?' asked Michael.

'Oh yes. But up to now they've only been using inmates from the Workhouse. Now they're planning to really improve it this time with hundreds more people working on it from all around here.'

'Well, it'll help, that's for sure,' Michael said. 'Still, it won't matter much to us. You won't see us working as labourers for the Union. The early harvest can be good or bad, but there's no way we'd do that.'

Later McKinnon left to travel to Knockanure. Luke saw him out, and then they walked along, leading the horse for some time.

'Your father's a proud man,' McKinnon said. 'I can understand him too, so let's hope the early harvest is good. Have ye enough planted?'

'Now what do you think?' Luke answered. 'Do you think Father would let us eat the seed potatoes? If there's no blight, we'll have plenty to eat. That's for certain.'

'Let's hope there's not. But I'll tell you this, blight or not, there's going to be hunger around here. I reckon the early planting was well down.'

'I know,' Luke said. 'Not that I blame them. Some of them reckon that if they don't eat the seed potato, they won't live long enough to eat any potato.'

'Aye,' McKinnon said. 'And that will cause more trouble.'

'Like what?' Luke asked.

'The Mollys.'

'The Molly Maguires?'

'Who else?' McKinnon said. 'People are getting desperate. They're causing trouble around Westport, those fellows, hundreds at a time I hear. The peelers can't control them. If it goes on like this, there'll be men killed.'

They crossed the bridge and went on towards the Union Works. He could hear it before he saw it – the sound of picks and shovels working without a break. As they came around a corner, he stopped and stared. There were hundreds of men and women levelling the road and digging ditches.

'I see what you mean,' Luke said. 'I never knew it was like this.'

'Come closer, and you'll see the need for it.'

But Luke stopped. 'I don't want to go any closer. I can see enough from here. I'm afraid I'd know some of them.'

What he saw was hunger. Gaunt figures, pinched faces, wasted arms.

'Where have they all come from?' he asked.

'Further up the Mountain. They walked down here this morning.'

McKinnon mounted his horse. Luke watched him riding through the Works until the crowd of people closed in behind him.

In Castle Bromwich, they were out with the potatoes before dawn. Pat was with Murtybeg and Fergus Brennan, digging out the potatoes and piling them up into heaps for collection.

'I'll be leaving soon,' Murtybeg said.

'I was half expecting that,' Pat said. 'For Leeds?'

'Where else?' Murtybeg said. 'And before you say it, I know it's going to upset my mother, but there's no helping that. You've got to ask yourself, what's the real reason she's so miserable. She knows the new schools are coming, and when they do, Da won't be able to go on working. He won't have a job, and neither will I if I stay with him. So I reckon my duty is to make enough money to keep them until they decide what to do.'

'And what do you reckon that's going to be,' Pat asked.

'I don't know, but they might have to come to England themselves.'

'England? They won't like that.'

'They'll have to face up to it. What else is there?'

After sunup, they spotted their master coming across the field towards them. He was accompanied by another man, who was very well dressed, far too well for working in the fields. He wore a high-necked jacket over a check waistcoat. His shirt was topped by a cravat, which Pat knew could not have been bought in Castle Bromwich. His knee-high riding boots were half covered in dust and well dried mud, flecks of it showing on his beige cavalry twills. They stopped three ridges away.

The man took his knife and cut a stem from one of the potato plants. He held the leaf up, looking at it closely. Then he folded it and inserted it into the top pocket of his jacket.

He came to the ridge where Pat and Murtybeg were working. He picked out a potato and held it up, again observing it closely. He cut straight through it. Then he picked up another and slit it, then another and another. The fifth one he did not bother cutting. He held it out for them to see. Around one of the eyes of the potato there were small, sunken, brown-grey spots, hard to see, but unmistakeable. Then he strode away.

'I wonder who that was?' Fergus Brennan asked.

'God only knows,' Murtybeg said. 'But I think the blight is back.'

The man's name was Edward Yardley. He was a landowner from Staffordshire. The next day, he returned to his estate and wrote a letter to a friend in London.

As to – Sir Robert Peel
Houses of Parliament
Westminster
London

Shirecliffe House
Tamworth
Staffordshire

August 8th 1846

My Dear Robert,

I cannot convey to you how saddened I was to hear that you are no longer Prime Minister. But it must be a relief for you to have the heavy weight of Government taken from your shoulders. Caroline and I both hope that you will take the opportunity to rest some weeks, and we look forward to seeing you here in Tamworth shortly.

But these are difficult times, and I am not sure that Johnny Russell will have the commitment or the ability to continue the hard work that will be needed. Should the blight return, it will be essential to press the Government to undertake whatever is necessary to alleviate suffering and perhaps outright starvation. Even in Opposition therefore, you will still require information on the situation, most especially in Ireland, I expect.

As you requested therefore, I have continued checking the potato crop here for you. Even before I left Tamworth, I saw early evidence of the rot with small patches of black here and there in the potato fields.

The farms along Watling Street were no better or worse than Shirecliffe. In the six farms I visited over the next two days there were no patches of black in the fields, though the white substance that your informant mentioned was evident on the leaves. It rained the other side of Coventry, and the substance seemed to disappear. The farms around Kenilworth and Warwick showed no evidence of it. As I continued back towards Dorridge and Solihull, it had reappeared, even upon the better leaves. I have no doubt that this is the same fungus we saw last year.

In Castle Bromwich, I clearly saw this substance on the leaves. One farmer told me that the potatoes showed no signs of rot on the potato itself, but I must tell you that this is not the case. Some of those that appear healthy are already showing tiny signs of rot, and while they may appear harmless now, I have no doubt that they will spread through the potato and may even infect those adjacent.

How many we will lose, I do not know. If the rot extends across England and Wales, the effects might be appalling. If it crosses to Ireland, it will be frightful. I intend therefore to cross to Dublin and spend perhaps a week examining the farms around the city to see whether there are any signs of blight at that early stage. This is something we can discuss over the next few weeks, either in London, or here in Tamworth.

Your suggestion of remuneration was most kind, but completely unnecessary. In any case, all funds raised should go directly to Irish famine relief, should the blight return there.

Please convey our respects to Lady Julia.

I remain, your true friend,

Edward Yardley

Chapter Eight

Mayo Constitution, August 1846:
We have been much alarmed during the past week of the fearful accounts of the potato crop. The work of destruction is going rapidly forward on every side of us. Within the last week, large quantities of tubers have become blackened, and the potatoes, when dug, are quite infected. The crops which a few days since were apparently safe, have, on investigation, been found diseased.

All through the summer, the weather in Mayo was still acting in strange ways. Sometimes it was warm, but even when the rains came it stayed warm and humid. When Luke was working with the hay, he stripped down to the waist before he even started, but even so his trousers were wet with sweat within minutes.

The damp caused more problems when the hay had been cut. It would not dry out. Luke and Michael turned it again and again, but it lay on the ground, dank and limp, slowly rotting.

The occasional storm cleared the air, but not for long. After each storm, there would be an unnatural silence. Often mist would appear. Not the fogs of winter, but a warm summer mist; sometimes low lying, just covering the growing crops.

But the late potato crop was abundant. Michael was delighted. 'Didn't I tell you it'd come back,' he said to Luke. 'We were right to keep enough of the seed potatoes. Make sure we'd have enough across the winter.'

'Yes, Father,' Luke said, thinking how many times he had heard this before.

The next few days, he spent in the quarry with Michael, smashing stone in preparation for road repair in the autumn and winter. He still felt the emptiness inside. If the rain was heavy, he stayed in the quarry. Sometimes he sheltered under the whin bush, his coat over his head. Other times he just went on breaking stone, rain drenching his hair and shirt and dripping from his eyes and nose.

He noticed the strange damp and misty days, but paid little attention to them. Sometimes it was warm, sometimes wet. They got some of the hay in when the days were dry, but most of it rotted. The potato crop looked good though. They began harvesting it.

Luke was the first to spot it. The morning was already warm. As he dug his fork into the ground and started to ease up the potatoes, he spotted a fluffy white growth on the underside of the leaves beside him. He stopped and pulled off a leaf.

'Have you ever seen this before, Father?'

Michael looked at the leaf. 'Oh, Christ Almighty.'

'What is it, Father?'

'This is the way it starts.'

A few days later, Luke noticed something else. The edges of the leaves were turning into a darker green which seemed to attract water in the humid conditions. Soon the edges were turning brown. The leaves were no longer wet, but had gone brittle.

'Are they going to rot, Father?' Luke asked.

'I think they will. It's the kind of weather that would rot potatoes anyhow. But this thing of the leaves, I reckon it's blight. There's hunger coming.'

When he woke one morning, he could hear the rain drumming on the slate. They worked in the rain that day, digging potatoes from dark to dark. Luke dug alongside Sorcha in the rain.

'*Do you remember 1839?*' she asked, without breaking her rhythm. '*The year the rain never stopped. In all my years, I never saw a summer like it.*'

'No? As old as you are?'

'*Never in all my life. Even '39. First the Big Wind, then the endless rain, then the rot and the hunger. The rain killed the potatoes. It was the rain brought the rot, and it will do the same now.*'

'*It will,*' Luke said.

'*My father, he used to tell us about the year of the Great Frost when he was a child. It killed the potato, just as surely as the rain. They died then too, they died in their hundreds and in their thousands.*'

'*That was a long time ago,*' Luke said.

'*Indeed it was,*' she said. '*A long, long time ago.*'

As they walked back that evening, he asked his father about the Great Frost.

'Was Sorcha telling you about that?' Michael asked.

'She was. She said her father told her about it. He remembered it.'

'I wouldn't have thought her father would have been that old. Though he might have been.'

'How long ago was it, Father?'

'A hundred years now. More maybe. They still spoke about it when I was young. I remember my grandfather going on about it, but I didn't pay much heed.'

'Was it that bad?'

'I don't know just how bad it was. The old people were inclined to lay it on a bit. They used to say that half the people around here died that year. I'm not sure I'd believe them. But one way or another, an awful lot died.'

'An awful lot died in 1840,' Luke said.

'They did,' Michael said, 'but it was nothing like that. I'll tell you this though, none of us are going to die, whether the potato fails or it doesn't. One way or another, we're going to live. We'll make sure of that, me and you.'

When they reached the house, Eleanor was sitting at the table. 'Come, and have a look at this,' she said. She held up a potato.

Michael held it beside the window. Then he handed it to Luke.

Around each of the potato's eyes there were sunken patches of purple and brown.

At the end of the corn harvest, Murtybeg left Bromwich with some of the other men and travelled, not to Liverpool, but to Leeds. When he arrived, he walked north along the new railroad towards Thirsk. Within a few hours, he found the lodging houses where the Mayo gangs were staying.

A few days later, Pat left Bromwich with the rest of the gang. They walked into Birmingham and took a train to Liverpool. Once or twice Pat thought he saw withered leaves in potato fields, but he dismissed them from his mind.

They crossed to Dublin by steamer. Sometimes they fell in with other returning harvesters. The blight in the potato fields was becoming more widespread as they travelled west.

When they crossed into Connaught, the potatoes were being dug. The men were digging, the women following, picking out rotten potatoes and keening. It was a weird, unnerving sound. No one said anything.

Pat wondered what he should do. Perhaps the sensible thing would be to write a quick note to his father, and return to England to find work on the rails. But since he was so near to Mayo, he decided to go on. Two days later, he arrived at Carrigard.

That evening Murty and Aileen came down to the house.

'Where's Murteen?' Murty asked him directly.

'Did he not write to you?'

'We haven't heard from him for over a month. Where is he?'

Aileen's eyes were fixed on the flagstones at her feet.

'He's gone to Leeds,' Pat answered.

'Leeds?' Murty exclaimed. 'But why didn't he tell us?'

'I don't know,' Pat said. 'I'd thought he had.'

'Well. he didn't.'

Eleanor was standing behind Aileen, her hand on Aileen's shoulder.

'He promised,' Aileen whispered. *'He said he'd come back. He promised us all.'*

'I know,' Eleanor said.

There was a long silence again, until Michael spoke. 'I know it's hard on you,' he said. 'None of us wanted him to stay away. But he'll be sending you money too. God knows, you'll need that.'

'We will,' Murty said. 'With the potatoes looking the way they are, we'll need as much as we can get.'

'He promised,' Aileen whispered again.

'Shush there, now,' Eleanor said, running her hand through her sister's hair.

For a few moments, no one said anything. Aileen was weeping. When he could bear it no longer, Luke spoke. 'Did the rest of them come home with you?'

'Not all of them,' Pat answered. 'Jamesy McManus, Mikey Jordan, Johnny Roughneen and Bernie McDonnell – they're all gone up to Leeds to join Danny and Martin. They went with Murtybeg.'

'So who did you travel home with?'

'Eddie Roughneen...'

'Eddie came home, and Johnny went to Leeds?'

'That's right. Michael O'Brien came back with us though. Johnny Walsh and Fergus Brennan too.'

Eleanor brought a bottle of *poitín* and handed a mug to Pat. He drained it in one gulp. She handed a second mug to Luke. She noticed his hands were trembling. 'Are you alright, Luke?'

'Yes, Mother, I'm fine.' No one else had noticed.

'What about ye, though?' Pat asked as Eleanor refilled his mug. 'How's the potatoes?'

'Bad enough,' Michael said.

'So what will we do now?'

'We'll wait it out a few days. We've money enough to last for a month or two, buy a little corn.'

'And little enough too,' Eleanor said, still stroking Aileen's hair. 'The price is going to rise, you know that as well as I do.'

'Let's see how much it does. In a few days, we'll have a better idea – see what the reports on the crop are like from around the county. I hope to God they don't all have the same story as us.'

'And what if they do, Father?' Luke asked.

'Pat might have to return to England, go on the railways too. We'll need money, a lot more than we have now.'

'After me just coming home?' Pat said.

'We'll see,' Michael said. 'If it has to be done, it can't be helped, and that's all about it.'

'Yes,' Murty said, 'and it's just as well Murtybeg decided to stay on too, even if he did break his promise. Danny says there's no problem getting work on the rails. It's like last year, they're building railway lines in every direction. We'll be fine, one way or another we'll have food to eat.'

'We will,' Eleanor said. 'But what about everyone else around?'

'God alone knows the answer to that,' Murty said.

Luke was repairing one of the walls when he saw Fergus Brennan walking across the field. His heart started to race. There's no need for this, he thought. Just act as if nothing happened.

'Fergus. I'd heard you were back,'.

'I am,' Brennan answered in a voice both non-committal and menacing.

'How was Bromwich?'

'Alright.' He looked Luke straight in the eye. 'I've been hearing stories.'

Luke stared at him, not knowing how to answer. He thought of denying the stories, but realised Fergus would have heard and checked them through different sources. He decided to be honest.

'They're old stories. It's all in the past now.'

'Yes, I'd heard that too.'

'What can I say, Fergus. I'm sorry.'

''Sorry' isn't enough.'

Luke saw the left fist move. Instinctively he brought his hands across to protect himself. He never saw the right hook coming.

'Where's Luke?' Eleanor asked.

'Up the top meadow,' Michael said. 'I sent him up repairing the wall there.'

'He should be back now.'

'It's not late.'

'He's always back for his supper,' she said.

Michael cut into a potato, raising half of it to his mouth. '*Arra*, don't worry. He'll be back soon enough.'

Eleanor fixed her shawl over her head. 'But I do worry,' she said. She left Michael at his dinner and walked up to the meadow.

At first she was alarmed when she could not see him. She started to follow the wall and came to him at the far corner, sitting on the ground, trembling, his arms around his shins, his head hunched into his knees.

'Luke,' she said. He looked at her, but said nothing. She knelt beside him, holding his head into her breast. '*You're cold, alanna. You shouldn't be sitting here like this.*' But she knew the trembling was not just from the cold. She tried to get him to stand, but he stayed hunched. She thought of going back to get Michael, but preferred to stay. She saw his tongue was bleeding. She stayed kneeling beside him, watching the bright harvest moon rising over the rath.

She heard Michael's voice in the distance. 'Over here,' she shouted.

He came and looked at Luke. 'What's wrong with him?'

'He can't stand.'

'Of course he can. Come on there, Luke.' He tried to lift him, but Luke fell away from him.

'I'll go and get Pat,' Eleanor said.

A few minutes later, Pat and Michael took Luke's arms around their shoulders, stood him up, and half walked, half dragged him back to the house. They laid him on his bed in the outshot. Within seconds he was asleep. Eleanor took off his boots and laid a blanket over him.

He slept for most of the following morning. Eleanor would not permit Michael to disturb him. Later, when Michael and Pat came in for their midday meal, she fed Luke porridge. Michael went to speak, but Eleanor shushed him with a finger to her lips.

For the rest of the afternoon, Luke stayed indoors. Eleanor had seen the bruises under his chin. She guessed what had happened, but said nothing.

After midnight, long after the family had gone to bed, he lay awake, staring into the darkness. There was a movement outside the curtain.

'Luke,' his father whispered.

'Yes, Father.' The curtain was drawn back.

'Are you better?'

'Yes, much better.'

'Was it Fergus?'

'Yes, Father.'

'He knows so?'

'Of course he knows.'

There was a silence. Luke could see the outline of his father's head against the moonlit window.

'Who else was there?'

'No one, Father.'

'So he just left you there?'

'He did.'

'It's as well he did. If you were out cold, he had plenty of time to smash your legs if he wanted. Killed you. Or worse.'

Luke flinched. There was only one thing worse than killing. 'I wonder why he didn't.'

'I don't know,' Michael said, 'and I don't want to know. I reckon it's over though. If he wanted to go further, he had his chance then. But he's done what he wanted to do, and soon everyone will know it.'

Luke thought about that. 'I suppose I can put up with that.'

'You'll have to. And just remember this – you were lucky this time. Damned lucky. Now go back to sleep, and don't ever get into trouble like that again.'

One wet morning, there was a knock on the door. Kitty stood outside.

Eleanor stared at her in a mixture of delight and horror. She looked thinner than before, and her shift hung loose. Neither said anything. Eleanor opened the door wider and let her in.

'*You shouldn't be here, child.*'

'*I know, I know. It's just how I couldn't stay away.*'

'*We'll be in terrible trouble if they find out.*'

'*Do you think I should go?*'

'*Sure, stay on a while,*' Eleanor said. '*We'll keep a good eye out for them. Sit here.*' She went behind the curtain and brought the baby out. Kitty took Brigid in her lap and hugged her.

'*Brigid, alanna,*' she whispered, '*do you know how I've missed you?*'

Eleanor sat beside Kitty, trying hard not to stare at her face. One of her eyes was puffy, a slight but discernible gash on the cheekbone just below it. Her other cheek and her chin showed definite bruising. Eleanor decided to be direct. '*Is he beating you, child?*'

Kitty nodded and went on rocking the baby, crooning in Irish. Her eyes welled with tears. After a few minutes, she spoke.

'*And Luke,*' she asked, '*how's Luke?*'

'*He's alright now,*' Eleanor replied.

'*Fergus said he beat him. He said he near killed him.*'

'*He beat him right enough, but it wasn't as bad as all that. He was up and on his feet after a day or two.*'

Now the tears were coming down her cheeks. '*I'm sorry,*' she whispered. '*I'm sorry for all the trouble I've caused.*'

'*Don't you be fretting yourself, child,*' Eleanor replied. '*It's the way we all are. You're no different to any of us.*'

After that, Kitty came by every week. Gradually her wit and spirit returned, and again it seemed like the old days. But Eleanor could sense the gloom in her. The bruises would disappear, and Eleanor kept hoping they would not return. But they would, and on such days she would do what she could to console her. She saw too how much thinner Kitty had become.

'*Are you not eating?*'

'*I am,*' Kitty said. '*But only corn and cabbage. What good can that do for anyone? We've little enough money with Fergus coming home, and what we have isn't enough to buy food for all the family with corn the price it is. And it's worse for the old man. He's not able to keep any of it in, he's only a shadow of a man now.*'

But there were better days too, days when Kitty would light up as soon as she saw Brigid. Some mornings she would spend hours playing with the child, swinging her around, sitting her on her lap, tickling her and telling her stories that the baby would not yet understand.

The need for secrecy was extreme. Always Eleanor sat by the window, keeping a sharp eye out for anyone coming. Once they were nearly surprised, but Kitty scaled the ladder into the loft, throwing herself down on the straw just as the door opened, and Luke came in with Michael. That episode gave Eleanor quite a fright, but she found that she was already infected with some of Kitty's wilder nature, and was almost beginning to enjoy the risk.

But one morning, they really were surprised. They were sitting close to the fire and did not see the door opening. Aileen was there. The three women looked at each other, stunned. Then Eleanor spoke. '*I was going to bring her up to you in a wee while,*' she said, nodding towards Brigid.

'*I thought I'd save you the trouble,*' Aileen said.

'*Wasn't it the right hurry you had.*'

Aileen looked doubtful. Eleanor stood, and put her hand on her sister's shoulder. '*It's alright now. Kitty is her godmother, and she has a right to see her. The thing with Luke is all in the past, so let's not worry about it.*'

Aileen sat at the table, looking directly at Kitty, still sitting by the fire.

'*I can't leave her,*' Kitty said, in reply to the unspoken question. '*And I won't.*'

Aileen nodded as Eleanor handed her a small mug of buttermilk. She made no direct comment on Kitty though. Instead she placed some coins on the table. Kitty looked at Eleanor, but said nothing.

'*We got the money from Danny yesterday,*' Aileen explained. '*Murty thought you might be needing some.*'

'*We might indeed,*' Eleanor said. '*It's good of ye to think of it.*'

'*And how are your potatoes now?*'

'*Luke and Michael are still reckoning they'll save the half of them, those of them that are clamped anyhow. They might have to kill the cow though. That will help us to the next harvest, please God. And after that, Pat will be sending money back from England again.*'

'*Well, this might help you with a little corn in the meantime.*'

'*It surely will.*'

Aileen looked from Eleanor back to Kitty, acknowledging her for the first time. '*And how about ye?*' she asked. '*Will ye make it to the harvest?*'

'*Not with what we've got,*' Kitty said.

'*So what will ye do then?*'

'*Fergus is talking of England again. He's thinking of joining Danny after Christmas. They say there's no end of money on the railways.*'

She saw the look of alarm in Aileen's eyes. '*But don't worry,*' she said, '*I'm not even thinking of Luke. I'll leave him alone, I swear it.*'

Now the balance of everything changed. There was still the risk, but it was easier with either Eleanor or Aileen standing at the window, or sometimes at the door in the mornings. Eleanor did not know if she was more concerned about making Michael angry or upsetting Luke. Twice more, the men returned early from the fields, but now the women had enough warning. Afterwards they laughed about it.

And it was this laughter that convinced Eleanor that they could not stop meeting. Kitty's stories, Brigid's childish smiles, all of this brought about a change in Aileen that Eleanor had once despaired of ever seeing. She thought of saying it to Murty and Michael, but dismissed it from her mind. Murty would not object, but Michael would never understand.

The hunger went on, and the women cut the rations for their families, determined that there would be enough seed potatoes left. The remittances from Danny and Murtybeg helped too. Eleanor promised Aileen that she would repay the money when Pat went to England again, but her sister only laughed at this. But the grim resolve to survive the hunger brought a change in the three women. They were determined that Brigid would have a different life.

It was Kitty who first brought up the subject. The price of corn had gone up again, and Eleanor had started cooking yellow meal instead. It was hard and flinty, taking hours of boiling to soften it.

'*Ye're eating meal too?*' Kitty said.

'*Of course we are,*' Eleanor said. '*We can't afford the corn.*'

'*It's hard to eat. Fergus's father, he's few enough teeth in his head without having to eat this stuff, and it won't be easy for the baby either.*'

The three women lapsed into silence, Eleanor stirring the pot of meal hanging over the turf fire.

'*Is this the kind of life we want for Brigid?*' Kitty asked suddenly.

'*What else is there?*' asked Eleanor

'*We'll make a start by sending her to Murty's school,*' Kitty replied.

'We will,' Aileen said. '*But what if the new schools come?*'

Eleanor saw the familiar look of depression return to her sister's eyes. '*Arra, they'll never come here.*'

'*Oh, but they will,*' Aileen said.

'*Don't worry about it,*' Eleanor said.

'*But it's not just us I'm thinking about,*' Aileen said. '*It's Brigid.*'

'*If that's your concern,*' Kitty said, '*I wouldn't worry. If the new schools come, then everyone will have to go to them, girls and boys, it doesn't matter. The Government men, they'll make them go, and the girls will get their schooling, whether their families want it or not.*'

'*Yes,*' Aileen said, '*but only for four years.*'

'*That's right,*' Kitty said.

'*So what are you saying, child?*' Eleanor asked.

'*Castlebar. They'd school her longer in Castlebar.*'

'*Castlebar!*' Aileen echoed.

'*Yes,*' Kitty said. '*And after that, Galway or Dublin even. Brigid is going to be a teacher.*'

'*A teacher!*' Eleanor exclaimed. '*That costs money.*'

'*So it does,*' Kitty said, '*but we'll find it. After the hunger is over, some way or the other, we'll find it.*'

Eleanor was feeding Brigid when she noticed McKinnon riding past in the direction of Knockanure. She thought a while. When she finished feeding the baby, she took her up, and walked down the Kilduff road. It was still early.

Sabina was washing down the tables when she arrived. There was no one else in the bar. She looked at Eleanor in surprise.

'I thought I'd bring the baby down for you to see,' Eleanor said.

Sabina dropped her cleaning rag and came over. 'Isn't she beautiful.'

'Of course she is,' Eleanor said. 'What did you expect?' She handed the baby to Sabina. Brigid smiled.

The next morning, after McKinnon had gone again, Sabina came down to the house. She was startled to see Kitty, but she too was sworn to secrecy. Even so, it was some weeks before the three women explained their plans about Brigid's education. Sabina was stunned. She looked from one face to the other in amazement.

'*A teacher! We can't afford food, and you're talking about training colleges for the child.*'

'We are,' Kitty said.

'*You're mad! Stark, raving, mad.*'

'That's right,' Eleanor said. 'Raving mad. All four of us.'

'Four,' echoed Sabina. '*Which four? You're not including me, I hope.*'

'Us three and the child,' Kitty said. 'What do you think, little Brigid? You too? We're all mad.'

The baby smiled – at Sabina. 'And you make five it seems,' Eleanor said.

It was a long time before Sabina could be convinced that the others were serious. Then she asked who would pay for Brigid's education. But Kitty deftly changed the subject, and it was only when Sabina was walking home that night that she realised the answer.

It had started to rain. After a while, they sheltered under a whin bush, their coats grasped tightly over their heads. The rain got heavier.

'Oh, to hell with this,' Michael said. 'We're not going to do much work this morning. We might as well go home.'

Luke followed Pat and Michael, their boots squelching in the mud. The morning was only half gone. Michael opened the door of the house, and Luke followed them in. There were four women at the table – Eleanor at one end, Aileen and Sabina beside her. Kitty was closest to the fire, cradling the baby.

Luke saw her, and drew back towards the door. Her face was grey and bruised.

'What the devil is she doing here,' his father shouted, glaring at her.

'She's here to see the baby,' Eleanor said.

'I want you to get out,' he shouted at Kitty. 'Now.'

No one moved.

'Did you not hear me?'

'She's the child's godmother,' Eleanor said. 'She's every right to be here.'

'Not in my house, she doesn't. Not after all the trouble she's caused.'

Still no one moved. Luke had never seen his father so furious. Aileen was crying.

'Shush there, Michael,' Eleanor said. 'You're upsetting everyone.'

'I won't be silenced in my own house, and not in front of a woman who has shamed my son.'

'It takes two,' Kitty whispered.

Luke thought Michael was going to strike her. 'No, Father...'

Michael stopped dead. 'And what are you on about?' he shouted. 'Aren't you the fool?'

'Maybe you're right,' Luke answered. 'Maybe we're both fools.' He nodded towards Kitty. 'We made fools of each other.'

'Two fools, is it?'

Luke dropped his eyes. 'Yes, Father,' he whispered.

For a few moments there was silence, only broken by the sound of Aileen's sobbing. Michael ignored her. He looked across to Sabina.

'And what are you doing here? What have you got to say about all this?'

'I'm here to help out with the child,' Sabina replied. 'And since you ask, I agree with Elly. Yes, Kitty was foolish. Yes, she's caused us all trouble. But she is the child's godmother, and she was Nessy's best friend too. Nessy died so this baby could live. Is it any wonder that Kitty might love her?'

'And what about her husband? What will Fergus Brennan think?'

'I doubt he'll care,' Sabina said.

'He cared enough to beat the hell out of Luke.'

'And his own wife too. And what does that prove?'

Michael stared at Sabina, taken quite by surprise. He turned to Kitty. Seeing the bruising, he drew back. 'He beat her?'

'He did,' Sabina said.

'And not for the first time,' Kitty added. 'Or the last.' Silence again.

'So that's the way it is,' Michael said at length.

'Yes, *a ghrá*' Eleanor answered him. She took her husband by both arms. 'That's the way it is,' she whispered, 'and that's the way it's always going to be. And there's nothing we can do about it.'

'And what about him?' Michael asked, pointing at Luke. 'You'll be worrying him with your goings on, dangling her in front of him.'

Eleanor hung a pot of meal on a crane and swung it over the fire. 'We're trying not to bother him,' she replied. 'She wouldn't have been here, only ye came in on us so sudden.'

Michael said nothing more.

'I'll leave early this morning, so,' Kitty said. She kissed the baby on the forehead. '*There you go, little Brigid,*' she said. She handed the child to Aileen, and crossed to the door.

'*I'll see ye all in a few days,*' she said to the women.

'*Of course you will, alanna,*' Eleanor said.

Chapter Nine

Telegraph or Connaught Ranger, August 1846:
The Potato Disease. The dreadful reality is beyond yea or nay in this County. From one end to the other the weal has gone forth that the rot is increasing with fearful ability. From our own personal knowledge as well as the reports we have received from the rural districts, we regret to say no description of potatoes have escaped – late as well as early planting are rapidly decomposing.

As to – Sir Robert Peel · · · · · · · · · · · · · · · · · Lawlors Hotel
Houses of Parliament · Naas
Westminster · Co. Kildare
London

August 28th 1846

My Dear Robert,

You will see from the address that I have now arrived in Ireland. As I had feared, the news is not good. Already I have met with a number of the Friends, in particular Goodbody and Odlum, who have briefed me well. Conditions in Dublin, Meath and Kildare are appalling. At least a half of the potato crop in the fields has been lost. The farmers here tell me that those that have been stored are rotting, and fear they may lose them all.

There are reports of much worse from further west. The Friends are talking of organising relief in the western counties, and I intend to travel with them. I have already written to Caroline to this effect.

I will send you further news as soon as I have it.

With true affection to Lady Julia and yourself,

Edward Yardley

Michael had sent Luke to continue digging the potatoes. It was raining. Michael had finished the milking and was shovelling the manure out of the shed when Luke returned.

'You're back early.'

'Yes, Father. I thought you'd like to look at the potatoes yourself.'

'Not good?'

'Not good at all. I think most all of them are gone.'

'All of them. That's impossible. Let's see.'

They walked back the rutted lane to the potato patch. Luke pointed to where he had been digging.

Michael looked at the potatoes. 'They look alright to me.'

Luke picked one up and squeezed it. Pulp seeped out through his fingers. Michael stared at it, his eyes widening. Then he picked a large lumper and squeezed, holding his fist to the sky. Pulp and fluid dripped down his forearm. 'Are they all like this?'

'Some of the ones over further aren't so bad yet. But the rot's there.'

Michael flung the putrefying mess against the stone wall. He watched as it fell away from the stones and into the ferns. 'We'll have to dig them all up. The good ones we'll clamp. Some of the others, we might be able to cut out the badness, but we'll have to eat those over the next few weeks.'

'And what about seed potatoes?'

'We'll have to keep them back. How many times do I tell you that?'

Over the next few days, the few potatoes they put into storage rotted. Any that were only half rotted, they brought back to Eleanor, and she cut out the good parts, but then these rotted too. By the end of another week, all the remaining potatoes in the ground were a brown, oozing mess.

One night they sat around the table, eating meal.

'They're all gone,' Luke said. 'We've nothing left. Nothing at all.'

'Let's wait,' Michael said. 'See how it's going with everyone else.'

Luke lay in bed that night, unable to sleep. He knew there was no point in waiting. He was home, Pat was home, and there was no money coming in from England. They had some left, but that would not last. They might make some money from selling oats, but that would hardly be enough to pay the rent. If they sold all the oats, the horse would have little food and would have to be sold. If they didn't, the cow would have to be slaughtered or sold. Someone would have to go to England. But the English harvest was over, and the only choice was the railways. Yes, Pat could go on the railways, but he had no experience of it. He would have to go to Leeds himself. Would Burke evict them if he went? If he stayed, they could not pay the rent, and they would be evicted anyhow. He suspected Burke would be happy enough to be paid the rent, and the only way that could be done was by working on the railways himself. Go to Leeds? Yes, and admit to Danny he had been wrong all along.

All through the summer, Eleanor and Aileen had joined the corn lines, paying for corn with money from England. Even now, Michael would not allow Eleanor to join the free line. Luke wondered when they would have to admit defeat, and be fed for free.

It did not work out that way. One evening, Eleanor returned from Kilduff. 'They've stopped the corn lines.'

'What!' Michael said.

'They've stopped them. They're gone. Nobody knows anything.'

'And what about Dillon?' Luke asked. 'Isn't he selling corn?'

'I don't know, the shop was closed. But I don't think it'd matter anyway with the price they say he's charging.'

'Damn it to hell,' Michael said, 'we've got to do something, we can't just wait around and starve.'

'I'll go up and see what's happening,' Luke said. He took some coins and left the house.

When he arrived in Kilduff, he saw a lamp burning inside Dillon's house. He knocked on the door.

'Go away,' shouted a voice from inside. He knocked again.

'Didn't I tell you to go away.' He knocked again, and the door opened. Dillon was there, furious. 'Can you not understand English? You're not wanted.'

'Let him be,' a voice came from inside. 'Come on in, Luke.'

Dillon still glared at him, but then he opened the door. Father Reilly was sitting at the table. 'Sit down, we're just having a little chat here.'

'I never invited him,' Dillon said.

'Well, he's here now.'

'I'm only looking to buy some corn,' Luke said.

'We'll see about that,' the priest said. 'How much did you say you have, Mr. Dillon?'

'Forty bushels left.'

'And what's coming?'

'I've eighty on order from Westport, but who knows when that's going to arrive. Or even if it will arrive.'

'We can only pray for that. But if we agree you have the corn, and we agree you're going to sell it, we still have to agree the price.'

'That's between me and the buyer.'

'Maybe it's between you and God, Mr. Dillon, and it most surely will be, if you're over-charging starving people. So what's your price?'

'A shilling and ninepence a stone.'

The priest looked up at him. 'A shilling and ninepence. What's that – a penny ha'pence a pound.'

'It is. It's the same all over the county. That's the price in Castlebar. And Claremorris. And Westport.'

'But I hear the depots are selling it at sixpence a stone.'

'Sevenpence, Father, but they've nothing left, and this is business. One and ninepence, that's my price.'

The priest thought for a moment. 'If that's your price, Mr. Dillon, then no sacraments, for you. Or your family.'

'You can't do that.'

'That's business too. God's business.'

'Damn you, that's excommunication. I'll write to the Bishop in Achonry.'

'I can't stop you, but he won't receive the letter for two days. And after Mass tomorrow the whole parish will know.' He stared into Dillon's eyes. 'Tenpence a stone is the price. That'll give you more profit than you need.'

'A shilling.'

'Tenpence.'

The merchant was silent. Finally he nodded. 'Tenpence.'

'And you'll open tomorrow.'

'I will, God damn it.'

A few minutes later, Luke and the priest left the merchant's house. Luke was carrying two pounds of American corn. 'You're a hard man, Father.'

'Hard times, Luke.'

He was in the quarry with his father. Pat was still digging rotten potatoes, though they knew there was little hope left. But Michael worked on as they always had. It was time to repair roads again. Once more they were levering rock out from the overhangs in the quarry, smashing it, breaking stones and piling heaps of it ready for filling ruts and repairing the damage from winter rains and frosts.

Luke was nervous. No matter what he did was wrong. Yes, he wanted to stay at home and take over the farm. Perhaps he would in time, but it was impossible now. Would it be impossible for ever? Was there no future in Mayo? Would he have to go to England and never return?

There was Michael too. If he wanted to leave, even for a year, he would have to defy his father. Would Michael accept it? Or would it create a rift between them so that he could never come home again, good times or bad? He decided he had to press ahead.

'It will have to be Leeds, Father.'

'What!'

'The railways. It's the only way. We need the money.'

'I know,' Michael said. 'I didn't tell you, I had a word about it with your mother last night when you were all asleep. It'll be hard on Pat and him only home, but he'll have no choice.'

'I wasn't thinking about Pat,' Luke said.

Michael put the sledgehammer down. He looked at him, eyes narrowing, whether in surprise or fury, Luke could not tell.

'You'll not go to Leeds,' Michael said. 'We've been through this before. You're to work this farm, and that's all about it. We'll send Pat, and there'll be no more argument.'

'I'd agree with you, Father, except for the times that are in it. We can't do it that way anymore.' He stopped. Perhaps he would have kept his mouth shut. No. His father was tough, but there would come a time he would have to be tough too.

'Go on,' Michael said. 'I'm listening.'

'It's the hunger, but it's not only that. The price of corn is rising, it's double what it was a few weeks back. Sure, Pat can go on the railways, but it's like what you said before, it'll take him months to work up to it, and we don't have months. I know one thing for certain, I can get to four shillings a day, five maybe, and I can do it fast. You'll need that money, and it's not just you. There's other people around will need money if we don't.'

He knew his mother still owed money to Aileen, and he knew his father did not know of it. He would have to find a way of getting that money to her, perhaps through Sabina. The problem was his father knew what he should be earning, and what he could expect. He wondered how many more hours he would have to work to pay Aileen too.

'Fine,' Michael said. 'Supposing we said you should go, what then? You know as well as I do, you'd never come back. You'll have the taste for it, and some girl in England will tempt you. No matter how much you say it, there's no way around that. And what about the lease? If they knew you weren't returning, what would happen then? What?'

'Would you take my word, Father?' he asked. 'If you think I'm fit to take over the farm, then you must know I'm fit to be believed.'

'And what would you promise? ' Michael asked. 'That you'd come home. When?'

'I'd be home as soon as the hunger is over.'

'And what if it isn't over?' Michael asked. He turned from Luke and went back to breaking stones.

They worked on. Luke was disturbed and angry. Was his father to have his own way for ever? Would he always have to give in to him? He had come back to Mayo because his father had demanded it. No asking, no request, just an order. He had given up Kitty on his father's demand too. But this was a test of wills now. His father would not believe his promise. And there would be a time when his father would not be able to run the farm. When that time came, would Michael let him run it without interference? There was no point in waiting. The time had come to stand up for himself.

117

He stopped smashing rock. 'If it isn't over, I'll come home next year, and we'll send Pat then.'

'You're staying, and that's an end to it,' Michael said. 'This argument is over.'

'No, it isn't over.'

Michael stared at him, disbelieving. 'You'll not argue with me.' He half made as if to strike him. Luke caught his wrist. 'I've always obeyed you, but you never listen to me. This time, you'll hear me out.'

'Let go of me.'

Luke released his wrist, and Michael moved away.

'By God, don't ever do that again.' He picked up his sledgehammer and started smashing rock again. Luke grasped the handle. Michael tried to wrench it back, but Luke still held it.

'If you want me to run this farm, Father, you'll have to respect me. Respect goes both ways.'

Michael glared at him in fury, but said nothing. Luke went on.

'Now I gave you my promise. If you don't believe me, you have no respect for me, and there's no point in us working together.'

'Murtybeg gave his promise, and look what happened.'

'Let Murteen please himself. I'll keep my word, and that's an end to it.'

'An end to what?'

'An end to the argument,' Luke said. 'If you respect me, we can work together. If you think I'm nothing but a poor *amadán*, then I'll go to Leeds and work with men who do respect me, and if I do that, I'll not be coming back. I prefer to go with your blessing, and if I do, then you have my word I'll be back. Now do you take it or not?'

'A father shouldn't be put in a position like this.'

'Do you take my word?'

No answer.

'Do you respect me as your son?'

'Damn it to hell,' Michael said, 'we shouldn't be having this quarrel.'

'I know.'

Michael picked up his hammer again and went back to smashing rock. Luke knew better than to press the matter, and waited.

Michael stopped. 'Are you working or not?'

'I'm waiting for an answer.'

Michael took his hammer and sat down on a ledge of rock beside him. Luke stayed standing.

'So what would you promise?' his father asked.

'I'd promise to come home if the early harvest is any good next year. One way or another, I'll come back for the late harvest. Pat can go then.'

'On your word?'

'On my word as a man,' Luke said. 'And as your son.'

Michael nodded 'So be it,' he said, 'and by God I'm warning you, if you break your word...'

'I'll not break my word.'

The next evening the land agent came. Eleanor brought him in to the table. Luke sat alongside his father. White's visit was unexpected, and Luke was nervous about what was coming. Whatever it was, he suspected it would not be pleasant.

White was direct. 'I'm afraid I must inform you that you are in breach of your lease,' he said.

Michael looked up sharply. 'In breach? Haven't we paid everything?'

'Oh, you have indeed,' White said, 'but that's not the problem. I don't know if you noticed on your new lease that there is a clause that expressly forbids subletting.'

Michael looked across to Luke.

'He's right, Father,' Luke said. 'But we're not subletting, Mr. White.'

'Oh, but you are. You have a cabin on your lower field, and it is most definitely occupied. I saw it myself.'

'But that's not sublet,' Luke said. 'They're only there for one crop. And there's nothing in writing, so how can it be a lease.'

'Yes,' Michael said. 'One crop only. Conacre maybe. A lease? No.'

'And how many years has this arrangement been running?'

No-one replied.

'You see, Mr. Ryan, long term conacre may establish certain rights in law. Some people may claim it as a sublease. We had legal advice from Mr. Dawson before we drafted the new contracts. If you have a subtenant, it puts you in the position of being a head tenant, and that puts you in a different situation legally. It's not something we can countenance.'

Michael looked out the window. 'It wasn't on the old lease,' he said at length. 'It never even mentioned conacre, let alone subletting.'

'It didn't,' White replied, 'but I'm afraid it's on all our new leases.'

'I'm sorry,' Michael said. 'I hadn't known.'

'I'm sorry too,' White said. 'I would have thought you'd have known about it. Bensons were subletting too. They finished with it before they even signed their new lease.'

Luke thought back. He had noticed the flattened remains of a mud cabin in one of his neighbour's fields, but the significance of it had not struck him.

'There was a whole family there,' Michael said.

'Not so many. A man and his wife with two children.'

'Where are they now?' Luke asked.

'Knockanure, I think. Bensons took them over to the Workhouse. That's what I heard.'

Luke thought he saw his father flinch.

'Well, we surely wouldn't want to be in breach,' Michael said.

White nodded. 'I am well aware of that, and so is Mr. Burke. It is not something we would like to come between us, but I am afraid you will have to terminate the arrangement.'

After White had left, Luke looked to his father, shocked at the way things had turned out.

'There's no other way,' Michael said. 'If Sorcha doesn't leave, we'll all leave.'

'You mean we're going to have to evict her?' Luke asked.

'It's not an eviction,' Michael replied. 'They're forcing us to do it, we've no choice.'

'That might be true,' Luke said, 'but at the end of the day, it's the same thing. We go on and on about Clanowen, and we're no better ourselves.'

Michael stood, leaning on the table and glaring across at Luke.

'Now, we'll have no more of that. We have to have her out because we are being forced to it, and that's all about it.'

Luke shook his head. 'So what should we do now?'

'We should tell her at once.'

'And who will do that?'

A few minutes later, he was standing outside the rough-built door of Sorcha's mud-cabin.

'*Are you there?*' he shouted. '*Is there anyone in?*'

The door opened. Sorcha squinted out.

'*Oh, it's you, alanna,*' she said. '*Come on in out of that.*'

Her frame was skeletal now; her long white hair uncombed and unwashed. Her eyes had sunk into their sockets, and her cheeks were hollow. He stepped inside the cabin. It stank of smoke. It was impossible to stand upright. At the back of the single room, the old man lay on straw. He stared open-eyed at Luke. He was gibbering and dribbling with fright.

'*Sit down, sit down,*' Sorcha said.

Luke sat on a rough stool that was far too low for him.

'*I've come to tell you something,*' he said.

There was a look of alarm in her eyes.

'*We're going to have to finish things,*' he said. '*The landlord is insisting.*'

Her eyes brimmed with tears. '*Who…? What…?*'

'*It's Mr. Burke. They're not allowing conacre anymore.*'

'They're not?'

'No. It's on our lease. No more conacre.'

'But what can I do then?' she asked.

'You've family up by Baile a' Cnoic.'

'I did. But that was many years ago.'

The next day, Luke took Sorcha and her husband to the Workhouse. It was not that he wanted to. He had thought of riding up to *Baile a' Cnoic*, but he doubted if he would find any of Sorcha's family there. Also, the rumours of blight from the Mountain were even worse than Kilduff.

He hitched the horse to the cart, and piled it with the few possessions from her mud cabin. Then they both lifted the old man into the cart. His eyes were rolling in terror. Three carts passed by. He swung out on the road, following behind the last one. On the back a mattress lay across the cart, an old woman lying on it in a huddle. A man sat on the side of the cart, driving the donkey. On the other side, there was a woman holding a baby to her breast. Between them, on the floor of the cart, there were six more children. None could have been more than eight, Luke reckoned. The youngest lay still between the other children, and did not move for the entire journey.

When they arrived at the Workhouse, there were hundreds of people there before them. He alighted, and pushed his way to the top of the crowd. The gates were locked.

'They're not letting anyone in,' an old woman told him. *'Only if you live in Knockanure or a mile of it.'*

He pushed his way out again, turned the cart around, and drove back towards Carrigard. He met people walking towards Knockanure, most walking, many on carts. He tried to turn them back, explaining what was happening at the Workhouse, but few believed him. He stopped trying. For the rest of the journey, neither he nor Sorcha exchanged a word.

The family were at their midday meal when he returned.

'What the devil do we do now?' his father asked.

'I don't know,' Luke said.

'We have to have her out.'

'I know, but we've got a few days yet.'

'That's little enough. We're supposed to tumble the cabin. And White will be along to see that it's done.'

Luke sat down and started to eat. Corn only with cabbage. He looked across at his father.

'It's all any of us are getting,' Michael said. 'At least until we see what's happening next.'

They finished their meal in silence.

'I've been thinking,' his father said at last. 'There's only one answer. You'll have to have a word with Ian.'

'What good would that do?'

'He knows the people in the Union. He'd be able to get her in.'

Later, Luke rode with McKinnon to Knockanure. They pushed their way to the gate. When McKinnon identified himself, they were both let in with their horses.

'They'd be stolen outside,' the gate-man told them. 'And eaten.'

Luke had never been inside a Workhouse before, but they saw little of it as they went straight to the administration block in the front.

The Workhouse Master was at his desk, dictating a letter to a young woman sitting beside him. She glanced at Luke in a matter-of-fact way. Then she stood up and offered him her seat.

'Oh no.' Luke said.

'Don't worry,' she said, 'I'll work over here for a while.' She sat at an open ledger on a table in the corner and began transcribing figures from worksheets.

The Master knew McKinnon well, and within a few minutes the matter was arranged. Luke and McKinnon left, carrying an admission ticket.

Next day, Luke brought Sorcha and her husband to the Workhouse again. This time, they were admitted with no difficulty, and he drove the horse and cart back towards Carrigard. He wondered if he would ever see Sorcha again.

When he arrived back, he saw that Michael had already started to knock down the mud cabin. They worked on through the afternoon. When the walls had been levelled, they piled the straw from the roof onto the cart, and brought it back to the cowshed for bedding.

What was left, they burned.

The Central Committee of the Office of Public Works in Dublin was in session. They had been sitting without break for nine hours. They had passed over a hundred applications for Famine Relief Works, sent twenty back for clarification, and rejected two. The committee secretary read out the next three applications:

'For the Barony of Clanowen –

Improving the road from Kilduff to Knockanure by making a new line of road at Carrigard to avoid the hill at the river. £600.'

'Making a road through the townland of Ardnagrena towards Brockagh. £350.'

'Making a road from Lisnadee to the road from Brockagh towards Knockanure. £250.'

'Clanowen?' a commissioner asked. 'Mayo again?'

'Yes, sir,' a clerk answered.

'Do we know which Union?'

'Knockanure, sir. The eastern part of the county, right up to the Ox Mountains.'

'I know Knockanure,' the chairman said. 'Voisey, he's the Poor Law Commissioner in the area.'

'That's right, sir. Mr. Voisey's signature is on the application.'

'A reliable man, James Voisey. Most reliable. I doubt he would put forward any scheme, if he didn't have the fullest confidence in it.'

'No, sir.'

'Haven't we received reports from this area of Mayo,' another commissioner asked.

'We have, sir,' the secretary said. 'Terrible conditions, they say.'

'And worst in the mountains?'

'Yes, sir.'

No one else spoke.

'If there are no objections, I will consider this application passed,' the chairman said.

'So noted,' the secretary said.

A week before Luke's intended departure, the land agent arrived at the cottage again. Eleanor called Michael in from the yard.

White was accompanied by a police constable from Knockanure. He came inside, while the constable stood at the door.

'If you're asking about our tenant, Mr. White, I can tell you she's gone,' Michael said. 'We've levelled the cabin.'

'Indeed,' White replied, 'I have seen that already, but that is not the reason for my being here this evening. I must tell you we are intending to expand the working of the quarry many times beyond its present capacity. We'll need your assistance. We will of course pay for it, since your duty labour is complete. A shilling and thruppence a day for direct labour; two shillings for labour with horse and cart.'

Michael thought about it. 'I accept of course, though I can't understand your reasons. The road is already in a good state of repair.'

'Under normal circumstances, that would be perfectly correct, Mr. Ryan, but this time we are not talking about repair and maintenance. The Barony has decided to proceed with substantial new Road Works in the townland as a Relief measure. It is intended to employ four hundred on building a new line of road so as to avoid the hill on either side of the river. I don't have to tell you how difficult it is for teams of horses pulling up the steep incline on either side of the ford. They have decided therefore to start a new line here at this house, to cross the river four hundred yards further south of the ford, where the land is flatter. It is also intended to build a bridge on the river at that point.'

'The land may be flatter, but it's also wetter. Isn't that why the road is where it is?'

'Again, you are perfectly correct Mr. Ryan, but the surveyors have already been out surveying the route. Perhaps you have noticed them. They say that the depth of bog is not so great as we might expect, and there is good clay and rock underneath. Also, it should be possible to drain it into the river. Their only problem is that they will need a large quantity of rock and gravel to build the road back again to the height of the land around it. This will be the largest contract that we'll ever have for stone from this quarry. Mr. Burke is most anxious that we handle the contract without any problems.'

'I'm sure we can do that. The question is, will there be anything left of the farm, or will we have quarried it all out?'

'I don't think we need to worry about that, Mr. Ryan. There are thousands of tons of rock in the quarry as it is. In any case, Mr. Burke has suggested we might be able to extend your farm elsewhere and failing that, there will be a reduction in your rent. Also, the quarry will provide plentiful employment for you and your sons through this difficult time.'

When Luke returned to the house late that evening with Pat, he found his father hunched over the table, studying the rough sketch map that White had left with him. Michael outlined what he had been told.

Luke whistled. 'Four hundred to be employed.'

'Yes,' Michael said, 'and I'm not even sure of that figure. I think the four hundred only applies to the part from here to the river. They may be using another four hundred on the other side.'

'But the road and the quarry will take more land from our own farm.'

'That's true,' Michael said, 'but White has promised work for the three of us and a reduction in rent. We'll also get first choice on other land that might be free.'

'But is there any other land free here?'

'Tolan's. Murtagh's. Byrne's. There's any god's amount.'

'Of course...of course there is.'

'Yes, and so long as it's no more than a half a mile away, we could surely farm more land. We might be able to get a second farm in the area for Pat perhaps.'

'Mr. Burke must be very anxious for this contract.'

'I think he is. I think he most certainly is.'

Michael said nothing about Leeds or railways over the next few days. But it was a subject that was always on Luke's mind. He had won the argument, his father had backed down, but circumstances were different now. Victory to defeat in a single week. Could he allow that?

All through his father's silence, he knew that the pressure was on him to change his mind. Michael was too intelligent to push him though, he knew Luke would have to draw his own conclusions. He was prepared to argue with him, perhaps even enforce discipline, but he reckoned it might not be necessary.

Luke realised that in spite of the horror of the hunger, he had almost been using it as an excuse because he wanted to get back to England. It was no longer because of the prospect of four or five shillings a day. Danny's argument had been fermenting in his mind; his own long talks with Kitty had helped the process. Danny was still working with Farrelly, but there would come a time when he would be a gangmaster on his own account. Luke thought of what it would be like working with him. He thought of Thomas Brassey and of Danny's comments. 'You might never be as rich as Brassey, but by God it's a hundred times better than starving in Carrigard.' Danny knew how to choose his words to hit home and hurt. But did it matter either way? He would only be going to Leeds for nine months, a year at the most. That was what he had promised, that was what his father had agreed. But now things could be very different. He and his father could be working on another contract with Mr. Burke, but it could be more extensive than anything they had done before. He knew that he would never earn as much as he could do working with Danny, but in its own way, it was an alternative. The quarry contract would bring in more money than it had before. Perhaps in time they could bid on other contracts. Make money from Famine Relief? From hunger and pain? Was it right or wrong? He did not know.

Kitty was another factor in his thoughts. Perhaps she had been right. Perhaps they should leave Mayo, and both of them go to Leeds. No, that would not work. He had promised to return. And anyhow the men on the gangs would never accept him if he brought another man's wife with him. France so? No, that was only a dream. Perhaps he could stay in Mayo and live with her. No, that was impossible, and he knew it. No one would ever accept that.

And then there was the question of his own family. Could he make more money in Leeds, help more that way? He was sure he could, but it would upset Eleanor. With the new quarry and road contracts, she would see that he no longer had an excuse. He could earn money in Carrigard, and while it might not be as much as in Leeds, it would be sufficient. She would be thinking – if he went to Leeds now, why would he not go to Leeds again later? Why would he not stay in Leeds?

He was torn both ways. He lay awake at night, trying to think it all out. Staying in Carrigard – that would just be giving in. Or would it be the sensible thing to do? Would Danny see him as a fool? More important, would his own father have less respect for him, see that he had lost the argument even as he seemed to have won it. He could not decide.

He worked in the bog and in the quarry, trying to forget what was happening around him, but always there were hungry people passing along the road towards Knockanure and Dublin. In the end, he started working in a part of the quarry where he could not see the road, and continued smashing rock.

A week later, White came again, this time accompanied by a stranger. He introduced him as George Gaffney, who would have responsibility for the new line of road. The three men sat around the table, and Eleanor listened while pretending not to.

'I understand from Mr. White here that your sons can read and write,' Gaffney remarked.

'Of course,' Michael answered. 'All of our family have done that for generations past.'

'Can they add and subtract as well?'

This time White answered. 'I should explain that Mr. Ryan's brother has been running a small school here for over twenty years. I understand they teach Latin and Greek too.'

'Excellent. As you can appreciate, we are very short of skilled men here, and much administration will be necessary for a contract of this size. Would they be prepared to work as clerks on a project like this, Mr. Ryan?'

'That depends on your conditions,' Michael replied,

'A shilling and ninepence a day is the rate.'

'I would be very happy so. My eldest son, Luke, has spent the past six years working in England. Pat has been working the harvests as well. Nothing would delight us more than to have them work here beside us.'

'I would like to meet them,' Gaffney said.

Eleanor walked across to the cow shed to bring in Pat and Luke. She was thinking. There was work in Carrigard. Leeds might not be necessary at all.

Luke and Pat sat at the table.

'I'm told you can both read and write,' Gaffney enquired.

'Yes,' Luke answered.

'You can add and subtract? Multiply and divide?'

'We can.'

'Let me test your ability. If I employ eight men for six days at one-and-sixpence a day, what is the total wage?'

'Three pounds and twelve shillings,' Luke answered without hesitation.

Gaffney stared at him. 'No one on earth could calculate that fast.'

When White and Gaffney had left, the family discussed the offer. It was clear now that the situation had changed again. Yes, the wages offered were still lower than what could be earned on the railways, but now Michael would also be earning money as well as hiring out the horse and cart. All told, they could be bringing in as much money as a man would working in England. There was no need for anyone to leave Carrigard.

Luke went outside and leaned on the fence of the haggard, trying to think. He was trapped again. Trapped by his own pride in showing how he could calculate. Perhaps he should have taken a few minutes, and given the wrong answer. No. There were footsteps behind him. Michael leant on the fence alongside him.

'It's the right thing, Luke, and you know it. And I want you to know this, I still respect you. I know you want to go to Leeds, but this is for the best.'

'Respect me, is it? You won the argument, Father.'

'No,' Michael said, 'you won the argument. I agreed with what you wanted. Not that I liked it, but like you said, respect goes both ways. But now everything has changed, and this is the right decision, and I respect you the more for it.'

He spent all the next day in the bog on his own. When he had finished, he walked towards the rath. It was still bright, the sun just descending by the shoulder of the Mountain.

He was weary and confused. Going to Leeds, it had been the obvious thing to do. But Michael was right too. The Relief Works had changed everything. McKinnon had already been surveying the Works on the other side of the river, but that was different. This was closer to home. The way Gaffney had put it had trapped him. They needed men like him to run the Works, and the Works were the only way that many of his neighbours could earn money now. The potatoes were gone. Day by day, famine was tightening its grip, and very soon the only alternative to the Relief Works would be death.

High up on the Mountain there was a fire. He wondered if it was a house burning. It seemed to be at *Gort na Móna*, but it was not close to the main settlement. He watched it for a few minutes more, then he saw a second one. This was higher up the Mountain, near *Baile a' Cnoic*. Then he saw another at *Árd na gCaiseal*. By now there were three around *Gort na Móna*, but none of them were near houses. He wondered at first whether the heather was burning, but some at least seemed to be in open fields. As the dusk advanced, more fires were lit across the Mountain. Soon there were twenty or more.

It was dark now. He heard his father's voice in the distance.

'I'm here,' Luke shouted.

His father ran up. 'What's wrong with you? Your mother was worried.'

'I was just watching the fires.'

'I know. And by God, they'll pay for that,' he said.

'Why? What's happening?'

'Coogan. He's been shot. '

'Who?'

'Coogan. Clanowen's agent. Someone got him at the bridge. Stood out right in front of his horse, and shot him dead.'

'But who shot him?'

'The Molly Maguires. That's what people are saying. Who knows?'

They walked on down to the house. Eleanor and Pat were standing with McKinnon, staring at the Mountain, fires burning from end to end.

'You've heard the news?' Pat asked.

'I have,' Luke said.

'The fools,' McKinnon said. 'The bloody, bloody fools.'

'At a time like this,' Michael said. 'He was a right bastard, Coogan, but they could at least have pretended they were sorry. All those fires – you'd think it was a feast day. They'll pay the price for this on the Mountain.'

'They will,' Eleanor said, 'but what price? That's the question?'

'Eviction,' Michael said. 'What else?'

Chapter Ten

Mayo Constitution, August 1846:
On last Tuesday night the dead body of a man named Anthony Donnelly who lived near Massbrook in the Parish of Adrigoole was found on the mountains about a mile distance from his residence. It appeared from the evidence of some members of his family at the inquest that their food for the previous week was nothing better than rotten potatoes, and that he went on the day before his body was found to Castlebar to purchase some trifling articles for a few pennies, the only money in his possession. It is stated that Donnelly was employed for 8 or 10 days on the Public Works, but was stopped a week before his death, and he had not since received any payment. The Coroner's Jury found a verdict that the deceased came by his death in consequence of want of a sufficient supply of food.

Luke and Pat found the next few weeks to be as tough as any they had worked in England. In terms of sheer physical effort, it was not as demanding, but there was an endless struggle with growing chaos against a background of mounting horror. Within days, Luke thought Gaffney to be the toughest supervisor he had ever worked under, even more than Farrelly. At times he feared him, at times he almost hated him. As he began to know him better, he found out more about him, and the kind of man he was.

Gaffney had been a ganger on the railways in England, and he had gotten ahead on merit and hard work, managing hundreds of men. He had worked for Brassey in England, Scotland and France. He had a reputation for toughness, but if he drove men hard, he drove himself harder. He was scrupulous, fair and honest, and he expected others to be the same. Now, in the midst of the devastating crisis, he demanded total commitment and responsibility from the supervisors, gangers and clerks working under him, never ceasing to remind them that desperate measures were called for in desperate times.

As the days grew shorter, Pat and Luke were up before dawn, doing the farm work before going off to meet the surveyors; spending hours measuring out the route, driving metal spikes into the ground to find the bedrock, marking off the edge of the quarry, estimating rock requirements by the cubic yard and ton, estimating hours required for breaking rock and laying gravel. Evenings were spent by candlelight over the kitchen table, bringing all the plans together, estimating men and wages required, tools and materials required, overall costs and time-scale. Luke would start to put together the orders and requisitions for materials, writing them out longhand, multiplying and adding endless rows and columns of figures and then checking them again and again, because Gaffney would not accept mistakes.

One day, a convoy of carts arrived carrying hundreds of picks, shovels and hammers. Since there was nowhere else to store them, they were piled up in the cowshed. It didn't leave much room for the milking, but it was more secure. That evening, Luke saw a figure beside the shed. He ran over, but the figure had disappeared. He made up an improvised bed of straw, brought a blanket from the house, and for the rest of the week he slept in the shed.

Both Luke and Pat had accepted their positions on the basis of a shilling and ninepence a day. It was little compared to England, but there were no costs for transport or for digs to be paid. For the wage estimates though, they were using a daily rate of eight pence for the men and seven pence for the women. Pat doubted that anyone would work on these wages, but Luke felt otherwise. 'We won't have a shortage of workers,' he told Pat. 'A hungry man will work for any wage.'

As soon as news of the Relief Works had become known, men and women had started to approach Gaffney for employment, and when he would not see them, they approached Luke or Pat. Then Gaffney instituted the rule – canvassing will disqualify.

'What does that mean?' Pat asked Luke.

'It means that if you ask for work, you won't get it.'

'That's daft. You have to ask.'

'Sure, you do, but only through official channels. Otherwise it's canvassing.'

Gaffney would not be moved on this point. One night he said to Luke – 'You are either fair to all or fair to none. If it becomes known that we have our favourites, our task will be impossible. Remember – people are starving. You have a job to do, and I expect you to do it right.'

Later Luke explained it to Pat. 'Gaffney is right. We have to help those who need it most. If we only help our family and friends, then we're being unfair, and the weakest die.'

Gaffney had let it be known that the Works would be opened ten days later, early on a Monday morning. He had requisitioned a derelict cottage about a hundred yards from the quarry, and this had been patched up as a rough office. He asked Luke and Pat to be over early on that morning so that all the wage sheets and the work tickets could be prepared.

It was still dark as they left the house. There were many other figures shuffling along the road in total silence. As they walked the few hundred yards to the old cottage, they realised that there was already an enormous crowd in front of it and around it. There was no need to push. As they approached, the crowd parted to let them through. Even in the dark Luke could see faces he knew, but no one looked at him. It was as if neither he nor Pat were there.

When they entered, Gaffney and three of his supervisors were already there. Gaffney looked up as they came in. 'How many do you think are outside, Luke?'

'I don't know – hundreds surely.'

'When it's light, I want you to go outside and try to make some sort of estimate.'

Later, Luke slipped out the back door, scrambled up the small lean-to at the end and pulled his way over the decaying thatch to the top. The crowd was vast now, and it was with a shock he realised how many people he knew. Relatives, friends and many other people he knew were looking at him, their faces etched deep from a year of hunger. They were staring at him with a mixture of hope and something more. A respect for authority perhaps, or a contempt for it. If he caught their eyes, they looked away from him. He felt puzzled and hurt, but tried to ignore his own feelings. He forced himself to concentrate on the task in hand, counting across and counting down and multiplying in order to estimate numbers in any particular section of road or field. He knew it was very rough, but he had to get some kind of figure. There were many family groups, fathers with sons, a few with their wives and daughters as well. There were also many women he knew to be widows, mostly there on their own, though he knew some to be supporting young families.

When he was satisfied with his estimate, he scrambled down and went back in. 'Two thousand three hundred I estimate,' he told Gaffney. 'Between two thousand and two and a half for sure.'

'Would you say there were many families? Wives? Sons? Brothers?'

'Yes, there were. I wouldn't know them all, but there must be hundreds.'

'Well, we only have four hundred work tickets. The first rule we apply is this – only one ticket per family. After that we must decide by need, and that will be almost impossible to assess. We'll need assistance on that.'

He signalled to Pat. 'I want you to run into Kilduff and tell Father Reilly, Sergeant Kavanagh and Doctor Stone that we need them here within the hour. And tell the Sergeant to bring some men along.'

Over the next hour Luke, together with the other clerks and supervisors, made their way through the crowd, explaining the one ticket per family rule and asking each group to select who it should be. Again and again it was stressed that the fittest within the family should be selected, though the decision was left up to each family. All this time Luke kept wondering where the enormous crowd had come from. Most were from the immediate vicinity of Kilduff, but there were families from further up the Mountain, where he knew only a few.

What struck him most forcibly though was how invisible hunger and fever had been. The hungry and the sick lived and died at home, it was not talked about. But the Relief Works had brought all the suffering together, and it could not be ignored.

By the time he arrived back at the cottage, many of the crowd had left, but more had arrived. Again he scrambled on to the roof and made a quick count. When he went in, Pat was working on wage sheets in the corner, and the only other men were Gaffney and Father Reilly.

'How many now, Luke?'

'About fifteen hundred, Mr. Gaffney.'

Gaffney looked back at the young priest, who seemed to be trembling.

'Decisions will have to be made shortly, Father.'

'There must be some better way, Mr. Gaffney.'

'The only better way is another thousand tickets, and those I do not have. It is four hundred tickets, Father. Or none.'

In the next few minutes, the doctor arrived, followed by the Sergeant with three other constables. Gaffney asked the Sergeant to have his men form the crowd into four lines, and maintain order. To the doctor, he explained the necessity for Selection, and requested his assistance. They would have to decide which families required assistance the most, and reject the rest. He explained that on the basis of Luke's count, three-quarters of those outside would have to be rejected.

'There's another problem,' the doctor said. 'While we must select on the basis of need, many of the most needy are incapable of work.'

'I understand that,' Gaffney said, 'but we will only expect each man to work according to his capacity. Yes, we must have the road built, but we must all remember that our first objective is the relief of distress.'

'Many of these people are far too weak, they'll die in these conditions.'

'That's what we must decide over the next few hours. Do we employ a man, knowing that he isn't capable of it, or do we take a man who can do the work and send the others home?'

A few minutes later, the Selection began. Four rough tables had been erected outside the cottage. They were occupied by the three supervisors, with Luke on the fourth table at Gaffney's specific request. Gaffney himself, together with the priest and the doctor were behind the four men, being called on for advice or for verification of facts. Pat flitted from place to place, bringing work tickets to the desks and doing anything else he was requested.

It had now been agreed that no more than one in four should be accepted, but at first it seemed impossible to keep it to this level. Then a rough and ready system developed. In spite of Stone's fears, it was decided to accept the weakest unless it was clearly impossible. Widows with families were accepted almost at once, and those with very young children. Preference was given to those with large families over small. With Pat's assistance, Gaffney kept a rough running total of the numbers accepted against those rejected, and the criteria for acceptance were adjusted until he was happy that they had it right. A minimum of four young children per family was set, except for widows, where the minimum was two. This time though, no children were allowed on the works.

What surprised Luke now was the continuing quietness. He had feared there might be a riot, but there seemed to be very little threat of this. In part, this was due to Kavanagh's efficient policing, but it also seemed that there was a certain hopeless apathy among those rejected. Many times he saw the despair in men's eyes, men he knew, but he could no longer afford to think about this. On one occasion, a man in front of him broke down in tears and ran away. Without a word, the next man stood into position. He was wearing worn and broken boots, with one sole coming away from the upper. His trousers were torn beneath the knees, one still trailing a thorny bramble.

'How many children?' Luke asked, too weary to look up.

'Luke, it's me. Matt.' It was Matt McGlinn.

'You've no children, Matt.'

'For Christ's sake, Luke.'

'I can't do it, Matt. I just won't be let.'

'For your own friends. For the love of God.'

Gaffney walked over. 'What's wrong?' He looked at Matt. 'Does he have four children?'

Luke said nothing. Neither did McGlinn. The next man pushed him aside and stood forward.

As the Selection went on, those with work tickets formed a growing crowd to the side of the house. Some of those rejected stood in shock, but Kavanagh's men persuaded them to leave without any trouble.

When the Selection was complete, Gaffney started the allocation of gangs to various tasks. Then one of the men ran over from the hundreds waiting, and came up to him.

'John McDonagh, he's fallen over, Sir. We can't wake him.'

Gaffney scarcely glanced up.

'Luke,' he called, 'can you go over and see what's wrong.'

Luke went over. He saw a man lying on his side. He turned him on his back. He was quite dead.

The operation of the quarry was done on a different basis. Edmond White negotiated a direct contract with the authorities in Castlebar, the amount per ton of shale and rock being agreed, and a single contract price given. It was also agreed that workers from the Relief Works would be used, but Burke would pay them directly.

In spite of Michael being an educated man, he was not asked to operate the quarry. For this purpose a supervisor was sent from Galway by Mr. Burke.

The work in the quarry was split in two. At one end, twenty men were working with picks and shovels, loosening the shale and filling the carts. At the other end, another twenty worked with spikes and sledgehammers, loosening the rock and breaking it into smaller rocks. The rock was then taken to the working end of the new road, where dozens of people smashed it into smaller fragments, using hammers. The work was long, hard and tedious. Michael himself worked with his horse and cart, carrying rock and shale from the quarry.

Murty was not employed on the Works, either as a clerk or as a labourer. He wrote to Murtybeg and to Danny, telling them of the desperate situation in Mayo. Their postal order arrived every two weeks.

Over the next five days, the Works settled into a steady rhythm. Pat spent most of the time in the old cottage with Gaffney, while Luke worked on the new line or in the quarry; making out the rolls, checking on those present and ensuring enough implements were in position each morning. As the work progressed, it struck him how similar it was to the work on the rails, except that the physical labour carried out was only a fraction of what would be expected of good workmen on a rail cutting. There were the same long lines of workers shovelling mud, digging trenches and breaking stones, but in England, it would have been at least three times faster. On thinking about it, he realised that the main purpose was to supply work, not to be efficient.

One other difference was the women and working, something he had never seen on the rails.

What he had found most disturbing though was the Selection. He told himself that he had done what had to be done. It was better to employ four hundred than none at all. Despite this, the faces of those he had rejected were always in his mind; men and women who he had known over the years. Once again, they had disappeared, but he felt this was even worse, as if they were already dead. It had been easier for Pat; he had not been forced to make decisions. But for Luke things could never be the same again. His family were still with him, he slept at home every night, but he was becoming a stranger to his own people.

Payday was a busy day. Pat was sent out to bring in the time-sheets from the gangers, while Luke calculated the sums due. He noted that while some had worked the full six days, many had missed days or half days, though he did not question why. During the afternoon the pay clerk arrived from the Union, and they began to distribute the coins to the lengthening lines of men and women. It was a requirement that each should sign his or her name alongside the capitalised version of the name on the list that Pat had prepared. Very few could do so, most only marked an X. Luke wrote the words 'his mark' or 'her mark' – one word above the X and one below, and followed it with his own signature as witness.

He was feeling more and more isolated. People he had known for years refused to look him in the eyes. At first Luke thought that this was because of shame in that they could not sign their name, but many could, having attended Murty's school. No, the shame was not that. The shame was in having to work on the Relief Works at all. Having to sign in front of Luke made it worse, and they hated him for it.

Afterwards Gaffney dismissed all the supervisors and clerks, but asked Luke to remain behind. He held a letter in his hand.

'Luke, I've a request to make of you. It would appear that the Union in Knockanure is losing control of the situation, and they've asked for my assistance. They say there are Works to be opened in Knockanure and around Brockagh over the next three weeks, but they have no experienced men to operate them. I am very much afraid that I'll have to ask you to assist them for a short period. Pat too, maybe. I can't spare either of you, but they have no one else with experience.'

'But I have no experience either, Mr. Gaffney.'

'You under-estimate yourself. You're educated. And I know you've worked on the railways in England. Any man who worked there is experienced.'

'Yes, Mr. Gaffney. But I was only a labourer.'

'None the less, you know the system, and you've learnt a lot over the past two weeks. Also, you are responsible. There are few as capable in Mayo.'

'I don't know about that,' Luke said.

'Oh, but I do,' Gaffney said. 'I've heard a lot about you. I know more than you might think. Do you remember the first time we met, I tried you on a computation. Do you remember that?'

'Yes, Mr. Gaffney.'

'It wasn't just my idea either. I'd been talking to your uncle Ian about you. Did you know that?'

Luke looked at him in surprise. 'No, Mr. Gaffney.'

'Well, I did, and he told me you were the fastest computer this side of Lahore. You reckon faster than the best, that's what he told me. I didn't believe him, but that day in your kitchen, I tested you, and by God, you're fast. I couldn't do that myself.'

'If it's that you're looking for,' Luke said, 'you'll find plenty more around. It was my uncle taught us that. When we were at school, he used to keep a few of us back every night, throwing us questions like that.'

'There's more like you then?'

'There are, but I think the most of them are in England.'

'So you see, it does come back to you, doesn't it?'

But Luke was thinking of other things too. The deaths on the Works had shaken him at first, but he was used to it now. There had been two more in the past few days.

What still gnawed at him though was McGlinn. He knew he had to turn him down, he knew he had no choice, but who else would see it that way. No-one. There was no longer any reason to stay. Knockanure was the only way out.

'What are my instructions, Mr. Gaffney?'

'You are to present yourself at the Union at seven o'clock on Thursday morning. The Poor Law Commissioner is a Mr. Voisey. He's the fellow who asked for our assistance. It's up to Voisey to decide, but I understand he'll be sending you to Brockagh to establish a Works in a week or so. You're to have a horse, and your wages will be raised to two shillings. They may give an allowance for lodgings, but you'll have to talk to Voisey about that.'

That evening, Luke discussed the offer with Michael. Their position was secure for the next year. Michael could still work hard, loading and unloading the cart with men half his age. Combined with the payment for the horse and cart, he was already earning two shillings a day. Among the three of them, they were now earning over thirty shillings a week. This would be enough to pay the total rent for the year in just over five weeks, and even with the higher price of corn, food was no longer a problem.

Michael had his reservations too though. Most of the men and women on the Works did not own a horse, and Gaffney would not use donkeys or mules. There were only five other horses carting stone. Michael had heard mutterings at the quarry about men wealthy enough to own a horse, and to rent it out for more than a man's wage.

A second factor was the 'one worker per family' rule. Gaffney had instituted this on the spur of the moment to overcome an immediate crisis, but it reflected very badly on a family who had three men working – all on higher wages. Luke knew that in total, they were earning nearly as much as

Gaffney himself, but he did not mention this to his father.

Still, the Selection was the worst of all. It had pained Michael too. Apart from Matt McGlinn, a number of other friends and relatives who had been rejected had spoken to him on the afternoon of the Selection. Michael assured Luke that he had done the right thing, but he too knew the consequences. They both agreed therefore that the request from the Knockanure Union would be for the best. Michael thought that the Barony might institute further Works in Carrigard to employ those who had been rejected, and by the time Luke and Pat returned the harsh feelings might have abated. Perhaps.

Pat and Luke arrived in Knockanure just after dawn. There was already a crowd of hundreds outside the Workhouse. At the front of the crowd, there were men and women clamouring to be allowed in or to be given food. The gate was guarded on the inside by two men, inmates, Luke guessed. One was carrying a heavy stick which he used on the fingers of men who were trying to clamber to the top of the gate. As they came to the edge of the crowd, he could see again the thin faces and loose-hanging clothes that signified hunger. He could also smell the nauseating stench of unwashed bodies.

He was horrified. It brought back to him the day he had brought Sorcha and her husband to the Workhouse. But there were more people now. He and Pat started to push their way through the crowd, and women screeched at them, trying to hold them back. But they fought their way through the crowd until they got to the gate, and Luke shouted at one of the inmates who was guarding it. At first he ignored him, but when he understood what their business was, he nodded to them, but he did not open the gate. Luke and Pat clambered up to the top, kicking away hands that grasped their ankles. They dropped down the other side and went to the administration building beside the Workhouse. Luke knocked. An elderly man answered.

'Luke and Patrick Ryan, from Kilduff. Mr. Gaffney sent us over. We're looking for Mr. Voisey.'

'Oh yes, I was expecting you. Which one of you is Luke?'

'I am,' said Luke.

'I'm glad you could both come. We will certainly need you. Can I ask you to wait in this office, and I will be with you presently.'

They entered the office. There was another man already seated at the table, working on maps. He stood up as they entered. It was McKinnon.

'I thought you two were in Carrigard,' McKinnon said in surprise.

'And we thought you were in Castlebar,' Luke said

'That was last week. They sent me over here to help Voisey and the other Poor Law fellows to get the Relief Works going.'

'And what about Sabina?' Pat asked.

'I told her to stay in Kilduff. Might be healthier for her than the Union in Castlebar. Or here, for that matter.'

Luke looked out the rear window at the crowd. 'It seems you're selecting for the Works today.'

'Oh no, the Selection was a week ago. It was a terrible day, there were thousands here. We only had work for one in ten, and we near had a riot. They were threatening Voisey's life. The peelers had to be called. It's calmed down a bit now.'

'If the Selection is done, who are all these people?'

'Some of them are those who didn't go home. The peelers tried to move them, but they gave up.'

'They've been here all week!'

'They have, and the crowd has been growing since. They're all looking for admission to the Workhouse, but it's already taken near double its capacity. Voisey fed them for a few days, but that only attracted more.'

'I thought they didn't allow Outdoor Relief without work.'

'They don't, and the Master here is a great man for the rules. It offended Voisey's Christian sensibilities though, he just couldn't turn hungry people away. But the Master had to put a stop to it, the Workhouse hasn't enough food to feed the inmates. I think they're just hoping the crowd will disappear.'

'Where will they go?' Pat asked.

'God only knows, Pat. God only knows.'

'What's Voisey like to work for?' Luke asked.

'He's a good man, a decent man. His brother is an Anglican minister in England. He'd have made a good vicar himself. Deeply Christian, as I say. The problem is he finds it hard to manage men, perhaps he's too gentle for it. I think all this will break his heart, poor fellow.'

'And the Master?' Luke asked. 'What's he like?'

'Cronin – oh, he's not bad. Strict, hard-working, a man has to be to run a Workhouse. A lot of experience, I understand, Dublin and everywhere else. His wife is the Matron, she'll have her work cut out for her now, poor woman.'

Luke glanced back to McKinnon and to the window behind. There was a hammering sound coming from the back yard.

'What are these sheds they're building along the wall?'

McKinnon followed his gaze. 'Fever sheds. They've no money for a proper building.'

'Have you fever here?'

'Black Fever. Only a few yet, but it's growing.'

Voisey entered, and they all sat down. 'You come well commended, both of you. Mr. Gaffney thinks very highly of you, and he is a man not easily pleased.

He writes to say that he cannot spare either of you, but he knows he must. I have much work for you. As you have heard, we are starting new Works in the area around Brockagh. I would send Ian, but I cannot spare him. We haven't enough good men for all we need, the work never ceases, and still it is not enough.'

He turned to McKinnon. 'Do you have the maps there?'

When they were spread out on the table, he turned to Luke.

'You can read maps?'

'Yes, I've studied geography.'

'I should explain,' McKinnon said, 'young Luke here is my nephew. Used to help me out with the Ordnance Survey when he was a young fellow back in '38. He knows all about maps and surveying.'

'Just the kind of man we want. Now, these are the two Works we must start around Brockagh. As you can see, the first is Ardnagrena, which we intend to open on Monday.'

'On Monday?' Luke exclaimed. 'With respect, Mr. Voisey, that's impossible.'

'I know that. Every day, we are expected to do the impossible. Every day, we must feed the Five Thousand, but miracles are not given to us. You must do what you can. And further, we must commence the Works at Lisnadee as soon as possible.'

'But how can I do all this?'

'I would suggest first you go to Brockagh and find the Catholic priest, Father Nugent. He is an excellent man, we worked together in '40. You will need at least seven men – one supervisor and three gangers for each of the Works. I'm sure he'll advise you on that.'

'I'll do what I can.'

'I'm certain of that.'

'And what about me?' Pat asked.

'Can you stay and help us here?'

'Well…yes.'

'Excellent. But now I must leave you. We have a meeting of the Guardians this morning, and I must prepare. Ian here will explain everything to you. Goodbye and Godspeed.'

For the next hour, McKinnon explained the maps, the estimates and the requisitions in detail. He explained the system of payment and the days on which the pay clerk would be expected to arrive at each Works. Then he brought them into the Workhouse block to meet the Workhouse Master. A young woman was working at the edge of the desk beside him. Luke recognised her as the one he had seen when he had brought Sorcha over.

Afterwards McKinnon gave Luke a five pound advance which he had to sign for, together with a quantity of cold cooked Indian meal. He brought him out to the stables to saddle a horse. Luke led it by the reins to the front gate. McKinnon took his hand. 'Good luck now. Just do the best you can. I hope to visit you in Brockagh over the next few weeks.'

He unlocked the gate and opened it. Two inmates held back the crowd, as Luke pulled his horse through gaunt men and women, mounted it, and rode away.

On the Leeds & Thirsk Railway, Danny had other concerns. He sought out the Erris men in their lodgings. They seemed happy enough to see him, and invited him into the shack for *poitín*. He was a little drunk when he left, but he had vital information. The wages on the gang had dropped to ninepence a day. The famine was forcing thousands of men out of Ireland, and wages were being driven down fast. The opportunity was better – far better – than he had anticipated.

A week later, as the Works finished, he walked from Bramhope into Leeds. He had mentioned to Farrelly that he had friends in Sheffield, and wanted to spend a few days there. Murtybeg asked about these friends, but Danny gave no answer, and Murtybeg knew that it would be useless to press him.

Danny was in time for the last train to Sheffield, and stayed in a rough boarding house that night. Very early the following morning, he took the first train across the Pennines to Manchester. He was in time to catch a stagecoach to Stockport, some miles south of the city. He stayed in a boarding house on the outskirts of the town.

He was awake before dawn and left as the sun was rising. He walked out the new Works on the Stockport & Warrington line. Again and again he stopped at various gangs, talking to gangmasters and subcontractors, talking to the men on their own and assessing the work involved with a practiced eye. But he was short of time and barely managed to get the stagecoach back into Manchester that night. The next day was all travel, Manchester to Sheffield, Sheffield to Leeds and then walking along the rails to Bramhope. It was the early hours of the morning before he arrived back in the lodging house. The next evening he wrote a letter to Luke.

Mr. Luke Ryan   Price's Lodging House
C/o Knockanure Union   Bramhope
Knockanure   Yorkshire
Co. Mayo

                                                   6th of September 1846
Dear Luke,
I was surprised to hear that you are working for the Union, and I hope this letter will find you.

It seems to me that the news from Mayo becomes more gloomy every day. Father has written to me, telling me terrible stories of fever and hunger. I understand though that you, Pat and uncle Michael all have good positions on the Relief Works, and I am happy to hear this. Here in Yorkshire we see the effects of the famine every day. There are many hungry people in England, but that is as nothing compared to the thousands of Irish flooding into this country.

Railway construction is growing very fast and attracts many Irishmen, but the English workers complain, because they say the Irish are driving down wages. This certainly seems to be true. In spite of all the rail building, the deals we have been able to negotiate are less than before. I have thought for a long time on these matters, and I have concluded that the future in this country is in general contracting as I already told you. Since wages are low, there are good gains to be made by any contractor, and the margin they add makes contracting even more profitable. If we were able to find men who had just arrived in England, perhaps men from Erris or the Ox Mountains who do not speak English, then we should be able to pay lower wages, and margins would be even higher. It would also be possible to employ many more men, making even more profit. Mayo men – that is the key.

This was something I had mentioned to Martin, but he feels it is too dangerous a course for us, and prefers to stay working as we are until we all have enough to go home with, though why anyone would want to go to Mayo now, I cannot imagine. So I have decided if anything is to be done I will have to do it myself. Of course, the problem is money. I estimate it would be necessary to have £100 in order to pay for workers and implements before an invoice could be raised. I have already been saving. I have £65 invested and would hope to increase that sum over the next few months. Please not to mention that to anyone in Carrigard or anywhere else.

So why am I writing to you? It is because you are my cousin and my friend. I feel the need for a good partner to work alongside me in developing this business. Such a partner would have to be someone I could trust, and God knows there are few enough of them. He would also have to have experience on the railways and be capable of dealing with accounts and dealing with men. As I say, it is vital to have a good supply of men from Mayo – they are where the profit lies. If this were part of your responsibility as partner, then it would involve travelling back to Mayo almost as often as you like. I know this is important to you.

I know too you have little enough money to invest, perhaps none, but I do not see that that should be a problem. If you wish to come in with me, I am willing to lend you the money to buy a one-quarter share with perhaps the option of purchasing a further one-quarter on account at a later stage. From my calculations, I reckon that we could together grow a business running a profit of £10, £20 or even £30 per month, and after that, who knows.

And so Luke, I would appeal to you to consider my offer. There is no future in Ireland. The blight has hit Mayo for a second time, and there is no guarantee that it will not come back. There is money to be made in this country.

As ever, your cousin,
Daniel

Chapter Eleven

Telegraph or Connaught Ranger, September 1846:
Our Foxford correspondent states that never in his memory
was fever so prevalent in that locality as at present. In the
villages between that town and the Pontoon entire families
are lying, and many dying. He mentions one family in particular, 8 of whom are confined to the bed of sickness, their
only attendant being a boy 6 years old.

Luke rode for four hours. The blackened stalks were still in the fields, flattened now. Some of the fields had been part dug, many in random spots across the field as the farmers had searched for any ridge where the blight might have been less. Most of the fields were undug though. There was no further point. This was total blight. 1845 had not been like this, nor 1840.

As it started to rain, he stopped by a stream and led the horse down to drink. Then he let it feed along the side of the road. He sat down under a thorn bush and started to eat the Indian meal. As he ate, he noticed the door of a cabin opening two fields away. A woman came down a track towards him, carrying an infant, another child walking behind, holding her skirts.

'*Tá an ocras orainn.*' The hunger is on us.

He asked her how many children she had. Eleven. He gave her the rest of the meal. He thought of the meal in his pack, but then he thought better of it. He did not know where he would be able to buy food again. He had been generous enough already.

He rode on through the afternoon, sometimes passing people on the roads, but no one addressed him. He met a horseman coming the other way, and he recognised him as the pay clerk he had met in Carrigard. They both stopped.

'It's a dangerous job,' he told Luke. 'One of the clerks was robbed as he rode into Foxford. There's stories too of clerks being robbed further west. One of them got a knock on the head, I hear he's still in Castlebar Infirmary.'

'Thank God I'm not a pay clerk so.'

'Oh, it's not just us. It's you fellows too. Have you been through a Selection yet?'

'Of course. Back in Carrigard.'

'Had any riots?'

'Not in Carrigard. But we had the peelers in, kept order pretty well.'

'They weren't so lucky in Castlebar. Had a riot at the Selection there. A few of the clerks got roughed up. You need a tough man to oversee the process.'

'Gaffney's tough.'

'Damned right he is. Tell me though, how did you decide who was to get tickets in Carrigard?'

'Gaffney's decision. He didn't take single people nor any children. And he wouldn't take anyone with less than four children in the family, excepting widows.'

The pay clerk nodded. 'Yes, I suppose that's fair. Not like what they did back in Roscommon.'

'What did they do there?'

'Oh, the landlord decided it was a great way to get their back-rent in. They only gave tickets to fellows who were behind in their rent, and then they deducted the back rent on pay day. Caused riots I can tell you. They had to call the militia in.'

'I'm not surprised.'

'No. The landlords are terrified though, and not just in Roscommon. They reckon the Molly Maguires would string them up if they got half a chance. Tough fellows, those bastards.'

'They are,' Luke said, 'There's some question that they were the ones shot Coogan.'

'Yes, I'd heard that.'

He asked Luke where he was going. Luke told him of the two new Works he was expected to start around Brockagh.

'That's impossible,' the other man said.

'I know.'

'Just be careful with your selecting.'

'I will,' Luke said.

As the sun set, he looked for a shed with hay in it, but could find none. He lay in a derelict cabin, his back against a clamp of turf, the horse blanket wrapped around him, and he slept until morning.

It was still raining when he started out again. As he rode, he saw a corpse near the middle of the road. He halted his horse, staring at it, undecided what to do. He thought of putting it over his saddle and carrying it to Brockagh. But what if the man had died of fever? He dismounted, and walked to the other side to see the face. It was a white, yellowish colour, not purple or black as he would have expected with black fever. But was he sure of that? It could be another form of fever. In the end, he pulled the corpse to the side and left it on the bank beside the drain for someone else to notice. Then he crouched down and washed his hands in the rivulet. He mounted his horse and rode on.

When he arrived at Brockagh, the rain had stopped. The mountains rose behind the town, trailing grey rain still clinging to the peaks of the Ox. There was no one outside, no sound.

As he rode through the town, he felt he was being watched, but he could see no eyes. He saw the church, a little larger than the houses. There was a small house beside it. He tied his horse to the bush outside, and knocked.

The priest who answered was tall and elderly, dressed in a stained and patched soutane. His face was gaunt.

'I'm looking for Father Nugent.'

'You've found him.'

'I'm Luke Ryan from Kilduff. I've been sent over by Mr. Voisey in Knockanure to start with the surveying.'

'Not Jim Voisey, surely?'

'Yes, Father. He's one of the Commissioners...'

'I know well who Jim Voisey is. So he sent you over? Surveying you say.'

'For the Works, Father. They're planning for Relief...'

'Now, that is good news.'

'...and I'm supposed to get it all started. The roads have to be surveyed...'

'The explanations will do later. If you don't dry off those clothes, there won't be much surveying done.'

He followed the priest inside. There was a turf fire burning. There was a table with an empty plate, three stools, a dresser and little else. The priest took a bottle from the fireside, uncorked it, and poured two small measures of a clear spirit into mugs.

'Here, this should warm you.'

Luke tasted it, rolling it on his tongue.

'It's good, Father. The man who made this knew what he was doing.'

'He did – he's the best in the Ox. Always one step ahead of the Excise too.' He raised his mug and drank. 'Your health.'

'Good health, Father.' Luke drained the rest of his mug, fire scorching his throat and lungs. He ignored the searing pain as all men did, and shook his head in ritual appreciation. Already, he felt warmer.

'But back to serious matters now,' the priest said. 'How's Knockanure these past weeks.'

'Not good, Father. Far worse than last year – there's scarce a potato left. The people have nothing. Now even the Workhouse is turning families away, they've no room, not even for children. And I hear they've no money to buy food for those inside.'

'Have you seen any sign of fever?'

'No, but I believe it's started. They're building sheds for fever by the Workhouse. It follows the hunger.'

'It does, it does,' the priest said. He stared into the fire, as if looking for answers. 'But what about Jim Voisey, I haven't met him in many years.'

'Not since '40 he says.'

'God, is it so long?'

'He remembers you well though, Father.'

'How's he coping with all this?'

'I think he's worn out, from all I hear. They say the Workhouse is bankrupt. He wants to feed everyone, but it just isn't possible.'

'It won't be possible here either. And we don't even have a Workhouse.'

'That's why Mr. Voisey sent me, Father. But I can't do it all on my own.'

'I'll do what I can, though it mightn't be much. Relief Works, you say?'

'Yes, Father. They're still against Outdoor Relief, unless the people work for it. They're starting Works all across the barony. The committee has decided to build two sections of new road around here – Ardnagrena and Lisnadee. They're intending to employ two hundred.'

'What will they pay?'

'Eight pence a day for the men. Seven pence for the women.'

'It's little enough, isn't it?'

'Very little, Father.'

'Still, it's not your fault – we must take what we're given. What can I do?'

'The hardest thing I'd ask of you is to help us with Selection. I know it's not easy – I've been through it myself. The instructions are no more than a hundred for the Ardnagrena Works and a hundred for Lisnadee. They're supposed to be the neediest according to Castlebar. Those who have suffered the most from the failure.'

'How do we decide that?' the priest asked. 'There's thousands starving in this parish.'

'I don't know the answer to that,' Luke said. 'When they did it in Knockanure, they had to call the peelers in. It wasn't much better back home around Carrigard and Kilduff. People are desperate. It's impossible to make a Selection, but a Selection has to be made. Around Kilduff we took only one from each family, and only from families with four children, two for widows. The older people living on their own were left to die. So no matter what we do, we'll be wrong. There are just too many hungry, and we can't help them all. It's a dirty business, this Selection.'

'Well, I hope I'll be able to help you, Luke. But first, you must dry those clothes.'

Luke brought in the horse blanket. He stripped down and wrapped it around him. The priest hung his clothes alongside the fire, then both pulled stools over and sat close to the heat.

'What age are you, Luke?'

'Twenty.'

'Why did they choose you?'

'I don't know. Gaffney, he's the Chief Supervisor in Kilduff, he reckoned I could help. When he heard I could write and add, he asked me to help him. They've not enough surveyors or clerks, so Gaffney decided to use me instead; writing down names, adding wages, measuring out the roads, all that class of thing. Then he told me and my brother to go over to Knockanure because they needed us more there, and then Mr. Voisey asked me to come up here and get everything started.'

'And what are you supposed to do?'

'Select the workers, like I said. Find shovels and picks and hammers, mark out the roads. But first I must find some good men for gangers. That's why I need your help. That and the Selection. You know the people here.'

'If it's gangers you're looking for, John Gallagher is the best man to talk to,' the priest said. 'He's a reliable fellow, spent a long time in England – Liverpool, Manchester and the rest. He hasn't much schooling, I'm afraid, but he's well respected around Brockagh. '

'He sounds like the kind of man we need.'

'One way or another, you'll need him on your side. You should go over and see him straight away. I'd take you across, but I've got a few sick calls. But you can come back in the morning. We'll work it all out then. And bring John with you. If he'll come.'

'Why wouldn't he?'

'I don't know. He can get suspicious of outsiders at times. He hates Government men.'

Luke did not respond. Government men? He dressed himself.

'You'll have no problem finding Gallagher's,' the priest said. 'Just ride back the street you came, turn second left, and you'll see Gallagher's over on the right. The house with the wagon outside. He might lodge you. If he doesn't, come back, and I'll see what I can do.'

He followed the priest's directions. As he rode down the street, two women stood by the door of a mud cabin, watching him in silence.

The second street seemed more prosperous than the rest of Brockagh. The houses were built out of rough stone; a little more solid than the cabins. There was no-one about.

He found the house with the wagon alongside. It was chained into an iron ring in the wall and padlocked. The wheels were high, rimmed with steel, and were chained onto the body of the wagon. Curious, he stooped to examine the axles. They were both forged, and carried the name of a foundry in Shropshire. He knew this was no ordinary cart from Mayo. It was similar to the heavy road wagons used for carrying brick to the railway construction sites, but not as heavy. It had been designed for lighter loads than brick, but for longer distances. From the way that the wood had been bolted together, he knew it had been designed to last. He wondered how it came to be in Brockagh.

He knocked on the door, and waited.

The young woman who opened it was dressed in a shift. She was his own age, maybe a little younger. Under her eyes were high cheekbones over thin cheeks. On one side her long hair was flung back by her neck, the other side hanging forward loose. The skirt of her shift covered little more than her knees. It was sprinkled with flour, and her hands were white with flour.

She held his gaze with grey eyes, unwavering, almost challenging him. Penetrating eyes, testing his strength. He thought of all the fashionable ladies he had seen in Dublin and Liverpool and London and Bath. Trying to make up for all they would never have, but that could be carried by a girl in a worn out dress, in an unknown village in Mayo.

A girl? Or a woman?

Kitty, bare feet, a patched grey shawl and the walk of a queen.

Aileen once, laughing as she mixed the bread; rays of flour suspended in sunlight.

Nessa in childbirth, her moans growing feebler as the wailing grew louder.

Sorcha, ancient and stooped, outpacing the digging men through brute strength.

Sabina, asleep by McKinnon after the storm, his old army greatcoat flung over them.

Eleanor softly singing; gently rocking her youngest child, no longer breathing.

Grey eyes.

'And what might you be looking for, sir?' she asked.

'The priest sent me,' he answered. 'I'm looking for Gallagher's.'

'Gallagher's,' she said with a smile. 'We're all Gallaghers here. Half the street is Gallagher.'

'It's John Gallagher I'm looking for, but I suppose you're going to tell me half the family are John.'

'Two at least,' she said. 'But since my brother is only eight, you'll be looking for my Pa. Come on in out of that. How do they call you?'

'Ryan's the name, Luke Ryan.'

He entered, closing the door behind him. The hallway was dark. He could just see her profile against a chink of light from the door into the room behind. He could not see how close she was. He waited for her to name herself, but she did not.

'Hold on here, Luke,' she said. As she moved back, she brushed against him. He said nothing, lost to words.

She went into the room, closing the inside door. Now there was no light at all. He felt unsteady. He could just hear whispered voices questioning. Then silence.

At last, the door opened. A man came out. The girl had not followed him.

'I'm told there's a Mr. Ryan looking for me.'

'That's right. Luke Ryan.' He held out his hand. It was not taken. The man opened the outer door, indicating to Luke to step outside. He leaned against the wagon.

'Father Nugent sent you?'

'He did. He spoke well of you.'

'I'm happy to hear that. But I'm sure he didn't send you just to say that.'

'No, no, not just that. Like I told him, they've decided to start Relief Works in Ardnagrena and Lisnadee on account of the hunger.'

'Relief?' He was questioning and suspicious.

'Yes. And I've been sent up from Knockanure to get it all started. I need a good supervisor to help me. I'm looking for a man with numbers.'

'I have that.' No further information was offered.

'You learnt it in England, the priest says.'

'A long time ago. On the Navigation back in the 'twenties. And the railways later.'

'So will you do it?'

'Maybe, maybe not. I'm out of practice, and I don't read too well.'

'That's no problem – I'm able enough with reading. What I'm looking for is a man who can add – pounds, shillings and pence. And measure distance. Someone who can supervise the work and the workers.'

The priest was right, he thought. This is the man. And this is the crisis. If he comes with me now, we have the village. If he goes against? He thought of Selection in Carrigard. Near rioting in Knockanure. Clerks attacked in Castlebar. Gaffney would know how to handle it. Would I?

'How much are they paying?' the man asked.

'Eight pence a day for the men, seven for the women.'

'God, it's not much, is it?'

'Damned little. More for a supervisor though.' That was a stupid thing to say, he thought. Sounds like a bribe.

'I've heard men on the railways can earn four shillings a day.'

'I know,' Luke said. 'I've done it myself. Good wages, like you say, but we were working fourteen hours a day. And the railways had the money.'

The man said nothing. He seemed to be thinking, staring at Luke. Weighing him up, testing him too. Luke thought of saying something, but reckoned it better to wait and force a response. The silence dragged.

Then Gallagher spoke.

'Well, there's nothing to be done about the pay today,' he said. 'Come on in and rest yourself. Have you anywhere to stay tonight?'

'Not yet. I should have asked the priest about that.'

'Don't bother him now. We'll find something here for you. It's not much, but it's dry.'

Luke followed him back into the house. The moment had passed. He was in.

In the main room, there was a single rush lamp at one end and a turf fire at the other. There were three young boys close to the fire and a woman sitting with the girl at the table, both mixing dough.

'This is my wife, Una,' Gallagher said. 'This is Luke Ryan up from Knockanure. He tells me they're starting with Relief around here.'

'Thank God for that,' she said. The same eyes as the girl. Grey. Older, wiser perhaps, more haggard. She might have been forty.

Gallagher gestured towards the table. The girl, who had left the room, came back with a bottle. She poured the drink, and then she stood at the far end of the table, still making bread. Luke sipped the clear spirit, feeling again the delicate yet burning sensation on his tongue. 'From the Ox, no doubt?'

'Of course,' Gallagher said. 'The best in Connaught. Times are rough, but we might as well enjoy the little we can.'

The three boys crowded around the table, still staring at the stranger.

'What's your name?' Luke asked of the youngest one.

There was no answer.

'He's shy,' the oldest said. 'Aren't you, Frankie?'

'Francis,' the woman corrected.

'How old are they all?' asked Luke.

This time the man answered. 'Young John here is our oldest – eight years now. Bernard and Francis are twins – they're only four yet.'

The girl had not been mentioned. He glanced at her, but said nothing.

They talked into the night. He told them all he had seen over the past two months. The potato crop in Brockagh was the same as Knockanure and Kilduff – complete failure. They talked about Relief and the help it might give to the starving, though Gallagher's opinion was that it would be no use to many families in the high Ox Mountains where men were already too weak to walk, let alone work.

Later he joined the younger lads in a room at the back. He stretched out in a blanket on the floor, his head on his pack. It was cold, but the *poitín* and the exhaustion of the ride overcame him, and he slept until the girl shook him awake in the morning.

Chapter Twelve

Mayo Constitution, September 1846:
A multitude of people also assembled in Mayo, exceeding, we should think, 5000. The assemblage of such a vast number of people, declaring themselves on the brink of starvation, was truly deplorable.

Gallagher accompanied him back to the priest's house, and they sat around the small table. The priest spoke first.

'I've been thinking about what you told me yesterday,' he said. 'I've some ideas I'd like to put to you. Given that we can't take everyone who will apply for work, I thought of the way you did it in Kilduff, and we could use that here. If we've not enough work tickets, we must help to feed those most in need. If we apply the same rules here, one person per family and only for those with four children, then these are the ones we would take.'

He handed him a sheaf of papers, each with a list of names of families. Luke glanced down the first page. 'You've been up all night, Father.'

'I have.'

'But how could you remember all these names? How did you think of them?'

'I've been here for thirty years. I just think of the roads, think of the cabins to left and right, and remember the names. My only worry is the small lanes and boreens. There's so many of them, I can't remember every one. There'll be more names before we finish this.'

Gallagher pointed to one of the names on the list. 'This name. Is this Gallagher?'

'It is,' the priest said. 'Eileen Gallagher from up by Burrenabawn. She's a widow.'

'She doesn't have four children anymore,' Gallagher said.

'She had five.'

'Two died in the last few weeks. And the older ones are gone to England.'

'I hadn't heard that.' A look of horror came into his eyes. 'But why didn't anyone tell me, John? Why did nobody say anything?'

'I don't know, Father.'

Luke was not listening to the others. He was still counting down the columns, front and back on each page.

'This list is terrible, Father. There must be three hundred families here.'

But the priest was staring into space. He turned towards Luke. 'You see what it's like here. I can't give the sacraments to the dying or even the dead. There's too many. Hundreds of them. Hundreds.' He shook his head. 'I'm sorry, Luke, what did you say?'

'The list, Father. We can't take more than a fraction of these.'

'Why? How many tickets did you say we have for Ardnagrena.'

'A hundred, no more. One supervisor, three gangers and three gangs, each of thirty-two.'

The priest started to read through the list again, tracing down the columns with his finger, whispering the names to himself.

'I see,' he said at length. 'A hundred.'

'A hundred,' Luke said.

'So what we must do now is go through all these names again, the three of us. We must decide which families need relief the most.'

'Yes, Father.'

'Widows,' the priest continued. 'Very large families, whatever we think best. When we have a hundred names, then we stop. Those names, and those names only, can be announced, perhaps at Mass on Sunday. That way, we'll not bring in anyone with false hopes.'

'It may be too rough, Father,' Gallagher said. 'Family size won't measure hunger. Or fever.'

'What other way is possible?' asked Luke.

'Death.'

'Death?' echoed the priest.

'Yes,' Gallagher said. 'Death for three months past perhaps. Any family who has already lost someone to fever or hunger, they're already in a bad way. They're already hungry.'

For a few seconds no-one spoke, the priest and Luke looking at each other in surprise. Death, Luke thought. The measure of everything.

'You're right,' the priest whispered. 'Lord, you're right, why didn't I think of it. It's so clear. We already know where people are dying. So let's go through these names and see how much we know.'

For the next hour they worked on the list. Father Nugent already knew many families where he had been called out for the last rites. Gallagher knew many more who had died in his own area without any sacrament. When they could remember no more, they stopped.

'Seventy-six families,' Luke said.

'But I'm sure there are many more we don't know about,' the priest said. 'Out towards the mountains – Teenashilla. Burrenabawn.'

'If I can make a suggestion,' Luke said, 'we still need three more men for gangers around Ardnagrena. If we knew one man in each area, we might be able to send for them, and they might be able to help us.'

The priest and Gallagher agreed three names. Then the priest went outside, and three young men were despatched to bring them back. Within two hours, two men had arrived. Another fifteen families were added to the list, representing thirty dead. Both men were signed up as gangers.

When the gangers had left, Father Nugent sat back at the table, staring down at the ticks made against each family.

'Thirty more dead,' he said. 'Most of them I hadn't even known about. What kind of priest am I? I can't even minister to my own. They die, and I don't even hear about it.'

'That's because they don't send for you, Father,' Gallagher said. 'They're too weak. They're not able to send for a priest.'

They left.

Later that evening, there was a knock at the door. The girl went to answer it and came back. 'There's a message for you, Mr. Ryan.'

He went to the door. A small boy stood there, dressed in rags, his trousers hanging in tatters just below his knees. His feet were bare, spattered with mud.

'What's this about?' Luke asked. The boy did not reply, but just turned his head to one side to indicate to Luke to follow him.

Gallagher had come out. 'I'd better go with you,' he said. '*Who sent you*,' he asked the boy.

'*The priest.*'

When they reached the priest's house, they saw the third man had arrived. 'You're most welcome here,' he said to Luke. 'We never thought we'd see Relief around here.'

'Let's wait, and see how it works out,' Luke said.

'Don't be like that,' the priest said. 'Tim here, he's one of the Durcans – there's a big crowd of them up in Knocklenagh. He's worked on the railways too. You won't get better than Tim nor John around Brockagh. Now let's get going – we're trying to find another nine for Relief between Ardnagrena and Knocklenagh.'

Luke explained the new system of Selection to Durcan. Within a few minutes the list had reached a hundred.

He slept at Gallaghers again.

It was only the next morning that he picked up the girl's name when Mrs. Gallagher addressed her as 'Winnie.' Winifred he thought. An English name. Why Winifred, why not Una? Perhaps it was a name that Gallagher picked up when he was working in England.

154

And she was attractive. Her grey eyes still transfixed him, he could not say why. Once or twice he thought he saw her glancing at him. He wondered if she felt the same as he did, but he had no way of finding out. On one occasion he thought he saw Gallagher looking at him, but with a different expression. Perhaps he had imagined it, but it put him on his guard.

He went to Sunday Mass with the family. The church was tiny – larger than most of the cabins and houses in Brockagh, but small compared to the church in Kilduff. Like the cabins around it, it had a rough thatched roof. Most of the men stood outside the entrance, a few standing inside at the back of the church.

During the Kyrie one of the men clutched his hand to his chest and collapsed. The priest looked up and signalled to the altar boys to wait. Then he walked down the narrow aisle to where the man lay. He turned him on his back. The man was gasping. A woman had come back from the front of the church. She knelt beside the man, holding his hand.

'*Will he live, Father?*'

'*Of course he will,*' the priest replied, though even from where he stood, Luke could hear the lack of conviction in his voice. '*Can you carry him home now?*'

Two men lifted him with his arms around their shoulders, and two more grasped their hands under him to form a rough seat. The priest walked back to the altar and went on with the Mass.

At the end, he explained about the new Relief Works, and gave the names of the families selected. Luke could feel a marked atmosphere of tension as the names of each family selected were read out, road by road. The one workman per family rule was explained. Selection by death was not mentioned.

A queue started to build up at a small table at the back of the church, where Luke sat with Gallagher. He had a single sheet of paper headed 'Checklist of Workmen employed on the New Line of Road at Ardnagrena.' He started to write the names, followed by the daily wage.

Patrick Lynagh, 8d.

Bridget Murtagh, 7d.

Edward Richards, child, 5d.

He hesitated. Should they have children working? Gaffney had not allowed it.

Martin Mullan, 8d.

Michael Meagher, 8d.

Jamy Judge…

He stopped. This was another child, ten years old perhaps. His bare arms were like sticks, thin ribbons of wasted muscle showing through. Much of the hair on the top of his head was missing, bald patches showing through where it had fallen out. But on his forehead, on his cheeks and on the rest of his face, there was a light covering of hair, as if trying to make up for the lack of hair elsewhere. The face of a fox, Luke thought.

'*Is this the strongest man in this family?*' asked Gallagher.

'*He is,*' one of the waiting men answered. '*His father's dead, his mother can't walk, and all the other children are younger.*'

...child, 5d.

Martin Dunne, 8d.

Thomas Flynn, 8d.

Anthony Meero, child, 5d.

Catherine Brown...

'A widow,' Gallagher said.

...7d.

Patrick Foley, 8d.

Margaret Conlon...

'She's not a widow yet,' Gallagher whispered, 'but she soon will be.'

...7d.

Eileen Dunne, 7d.

Michael Padden, 8d.

Eileen Monaghan...

A girl with the same baldness and the same facial hair, darker this time. The bare skull and hair strewn face gave her the appearance of a boy in girl's clothes.

'*Surely she's not the strongest...*'

'*There's no-one else left.*'

...child, 5d.

'*That's unfair to the men who have families to feed,*' the next man in line said.

'*Five pence is the rate for a child,*' Luke replied.

'*You won't get five pence of work from her.*'

'*That's no business of yours.*'

'*It's not right.*'

'*Do you want a ticket or not?*'

'*I do.*'

'*Name?*'

'Edward Reilly,' the man said in English.

Edward Reilly, 8d.

That shut him up, the bastard. He's right though. She's not worth fivepence. But she'll never last it out, she'll be dead soon. She won't affect the work-rate for long. Oh God, now I'm thinking like a Government man. And sounding like one too. How in hell did I get to this?

The two men went on working, not even stopping when the next Mass started. More bald, bearded children appeared in the line. Luke felt horrified, but forced himself to concentrate on his task. As for the children, many were the only ones in the family who could work. He had to take them.

When they finished, they had eighty names. There were twenty tickets left. The priest joined them. They went through the names again, and the priest undertook to find those who would receive the remaining tickets.

They returned to Gallaghers. Dinner was a silent affair. Luke was torn. Winnie excited him. The Selection had horrified and sickened him. Fox-children. He felt his mind was dividing in two.

They went to bed early. Then the foxes came. The vixen, huge and terrifying. Dry dugs. The cubs, red-eyed and starving. Ribs showing through. He was running. The cubs were at his heels, grabbing at them. The vixen leaped on him.

He woke with a cry. He was trembling. The quiet breathing of the three sleeping boys brought him back. No one had heard.

He thought of Winnie. Grey eyes, laughing at him. The nightmare died. The trembling stopped. He slept.

Pat put his pen down and stared out the window of the small office in the administration building. He could see across the lawns to the front gate of the Union. They were still there, as they had been for weeks, hundreds of people waiting in silence. He was feeling low and lonesome, homesick for Carrigard in a way he had never felt in Castle Bromwich. Home was six miles away – two hours walking only.

The administration block was in front of the Workhouse and faced onto one of the streets of Knockanure. It was where the crowd was densest. Pat knew that there were more at the back gate, but he preferred not to go there unless there was a reason to do so. He only went out when he had to; it was hard enough to get in and out through the crowds. His first morning had taught him that lesson. As he had let McKinnon and his horse out, three men had broken in past him, and had to be rounded up by the inmates and ejected. Pat was agile enough to get in and out by climbing over the gate. There were two inmates on guard at either end to prevent anyone else from following him.

His work left him in a strange position. He was supposed to be working for the Poor Law Union, not the Workhouse. The Union covered the barony, and while it included the Workhouse, it was also responsible for the Relief Works outside. But in the deepening crisis his official position no longer mattered, and Pat found himself pressed into working on the accounts and administration of the Workhouse as well as the Union.

He had been given an assistant, an inmate of the Workhouse. He was an elderly man who had spent many years in Liverpool. He spoke little, but from what Pat could determine he had been an inmate of the Liverpool Workhouse too. The old man had a morbid fear of death and an obsessive wish to die in his own county rather than an English city. The Workhouse in Liverpool had obliged him by putting him on a ship to Dublin with dozens of other Irish who had been expelled from England because the local Unions saw no need to support Irish beggars. He had walked across Ireland, and had been in a famished state when he reached Knockanure. He had arrived ahead of the rush to the Workhouse and had been admitted. When they discovered that he could add and subtract, he had been taken off stone-breaking and put working on accounts.

At first he resented Pat. At sixty he was over three times Pat's age, and it rankled him to be working under him. For the first few weeks he was sour and quiet, but then he opened up, and if he didn't like the situation, he at least tolerated it.

Voisey came through once a week for the meeting of the Guardians, together with Sir Albert Clanowen, whose estate stretched from the Mountain to the other side of Knockanure. Voisey would scrutinise every detail of Pat's work, and Pat expected to be called in front of the meeting, but he never was.

Every few weeks, McKinnon called by. This was Pat's only real source of information on Carrigard and Kilduff. He had no use for his wages in the Union, and he would give them to McKinnon, together with a brief letter to take back to Michael. At first he looked forward to McKinnon's visits, but as time went on the reports on what was happening around Carrigard became more and more terrible. He questioned McKinnon too on what he saw in other parts of the county, and this depressed him more. He began to realise that the Workhouses were only taking in a fraction of the people who were hungry.

News from the outside world filtered through in other ways too, becoming more horrifying as time progressed. Other surveyors from Castlebar stopped at the Union; pay clerks too. It was far too dangerous for them to stay outside when they were travelling from Castlebar with large sums of money. Regardless of which barony they were travelling to, the Union put them all up, giving them dinner and a bed for the night. By preference they slept in the administration block rather than the Workhouse. Many nights Pat had to share his bed with strangers. It struck him that some of these men might be in the early stages of fever without knowing it and could pass it on to him, but there was nowhere else to sleep in the Union buildings. One night, one of the men tried to grope him in the crotch. After that, he slept in his office sitting in his chair, slumped over the desk. At first he found it impossible to sleep this way, but he got used

158

to it and slept as well as he would have in his own bed.

His work for the Union was paid, his work for the Workhouse was not. He knew he could refuse, but he also knew that he was lucky to have good dinners in the administration block, and he felt in conscience he had to do what he was asked. Then the old man disappeared into the fever sheds, and Pat never saw him again. With all the extra work now, he was working seven days a week, adding long columns of figures and writing out requisitions in the guttering candlelight, his eyes red and raw by the evening.

Conditions in the Workhouse shocked him. It was overcrowded, with twice the number of inmates it was designed for. The latrine shed stank, but a pit was being dug for a new one. At the side wall on the other side of the Workhouse, another pit was dug as a mass grave. Every night corpses were thrown into it, every morning more was dug, and the grave grew longer.

Inside the Workhouse building families had been split into male and female, each separate. In the dormitories, the inmates were sleeping sometimes two or three to a bed, sometimes on straw on the floor with rough blankets thrown over them. The refectory was just as bad. The old system of using tables and benches could no longer cope, and the Master had instituted a new system to run alongside it. Only children were fed at the tables. For the men and women a sort of shelf had been installed along three walls of the refectory. Their food was ladled into their bowls, and a mug of buttermilk given to them. As they ate and drank, they shuffled along the shelves, and when they got to the end, the bowls and mugs were returned, washed in a greasy barrel, and transferred to the start of the shelf again.

Worst of all though were the fever sheds. Pat tried to avoid these as much as possible. The inmates were not being treated, they were only brought to the sheds to separate them from the rest of the Workhouse. Here too, beds were occupied by two or three patients. Pat always associated the sheds with the smell of urine, gangrene and decaying flesh. He wondered how the inmates cleaning the sheds survived. He was surprised though when the Workhouse doctor died, since he had spent little time in the sheds. Checking patients for illness seemed to be dangerous enough in itself.

Most of the patients had black fever, but some had other diseases, and some were showing the advanced signs of hunger, including diarrhoea. Thinking of his own fears of fever, he wondered whether it was wise to have more than one in a bed. Black fever was contagious. But then it struck him that those who did not have it were dying from other causes anyhow, and picking up black fever too might not matter much. The thought shocked him. He felt that he himself was becoming uncaring. But he knew there was no other way. If he worried about the horror he was seeing, he would not be able to do his job. Which was worse?

Once he thought he recognised Sorcha in a thin old woman outside the fever sheds, but he could not be certain, and he never saw her again. Her face kept coming back to him in his dreams, and over time he became more certain that it had been her.

The only aspect of the Workhouse that cheered him was dinner on Sundays. This was for his unpaid work at the Workhouse, and while it was not as appetising as he had been used to, even in Castle Bromwich, it was a welcome change from the weekday fare. It was the only time of the week that he would taste meat.

Sunday dinner was another source of information since it was attended, not only by the Master and Matron, but also any guardians, surveyors or pay clerks who happened to be in the area. Doctor Connolly had been there until he died. Doctor Short had replaced him two weeks later. Pat liked these discussions. He enjoyed listening to educated men, even if most of the discussion was about the administration of Relief and the working of Workhouses and fever sheds. Most of all, though, he enjoyed the company of the Cronins' daughter.

She was attractive, there was no doubt of that. But she was older than him and of a different class. At nights, he found himself thinking about her and seeing her face. He dreamed of what it might be like to have a woman like that. But he was only dreaming dreams, and every morning brought him back to the harsh reality of the Workhouse.

Then one day, she came to his office.

'You're working too hard,' she told him.

He looked at her, not knowing what to say. 'You think...you think I'm working too hard?'

'I know you are. I've been watching you.' She crossed the room. 'Now push over and show me what you're doing. I can add too, you know.'

As to – Sir Robert Peel   Knockanure Union
Drayton Manor   Knockanure
Tamworth   Co. Mayo
Staffordshire

September 19th 1846

My Dear Robert

I regret that I had not written to you earlier, but since I arrived in Mayo, I have been travelling and examining potatoes every day.

Last week I visited the area around Kilduff, a small village in the eastern part of Mayo. I met with a Mr. Ryan, a schoolmaster from outside the town, and what he told me was shocking. The situation here is even worse than Kildare. It appears that the potato crop has failed, and failed totally.

160

Already the death toll from fever and hunger is terrible and increasing daily. What now lies in store for Mayo, I truly cannot conceive.

Today, I came to the Poor Law Union in Knockanure and met with a Mr. James Voisey, a man recommended to me by the Friends in Kildare. He tells me that the Workhouse in Knockanure is hugely over-crowded, and they are turning hundreds away every day. He brought me around the Workhouse, and it is in an appalling condition.

I am now writing to the Friends in Staffordshire to request aid for this part of Mayo. I intend then to stay in Knockanure, so that I can organise our relief efforts from this end. You may of course write to me here, care of James Voisey at the Poor Law Union.

I understand from Caroline that you and Julia visit her every week, and I appreciate this more than I can tell. In her last letter, she said she would join me here in Mayo. I have written asking her not to, and I know that you will do all in your power to dissuade her.

She is too gentle for this place. Mayo would break her heart.

I remain, your true friend,

Edward Yardley

Chapter Thirteen

Tyrawly Herald, November 1846:
On Friday morning last a woman named Melody died of
starvation near Palmerstown. The unfortunate creature
procured shelter during the previous night in the cabin of
another poor woman, and, while there, drank a mixture of
a very small quantity of meal she had with her and some
water. She slept on some straw, and, in the morning, when
she made an effort to get up, she fell from exhaustion, and
died shortly afterwards.

Luke spent the next afternoon and evening at the table with his papers,
calculating how much money he would need for wages and for supplies.
Later on he joined the Gallaghers at the fire, talking about the Selection and
hunger around Brockagh.

Through it all though, he still felt the attraction to Winnie. He wondered
what it was about her, what was different. Face, legs, breasts? Her hair?
Everything and nothing. She looked no different to many other women of
her age. He could not stop glimpsing at her when he thought no-one was
looking, but often she would catch his eye.

Gallagher was suspicious, he was sure of it. Yet there was no need, nothing
had passed between them. Gallagher could not know, he could not see into
his thoughts. And her glances? What did they mean? Nothing, he was just
imagining it. Gallagher had no need to be suspicious of either of them. And
even if he was suspicious, why would he be worried? Luke thought back to
Kilduff and Carrigard. All the women – and men – who would have seen him
as an excellent match for their daughters. What possible reason could there
be for Gallagher not to see things the same way? He thought about that.
There were many.

Gallagher knew nothing of him. Luke was a stranger who had come into
Brockagh, and, even worse, a Government man. Perhaps Mrs. Gallagher
had her fears too, afraid that he would take her daughter away from her
and away from Brockagh. Perhaps they had other plans for their daughter.
Perhaps they had another match in mind. Perhaps it was just the natural
instinct of the father to protect his daughter, the thought of any man having

her. Or perhaps it was the thought of the dowry. Who could afford a dowry now? He would be able to reassure Gallagher on that point, no dowry was necessary. If things ever got that far. If, if, if.

Or perhaps it was not the girl at all. Gallagher was a tough man, a proud one too. He thought of other tough men he had known – his father, Farrelly, Gaffney and more. Such men would find it hard to work under a younger man. They would be ashamed too of their families going hungry, ashamed of being on Relief and the need for it. He thought again of his father six years ago, the humiliation, the shattered pride. Yes, perhaps that was it. Gallagher resented him. And that gave him even more reason to protect his daughter against a man like him.

Luke and Gallagher took the other gangers into Castlebar to buy hardware and other supplies. They took Gallagher's horse and wagon, together with three carts with donkeys. Gallagher had found another horse to make a pair for the wagon, but the second one was weaker, and kept dragging the wagon to the side.

Luke walked alongside it, holding it close to the bit and leading it along. Gallagher walked alongside, explaining about the road, the hardware stores in Castlebar, and the carrying capacity of the carts and wagon. Luke was only half conscious of what he was saying. He was thinking of other things. Grey eyes! He glanced at Gallagher, he wanted to ask him about her, but every time he thought of her, his resolve died. He tried a different approach.

'Young John seems a sharp lad.'

'He is,' Gallagher replied. 'Another year or two, he'll be able to help me with this carting business. We'll build it back up again to what it was last year. Maybe we'll start sending wagons to Castlebar again. Westport even. Who knows?'

Yes, he thought, the wagon. And not just one.

'Wagons to Westport,' he exclaimed, pretending surprise.

'Yes,' Gallagher answered. 'Westport, Galway even. And why not? There's a need for transport around here. Or at least there will be as soon as this damned hunger is over.'

Transport? He was right. That wagon hadn't just appeared. Gallagher had ambitions, or at least he once had. He decided to change the subject.

'And Bernie and Frankie. What will they do?'

'Damned if I know. A year or two ago I thought they'd work with me here. But things are different now. I suppose they'll go to England when the time comes. They'll be working on the rails. Just like you did, and I did. Nothing changes.'

They had come to a deeply rutted part of the road. They tried to lead the horse and donkeys along the edge of the road, the wheels crunching on one side and along the raised centre. The road was getting steep, and the men led the animals forward at speed. But the horse went too close to the edge, and the wagon wheels slipped into the ditch. Gallagher urged it forward and out as the other men pushed hard at the rear. After much cursing and swearing, they brought it clear and reached the brow of the hill.

They walked along in silence for a few moments. Then Gallagher spoke. 'I've seen the way you look at my daughter, and I know what you're thinking.'

'I'm not thinking anything,' Luke replied. 'She's a good looking girl, your daughter, and any man might look at her for that. But there's nothing more than that to it.'

'There had better not be.'

Luke said nothing. The wagon and carts rattled along the road. The horse's hooves were striking the stones and crunching the gravel. He could see the potato patches interspersed between the corn, leaves blackened and withered. He could smell the stink of blight. They passed a mud cabin. There was a ragged woman with four children standing outside it. They watched the wagon and carts in silence.

The day after, they measured out the road. This was easier than it had been at Carrigard. It involved road improvement, with only a few hundred yards of new road. Some corners were to be straightened, potholes and ruts filled in, and in some places the undulating road was to be levelled by excavation and infilling. The main work was digging new drains on either side. The surveying did not take very long, and Luke was able to explain their duties to each of the gangers. It had been agreed that Gallagher would take responsibility for this site, while Luke and Durcan would establish the new Works at Lisnadee two weeks later.

Next day, the Works commenced. As they were allocating the workmen, including the women and children, he noticed a number of marked differences from Carrigard. There were more women on the Works. There were children too. Should he have allowed it. But the people here were much weaker anyhow. Hunger was carved into their faces, disease too. He had not thought of that before. Was it wise to have feverish people working alongside others, where infection could be spread? He did not know the answer to that. Nor did he know why the children had the growth on their faces, but he was starting to link it with the extreme stages of hunger rather than fever.

He wondered why Ardnagrena should be so much worse than Carrigard. He felt it was because of the more remote location; the land was worse and the farms smaller. Also it was now later in the year, and the hunger was more advanced. But most of all, he felt that it was Gallagher's method of Selection that explained the difference – it had been more successful in locating real hunger and want. The Selection system that Gaffney had applied in Carrigard had been more random. Gallagher's approach not only identified those most in need, but even found those higher in the mountains who would not even have applied for relief.

As the Works proceeded, he noticed that they were slower again than at Carrigard. Some of the men seemed to have difficulty raising the picks or even shovelling the loosened soil and gravel. He and Gallagher had allocated the women and children to lighter tasks, helping the gangers to mark out the drains in detail and later on cooking the Indian meal for food at midday. Even these actions were carried out very slowly. Luke was now worried whether the Works could be carried out either in time, or at the agreed budget. He wondered what Gaffney might have done in the situation, but Gaffney was not here, and he found it hard to think as Gaffney might have. He had been sent to Brockagh to improve roads and to relieve hunger, but it might be impossible to do both.

As they ate at midday, he noticed that one of the young boys was refusing food. The child's thighs showed bare through the remains of the rags he was wearing. They were thin, with very little muscle left. His ankles were swollen and purple. As the Works started again, he stayed sitting. Luke saw he was shivering. One of the gangers came over and placed his own coat around him.

'*What's wrong?*' Luke asked.

'*He's no longer able to work, Sir. He's not putting it on, he just can't do it.*'

Later in the afternoon the boy was lying down. One of the women came over and sat beside him, holding his head on her lap. Luke sent one of the men into Brockagh to call the priest, but he came back and told him that the priest had gone out towards Knocklenagh, no one knew where. Soon the boy was dead.

That evening, he rode back with Gallagher. As agreed at Knockanure, he had offered Mrs. Gallagher three pence per night for dinner and lodgings, and she had accepted. Every evening she and Winnie would cook. He found himself looking forward to dinner; he had become more relaxed about Winnie. He wondered what she thought about him.

A rough bed with hay had now been made up for him in the boys' room. Every night he wrapped himself in his blanket and slept with his pack. He was always too tired to worry about the lack of comfort.

Every day, he would go down the line, visiting each ganger in turn and going down his section, calling out the roll. On the first day, he had already noticed that some of the men who had been there in the morning were missing in the evening. After that, he did the roll call twice each day.

On payday, Luke called the roll early and started to calculate the wages due. Afterwards he walked down to Durcan's section.

'I've noticed there's four in your gang haven't finished the week, Tim.'

'I know. I'd expected it. Anthony Meero, I don't know why. For the rest, they all had fever, even when they began. Eleanor Lavelle, I think she was dying when she started. I'd not expected to see her here on the first day.'

'How can we pay them for the days they've worked? I have to get their signatures or marks. I can't do that if they aren't here.'

'I don't know what the answer to that is.'

He checked out the payroll with the other gangers. There were seventeen workers missing. He wondered how many would return.

Invisible pain.

When the pay clerk arrived from Castlebar, he was accompanied by two constables. It was the same man he had met at Carrigard and on the road from Knockanure. This time he introduced himself as Martin Davitt. He was from Straide, a small village closer to Kilduff than Brockagh.

'How are things there?' Luke asked him.

'I haven't been there this month past, but even then the blight had destroyed everything. I don't know what'll happen now, no idea.'

'What'll you do?'

'Just as always. I do my work, send the money whenever there's anyone going over that way, and hope for the best.'

'You have children?' Luke asked.

'Two only, thank God. The youngest is only six months though. Great time to come along, eh?'

'Just great,' Luke said.

They started to organise the payment of the workers. This was a rapid procedure now. Luke, Davitt and Gallagher sat behind a single table. Each of the gangers came up in turn, and were asked to identify each worker. Luke witnessed each cross or signature, while Gallagher and Davitt paid out the amount due.

When all the workers had been paid, Luke and Davitt sat at the table, checking the cash.

'What about the people who didn't turn up,' Luke asked. 'How can I pay them?'

'I'll give you an advance on that,' Davitt answered. 'How much do you need?'

Luke added a column. 'One pound, seventeen and nine.'

Davitt counted out the amount. 'Can you check it?'

Luke counted the coins. 'To the penny. But I mightn't need it all.'

'Why not?'

'They mightn't come back. In fact, I'm sure they won't, the most of them.'

'If they don't come back, you'll have to go to their houses.'

'Will I?'

'You will,' Davitt said. 'And there's one other little thing too. If you're not careful, Knockanure might accuse you of fraud.'

'Fraud?'

'How do they know you've paid them?'

'I'll get their marks.'

'That won't be enough. When you're paying out on the Works, you've got witnesses – myself and the peelers. You've none when you're riding about.'

'What can I do so?'

'That's simple,' Davitt said. 'All you do is get the priest's signature. The Union have always recognised a clergyman's signature.'

'Even a Catholic priest?'

'It's no matter to them what religion he is.'

After Davitt had left, Luke rode with Gallagher towards Brockagh. They noticed a crowd of about fifty gathered around a very rough shed which had not been there in the morning. When they came closer, he realised that many of the crowd were drinking out of bottles. As they rode up, the man behind the rough bar looked to them, and turned back to serving his customers. Between times, he was shouting 'whiskey, two shillings a bottle, shilling and thruppence a half.' Many of the people were carrying half bottles, some were empty. A few who had been paid an hour earlier were already drunk. Luke noticed two of the gangers sitting on the wall on the other side. Durcan was not with them. Luke rode over.

'What's going on here?' he asked the gangers.

'Our friends are buying drinks for us.'

He looked at them, almost too stunned to speak. He pulled the reins on his horse and rode over to the shebeen. This time, the man behind the bar did not even glance up.

'I want you to get out of here,' Luke said.

The man did not answer him. 'French Brandy, three shillings the bottle.'

'Did you hear what I said? GET OUT.'

'Why should I?' answered the man, still not looking at him. He put a half bottle of whiskey on the counter for one of the workers. 'I'm legal. I'm only selling spirits, duty paid. The Excise are happy.'

'Get out,' Luke repeated. 'Now.' The man said nothing, as his customer counted out his coins. Fifteen pennies, each observed closely. Eleven heads of Victoria and four of King George.

Luke turned to the crowd.

'Go home to your families.'

No one moved.

Gallagher rode over. 'Come on, Luke. There's nothing we can do.'

He looked at Gallagher in fury. Then he realised it was pointless. He pulled his horse away.

'Like he says, it's legal,' Gallagher said, as they rode away. 'It's like they did on the Works on the Shannon, and that wasn't even Relief. I've heard about this in Sligo and Roscommon too.'

'And what about the gangers.'

'They get free whiskey.'

'Damned sure they do. And a share of the profits too?'

'Look, I'm sorry. John Luby – I recommended him. Hanrahan – he was Father Nugent's suggestion. We both thought they'd make good gangers.'

'Damned right they would. Just like the bastards on the railways. Get every penny out of you – grind you into the mud.'

'Don't I know.'

'One and thruppence a half bottle of whiskey, though. That's a hell of a profit, John. These people are starving, they can't afford that, they need the money for food. And if they don't, there's others who do. I'll fire those bloody gangers – that'll do for a start.'

As they rode on towards Brockagh, the shebeen preyed on his mind. How could it happen? How could starving people even think of buying drink? And how could any man even think of battening on their misery for profit?

That night he went to see Father Nugent. He told him about the shebeen, the deaths on the Works and the workers who had not completed the week.

'Do you know who the seventeen are?' the priest asked.

'Of course. They're all on the payroll here.'

'The priest went down the names. 'Seven of these are dead.'

'Dead?'

'Yes, Luke, dead.'

'That's nine in a week.'

'I know.'

'So what can we do now?' Luke asked.

'Not much if they're dead. It's their families I'm worried about, they're the ones who'll need us. We'll just have to visit them all on Sunday. Both of us.'

'Yes,' Luke said, 'and you can help with another matter too. I'll need a clergyman's signature as a witness each time I make a payment. Otherwise they'd accuse me of fraud.'

'Fine so.'

'But on a Sunday, Father? You've Masses on Sunday.'

'I have, but that's no excuse. We'll have to do it. You've no choice, and neither do I. I'm a priest, I'm supposed to give the rites to the dying.'

'If you can,' Luke said.

'It's not a question of 'can' any more – it's a question of 'must.' That day with you and John showed me how many I was missing, and I've decided not to wait. I've spent the last two days riding around, asking who was near dying or dead already. I'll do the same for the next few days, and we'll do the same on Sunday, you and me. Perhaps we can find these people. That way you can pay them or their people, while I do the praying.'

It was late when he left the priest-house. As he walked back towards Gallaghers, he thought again about the shebeen. His anger flared. He led out his horse, not waiting to saddle it. As he rode up towards the shebeen, he saw men and women walking back. He noticed a few men and one woman stretched out on the road or in the ditches. When he arrived, there was no one there except the owner, huddled around a fire, counting his coins.

'I told you to get out of here,' Luke said.

'And I told you, I'm legal. There's no *poitín* here. You can check if you want.'

Luke walked around the side of the bar. He brought out two bottles of whiskey and smashed them on a rock.

'What are you doing, you damned bastard,' the other man screamed. He broke an empty bottle, holding the jagged glass, he rushed at Luke. Luke ducked, then punched his right fist under the man's chin. The man staggered, eyes glazing, mouth slackening, as his knees fought to stay upright. Luke drew back, aimed again, and smashed his fist up again into the hanging jaw. He heard the crunch as the front teeth broke. The man slumped onto the road, face down, and did not move.

Luke pulled the prostrate body across the road and dumped it in the ditch. He listened for a few moments to see that he was still breathing. Then he went back to the shed and smashed more bottles. He smelt the fumes, strong and pungent. Brandy perhaps. He thought he felt light-headed, even drunk.

He hesitated. He looked to the fire.

Then he took a burning log. Standing back, he threw it into the shed. There was a purple flash. Within seconds, the whole structure was ablaze.

He mounted his horse and rode towards Brockagh. The shebeen lit the night sky, bottles exploding in the flames.

As he rode with Gallagher to the Works the next morning, he told him what had happened.

Gallagher looked at him in surprise. 'You knocked him senseless?'

'I did.'

'And burned the shack?'

'That's right. The shack and all that was in it.'

'Well, by God. I never thought you had it in you.'

Luke thought about that. He did not know whether it was praise or condemnation. Perhaps it was a bit of both.

Later they passed the burnt remnants of the hut, shattered glass lying around.

'You did a good job.'

'I didn't do half enough to the bastard.'

'You must be more careful though. You could have killed him.'

'I wish I had.'

'No you don't. You don't want to be hung. And we don't want you hung either. Brockagh can't afford to lose you. Too many people depend on you.'

'I know, John, I know.'

They rode on.

'I was talking to Father Nugent last night,' Luke said. 'He was worried about people dying, wants to ride around the mountains to give them Extreme Unction. I'm going with him.'

'For what?'

'It's just we owe them money. Whether they're dying or dead, we still owe them. I'll have to go and pay them what they're owed. Them or their widows.'

'Or mothers? Or children?'

'Whatever.'

As they arrived at the Works, the men and women seemed to look at him with a new respect. Again he watched the workers, concerned about how weak and slow they were. A small gang were filling a wagon with shale. He doubted they were doing a twentieth as much as would be done on a railway cutting in England.

England had been different.

They had earned more in England, but it was hard work, and filling wagons was the hardest of all. Many men in other gangs found it impossible to keep up with the physical effort required. The full shovel load had to be lifted well over a man's height. The men worked in pairs; two men together could fill ten or twelve wagon loads in a day. But the Mayo men worked longer hours – Farrelly and Corrigan often filled sixteen or seventeen wagon loads a day. On one long summer evening, they filled twenty.

Tunnelling in England was tough work too. The tunnels always seemed to be damp, and the sputtering lamps did little to allay the darkness. The rail had to keep up with the tunnelling, close enough for the wagons to be filled, but not too close. There was always the danger of rock falling from the roof. From time to time, the blast of the explosions echoed along the tunnel. In every tunnel they worked, there seemed to be a permanent smell of explosive, mixed in with the raw stink of urine and horse manure. The rail men followed the tunnellers, and the bricklayers followed both. The work continued day and night.

In the tunnels, the other Irish gangs were in an endless struggle with their supervisors, many of whom were Welshmen from the coalmines of the Rhondda. The Irish men – Donegal and Mayo – hated the Welsh with passion. Mayo men saw their supervisors as the scum of the earth. Sometimes in the tunnels Luke had heard plans of murder, but he had reckoned it was only talk, and paid little heed to any of it.

But it was different here.

Now he was the supervisor.

When he arrived back at Gallagher's, he was exhausted. There were two other men there. One was the shebeen owner, now missing three front teeth, his tongue scarred. Beside him was a constable.

'We've had a complaint of assault and arson, Mr. Ryan.'

'What do you mean?'

'Mr. Clarke states that you assaulted him last night and burned out his business. A very serious charge.'

'I told him to move out yesterday, but I haven't seen him since.'

The constable ignored him. 'Mr. Clarke had every right to be there,' he went on. 'All his stock has always been duty paid.'

'I know. He told me. I accepted what he said and left him to it.'

'And where were you after you left?'

'I rode back here with Mr. Gallagher.'

Behind the two men, Winnie nodded at him.

'And after you rode back, where were you then?'

From the shadows, Winnie pointed to her open mouth; then she made a pillow of both her hands, leaning her cheek into them.

'I stayed here,' Luke replied. 'I had dinner with these people, and then I slept.'

'Perjury is a very serious offence, Mr. Ryan.'

'You heard what Mr. Ryan said, constable,' Winnie said. 'He's an honest man, and if you think he's not, then everyone here is a liar too.'

The constable looked at each of them in turn. He went to each of the children, holding their faces up to look into their eyes. No one flinched. He turned to leave.

'Come on, there's nothing to be done here.'

Clarke followed him. 'You damned bastard,' he said to Luke, lisping. 'You'll hear more of this.'

When the two men had left, Mrs. Gallagher sent the younger children back to sleep. Winnie reheated some meal and cabbage for Luke, and the four sat down again.

'You needn't worry about Father Nugent,' Gallagher told him. 'I spoke with him after Clarke's first visit. He doesn't remember seeing you last night at all.'

Afterwards Mrs. Gallagher made up four cups of *poitín* punch. She raised her cup to Luke.

'To our own apostle of temperance,' she said. Luke sipped the *poitín*, saying nothing.

On Sunday, he accompanied the Gallagher family to early Mass. He sat with Gallagher, Young John and the younger boys on the right hand side of the church, while Winnie and Una sat with the women on the left. Before the Mass began a man and woman came in, carrying another woman. Luke was horrified to see that she was in the last stages of fever. Her face was black. Even from where he sat, he could smell the gangrene.

The couple stopped at the top of the aisle, and one of the men whispered to another man, who walked back into the rough shed adjoining the church which served as a sacristy. Already people were edging back. The priest came out. He administered the Last Rites to the sick woman, and she was carried out again.

During the mass, the priest read out the prayers for the dead, listing those deceased during the week. The list seemed endless. Then he faced the congregation. 'I want you all to know that bringing people with fever into a crowded church is dangerous. You must send a message to me, and I will come as soon as I can. If I cannot come in time, do not worry. God knows when we are doing our best, He will not blame us for being late.'

At the end of the Mass, he read out the names of more families who had been selected for tickets for the Works, and told them to report to the Works direct the next morning. Again he looked at the congregation.

'Two men – John Luby and Michael Hanrahan – have been dismissed from the Works. God bless you all.'

Luke went back to the priest-house after Mass to discuss the new workers with the priest. When they were finished, the priest shook his head in despair.

'That business with the old woman in the church shows you what I'm up against,' he said. 'Even riding around the mountains, I won't be able get to everyone. I know I said that God will wait – but how do I know that? And with all that's going on now, He'll be waiting for ever. I just can't go to everyone who is dying or dead, it's not possible for any man.'

'I know,' Luke said. 'But bringing her to the church, that could have been deadly.'

'Deadly is right. I gave her the shortest and fastest Last Rites anyone ever got. I just had to get her out fast.'

When Luke came out, the church was empty, but Winnie was still at the door.

'What are you doing here?' he exclaimed.

'I only thought I'd wait on you. And what's wrong with that?'

'What's wrong indeed. I'll be in trouble with your father if he finds out. He's already warned me off you once.'

'What!'

'Yes, the time we went to Castlebar, he reckoned there was too much 'making eyes' between us. He told me he was watching us. If he sees us talking together, there'll be all hell to pay.'

'Well, I don't know what he's watching for,' she said. 'There's nothing between us, and there's no harm in talking together surely?'

'I don't know that he thinks that way. And I'm sure of one thing, he doesn't like me. He'll put up with me, but that's only because he has to.'

She thought about that. 'Perhaps you're right,' she said, 'but I don't think it's so much that he dislikes you. You've got to understand it's hard for him working under a younger man. All the time he was working in England, he had fellows working under him. He's used to having things all his own way. He doesn't like taking orders from anyone.'

'And sure as hell not from me.'

They walked the long way around to the Gallagher house. Luke wondered at how many eyes were observing them, though the street was quiet.

'You're a tough man, Luke!'

'Not half tough enough.'

'What about that business with Clarke the other night?'

'He only got what he deserved.'

'And I thought you were a gentle fellow.'

'I am, and that's the worst of it. Did your father tell you why I did it? Did he tell you what was going on up there?'

'He did,' she said. 'I never knew things like that happened.'

'We saw it all the time on the railways, but men had money there. I didn't think I'd see it here. Clarke was a right bastard.'

'But you did what you had to do. Isn't that all?'

'Perhaps it is,' he said. 'But I don't have it in me for this. We had tough men managing us on the railways in England, but they were our own fellows.

Older too, well used to it. I never knew I'd end up like this.'

'I think you're well able for it.'

'I don't think so,' he said. 'I'm not sure I can last this out.'

They walked on. Beside a mud cabin, a man was scrabbling at a clamp of potatoes, a woman standing beside him. Both were thin and gaunt. The woman was holding out her apron to hold the potatoes that the man was passing to her. Luke could see that every one was rotten. Yet she was hoarding them in to herself. She backed away from them as they approached, as if fearing they would steal them.

'They're going to eat those,' Winnie said.

'They are.'

They stopped at a small bridge in the village. They both leant against it, staring at the water.

'What will you do when this is all over?' she asked him.

'I don't know,' he said. 'I've been thinking of America.'

He thought about that. It was not true. It was the first time he had said it to anyone. Even himself. Yes, Kitty had said it, but he had almost forgotten that. He had told Kitty it was impossible. But was it?

It might be one way out, and not just because of the hunger. When he had started working on Relief, he had felt he had to do it. It wasn't a matter of money either, he could earn more in England. People were starving, and he had to help. But it had all come back in his face. Selection – he had never even thought of that. Refusing desperate men in Carrigard, refusing family and friends. And the shebeen. Already, after only a few weeks in Brockagh, there were men who would see him dead.

It was cold. He shivered, and put his arm around her shoulders. She said nothing.

'Come on, Winnie. Come on home.'

He held his arm around her. She leaned her head into his shoulder as they walked. They might be seen, but he no longer cared. He was silent, thinking of her and thinking of other places.

America?

Later he called back to the priest-house, and he and the priest rode towards the hills above Ardnagrena. Luke was carrying his payrolls, the priest his viaticum for the last rites. They rode for half an hour, talking about many things. Higher up, the land was much rougher; long stretches of heather with the odd patch of rotten potatoes between. The roads grew smaller until they were following mere tracks in the ground. There were very few houses of stone now, most were mud cabins with rough roofs of sod and heather rather than thatch. They rode through the remote mud *clocháns* of Benstreeva and

Croghancoe, high above Ardnagrena and Lisnadee. They stopped.

'Patrick Lynagh,' the priest said to him. They went in. There was only a single room. In one corner was a large bed. There was a man in it and two children. The man was shivering. The priest walked over and started to give him the Last Rites. There were four other children in the room and a woman sitting at a rough table. 'Mrs. Lynagh?' Luke asked. She did not reply. He counted out fourteen pennies.

'*I need your mark here.*' She made an X. Alongside he wrote – Wages for Patrick Lynagh, now in fever. The mark of his wife.

He handed the pen to the priest as witness.

Fr. Matthew Nugent, Parish Priest.

In the next house, a small rough built mud cabin, the man was already dead and buried. Father Nugent had given him the last rites three days before. Luke counted out seven pence, and again he asked for the woman's mark. He was surprised when she signed her full name, in elegant copperplate style, as Edwina Anastasia Hughes, but he said nothing. Alongside he wrote – Patrick Hughes, deceased. The signature of his widow. Again the priest witnessed it. Fr. Matthew Nugent, PP.

As the afternoon progressed, Luke noticed many other things. Higher up the mountains, many of the people were not even living in mud cabins. Rough *sceilps* had been built instead, branches covered with heather and sods of turf, leaning against banks of turf with holes dug out for shelter. The living showed all the signs of hunger. He saw the thin women, suckling infants at breasts that had no milk. Again and again he saw the bald children with the light hair on their faces. No matter how often he saw them, it still sickened him. The fox-children.

There was worse. Everywhere he saw lice and fleas, but he thought nothing of this. In the cabins and *sceilps,* he saw the unmistakeable signs of black fever, or as he knew it from Doctor Stone – typhus. It brought him back to 1839 and the horror of Alicia's death. Again he saw the dark faces. He saw the 'rice water' diarrhoea on the floor, which many families no longer cared to clear. He saw the convulsing limbs of people in delirium. Many times he knew the black fever was present before they entered a cabin – the screams and the unmistakeable rotting stench of gangrene.

Later they came back from the mountains and rode around some of the nearer areas. They had not covered all the houses, but the priest suggested they continue during the week. Luke agreed. He was feeling shaken and depressed, though through it all the thought of Winnie still cheered him.

America?

Would she come?

*

With advice from Gallagher and Durcan, he appointed two new gangers at the Brockagh Works.

The planning for Lisnadee was finalised. A message had been sent to Knocklenagh, and Timothy Durcan joined them in the priest's house.

This time, with Durcan's assistance, they were able to mark down the families to be relieved from their own direct experience, and also from what Durcan knew from asking around Knocklenagh and Lisnadee.

Because of the greater distance, it was decided that the list would not be read out from the church in Brockagh. Instead Timothy Durcan was delegated to return to the mountains, and either visit or send messages to those who had been selected. Later that week, Luke arrived at Durcan's. They filled in the worksheets in Durcan's house, a long line forming in the cold outside.

Two days later, they opened the new Works at Lisnadee.

One day in November, he saw two horsemen riding towards them. He recognised one as Ian McKinnon. They dismounted, and all three sat down away from the workers. Luke explained his expenditure to date, showing what he had paid and what he still owed to the various merchants. McKinnon paid out the amount still owing, and gave him five pounds as an advance.

It was only then he introduced the other man as Henry Morton, a senior surveyor sent over from London. He wanted to examine the site. Over the next half hour the three men moved around measuring the work done.

'How many days work does this represent?' Morton asked.

'Four, though we've not had all the workers for every day.'

'Can you tell me the attendance rate?' Luke showed him the payrolls. Morton went through them, examining them and checking calculations at random.

'You make an excellent accounts clerk, Mr. Ryan, but we need better management here. With these days worked, we should be twice as far advanced. There is no excuse for this.'

'There's little else I can do, Mr. Morton. You know it yourself. Many of these people have fever. I've watched them. They can't work faster.'

'There are ways of making them work faster,' Morton replied. 'And we will succeed. We're going to introduce piecework.'

'Piecework?'

'Yes. Piecework. A basic wage of tuppence three-farthings per day for the men, tuppence ha'penny for the women and tuppence farthing for the children under twelve. The rest by work measured.'

'Work measured?'

'Yes, Mr. Ryan. We're offering them an excellent rate – tuppence per cubic yard of earth shifted and thruppence per cubic yard of gravel.'

'What?'

'Hear me out. We're also offering them a further ha'penny per perch for lock-spitting and a penny per perch for digging drains.'

'But that's nothing.'

'On the contrary, Mr. Ryan. For people who are willing to work, it is an excellent system. These people are lazy beyond belief. They will not work unless they are forced to it.'

'They're not able for it,' Luke said. 'You know that. You'll kill them or starve them.'

'I won't argue with you, Mr. Ryan. Those are the instructions from Castlebar. They are to be applied this week, as from yesterday morning. And if you do not wish to carry out your orders, you will be replaced.'

Behind Morton, McKinnon shook his head, but said nothing.

'Now Mr. McKinnon will explain the system to you,' Morton continued, 'while I observe these damned beggars.'

As Morton rode along the line, McKinnon and Luke sat on a flagstone, going through the new system and the way that piecework would be calculated.

'I can't believe this,' Luke said. 'Savage is the only word for it.'

'What can I say?' McKinnon said. 'It's what Castlebar demands, and there's damned little we can do to stop it.'

'And they're doing this at home too?'

'I don't know about Carrigard. There was no question of piecework when I was last there, but I'll tell you this, there'll be trouble if they try it. Gaffney's not the class of man to give in to that kind of thing too easy.'

Luke thought about that. Gaffney? Yes, he had the strength to resist Castlebar. But what could Luke Ryan do? Nothing. Nothing at all.

'You reckon Gaffney's tough enough to face them down?' he asked.

'I know he is,' McKinnon said. 'He faced down Clanowen, and no one expected that.'

'Clanowen? Was he going to evict...?'

'Oh no, it wasn't a question of evictions. He hasn't got around to that yet. It was the Works. He was demanding that the people from the Mountain should all be dismissed for Coogan's murder.'

'But Gaffney wouldn't have it?'

'No way, would he have it. I was in the cottage when Clanowen came in, furious that his tenants were on the Works. Damned near screaming, he was, but Gaffney just sat there, shaking his head, wouldn't be moved. In the end, Clanowen just stormed out again.'

'That's hard to believe,' Luke said.

'It is,' McKinnon said, 'and I wouldn't believe it myself, excepting I saw it. But you know Clanowen, he's not the man to give up easy. If he can't get his revenge one way, he'll get it another.'

It had started to rain. As they stood sheltering under a tree, McKinnon handed him a letter.

'Cronin asked me to give you this,' he said. 'It's been in the office in the Workhouse for a few weeks. They didn't know rightly where you were.'

Luke looked at the Leeds postmark. It was dated September. 'You'd think they'd have asked Pat where I was,' he said. 'Or even Voisey. Have they no sense?'

'Oh, I'm not surprised,' McKinnon said. 'They've far too much to do as it is. What with thousands of people trying to get into the Workhouse and hundreds of new Works to be started, I'm afraid Luke Ryan's personal correspondence rates very low in the order of things.'

After McKinnon and Morton had left, Luke called John Gallagher over, and both men walked down the road to each gang. When the gangers had called the men and women together, Luke tried, as best he could, to explain the new system of lower wages and piecework.

He was greeted with silence. He could see the fear in their eyes, but also the contempt and hatred.

That evening, he rode to the priest's house to sign up more workers to replace the dead and dying. Again the news of the new system was received in silence.

James Kilgallon, 2¾d.

Anne Carr, child, 2¼d.

Patrick McEllin, 2¾d.

Alicia Byrne, 2½d.

Robert Carroll, child, 2¼d.

Bee Feely, 2½d.

Catherine Mullany, child, 2¼d.

Michael Morrisroe, 2¾d.

Brigid Brannan, 2½d.

Later that night, he read Danny's letter as the women were preparing dinner. Long afterwards, when the family had gone to bed, he stayed up, sitting on a stool beside the embers of the fire. He was more torn than ever.

He knew Danny was serious. He knew that for the first time – perhaps the only time – he was being offered the opportunity of making real money. He knew too that Danny had the ability to do it, the combination of experience with the native cunning of so many from Mayo. His sheer forcefulness and ruthlessness would ensure that he would succeed. He would go far, further than any of them, and he – Luke Ryan – was being offered a share in all this. 'Specialising in Mayo men.' Yes, and working them into the ground on starvation wages. He thought of the Works. Brockagh or Leeds? What was the difference? Profit, that was the only difference. But which of the two was worse?

To hell with Danny. There was someone else too. Winnie. What might happen between them? If he left Brockagh, he would never know.

He folded the letter. Then he put it in the pocket of his greatcoat and went to bed.

The Killing Snows

Blight and death alone
No summer shines
Night is interblent with day
In Siberia's wastes always
The blood blackens, the heart pines.

In Siberia's wastes
Are sands and rocks
Nothing blooms of green or soft
But the snow-peaks rise aloft
And the gaunt ice-blocks.

And the exile there
Is one with those
They are part, and he is part
For the sands are in his heart
And the Killing Snows.

Extract from 'Siberia' by James Clarence Mangan
Published in Dublin in 1846

Chapter Fourteen

Tyrawly Herald, November 1846:
We regret to state that on Tuesday last a worker named Bridget Thomash died of actual starvation within a short distance of Ballycastle. It was sworn to at the Inquest that she had not partaken of more than one scanty meal per day for the last fortnight, and on some occasions she had nothing whatever to support nature. There are hundreds of poor creatures in the same locality who are similarly circumstanced, and if immediate relief is not afforded, they too shall meet with the same dreadful death.

For three days, the sky was grey, and the air was still. Then it began to snow. At first it fell in large flakes, drifting to the ground and melting at once. That evening Luke rode home through the slush. Above him, the mountain and village of Croghancoe were white.

The next morning, the slush had frozen hard. As he rode towards the Works, it snowed again, and that day it did not stop. By evening the land lay white, all the way from the mountains to the sea.

The following day dawned bright and clear. It did not snow again, but it was bitterly cold. Then the wind began to blow. As he rode around the Works, he could feel the stabbing pain of the cold on his face and hands. At Ardnagrena, he called an early break at mid-morning, but the men in one gang protested that they would not make enough piecework if the Works were halted too often.

The Works continued through the cold and the wind. At Lisnadee the gangs refused to work at the top, where the road ran through the pass. The north-easterly wind was blowing across the lake below Croghancoe before it was funnelled through the narrow pass. The cold here was extreme. He decided that that part of the road could be left until later. Even lower down though, the people were fighting to work in the more sheltered sections. As the quarries deepened, many of the gangs were asking Durcan for the right to work in them. Luke agreed to this, and heaps of stones began to grow at the edges of the quarries. He decided that the laying of the stone could wait until later.

Then the weather improved as the wind swung to the south-west. He was relieved at this, and at Lisnadee they continued building the road across the pass. After a few days though, the snows returned, blown on another north-easterly gale. Again Lisnadee was worst because of its height. He thought of closing the Works, but when Durcan mentioned this to the gangs, it brought strong protests from the people. Luke was relieved. He knew that Morton would not listen to any excuses for the road not being built.

Again the wind swung to the south-west, and the snow melted, except for the white peaks above Ardnagrena and Croghancoe. The Works went on. When the snows returned, it was even colder than before. The people started to light fires, stealing turf from cottages nearby. This caused fighting, as the local people saw their only source of heat for the winter disappear. But it no longer mattered to the men on the gangs. He tried to have the stealing stopped, but survival was more important to desperate men and women.

One payday, he rode to Ardnagrena. The winds had died, but it was as cold as before. He noticed that the shebeen was back. He rode past without a word. When he arrived at the Works, he called Gallagher over.

'Our friend Clarke is back again, John.'

'I know. I'd noticed.'

'We're going to have to find some way of dealing with him, but I think we'll wait until Davitt comes.'

For the next two hours, Gallagher measured out the work done with the ganger for each section. As he finished, he sent the gangers back to Luke to calculate each worksheet. Luke was surprised to notice that some of the payments had increased. In one gang, the men were to be paid a shilling a day each and the women ten pence. Even the women were earning more than men in the other gangs. At the end of his calculations, he commented on this to Gallagher.

'There's a simple explanation,' Gallagher said. 'If you examine it, you'll see that the number in the gang dropped the day after Morton was here.'

'Why was that?'

'Nobody seems to know why, but I know the reason damned well. We're paying the piecework on a gang-by-gang basis. So no one wants weak fellows in their gang. It drags everybody's wages down.'

'You mean they've been threatened? Run off the gang?'

'I can't prove it, and you can't either. I've spoken to a few in their homes, and they just tell me they can't do the work. And three of them are already dead.'

Davitt arrived, again with the two constables, both of whom seemed to regard Luke with some disdain. They too had noticed the shebeen. Luke brought Davitt and Gallagher aside for a few minutes, and spoke to them.

This time, things were done differently. Davitt and Gallagher, together with the constables, carried the table out of the tiny cottage which had been used as Luke's office. Instead of setting it up outside the cottage, they started to carry it away. Some of the nearby workers were concerned by this, and grew more so when Gallagher and one of the constables returned for the bench and carried it away too. When he judged all was ready, and the working day was over, he walked down the line, and told each of the gangers that everyone was to assemble at the old cottage before being paid. Then he scrambled through the snow to the top of the thatch, and addressed the crowd.

'I know it has been a very hard week for you all. I'm sorry that this way of working has been started, and I know some could not finish the week. For the rest of you, it has been very tough. As you all now know, we only have a hundred work tickets for Ardnagrena. That too, I can do nothing about.'

He hesitated.

'I know too that there are many other families who need work tickets. Father Nugent has told me about them. Because of this, I am asking any of you who do not need your ticket next week to step forward. We'll then be able to give your place to someone who needs it more.'

As he expected, no one moved.

'I must also tell you that these Works are for the relief of hunger. The money you earn is not much, but it will help you to feed your families. If we see that you do not need it for this, we'll know that you no longer need a work ticket, and again we'll give it to a family that needs it more.'

He climbed down and walked to the pay station. No one spoke to him. Once or twice he heard hostile murmurs, but he ignored them. He joined Gallagher and Davitt on the bench which had been set up just across from the shebeen. The first ten or twelve workers were paid and walked towards Brockagh. Then one man took his wages and walked to the shebeen. All eyes turned to Luke. He crossed out the man's name on the payroll. A woman ran across to the shebeen and spoke to the man. They both looked to Luke, the Government man. He looked back at them, holding his pen, waiting. Then they turned their backs on the shebeen.

He re-entered the name.

He rode back to the priest-house on his own. He and the priest had almost agreed the list of a hundred families to be announced for Lisnadee, and it did not take long to finish. A half an hour later, he left and rode back towards Gallaghers.

There was a movement in the shadows. Then there were two women grabbing at his leg and jacket, and he was pulled to the ground. They dragged him up into a half kneeling position, while a third woman punched him on the nose and mouth and eyes. He screamed through the red flashes of pain. Between blows, he could see half a blackened face, rough rags covering the mouth and nose. He heard men's voices and realised his assailants were all men. He was held prostrate on the ground, one man on his chest, his dress rucked high. Another held his feet as the third lifted a rock and smashed it on his knee. Again he screamed. They lifted him up, and he was cudgelled from behind. He passed out.

When he came to, his head was spinning and throbbing as he lay on the hard ice, unable to see or hear through the pain. After a few minutes, his senses returned. His knee was aching, his horse was gone, and there was no one around. He was cold, shivering and convulsing. He shouted for help, he screamed. Nothing. He knew he could not stand and tried to roll over on his stomach, but the pain was too much. He waited, then tried again. Forcing himself through the wall of pain, he rolled over. For some time he lay gasping, his face to the mud until the pain waned. Then he started to drag himself over the frozen snow. He tried not to pull his injured knee, but he could not avoid it, and again the pain got worse.

At the nearest cabin, he tried to knock on the door, but could not. He shouted. The door opened – and slammed.

Again he lost consciousness. When he came to his senses, he was shaking, and his tongue was bleeding. He had no idea of how long he had lain there. When the shaking stopped, he started to drag himself again.

At the next cabin, a dog barked, but no one came. At the third cabin, the door opened, and there was a woman's cry. He was aware of people handling him as he passed out again.

When he came conscious again, he could still feel the pain in his knee. He saw he was back in Gallagher's. Winnie and Mrs. Gallagher were both there and another woman, very old. He had no idea who she was. She spoke in a rough, guttural Irish.

'She says to tell you that you'll be alright,' Winnie said in English. 'You'll walk in time.'

'I know, I understood.'

'Our friend Mr. Clarke, I suppose?'

'Yes, and two other bastards dressed as women. I couldn't see their faces. Could have been the Molly Maguires for all I know.'

'Don't say that,' Winnie said.

'Sorry.'

It was then he realised that the lower part of his body was bare.

'What happened my trousers?'

'We had to cut them off you,' Mrs. Gallagher said, 'but don't worry. John will get you another pair, and I'm washing and stitching your old ones for rough use.'

'You could have put the blanket over me.'

After the old woman had gone, Winnie brought him porridge. He was still unable to sit up, but this time the blanket covered him.

She fed him through his battered lips. 'They could have killed you.'

'They tried their damnedest.'

'I know,' she said.' You'll have to be more careful. Take care of yourself better.'

'You've been crying.'

'You're quick to notice. And anyhow, why shouldn't I?'

She turned her face away and said nothing. She fed him for a few minutes before she spoke again.

'You'll have to rest two weeks at least.'

'I can't do that. There's people depending on me. I can't stop now.'

'You'll have to. You have to think of yourself. And if you don't, I will.'

He smiled at her. 'Well, you think of me, and I'll think of other people. Is that a deal?'

'It's a deal.'

'And talking of other people, whose bed is this?'

'Bernie and Frankie and Young John, they share it. Surely you remember that.'

'I think the belt on the head knocked some of the remembering out of me.'

'I'll have to do the remembering for you too, so.'

'But I can't be taking a bed from the lads. Where will they sleep?'

'They'll find somewhere.'

That evening, John Gallagher and Father Nugent came.

'The bastards really got you,' Gallagher said.

'They took no half measures, that's for sure.'

'I gave you the Last Rites last night,' the priest said. 'That's how bad it was. That blow on your head was enough to kill a man.'

'Maybe that's what they wanted,' Luke said.

'You're going to be in bed a few weeks,' Gallagher said.

'I can't do that. You know that as well as I do.'

'You'll have to. We're just going to have to take care of things while you're recovering.'

'But what about Lisnadee?'

'One or two little matters to straighten out. Nothing that won't wait a week.'

'And how's Ardnagrena?'

'No different to yesterday,' Gallagher replied. 'One of the gangers left, but I've replaced him.'

'Why did he leave?'

'He couldn't take the hate from his own people. He told me he'd die sooner. Starving's better.'

'It must be tough on you too.'

'I've less friends than I used to, that's for sure. Even some of my own cousins don't seem to know me anymore.'

'I'm sorry,' Luke said. 'I should have warned you of all this.'

'It's not your fault. I'd have done it anyhow.'

'I know you would.'

'Now you're to stop worrying,' the priest said. 'John will look after the Ardnagrena Works as we agreed. Tim is looking after Lisnadee, and I'm helping him. And you're to just rest.'

Winnie fed him again that night. There was some meat mixed in with the meal, cut very fine.

'Does your father know you're here?' he asked.

'You're not on about that again.'

'I'm just worried, that's all.'

'Well, you needn't. I've told him already there's nothing between us, and he's not to be worrying his head about it. And anyhow, aren't you a sick man. What trouble would you be causing the way you are.'

'Just so long as he understands that.'

He opened his mouth as she held the spoon of meal to him.

'I'm sorry about this morning,' she said.

'Why's that?'

'We didn't mean to shame you like that. We should have covered you up.'

'Oh, don't worry about that.'

'No, no, you're right. It's just that us women are more used to it. That's what Ma always says. We're always nursing – nursing the children, nursing the men. We never worry about it.'

'I'm sure I took a lot of nursing.'

'More than you think. You were in a terrible way when they brought you in. We had to wash you down well.'

'Yes, I'd noticed.'

'Ma didn't want you catching fever.'

'It's nice to know that one of you was worried.'

186

She hesitated, holding the spoon a few inches from his mouth.

'Now you're to stop teasing. If you want to be fed, you'll have to be nice to me.'

'Sorry,' he said. 'I'll be nice. I promise.'

His horse was never found. Rumours in Brockagh had it that it was taken to Ballina and sold. Gallagher was able to borrow a donkey for a few weeks. Its owner had no oats to feed it.

When he brought it home, Gallagher told him that he would be happy to use the donkey himself and let Luke, as the senior officer, use the horse. But as they all realised, a donkey was easier to mount for a man with a twisted knee.

The next day, he insisted on visiting the Works. When Winnie and Mrs. Gallagher saw that he would not be put off, they prepared him for the journey. Mrs. Gallagher tied a branch as a splint for his knee. Luke winced with pain as it was tied tight. Then Winnie made up a rough crutch, and together they managed to get him on the donkey from a kitchen chair.

He rode up towards Ardnagrena.

It was grey and overcast, but it was not raining or snowing, and for the past few days at least the freezing cold had disappeared. As he rode down the line now, people stopped working and turned to stare at him, anger and hate in their eyes. The Government man, the man who kept them working regardless, the man who killed them in the cold.

When he came to the end of the line, John Gallagher came over.

'I'm not getting off,' Luke said.

'You're right, you're not,' Gallagher said. 'And you shouldn't be here at all.'

'How did this morning go?'

'Well. We only had eighty nine starting the week, but Father Nugent got it back to a hundred this morning.'

'So you've got everything under control?'

'We have.'

'That's great. I'm just going to go up to Lisnadee now.'

'Don't be crazy,' Gallagher responded. 'Go back to bed. That's an order.'

'I thought I was supposed to be supervising you.'

'Not as far as your health is concerned. Go on home now.'

'Do you have the worksheets for the last two days? I might as well work on them when I'm resting.'

Gallagher gave them to him. He rode back through the accusing lines of gaunt, starving people, and on towards Brockagh.

When he arrived at Gallaghers, he spread his papers over one end of the table, away from where Winnie and Mrs. Gallagher were working. Then he took out Danny's letter, knowing that the women would not notice it among the other papers. For a few minutes he stared at it. He had come to a decision, and he knew it. The whole business of exploiting starving people nauseated him. But Danny was his cousin, and had been his best friend for all the years on the rails. He could not go with Danny, but there was no point in annoying him. So he wrote him a letter, a polite and friendly one, refusing his generous offer. He gave no reason for his refusal beyond the fact that he was very busy, and could not spare the time. He put it in an envelope. When he had written the address, he stared at the envelope. Then he put it in his coat, and dismissed it from his mind.

When Gallagher came back that evening, Luke was still hunched over his papers.

'Still working?' Gallagher asked.

'No,' Luke said. 'I'm just trying to think it all through. This business of the weakest being run off the gangs – that worries me.'

'I don't think it's going to be as bad as we thought. Father Nugent sorted them out this afternoon.'

'He did?'

'Well and truly. He came along at the end of work, collected everyone together, and gave fire and brimstone to the fellows on that gang. He told everyone that running the weakest off the Works was murder, pure and simple.'

'So what happened?' Luke asked. 'How did they take it?'

'They gave in, what else could they do. All the others turned against them. They began to call them murderers too. In the end, Father Nugent agreed to give them absolution, but only if they took back the fellows who'd left.'

'So there's decent people in the world yet.'

'There are,' Gallagher said, 'and if there's them that forget it, we have a priest who won't stop reminding them.'

One morning, he rode towards Lisnadee. An early mist had lifted, the sun was shining. The cold was less than before. The pain in his knee had eased, and he knew that while he would hobble for a few weeks, there was no permanent damage. He almost began to feel happy.

The shebeen might still be a problem, but he now thought this was unlikely. Refusing to retain men and women who used the shebeen had been a tough and dangerous course, but it had worked. Many would have resented his actions as unnecessary interference, but he felt certain that some at least would understand it as the only way in a time of fever and famine. He knew that Clarke had orchestrated the assault on him, but he reckoned that this was the high tide mark of the violence, and it would not be repeated.

Gallagher's comments had cheered him too. If the weakest were run off the Works, the whole exercise would have been pointless. He realised that he had let the single episode dominate his thinking, but what Father Nugent had done, and the reaction of the men and women in the other gangs, confirmed what he had known all along. Even now, people supported one another.

He could see Lisnadee in the distance – the listless lines of men and women working with their picks and shovels. He thought of the Great Western Railway and the South Eastern, it all seemed so long ago. Enormous Works, thousands of men. Compared to the rails, Lisnadee was nothing, but the way of working was the same. Under Farrelly's system the strong supported the weak, though men earning three, four or five shillings a day could not be described as weak.

But there were weak people here. Feverish men, gaunt starving women, children unable to lift a pick. If the rest of their gang abandoned them, they would die.

As soon as he arrived, he could see that everything was running well. He dismounted. Close by, a man stopped working, and turned to face him, saying nothing. Luke could see the lice in the dirty blanket wrapped around him. He could see too the look of contempt in his eyes. After a few moments, the man shook his head, and turned back to his work.

Durcan came up to him. 'I'm surprised to see you. Shouldn't you be in bed a few days yet.'

'Too many things to be doing,' Luke said. 'Though from all I can see here, I don't know that you'll be needing me at all.'

'Oh, we'll need you alright. Father Nugent helped out a lot, but he's too much to do as it is.'

'Maybe you'd give me a quick look down the Works. I don't want to get off.'

Durcan took the bridle, and led the donkey along, explaining how far each operation was advanced.

'Do you have all the papers there?' Luke asked.

'Of course. All filled out, just as you'd want.'

He took the work sheets, and started to check through them, doing rough estimates on the piecework as he did.

'Have you had any trouble with piecework here?' he asked.

'Not in carrying it out. I heard from Father Nugent that you had some trouble with it in Ardnagrena. Running fellows off the gangs.'

'He told you about that, did he?'

'He did, but he told me to keep it to myself. No point in causing trouble.'

'So why do you think you've had no trouble?'

189

'I've been thinking about that too. Two reasons. First, we had piecework here from the beginning; they never knew any other way of doing things. And second, no one got the idea of forcing the weaker off the gangs.'

'It only takes one man to start trouble with that.'

'That's true. Maybe it's because people here are more used to helping each other, they wouldn't force people out and let them die. They even share out the little corn they have. But it's not that that worries me.'

'What then?' Luke asked.

'The fever is going to be the real killer here. At times I wonder about bringing people together so as fever can spread among them.'

'Yes,' Luke said. 'I think you're right.'

He looked at the scene around him. The sun was sparkling off the lake, birds singing. Only people were suffering.

'And we're going to have another problem too,' he said. 'The piecework payments are going to be very little. Damned little.'

'Yes,' Durcan agreed, 'Father Nugent had noticed that. These figures aren't great.'

Luke rode back between the lines of workers. Whenever he caught people's eyes, he nodded at them. Some just stared at him, most looked away. Their bodies were skeletal now, eyes and cheeks sunken so deep that their faces seemed like skulls. When he got to the end of the line, a young boy turned around and spat in front of him. Luke rode on.

He spent that evening calculating the wages and the piecework payments. It was as he had feared. In each of the gangs, the workers were not earning much more than five pence a day. Again he thought back to the railways. There they had worked piecework on the South-Eastern with no basic wage at all. No one had ever bothered much when they did, they earned more that way. They had been young and strong, and earning money, more than they could ever have earned in Mayo. But piecework was different here. It didn't reward the strong, it only punished the weak.

The snow returned, blown on a powerful gale that scoured the fields, dumping drifts against the walls and across the roads. The people still came, tramping across fields and along the lee side of walls. Luke had the work continued where there were no drifts, but many of the worksites were buried, and he had to have the snow shovelled away before some of the gangs could start work.

The next payday was busy. He had to supervise payments at both locations. When Martin Davitt arrived, he had already heard of the attack.

'Dangerous men around here, Luke.'

'Aye, there are.'

'Didn't I tell you to be careful about the Selection.'

'Oh, it was nothing to do with that.'

'What then?'

'The shebeen. The fellow who was running it, I don't think he liked me.'

Davitt laughed. 'Damned sure he didn't like you. Not after you burning his business premises, eh?'

'Who told you that?'

'Everyone knows.'

'Yes,' Luke said. 'I suppose he had his reasons. Not that he'll ever prove it, the bastard. And don't say I said that.'

'Of course not.'

When they had finished the payments at Ardnagrena, he rode with Davitt towards Lisnadee.

'I didn't tell you about Morton,' Davitt said. 'He saw your wage sheets. Told us you were getting the best results in Mayo.'

'Damned bastard!'

'Yes, he kept lecturing us on how we should achieve the same results all over the county. He said you knew how to do it.'

'I don't know how to do it,' Luke said. 'I'm just doing what he told me I had to. I've no choice. Isn't everyone else doing the same?'

'Not yet. Seems Morton was using you as an experiment. They'll be applying piecework alright, but only starting next week.'

'He never told me that,' Luke exclaimed.

'He wouldn't, would he?' Davitt said. 'But I'm afraid there's more bad news to come. He wants the basic reduced.'

'What!'

'Yes, from next week. Only by a farthing – tuppence ha'penny is the new rate for the men, tuppence farthing for the women and tuppence for the children.'

'And is there an increase on the piece-work rate?'

'Now what do you think?'

They rode on through Knocklenagh.

'The people won't stand for this,' Luke said.

'They will,' Davitt answered him. 'They'll have to. They've no choice.'

'They'll kill someone.'

'Not here, they won't. They haven't got it in them anymore.'

'What can they do, then? What the devil can we do?'

'Wait it out. Wait until the fever and hunger are over, wait till they've got their strength back. Then we'll see what we'll do. And there's many won't like it.'

'That sounds pretty rough,' Luke said.

'It's meant to be rough,' Davitt said.

As he rode one afternoon from Ardnagrena back to Brockagh, he saw a man in the distance carrying the body of a woman over his shoulder, her arms and long hair swinging as he staggered along, slipping and sliding over the compacted snow. Even from a quarter mile he could see that the body was so thin it could not have weighed much, but the old man had little strength left in him. Luke rode up to him and dismounted.

'Are ye going to the graveyard,' he asked. The old man looked at him in fright, and only nodded.

'Here, I'll take ye there,' Luke said.

The old man put the corpse down, and Luke helped him into the saddle. Then he took the corpse to place it on the donkey behind. As he lifted it, he dropped it in horror. It was already well decomposed. The face was black, the woman's ribs and stomach showing through. Maggots crawled through the pus on her ulcerated legs.

He was committed now. He would have to continue, but he was risking fever himself. He lifted the corpse again and hefted it onto the donkey behind the old man. Then he led the donkey along in silence. When they reached the graveyard, he helped the man down again and lifted the corpse, leaving it just inside the gate. The man nodded to him again, whether in gratitude or hate Luke could not tell, and started walking back towards Ardnagrena.

Luke did not remount. He stood leaning against the donkey, feeling his throat retching. He vomited onto the road and stood staring at the pool of half-digested corn and turnip in the snow. Then he took the donkey by the bridle and walked back to Gallaghers. He asked Mrs. Gallagher to prepare a bowl of hot water. He washed the donkey down well, then the saddle and his own arms and chest. For days, the episode nauseated and frightened him, but his luck stayed with him, and the black fever did not claim him.

For the next few weeks, both Works progressed at a slow pace, interrupted by blizzards day after day. He alternated between Ardnagrena and Lisnadee. Davitt's prediction had been correct. When he announced the farthing reduction in the basic pay, there was no response at all. The roads were being built as the system dictated, and everything was within budget, just as Morton had demanded. But he could still see the human cost. In Ardnagrena and Lisnadee, he was despised, but there was no trouble, only a mood of sullen acceptance. Men and women could no longer support their families from their farms. Their pride had been broken.

The silence unnerved him though. As he walked down the Works, no one spoke to him, no one looked at him. The horror of it all was affecting him more than ever. Many of the workers were earning only a little more than the basic wage, and he knew well that large families could not be fed on this kind of money. He knew too that the price of corn had increased; two, three and four times over.

The hunger deepened, and the workers became more emaciated. They were little more than walking skeletons now. The bald heads of the children, wisps and strands of hair blowing from the side, horrified him more than ever.

The cold went on. And the Killing Snows.

Chapter Fifteen

Mayo Constitution, December 1846:
More starvation. On the 16th, Mr. Rutledge, coroner, held an inquest at Robeen on the body of Catherine Walsh, who died of absolute starvation. One of the witnesses deposed that the deceased was able to work on the roads until the inclement weather set in, when, from her age, she was unable to withstand the cold, and therefore she could not procure food. Dr. Little declared the cause of her death to be from the absolute want of the necessaries of life.

The winds had died. The snow stopped too, and for a few days there were clear skies with heavy frost at night. It was still cold during the days, and the snow did not melt. The searing cold of the previous weeks had disappeared though, and the Works went on.

One day at Ardnagrena, as the Works stopped for feeding, he sat alone on a flagstone and took out his pack. It was cold, but fine.

'Mr. Ryan.'

He looked around. There was no one there. A voice came from behind the wall. 'Don't say a word, it's only me.'

'Who's me?'

'John Gallagher. Young John.'

He looked around again, fearful that he might be seen talking to himself. 'What's up, John?'

'I'm to take you for a walk.'

'A walk?' He looked back towards the gangers and workers, then turned his face sideways. 'I can't walk,' he said.

'Well, ride.'

'Where to?'

'Just go down to the crossroads and take the turn towards the hill.'

Curious, he hobbled across the snow to the donkey, and rode down towards the crossroads. He could see a faint movement in the brown, withered gorse. When he got to the crossroads, he saw a figure climbing over the wall, fifty yards on. He rode up.

'What's this all about?' he asked.

'It's a secret. I'm not to tell anyone. And I'm to stay near you all the time.'

'Near me?'

'Yes. But not too near.'

He ran on ahead. Intrigued, Luke rode after him. Young John had stopped by another small road going off to the right. He scrambled up the wall across from it on the left and sat facing the other road. When Luke arrived, he heard a voice from behind a whin bush.

'Good morning, Luke.' It was Winnie.

He stared at her, surprised. 'God, after one ambush, you'd think I'd have more sense than to walk into another!'

'That's very careless of you. I told you, you don't mind yourself well enough.'

He dismounted and tied the reins to the whin. 'What if we're seen?' he asked.

'We won't be seen. Young John, he's got eyes in his head, hasn't he? And who is there to see us, they're all down on the Works.'

She grasped his hands. He tried to move closer.

'Shhh, be careful. Young John's watching.'

He laughed. 'And whose idea was that, bringing him along?'

'No one's idea. Or mine maybe, but it's the way it's always done. He's the eldest son, he has a duty to protect his sister.'

'The eldest son, indeed,' Luke said. 'He's ten years younger than you if he's a day.'

'And what's wrong with that?'

'Nothing at all,' Luke replied. 'Does your mother know he's here?'

'Of course not! There's no need, he's well able to take care.'

'Is he?'

'Of course he is. He's eight years old.'

'God, you've an answer for everything! And Young John, who better?' Again he tried to draw her closer.

'No. Not now.'

'Sorry. I'm not supposed to hug you? What am I supposed to do?'

'Just talk to me,' she said. 'Tell me about yourself. You never talk about yourself.'

He stamped his feet on the snow and blew into his hands.

'No,' he said, 'you start.'

'But there's nothing to tell you. What you see is all there is of me. I've been brought up in Brockagh, never travelled. Well, Ballina once or twice. You know my family, we're hungry, but not so much as we were. You know the house we live in. That's all there is to us and to me. You're the one who came riding in from nowhere and changed all our lives.'

195

'Don't be silly,' he said. 'That was only because of the Relief. I was sent here by the powers-that-be.'

'Oh yes, they're the reason you're here, they sent you here. Because we were starving, that was why. But once you arrived, Brockagh could never stay the same, and not just because of the Relief. Look at the effect you've had on the family – Ma and Pa, Young John and everyone else. And me.'

'You!'

'Yes, me,' she said.

'I thought you said there was nothing between us.'

'Stop teasing.'

'But you said it. Only the other day.'

'No, I didn't. I only said that was what I told Pa.'

'But when...'

'Right from the moment you knocked on the door. And don't pretend you didn't notice.'

Yes, he thought. The door opening. Grey eyes. It was all in the eyes – but what? Teasing? Laughing? Defiant? Something more?

'Maybe you're right,' he said. 'I never believed in that kind of thing though. I thought it was all old wives' tales.'

'You men, you never believe anything until it's staring you in the face. You wouldn't believe it, but I always did. I knew it would happen. Someday.'

'I never believed it'd happen at all.'

'But it did, didn't it?'

'Yes,' he said. 'It did.'

Again she took his hands. 'Now tell me about you.'

He held her hands into his chest. 'You're cold.'

'No, I'm not. Now tell me.'

'What's there to tell? A little farm near Kilduff, that's where I come from, no different to most around. A brother, a sister dead of fever and another baby girl my mother is fostering. And I'm supposed to inherit the farm, at least I was supposed to before all this began. We've eight acres. My father works it. He's sixty three now, going on sixty four. I don't know what else to tell you.'

She cleared the snow from a flagstone and sat down, patting the space beside her. 'God, you're hopeless. So you spent all your life on the farm before the Relief started. Is that all there is to it?'

She took his hand and placed it on her knee. Through the thin shift he could feel the full shape of it, the roundness, soft hollows on either side. She put her hand on his. He said nothing, his mind was empty. He no longer noticed the cold.

'Well, come on,' she said. 'Have you been struck dumb?'

'Oh yes, I'm sorry. No, no, I didn't stay all the time on the farm. I had to go to England, just like everyone else. We needed the money to pay the rent, buy the food in the bad years. I worked on the railways. I went over by Liverpool.'

'I've heard of Liverpool.'

'Of course you've heard of Liverpool,' he exclaimed. 'Your father worked there, didn't he? Or near it anyhow.'

'I'm sure you're right. I just don't know.' She looked away.

'I'm sorry. I didn't mean to upset you.'

'I'm not upset. Anyhow you were saying you'd got to Liverpool.'

'Yes, and from Liverpool we went down to London, and then I worked on the Great Western Railway.'

'I haven't heard of that.'

'You haven't? But your father, he worked on the railways.'

'I don't know,' she said, shaking her head. 'He never spoke about England. I used to ask him, but he said it wasn't meant for little girls. All he'd say was that it was terrible, and that I wouldn't want to know about it.'

'Terrible? How did he mean, terrible?'

'I don't know. He never told me.'

In the distance, he could hear that the Works had started again. The sound of picks and shovels. He thought again of the gang on the Great Western – Danny and Owen and Martin and Bernie. Hard work. Good money. All the laughing and joking. Easy Sundays, always talking, long arguments into the night. Terrible?

'I don't understand,' he said. 'I'd been thinking of going back. Make more money. My cousin Danny, he keeps writing to me, telling me I should go back over.'

'Why don't you?'

'Only because all of this started. They were looking for fellows who could read and write and add. I was going to go back to England, but my father said I should stay on and work as a clerk. It was better than being a labourer on the railway, he said. Only a quarter the money but everyone looks up to clerks. I think Mother put him up to it.'

He knew he should be back at the Works. It was a bad example for the senior officer to be away chatting with a girl, but he was still curious.

'Your father is a tough man,' he said.

'You know, everyone says that. I don't know why?'

'He's a man of few words.'

'Not with us, he's not. Well, at least he wasn't. But he's been through a lot. I'm sure you can understand that.'

'There's just one thing I don't understand.'

197

'What's that?' she asked.

'The wagon.'

She shook her head. 'God, you're sharp. You come right to the heart of it. The wagon.'

'I couldn't help noticing it. We used wagons like that for building railways in England, but I never saw any of them around here. I wondered where he'd got it from.'

'Why didn't you ask him.'

'I reckoned he wouldn't tell me.'

'Maybe you're right. You see, it was when he was in England, he was a wagon driver there. Down along the docks and on the railways. Or at least that's what I understand. But he wanted to be more than that. Do you know, he's so much like you.'

'Me?'

'Yes,' she said, 'you. And don't pretend you don't know what I'm talking about. He wanted to get on, but he wanted to come home too. Home to Brockagh, but what could he do here? Everyone else wanted to farm, but he reckoned he could do better than that. So he decided to start his own little business. Do what he knew best – driving wagons. Hauling freight, as he would say. So he bought three carts in England.'

'Three?'

'Yes, three. He had them built; brought them home with him. He thought they'd be needed around here. And do you know, I think he was right. I remember them from back when I was a girl. Backwards and forwards to Ballina, Killala, Castlebar – sometimes even Westport. I'd always beg to go with him, sitting beside him in the driver's seat. So that's how I've been to Castlebar and all. But Ma didn't like it, so I didn't get out with him often.'

'So what happened to them? The wagons?'

'Oh, I don't know. Pa started to drink when he came back from England, more than was good for him. And when the first of the hunger came, he had to sell one of the wagons.'

'Last year?'

'No, no, years ago. 1840 I think. It was a terrible time here.'

'It was terrible all over Mayo,' he said.

'But he hung on to the other two wagons. He wanted one of them for Young John. He didn't like wasting money paying other fellows for driving. So sometimes he'd trust me enough to drive one of the wagons, following behind him. But I never drove too far – Killala was the furthest he'd let me. Not fit work for a girl, you see. But then the hunger came again. We had no money, and there was no call for wagons in Brockagh anymore. I remember he started drinking again, and then one day he disappeared.'

'Disappeared?'

'Yes, only a few months ago. Took two of the horses and one of the wagons, and went off. We still don't know where – Castlebar maybe. He was away five days. Ma near went mad.'

'Why didn't you tell me any of this before,' he asked.

'I don't like talking about it.'

'I'm sorry.'

'Oh, it's not your fault. But anyhow, after five days he came home, walking. But the wagon and horses had disappeared. He'd sold them. He looked terrible. He'd walked all the way back from wherever he'd been. Sleeping in ditches and God knows where. We all knew what had happened, but we didn't dare ask how. But anyhow he brought some money home. Thirty five shillings.'

'For a wagon and two horses?'

'Maybe they knew he was desperate. And I'm sure he drank the most of it. But anyhow, we had the thirty five shillings. Ma took it off him and hid it. She won't let him go drinking now. And she keeps a close eye on all he drinks at home.'

'So that's why he's so quiet.'

'Yes, that's why. Shame, I suppose you'd call it. And that's why he was so careful about you. He likes you a lot, but it took a long time. He was against you at the start.'

'Don't I know.'

'But he likes you now. That's very important.'

'Likes me,' he said. 'I don't believe that.'

'But it's true. He didn't like working under you at first, but he's got more respect for you now. Reckons you're more of a man than he thought you were, he even told my mother that. You might be young, but he reckons you're well able for things. Tough too. And that business with Clarke, he respected you for that.'

He thought about that. Beating a man, that's what it took to gain respect! Yes, that and being able to handle dying people on the Works.

He hugged her. This time, she did not resist for a few moments. Then she pushed him away. She kissed him lightly on the lips.

'Go on back now, we'll talk again later.'

She helped him to mount the donkey. He kept the animal still, and watched as she walked across the other road.

Young John jumped down from the wall. She took his hand, and walked back through the snow towards Brockagh.

199

Chapter Sixteen

Telegraph or Connaught Ranger, December, 1846:
Starvation. The accounts we have received from Clare Island are of the most distressing nature. The Reverend Peter Ward writes to say 'that a great majority of the inhabitants are literally starving – that many of them have perished for want of food – that the last victim was Catherine Malley of the village of Maan, and there are at the present time 200 families without the means of support, members of which have fruitlessly endeavoured to obtain employment.' The reverend gentleman describes them as resembling birds of prey screaming for something to feed on. He gives it as his opinion that unless immediate relief be afforded, the most appalling consequences may be expected to ensue.

For the rest of the week, he left Gallagher and Durcan in charge of the Works and accompanied the priest on his calls around the parish. Always he carried his worksheets with him. So they travelled the back roads and boreens, the Government man and the priest, searching out the houses of missing workers and dying parishioners. As before, the worst was the arc of mud cabins and sceilps stretching across the mountains from Benstreeva to Croghancoe. Again and again he paid out wages as the last rites were administered to the dying or the dead in the bitter cold.

A *sceilp* leaning against a dug-out bank of turf, one end half buried in snow. Inside the dug-out the ragged corpse of a woman lay on a pile of heather, a silent man seated beside her. The woman's shift was torn, her legs showing bare, the skin on her thighs hanging loose from the bone.

Catherine Devine. 1/2¼.

Luke added one stark word after the amount to be paid.

Deceased.

Then he handed the pen to the man.

'*I need your mark here.*'

X.

Luke wrote – Catherine Devine. The mark of her husband.

He handed the pen to Father Nugent, who scribbled his signature

200

alongside as witness. Then the priest knelt by the woman. He dubbed chrism on her forehead, whispering –

'*Per istam sanctam Unctionem...*'

Through this Holy Unction, may the Lord free you from sin and raise you up on the Last Day.

Another *sceilp*. One woman alone and frightened.

Widow Carney. 9½d.

She grasped the pen, he held it too to stop the trembling.

X.

Widow Carney. Her mark.

Again he handed the pen to the priest.

The woman took the coins. Luke said nothing.

A mud cabin, still standing, well thatched and white washed. One woman with three emaciated children.

Eileen Caulfield. 9½d.

'*Just here.*'

She signed as Eileen Caulfield.

Another cabin, blackened thatch showing through patches of snow. One woman, a child grasping at her ragged skirts.

Brigid Walsh, Child. 11¼d.

The woman grasped at the coins, but he held them away, pointing to the worksheet.

X.

Brigid Walsh. The mark of her mother.

A rough mud cabin. A woman, six children and a man's corpse in the outshot. The man's face was white, his lips blue and black. No sign of fever there. Killed by hunger. The woman pointed to the corpse. '*Only yesterday,*' she murmured. He nodded, and scribbled.

Edmond Ivers. 1/3. Deceased.

Then he handed her the pen.

Brigid Ivers.

Edmond Ivers. The signature of his widow.

'*Per istam sanctam Unctionem...*'

A mud cabin, thatch collapsing at one end. The stink of gangrene. One man, three children with the fox faces, and a heap of rags in the corner. Rats.

John Jennings. 8d.

He came close to vomiting. Unable to speak, he pointed to the space for the signature.

'John Jennings' the man wrote alongside.

He asked for Patt Jennings. The man pointed to the rags.

Patt Jennings, Child. 11¼d.

Again he scribbled one extra word in the jotter. Deceased.

He handed the pen to the man again. '*Here too*,' he whispered.

John Jennings, the man wrote again.

Patt Jennings. The signature of his father.

The priest signed twice, and knelt by the child –

'*Per istam sanctam Unctionem...*'

'I thought we were only supposed to take one from a family,' Luke said as they left.

'Isn't it hard enough getting a hundred a gang as it is?' the priest replied. 'There's few enough coming forward now, and there's still roads to be built. And God knows, they have more call for the money than the Union or Castlebar.'

They rode their horses across a bog to avoid the drifts on the roads. The surface was frozen, crunching under the horses' hooves, but they had to thread their way between icy pools of water and around the edges of turf banks to the other side of the bog.

He started to question the priest.

'There's something I can't understand here, Father. All these people who signed their full name, I wouldn't have expected it up here.'

'Yes, yes,' the priest answered, 'it's rare enough, but I'll tell you how it's done. Séamus Doherty, he's a fellow from up these parts, spent years on the harvest in England every summer from the age of eight. He learnt how to read and write over there. Don't ask me how, but he did. Then he came back here and started teaching it. No school, mind you. He just went from one place to another, the blackboard strapped to his back, and taught them their reading and writing. Adding and subtracting too. He's dead five years now, but they still remember what he taught them. And here's another thing that might surprise you. Eileen Caulfield and her family, they came from better land down towards Killala.'

'Killala!'

'Edwina Hughes too. Remember her a few weeks back?'

'What are they doing up here so?'

'They're the ones that didn't go to America after the evictions.'

'What evictions?'

'Oh, Lord Clanowen. Months back. The time his agent was murdered.'

'Coogan?'

'Yes, Coogan, that was the man. It seems his Lordship reckoned the people weren't sorry enough for his murder, but I'm not sure that that was true. That might have only been an excuse. Anyhow, they were evicted, and the most of them went through Sligo to America. But Eileen stayed back, Pat and Edwina too, God only knows why. And now this is all they have.'

At the next cabin, they helped an old man to bury his wife. Luke felt nauseated by the stink of decomposition, but he took the man's *sleán* and dug a shallow grave in his cabbage patch. The Coogan murder, he was thinking. Bonfires right across the Mountain. So Clanowen had got his revenge around Killala. But what about the Mountain?

No point in thinking about it. They had enough other problems trying to find more workers as the numbers in each gang dropped. He took the priest's advice on this, still trying to apply the same rule. Death for three months past. There were many more families now, but they would only offer a ticket to those who were able to work, and there were few such men or women anymore.

They laid the woman's corpse into the grave, and Luke shovelled clay and soil over her. Now he felt he was hardening himself to the sights he was seeing. As Gaffney had said, there was a job to be done, and he had to do it.

Through it all, he kept thinking of Winnie.

She might be his only anchor in a world gone mad.

December. It had been milder for a few days, and the snow around Brockagh had turned to slush, but now it froze again. Then it snowed. It was light, an inch deep on top of the frozen slush, but it did not melt. The cold intensified.

On the first Sunday, as he accompanied the priest around Brockagh and over towards Knocklenagh, they met a small cart coming down from Lisnadee. There were four corpses in it, two of which Luke had seen alive only a few days before. The priest gave all four the last rites, and directed them back to Durcan's house for burial to be organised.

'I'm intending to spend most of this week coming at Lisnadee, Father,' said Luke.

'It must be bad up there?'

'Desperate. I don't know what we're doing there. We're building a road, but how much we're helping the people, I just don't know. They keep right on dying.'

'Whatever you're doing, it's helping. I saw a cartload of corn going up towards Knocklenagh two days ago.'

'I didn't.'

'Well, I did. And they wouldn't be going there excepting they knew they could sell it.'

For the next two days, he rode from Brockagh to Lisnadee, until Durcan suggested it might be easier to stay over a few nights in Knocklenagh since it was closer than Brockagh. That evening he explained his plans to the Gallaghers. Winnie made up two loaves of brown bread for him. He would have protested, but he knew Winnie had decided and would not accept a refusal.

*

Wednesday. He rode towards Lisnadee. It was snowing. By the time he arrived at the Works, the light sprinkling of snow had turned the landscape white. A wan sun appeared, but it was intensely cold. Durcan had already sent some of the men out to collect dead wood in a small copse a mile away. They had also found a turf rick which they helped themselves to, without wanting to know who owned it. There were two fires burning. Every hour now the gangers called a break to allow the frozen people to warm themselves at the fires.

He was shocked to see that many of the workers were dressed no different than they had been before. Most of the children had no shoes, they had wrapped rags around their feet, but their shins still showed bare, and sometimes purple and black. Many of the women wore only shifts.

That afternoon two of the workers died, a woman and a young boy. He examined both bodies. Neither had any signs of fever. They had been killed by hunger and cold. At the end of the day, he counted the workers. Eighty-seven alive and two corpses.

'We're missing eleven more, Tim.'

'I know, I'd noticed. The ones I know, they're all from higher up the mountain. Must be that the snow is deeper there.'

He had all the workers called together before they left.

'I've decided to close...'

'You can't do that,' a woman screamed.

'Do you want to kill us all?' a man shouted. 'No money, no corn.'

Luke looked across to Durcan, who shook his head. He relented.

The two men walked back down towards Knocklenagh, leading the donkey and horse, each with a corpse slung over the saddle.

'There must be some other way,' Luke said.

'You heard what he said. No money, no corn.'

'And I don't suppose the merchants would give credit?'

'Would they, hell?'

They left the bodies inside the graveyard gates, and Durcan organised four village men for grave digging in the morning. That night they both rode around Knocklenagh and the lower parts of Lisnadee. Luke paid out wages to the families of those who had died, and wrote out thirteen more work tickets. By midnight it was snowing again.

Thursday. In spite of the new tickets, there were only eighty on the Works. The snow had stopped, but the cold went on. This time one of the women carried three blankets with her, and wore another. Each of them had a hole slit in the centre. She gave the others to one of the women and two of the fox-children. Luke could see the lice and fleas defying the cold. That day, two more workers died. Again the two men trudged back towards Knocklenagh, leading their animals and corpses. Again that night he paid out wages. Again he wrote out new tickets for the Works.

Friday. A light wind had sprung up, and the snow was starting to drift. It filled the road between the hedges, and they had to lead the horse and donkey into the fields. As they approached Lisnadee, it became easier to ride, since there were no hedges, and the wind swept the powdery snow away. But the cold was worse in the freshening wind. He reckoned there were less than sixty workers, he no longer bothered to count. The workers were shivering and trembling in the bitter cold.

That day, four workers died – a man, a woman and two young boys. Durcan had each of the bodies carried to an abandoned cottage, where they slowly froze. They didn't attempt to bring the bodies back. The snow was already deep, and it would be difficult enough for the donkey and horse as it was. Nor did they try to find any more to work and die on the Works.

In the evening, they sat around the table, eating Winnie's bread, and what little Durcan's wife could provide.

'We can't go on like this,' Luke said. 'This is madness.'

'What can I say?' Durcan answered. 'They need the money for food. Do they freeze or starve?'

The wind had died, but it snowed for most of the night.

Saturday. The snow lay deep and undisturbed. Many of the features of the landscape had disappeared under gentle curves of snow. The two men fought their way back to the Works without their animals. After the hedges gave out, it was almost impossible to follow the line of the road. When they arrived, there were less than twenty people there, and no fires. One man lay in the snow, face down.

Durcan went over, and examined him. He shook his head.

'It's no use.'

'I know. We'll just have to close it down. Can you get the gangers to do a roll call?'

'We only have one ganger. Thady Conlon's not here. Mike Murtagh neither.'

'Where're they gone?'

Durcan shook his head, saying nothing.

The roll call showed one ganger, eleven men, four women, two children and a corpse. Luke spoke to them.

'*We can all see there's no point in staying here today. There's no chance of working – we'd only freeze to death.*'

'*And what about our wages?*' asked one of the women.

'*Seeing as you're here I'll pay you the base wage for this morning.*'

'It's not our fault we can't work. And the base wage is nothing.'
'I know. And even that I'm not supposed to give you.'
'When will you pay us?'
'Tuesday.'

An old man stepped forward. He gestured at the endless ocean of snow drifts around them. 'You won't pay us on Tuesday,' he said, half-whispering. 'You can't pay us without money, and the money man won't come through this snow.'

'We'll pay you when we can,' Luke said. 'I promise you that.'

He carried the body with Durcan, and they brought it back to join the other four. There was very little weight in it. They stayed on in the freezing cottage for an hour. Two dead men, a dead woman and two dead children stared at the rotting rafters, eyes unseeing. Luke tried to close the eyelids, but those from the previous day were already frozen to the eyes.

Six more workers turned up. Their names were noted, and they were sent home. When they judged no more would come, the two men struggled back to Durcan's cabin through deep drifts of snow.

The priest was there.

'How did you get up here this morning?' Durcan asked, surprised.

'I didn't come this morning, Timothy. I came up last night.'

'But why...?'

'Too many sick calls. It's worse than Brockagh 'round here.'

'You should have told us you were here. You could have stayed with us.'

'No need. I was at Gill's. Eileen didn't want me leaving, so I stayed over.'

'What! Gill's? Who...?'

'Tommy. Him and the son. Son's dead.'

'Dead?'

'Dead.'

'And Tommy?'

'He's got fever, but he's over the worst. He'll live.'

'Well, thank God for that.'

'Thank God is right,' the priest replied. 'But it's not Gills I'm worried about. Eileen told me about people dying on the Works at Lisnadee. Says they've buried four in two days. She showed me the graves, but there were no names.'

'They were the ones we got down,' Luke said. 'And I've got the names.'

'The ones you got down!'

'There's another five up there now.'

'Five!'

'Yes, Father. We had to leave them there, we won't be able to get them down till the snow melts.'

'Can we get up to them?'

Luke stared at the priest in surprise.

'Could we not wait a few days, Father?'

'No,' the priest said. 'I've been waiting all my life. It's time to stop waiting.'

'I'll go with you, Father,' Durcan said.

'No, Tim, you'll stay here,' Luke said. 'You've got your family to be thinking of. Come on, Father, I'll go.'

'It'd be as well for ye to go at once, so,' Durcan said. 'There'll be more snow this evening.'

A few minutes later, they were trudging back through the snow to Lisnadee. Luke limped, staring at the snow underfoot, concentrating on following the prints he and Durcan had made on the way down. It was easier to walk that way. Once he glanced across at the mountains.

Benstreeva. Teenashilla. Burrenabawn. Croghancoe.

Now they frightened him. He did not know why.

'I don't want worrying you further,' the priest said, 'but Ian McKinnon came by two days back, and he had two messages for you. I was going to leave word with Mrs. Durcan.'

'What messages, Father?'

'One is that you're to return to Knockanure on Thursday. Morton wants to see you again. You're to make a report to him and the Guardians.'

'God damn him to hell, can't he stop interfering.'

'Don't be like that, it'll only be for a day or two.'

Luke shook his head. 'And what was the other message?'

'Your father has fever.'

When they reached the old cottage, the priest knelt, giving out the last rites to each of five corpses. '*Per istam sanctam Unctionem...*'

As the blessing was repeated and repeated, Luke tried to follow the words in Latin, but there were too many that he did not understand, and his mind was drifting, half conscious, half horrified. Father? Father dying? Dead already? Who knows? And Mother? How would she take it? What will she do? Maybe she has the fever too. Dead too? No, no. That could never happen. Father can't die. He's too strong. He's had the fever before. He didn't die then, why should he die now? And why should Mother get it? She didn't get it when Alicia died. If she didn't get it then, she won't get it now. But how do I know? Amn't I like a damned fool, only telling myself what I want to believe? But I'll have to get down there. But when, when? Oh God, this bloody snow.

'We'll have to move them soon,' the priest said. Luke started, surprised.

'I know,' he said at last. 'I've been keeping a watch for foxes. If they're frozen though, the foxes mightn't find them.'

'Why not?'

'No smell.'

'Maybe you're right, I don't know. Either way I won't be happy until I see them in consecrated ground in Knocklenagh.'

'Let's leave them here, Father.'

They started back through a desolate landscape. Luke was cold, his feet wet, his hands and face almost numb. Around him he could see little but grey sky, white earth and tiny plumes of smoke coming from the *sceilps* and mud cabins of Croghancoe. The smoke came together in a thin rising veil over the top of the white mountain.

It was still and silent.

He stopped and stared at the mountain. He sensed a vast endless power behind it, and felt a deep unreasoning terror.

He went rigid in cold shock.

'Easy, Luke!'

He turned around, startled. He was trembling violently now. The priest was gripping his arm.

'Easy, easy. I'm here, Luke. Easy now.'

Luke stared at him. He looked around. Everything seemed normal again. He could see white fields, cabins and mountains, but the power had gone. Slowly the fear drained away, and the trembling eased.

'I'm fine,' he said. 'It's only the cold.'

'Of course,' the priest replied. 'Sure 'tis bitter cold.'

He never forgot the long ghastly journey down to Knocklenagh. Many times they rested, leaning up against stone walls, desperately cold as they gasped freezing air into their lungs. When they arrived at Durcan's, it was already dark. A freshening breeze had sprung up from the north east, and it had begun to snow.

They stood at the fire as Mrs Durcan prepared the meal. Afterwards they sat at the table, sipping *poitín* and talking quietly. They had little heart for it though, and they lapsed into silence and retired early.

CREDO. Luke woke just before dawn and went outside. It had been snowing without cease during the night, driven by a high wind, but now both the wind and snow had stopped. For ten feet in front of the house there was no snow at all. Beyond that there was only a wall of white. Half asleep, he could not understand what it was. It brought back images of the mountains, but high above he could see the stars. Slowly he realised that he was looking at a giant snowdrift, sculpted away from the house by the barrelling effect of the wind along the wall. He reckoned it at twice his own height. He relieved himself on the half-hidden manure heap, and went back inside.

As he returned to his straw and blanket, he saw the priest getting up.

'Go back to sleep, Father.'

'I can't. I have to get down to Brockagh for the early Mass.'

'You won't get near Brockagh today. The snow is twelve feet deep.'

'But…'

'No 'buts'. It's impossible.'

'What about Brockagh? There'll be people turning up for Mass.'

'I doubt there'll be many. Have a look outside.'

The priest walked to the door and looked out. He shook his head and came back in. He lay on the straw again.

'Luke.'

'Yes, Father.'

'You gave me a terrible fright yesterday.'

'I'm sorry. I didn't mean to.'

'I thought you were going to die. I couldn't have taken that.'

'I told you it was the cold. It was enough for any man to shake.'

'It was more than that.'

Luke shook his head. 'Why should it worry you anyhow? One more dying wouldn't change much.'

'Don't say that. We need you for the others, and well you know it. And I didn't know what was happening to you.'

'I don't know what happened either,' Luke said. 'I don't even know how to explain it. There was something behind the mountain. Whatever it was, it scared the hell out of me.'

'I don't know what you saw there neither. All I know is that it was something I've never seen. But I'm only a priest.'

'Don't say that, Father. There's no 'only' about it.'

For twenty minutes neither said anything. Luke thought the priest was asleep. But then he started to speak, almost whispering so as not to be overheard by the family.

'Yes, Luke, I'm only a priest. Nothing more. It was all I ever wanted, you know, right from the time I could first understand it. Maybe it was because of my mother. I was the last of her sons, the last chance of a priest in the family. My father – he thought we were foolish, the both of us. He was a man of the world. County Meath. Good land, and he owned it all himself. Landlords you could have called us, nothing like Lucan or Clanowen though, we only farmed our own. Our house wasn't too far from the seminary at Maynooth. My mother wanted me to study there, and my father had to accept it. Not that he liked it. But he had the money, so I was sent. But an education wasn't what I was looking for, and even in a seminary I couldn't find what I wanted. Isn't that strange? They taught us everything they knew. They taught us Canon Law and Theology. Latin and Greek. The Gospels and the rest of the New Testament. Acts and Revelations. And the Old Testament, they taught us that too. They taught us to recite the Mass, to baptise and to hear confessions, to give out the Eucharist, to marry people and give them Extreme Unction when they were dying. They taught us the history of the Church too. They taught us about Paul's conversion and Peter's martyrdom. *'Tu es Petrus, et super hanc Petram...,'* but no one told Peter that Paul had broken the Rock. They didn't tell us either. But still we had to learn the names of all the popes, the successors of Peter and Caesar, right up to today, and all about the Curia and the Sacred Congregation and Propaganda Fidei. They taught us about all the old heresies, Arians and Donatists and Albigensians and all the others no one ever heard of in Brockagh, I'll tell you. And the new ones too, the ones we had to fight. The Protestants, and how we'd have to stop them converting all of Connaught. Nangle and his Achill Mission, that was the enemy, right here in Mayo. They told us all the great things McHale was supposed to be doing to fight Nangle and the forces of evil, and how all the schools should be Catholic, and the Protestants and Presbyterians could teach their own, we didn't want them. But through it all, there was only one thing they never taught us. They never told us how to find God. And do you know why they didn't? It was because they didn't know, they just did not know. But they made me a priest anyhow – a priest of the order of Melchisedech. And they sent me to Dublin, these godless men, to say the Mass to rich Catholics. They thought it was better for me. I was a rich farmer's son, I couldn't handle anything else. And I said the Mass in their big churches and their colleges and their private oratories, but I couldn't find Christ there. So I asked the Bishop for another parish – I asked for Donegal or Mayo or Galway or Kerry. He told me I was a lunatic. He said I'd never get anywhere in the Church, never make the Hierarchy. He said it would break me. But I insisted. So he gave in, the Bishop gave in. He wrote to McHale, and they tried me in a village near Tuam. But it wasn't enough for me. I could see what they were doing with the schools, the way they were driving people apart, driving away other Christians who were just like ourselves, and all in the name of Christ. So I asked for another parish again, and they told me they'd send me to Achonry Diocese, to a little place called Brockagh. They couldn't find anyone else who wanted to go. They were going to demand obedience of some poor young fellow, but with me there was no need. They thought that would cure me, but it didn't. Brockagh! For the first time I felt I was coming closer to Christ. Saying Mass in a church that was no more than a cowshed. We can't even fit everyone in it, but I knew when I first saw it, it was the kind of church that Christ would have wanted, the kind he would have known in Galilee. And I was happy there at first. We didn't even have a school, nor any

Protestants nor Presbyterians to keep out. It was only when Jim Voisey came here back in the famine of '40, then I saw that there were other Christians too, real Christians who understood the message. And he wasn't one of ours. He wasn't Catholic, he wasn't a priest, not even a parson. But he knew, yes he knew. And we worked hard, Jim and me. People died, but we did everything we could. Relief supplies, fever sheds, consoling the dying. And giving them Extreme Unction like they taught us in Maynooth. Again and again and again and again, I thought it'd never end. But it did end, even the worst things end. But then I slipped back. When it was over, I thought I'd done my penance. I thought one hunger was enough. After that I did my duty, that was all. I said the Mass and gave out Communion and married people in my little church. I only went to their houses when they were dying or dead. But it was when the hunger came again that I began to understand. It was when we started to ride around the mountains that I saw how people suffered and died. We went into so many houses, Luke, you and me. All of them, I knew where they were, but I hadn't been in them for years, or even not at all. But you brought the message, though you never knew it. But I did. I knew that Christ had sent you – no, don't argue. So I began to understand Christ's message again, and I swore I'd never forget it. 'Love your neighbour,' at least I can do that now. But 'Love God,' that's harder. Much harder. Do you know, for three Sundays now, we've had no Communion at Mass. They had no wheat, they couldn't send us white bread wafers, and they wouldn't let us use brown. I wrote to Killala and I wrote to Achonry. 'What does it matter if it's consecrated bread?' I asked them, but they wouldn't see it that way. They told me it was a terrible thought, that I would have to confess to the Bishop when the time came. The Body of Christ is white – the rich man's bread. The people in cabins, their bread won't be let used. It's not worthy of Christ they tell me. They don't understand. They don't understand, and they never will. Maybe it's unchristian of me to think like that, but like I said, I'm no saint, I'm only a man. I'm only just learning how to love my neighbour, but loving God – I'm still trying to do that.'

'But how...?'

'How? Well you might ask, Luke. Yes, how? By visiting the houses where they're dying, that's how. It's all in their faces – the faces of dead children. The pain is all in the dying, but Christ is with the dead. Maybe I'm hoping I'll get fever myself. All the pain, all the agony, spare me nothing, just suffer and die. And then, when there's no more living to be done and no more dying, then I might understand it all. Then I might see...'

He stopped.

'Then I might see...' he repeated, but he choked on the words, and said nothing more.

211

Chapter Seventeen

Telegraph or Connaught Ranger, December 1846:
Great Fall of Snow. We have not had for many years such a great fall of snow as that with which we are at present visited. On Friday it commenced to snow in Castlebar, and, with little intermission, it has since continued to fall. In some parts of the neighbourhood, the snow is from seven to ten feet deep. The Works under the Labour Act have been now checked, and thousands, whose only means of support depended on such labour, are left homeless, without fire, as fuel is so dear, none but the rich can think of buying it.

An hour later, the rest of the family got up. Before they ate, the priest told them he would say Mass. He consecrated the house.

'I didn't know you could do that,' Durcan said.

'Oh, you can do it alright, Timothy. It's just that it's not often done.'

They pulled the rough table to the side of the kitchen.

'*We've no wine,*' Mrs. Durcan said.

'*We'll have water so. Christ turned water into wine, didn't he?*'

'*Did he?*' she asked, uncertain.

'*He did. Now do you all want Communion?*'

'*Communion,*' Durcan echoed. '*We only do that at Easter.*'

'*No reason not to do it now.*'

'*We haven't been a day fasting.*'

'*We've all been fasting enough this long time.*'

The family stood as he started to say the Mass.

'*Introibo ad altare Dei...*' I enter to the altar of God.

For half an hour, he continued through the Latin liturgy. Then he stopped. He turned to Mrs. Durcan and asked for a small slice of brown bread. He broke it into separate parts and consecrated them. Then he motioned Mrs. Durcan to move forward. She did so, still carrying a small baby which had been suckling at her breast. She knelt.

'*Corpus Christi,*' the priest said. Body of Christ.

He laid the grey-brown fragment on her tongue.

She stood, and Durcan knelt.

'Corpus Christi.'

The three older Durcan children followed.

'Corpus Christi.'

'Corpus Christi.'

'Corpus Christi.'

Luke knelt last. The priest bent down to him.

'*Corp Chríost*,' he whispered in Luke's ear.

'*Corp Chríost*,' Luke repeated, and stood.

Next morning, Durcan shook him awake.

'I'll need a hand, we've work to do.'

Luke sat up. 'What's up?'

'We haven't enough wood in. You'll have to help me, it's too much for one man.'

Tired and groggy, Luke got up and put on his overcoat. He flinched as he stepped outside into the freezing cold. The storm had passed over, but there was still a strong wind.

'Where's the wood then?' he asked.

'It's around the corner. I should have thought of it before.' He handed Luke a shovel.

They worked at shovelling snow for the next hour. The fresh snow was lying on top of a hard crust of ice. It was hard work. After an hour, the priest joined them. There were only two shovels though, and Luke insisted that Durcan should go back inside to warm up, while he and the priest continued the work. 'I've never felt cold like this,' the priest exclaimed.

'No,' Luke said, 'and I think we've got it for the day. It isn't going to warm up too much, that's for sure.' They worked on. The hard labour warmed them against the intense cold. They stopped at last, gasping.

'Look,' the priest said, after he had got his breath back, 'I'm sorry about the other night. It was silly.'

'No, it wasn't.'

'Yes, it was. I want you to forget all about it.'

'How can I forget?'

'Now you're the one's being silly.'

'No, I'm not. I can't just order myself to forget, can I?'

'I suppose you can't,' the priest said. 'But you mustn't ever tell anyone.'

'I won't.'

'Promise me.'

'I promise,' Luke said.

They worked on. Then the priest stopped again. 'There's something else I have to say sorry for,' he said.

213

Luke stopped. 'You'll have a lot of penance for all these 'sorrys' of yours. What is it this time?'

'Your father.'

'That's not your fault.'

'No,' the priest said, 'but I should have thought of it all when I was going on with all that nonsense about dying the other day. It wasn't fair to you.'

'*Arra*, don't worry about it,' Luke said. 'I wasn't even thinking that way.'

Durcan came back out and took the shovel from the priest. Luke insisted on working on. Their path through the snow went over the manure heap where the snow was less deep. The manure was frozen solid. When they came to the gable, the snow was nearly the height of the house. As they dug through it, it kept collapsing, and there was more work in clearing it than there had been in front of the house. In the middle of the day, they came in, and Mrs. Durcan served them a thin meal of cabbage, turnip and gritty Indian corn.

'We're just about there,' Durcan said. 'All we've got to do now is to get the logs back.'

After eating, Luke and Durcan joined the priest and the rest of the family at the fire.

'*Ye'd better heat yourselves up first,*' Mrs. Durcan said. '*We don't want you dropping in the snow now.*'

'*You're right,*' Luke said, holding the his hands in towards the fire. '*Have ye ever seen anything like it though?*'

'*Never,*' Durcan replied. '*The cold's bad enough, and there's no sign of it stopping. But the snow is worse.*'

'*It is,*' the priest said. '*It's like it'll never stop. I heard an old fellow the other day saying it's as bad as the year of the Great Frost, and that was a hundred years ago. If it goes on like this, it'll be worse than they had then.*'

'*I reckon it's worse already,*' Durcan said.

The three men went back outside and began throwing the logs back towards the front corner of the house. As a pile built up there, Durcan started throwing it half the length of the house. As darkness fell, they were building up cords of logs along the front wall on either side of the door.

That afternoon the snow returned, blown on a violent gale. When Luke stepped out, his face was peppered with snow. The north end of the cabin had disappeared under a drift. Once again he relieved himself on the frozen manure heap, and fought his way back in.

'We can't be going out any more in this wind,' he said to the family.

'Sure why bother,' Durcan said. 'The cattle don't.'

Luke sat at the fire that evening, listening to the screaming storm. It brought back memories of the big wind of 1839 and Alicia's horrifying death. Carrigard? Fever?

At least the house was warm now. There was little extra work that could be done besides clearing out the manure from the cows' end of the house, and this did not take the three men very long. Sometimes over the next few days, Luke sat at the table, adding up columns and finishing out the worksheets. When he had done that, he started preparing the worksheets for the next few weeks. Again, there was little enough work involved, and he knew he was making work to keep his mind off other things.

At last the wind died, and the snow stopped. As the sky cleared, the surface of the drifts turned slushy, but that night there was a heavy frost, and it froze hard again. Next morning, Luke discovered that the drifts were rock solid on top. Gingerly he started to climb, and found that they held his weight. Slipping and scrambling, he made his way towards the gable end until he was higher than the cabin itself. At the other end, the chimney was surrounded by snow, but the smoke still drifted skywards.

To the west there was an unbroken blanket of snow all the way to the black ocean. He looked back towards Croghancoe. He could see no cabins at all, only tiny mounds in the snow. No smoke rose from the dead white mountain.

That day, the priest started to refuse food. 'It isn't fair,' he explained to Durcan. 'It's your food, you've got a family to feed, and ye weren't expecting us to come in on you like this.'

Mrs. Durcan protested, but he would not relent. 'A little penance might be good for me,' he said. 'The Lord knows, I've enough reason for it.'

That night, on Mrs. Durcan's request, he heard confessions for the entire family, and absolved them from all sin.

The next day, Luke too refused food. He reasoned that if the priest could fast, there was no reason he could not. He might have been less concerned about his eternal soul, but he too felt he could not take food from those who had little enough themselves. There were other reasons too. Pay back the debt and understand the suffering? Perhaps.

He felt the gnawing pain of hunger again. It brought him back too to 1840. Now he was eating nothing. But he was determined about it. He knew his body could survive another week or two. After three days, it became easier as his stomach shrank, and he no longer felt hungry.

The snow had returned, gentler now, infilling all hollows and climbing higher up the walls. Soon the house was covered, and only the heat of the fire kept the chimney open. Sometimes Luke would stare up to see if it was night or day. The silence outside was total. Inside, the air was a dank fug of smoke, sweat and the stink of cows, urine and manure.

Often they sat around the table, talking quietly in the light of the fire.

Sometimes it was about the hunger, the fever and the dying. Durcan and the priest would talk of those who had already died, the kind of men and women they were, and their role in the area around them. Luke hardly followed these conversations, he didn't know the people they talked about, though from time to time he would remember some that he had met on the Works or in the cabins on the mountains.

The priest started to question Luke about his time on the railways in England. At first this brought a welcome distraction to the whole family, and the elder Durcan children were fascinated by Luke's stories. But as time went on their interest lessened, and he lapsed into silence.

But even through their fasting, as he and the priest felt the effects of hunger, Luke continued to question the priest about his life and his beliefs. Some days they would sit on their stools nearer to the cattle, whispering. The priest started to talk of things that he would not discuss with anyone else. But he never again referred to what he had hoped to see when it was all over, and Luke was too wise to press him on the point.

At nights Luke often lay awake, staring into the darkness. It was no longer the lack of food that worried him though. He could not keep his mind away from Carrigard and the horror of fever. Perhaps they would all be dead by the time he arrived back. He knew that he had no way of knowing this, but the uncertainty only made it worse. It created a new nothingness inside him.

One night the foxes came again, this time with rats. He cried out in his nightmare, and bolted upright. The fear drained out of him, but he still sat, hunched over his knees, looking down to the glowing remnants of the fire. He thought of Winnie and a future when the snows and hunger would be gone. There was a way forward. There would come a time when life would be worth living again.

The next day, the snow started to thaw. That night, the three men sat around the fire, talking. In the corner, Mrs. Durcan was crooning to the youngest child. Even without Luke and the priest, what the family was eating was little enough. The children were hungry too.

'What will you do when the snow's over?' Durcan asked him.

'What can I do? We'll have to reopen the Works, you and me, as soon as the snow is gone. We just have to keep going.'

'And don't forget, you've got to go and see Morton,' the priest said.

'Aye,' Luke said. 'And a week late too. What will he think of that, the bastard?'

Two days later, they dug their way out. Fresh clean air flooded the cabin. Outside the sun was shining, reflecting off the wet snow. Luke scrambled up to the top of the manure heap, and looked across to the mountains. The cabins and *sceilps* of Croghancoe were visible again. Smoke was spiralling from two of the cabins. From the rest of the settlement there was nothing.

'Croghancoe?' He spun around. The priest was behind him.

'Yes. I was looking to see if they had fires burning.'

'They didn't have much money for fuel.'

'That's for certain,' said Luke. 'Nor any way of getting it if they had.'

'God help them all,' the priest murmured.

As the thaw continued, Durcan and the priest organised men to bring the bodies down from Lisnadee. Luke rode down towards Brockagh. As he rode, snow slid off branches, and water dripped off the trees into the melting drifts. The trees were wet, their skeletal branches showing black against a grey sky.

Mrs. Gallagher and Winnie helped him to dismount. He leant on Winnie's shoulder as she led him into the cabin. She sat him on a stool by the fire.

'We were worried about you,' she said. 'We'd heard there's terrible weather up the mountains.'

'The worst snow I've ever seen. We've had to stop the Works.'

'Was it that bad?'

'Terrible. Nine more dead, frozen to death on the Works. It's just murder. Bloody murder.'

He put his head in his hands, his body shaking. Winnie led him inside, She stood beside him, squeezing his shoulder as Mrs. Gallagher started to prepare corn and rice. Bernie and Frankie looked on in wonder. They had never seen a man cry before.

'What happened?' Winnie asked. 'Tell me about it.'

He put his hand on her hand, trying hard to stop shaking.

'I'm sorry. I haven't eaten for so long.'

'Maybe that's what's wrong with you, it'd be enough to worry any man. But don't worry, *a ghrá*, we'll have food inside you quick enough.'

'I know. But there's other things too. Father has fever, Father Nugent told me. I just can't get that out of my head. Who else will have it now? And I won't be able to find out anything till I get down to Knockanure.'

'Wouldn't your brother know? Why don't you send him a message to him.'

'No need. I'll be going down there tomorrow.'

'Well then, don't worry, you'll be knowing soon enough.' She sat at the table, and pulled him down onto the bench beside her. For a long time he said nothing, staring hard at the ground.

'You've got more on your mind, Luke.'

He shook his head.

'Go on,' she said, 'go on.'

'You're right, it's not just Father. It's what's been happening on the Works. I saw terrible things in the mountains, I never told you about that, I didn't want to. But I never saw anything like the last few weeks. I was the one who was supposed to be in charge. I was the one that was supposed to stop it, but I couldn't. What could I do? I couldn't feed them food I didn't have, I couldn't stop the cold. When the snow started, I tried to shut the Works, but they wouldn't have that. I thought it would be better for them, at least they could stay in their cabins, keep warm. But they were frightened. They thought I'd never come back. They had no money, and they thought they wouldn't be able to buy food again. Nor wood to burn neither, they've only scraws of heather and turf, and little enough of that. It's not just the fever and the hunger, it's the cold too.'

'I know,' she said. 'Father told me about Ardnagréna.'

'What did he tell you?'

'Oh, I don't know, but it wasn't as bad as what you're saying. One old woman died, and God knows, it's one too many. But you'll hear all about it soon enough. You go on, tell me what happened next.'

'We just had to continue, I couldn't stop it. But every day, there were less and less of them. I knew what was happening, I knew right well. You never see it though. The people, they keep to themselves. But I knew what it was like. The fever is a terrible thing. I saw my sister die of it in Carrigard. They stink when they're dying, Winnie, the fever eats them alive. It isn't a death that's fit for man nor child.'

'I know. I've seen it too.' He looked at her in surprise, but she waited for him to continue.

'But we went on,' he said. 'I reckoned as long as I could see some of them, they were still alive, and that was something. But it was nothing. They started to die on me, right there on the Works. Men and women and worst of all, the children, I couldn't take that. You know the ones with the hairy faces, they'd just look at you with their dead eyes. They used to hate me, but when they were like that they wouldn't know me, there'd be nothing in their eyes at all. So when they died, we just brought them down to Knocklenagh, Durcan and me, he'd get someone to bury them, and we'd go back up to Lisnadee to watch more of them die, and bring more of them back down.'

'Oh God, Luke, it must have been awful for you.'

'Never mind me,' he said, 'wasn't it worse to be dying.'

She said nothing, and waited.

'And even then,' he said, 'would you believe it, even then when it was still snowing, we were trying to get workers back up on the Works to make money for themselves, but I was wrong to do that, I shouldn't have done it, and in the end it was useless anyhow. We had to close them, the Works. I'll never forget the look in their eyes when I told them that. I had no choice, the snow was too deep, and they were still dying on me. And we couldn't get the last of the bodies down, we had to leave five of them there. It was bad enough that, but I was worried about the foxes coming too. With all the snow and the cold they're desperate enough, they're starving too.'

'You mean to eat...?'

'Oh, never mind,' he said. 'I shouldn't have told you that.'

'But did they? Do you know?'

'I don't know. The bodies, they were still up there, at least when I left. They were getting a gang of fellows to go up and bring them down, but God knows whether they'll get up there with the snow in the mountains as it is. When I saw them last, the foxes hadn't been at them. Not that it'd make much difference. I reckon the snow's killed hundreds more by now, and most of them won't have been buried either. But when we got down to Knocklenagh after closing the Works, Father Nugent was there, he wanted to go up to Lisnadee again, give Extreme Unction to the dead bodies there. Wouldn't hear of staying back in the warmth. So I had to go with him, no horses, just walking. I was frozen already, but what could I do, I couldn't let him go on his own. Oh God, it was cold, and then he told me about Father having fever, it was a hell of a shock I can tell you, and all I could think about was Father and fever. But then something happened. I don't know what it was. I was looking at the mountain as we walked back, and I felt frightened. Terrified. There was something awful powerful behind the mountain, but there was nothing there.'

'But what was it?' she asked.

'It was nothing, I'm telling you. Or like someone who knew everything there was to know about me. So after that, I thought I was mad, then I thought I was raving with fever, but I wasn't.

'It was the cold, that's what it was. It does that to people.'

'Maybe. It was very strange though. What happened next, that was strange too.'

'Strange?' she asked. 'What was so strange?

'I started talking to Father Nugent. He's quite a fellow you know, I never knew a man like that before. I think what happened to me on the mountain, it shook him too, more than seeing the dead bodies even. I couldn't explain it to him either, but it made him talk. Told me what decided him to be a priest. He comes from a big farm in Meath, you know, came here to Brockagh because he wanted to. Could have been preaching in big churches in Dublin, but he prefers it here. Reckons he's close to God here, they don't know what God means up in Dublin, that's what he told me.'

'He prefers to be in Brockagh!'

'That's what he said.'

'What else did he say?'

'Don't ask, that's between him and me. But anyhow, after that he started fasting, what else should a priest do he said when there's people starving. So that's when I stopped feeding too, that's why. That and because the Durcans had little enough for themselves. They'll last a few weeks yet, but I thought it was like taking the food from the little children, and I've seen enough of dead children for one lifetime. Oh God, I thought I was going mad, I really did, I could hardly stay standing. There was only one thing that held me back, only one thing I could think of that would bring me back again.'

'And what was that?' she asked.

He did not answer directly.

'Jesus Christ, Winnie,' he said at length, 'I need you. I knew someone once, I thought I knew what it was to need someone, but I didn't. It was only what I thought she was, but she wasn't that at all. But you're different, you're every bit the woman I know you are. It'd kill me to be without you.'

'You'll never be without me,' she said.

In the afternoon, Gallagher arrived back, and Luke worked on the Ardnagrena time sheets, calculating the piecework. Then he summarised it, detailing the payments for each gang there and at Lisnadee. He handed the sheets to Gallagher.

'I'll have to ask you to arrange the wages at Ardnagrena, John, and Lisnadee as well. I've paid a few already. You'll see all the amounts owing here.'

'What about you?' Gallagher asked.

'Morton wants to see me down in Knockanure. It was supposed to be last Thursday, but I'll go tomorrow. He should be there with the Guardians, they meet on Thursdays. He'll scream at me for missing last week, but I can't worry about that. Will you be alright here though?'

'I'll be fine,' Gallagher said. 'Don't you worry about it.'

'There's one other problem though. I haven't enough money. I'll leave what I have, but for the rest, you'll have to wait until Davitt arrives. If he arrives.'

'Don't be like that. He'll arrive, you know it. Just you go on down to Knockanure, and leave things to us for a few days.'

He rose very early, borrowed Gallagher's horse, and rode through the dawn towards Knockanure. He passed gaunt figures walking through slush. It was afternoon before he saw Knockanure; the Workhouse and the Church of

Ireland steeple standing clear over the houses and cabins.

He rode to the Workhouse and then to the back entrance. There was a small crowd, but he managed to struggle through the gates as they were unlocked for him, and he led the horse in after him. He went to the administration building.

He handed the reins of the horse to one of the inmates to bring to the stables. Voisey answered his knock. He looked puzzled as he greeted him.

'You've noticed the horse,' Luke said.

'A carthorse. Where did he come from?'

'I was attacked. They thrashed the hell out of me, and stole the horse. I had to borrow this one from the people I was staying with.'

'I'm sorry, Luke. You're not the only one though, we're hearing stories like that every day. It's a dangerous business working for the Union now.'

'It is.'

They walked into the building.

'How are things in the mountains?' Voisey asked.

'Desperate. The numbers are down at both of the Works, but I don't think I'll have difficulty getting them back now the snow is melting.'

'We're talking of two more Works. If you can manage them.'

'I don't know...'

'You did it once before Luke. I'm sure you can do it again.'

'Where?'

'As you say, in the mountains. Wherever you think it is needed most, the Guardians will go with it. You can have a word with McKinnon when you see him next. It might be some weeks yet though.'

Voisey went into the meeting room, while Luke waited outside. There were two clerks ahead of him. He asked what had happened the previous Thursday. He was relieved to hear that the meeting of the Guardians had not proceeded because of the snow all across the county. He knew well that Morton would not accept excuses from him for not carrying out his instructions, even if they had been impossible.

When the main meeting ended, and most of the other Guardians had left, he entered the meeting room. Morton was waiting for him impatiently, wanting to return to Castlebar as soon as possible. Once again he went through Luke's time sheets and calculations, and declared himself impressed by the results. Most impressed.

'With respect, Mr. Morton,' Luke said, 'I'm not impressed with my results at all. We're killing people with this system. I've seen them working until they die. I've seen the cold killing them in the mountains. This isn't Christian, it isn't Relief, it's a mockery of everything we're trying to do.'

Morton raised one eyebrow, staring at him. 'I'll have to ask you to calm yourself, Mr. Ryan. We won't achieve anything by talking this sort of nonsense. I was sent here to build roads, and roads I will build. Mr. Gaffney told me that you had worked on the railways, and you understand how it is done. That is the reason we have given you such responsibility.'

'Yes, Mr. Morton, but that was England. This is Mayo, and people are dying.'

'I am well aware where I am, Mr. Ryan, and I have no desire to spend any longer in this dreadful county than I have to. Now if you wish to resign, your resignation will be accepted. But if you wish to help these people of yours, I would advise you to treat your superiors with more respect. There are already questions regarding the theft of a horse, the property of this Union.'

'What? You're not suggesting...'

'Yes, Mr. Ryan. You were given a Union horse, and you bring back a carthorse. That is theft. For some reason, Mr. Voisey does not wish to prefer charges. But we are not all fools.'

Luke looked across to Voisey, who shook his head. He turned back to Morton.

'I was assaulted, Mr. Morton. The horse was stolen.'

'That's your story, Mr. Ryan. Just remember – we are watching you.'

Luke said nothing.

'Now there's one other matter,' Morton said. 'We need more Works opened in the mountains. I understand Mr. Voisey has told you about that.'

'He has. But when do we open them?'

'As soon as we inform you.' He handed him back his worksheets. 'Now kindly return to Brockagh, and continue your work.'

As he limped out of the room, there was a shout from the other office. 'Luke!'

'Pat! I was just going to try and find you.'

'Well, now you have.'

Luke walked across the room. He noticed the Master's daughter at a desk in the corner. She took the papers she had been working on, and left the room.

'Who was that?' Luke asked.

'Oh, Sarah. She was just giving me a hand with the accounts. Last fellow I had got the fever and died.'

'She seems a shy sort.'

'The devil, she is.'

'Good at sums, is she?'

'Yes, by God. Cronin has her well trained. She's worked with him for years, unpaid too. I don't know what I'd have done without her. They've me working night and day, adding and subtracting. I can't even sleep at night with all the numbers chasing through my head.'

'Yes,' Luke said. 'I know just what it's like. But tell me, what about Father? I'd heard he had fever.'

'I didn't think you knew about that. He had fever alright. Gave Mother quite a fright. But you know Father, he's had it before, and if it didn't kill him then, it wasn't going to kill him now. No, he's fine, he's even out working the quarry.'

'You were over?'

'Just for a day. Like you, I was half expecting to be going to a funeral.'

'Lucky I met you. I was just about to ride over to Carrigard.'

'Go on so, why don't you?'

'I can't. I would have, if I thought he was dying, but I've other things to be doing. I'll have to leave it a few weeks yet.'

'But why?' Pat asked him.

'Too much to do. I don't want to do it, believe me, I'd far prefer to go back home. But things are terrible, and I can't just run away. I've just come from a place called Lisnadee. We were running Works there until a week ago. I saw people frozen to death. It terrified me. I don't want to ever see anything like that again. But I have to do it, stop it happening again. If I can.'

'I'd heard things were bad in the mountains.'

'Worse than I could even tell you. Now I find I can't even talk about it. I tried to explain it all to Morton, but he doesn't want to know.'

'He doesn't want to know much, our Mr. Morton. There's nothing in his head except sums and accounts. God knows where they bred him, he's no mother's son.'

'So how do you manage working with him?' Luke asked.

'I just keep my mouth shut. It's poor old Voisey who takes it worse. Cronin too. They want to do more, feed the whole county, but Morton won't have a farthing out of place.'

Luke stared at the long columns of figures on the desk. For some time, neither spoke.

'Tell me about Lisnadee,' Pat whispered at length.

'I told you – I can't.'

'Try.'

He shook his head. 'What is there to tell you?'

'Where is it? How did you get there? What were you doing there?'

'You know Knocklenagh?'

'I think so. The little village up from Brockagh?'

'That's right. Well, Lisnadee is above Knocklenagh again. You couldn't call it a village. Just dozens of mud cabins, all across the mountain.'

'And why were you there?'

'That's where our second Works is. We had to start another once we got Ardnagrena running.'

'You're running two?'

'I have to,' Luke said. 'And there's some question it might even be four.'

'But why you?'

'Because there's no one else to do it, and people are dying.'

'It's impossible, isn't it?'

'Damned near. But I've a few good fellows working for me. And the priest.'

'But four Works. That puts you on a level with Gaffney.'

'Oh, to hell with that. What the devil does that matter?'

His brother said nothing. Pat glanced down the long list of columns, black and red ink. Then he looked back to Luke.

'Go on.'

'Yes, so we got the Works running at Lisnadee a few weeks ago. The priest, he found me a fellow in Knocklenagh – Tim Durcan is his name. Got it running in a few weeks, but God, it was slow. It was all piecework. They were earning near enough nothing.'

'Piecework!' Pat exclaimed. 'What piecework?'

'The new system Castlebar introduced. Morton insisted on it.'

'What are you talking about?'

'Just like the railways. Pay you for work done. And tuppence ha'pence basic.'

'Tuppence ha'pence for what?'

'Basic per day. Tuppence ha'pence for the men, tuppence farthing for the women, tuppence for children.'

Pat shook his head. 'Tuppence a day! I just can't believe this.'

'And then, when the snows came, the cold was killing them. I never saw anything like it in my life. The last few days in Lisnadee, they were nothing more than murder. Murder, pure and simple. I couldn't pay them a living wage, and they couldn't stop coming for the few pennies they got. We were running three gangs at Lisnadee – supposed to be a hundred people with Tim. But every morning there were less and less. Maybe some of them just couldn't get down through the snow, but I reckon with the hunger and the fever, most of them just couldn't face the cold again. Every night we'd go around trying to find more workers, but in the end I gave up. Oh, God...'

His hands were trembling. 'I'm sorry,' he said.

'There's no need to say sorry to me.'

'No. Well...then they started dying on me. Right there on the Works. Two of them died there one day, two the next day. Then four. We tried to bring their bodies down to Knocklenagh, but in the end we just left them there to freeze. On the very last day, we'd only nineteen workers. Can you understand it? Nineteen out of a hundred. And one was already dead.'

'So what did you do?'

'What could I do? I just closed the Works. There's no need killing people in the snow, they might as well die at home, and I reckon the most of them probably did. So I left the Works and stayed over in Knocklenagh until the snow stopped.'

Pat said nothing. He thought of the horror he had been seeing in the Workhouse and the fever sheds over the past months, but he reckoned Luke was already on the edge, and there was no point in burdening him with further stories of hunger, disease and death.

Luke was staring out the window at the crowd in front of the gates. He thought of saying more, but decided against it too. Pat would never understand Croghancoe – the power or the terror. At last he looked away, and turned back to his brother.

'Let's see what you're doing there. Perhaps I can give you a hand?'

For half an hour they worked in silence, Luke adding long columns as Pat transcribed new columns from wage sheets, payment slips, invoices, requisitions and other documents. When Luke had finished all the columns and checked them, he put his pen down.

'How long are you intending to stay here?' he asked.

'A long time yet. But I'm going back home in a few days, just for a day or two.'

'I've got forty-five shillings here. Would you take it back for me?'

'Of course.'

He stayed in Knockanure that evening, sharing a bed with his brother. The next day, Voisey gave him another Union horse, and he led Gallagher's horse back towards Brockagh.

Following his arrival, work continued for a few days more. As the priest had promised, the Works had been re-established, but in spite of more workers having been selected, the numbers were still down on what they had been at the start of the month. The rolls showed less than eighty at Ardnagrena and only sixty at Lisnadee.

Davitt had arrived with the wages the previous day, but looking through the rolls, Luke could see that many wages had not been paid because the workers had not arrived. Snow still blocked the mountain roads.

When he arrived at Lisnadee, there was already one body in the old cottage. He saw the dark blotchy face. The man's clothes were infested with lice.

On the Works, more men and women showed signs of typhus. He had these sent home at once. He was certain now that workers carrying fever spread it among the rest. From then, anyone complaining of headache was sent home. After that, no one complained of headache. That worried him even more.

A few days later, the Works closed for Christmas and St. Stephen's Day. He had thought of riding over to Carrigard, but he reckoned he would have spent all his time on the road, and he saw little point in this.

On Christmas morning, he accompanied the Gallagher family to Mass. There were many gaunt men, women and children in the tight packed congregation, and many darkened faces. And the fox-children.

Christmas dinner was a quiet affair. It consisted of corn, mixed in with turnip and cabbage. Gallagher had brought down a flitch of bacon which had been hanging from the rafters in a hessian wrapping. Mrs. Gallagher cooked two slices for everyone, and brought out a bottle of *poitín*. Gallagher raised his cup.

'To better Christmases than this.'

'Better Christmases,' Luke repeated.

Winnie started to wash the dishes and pots, as the younger children sat in the corner. Luke stood beside her, drying the plates. At one point, she brushed against him, holding her thigh against his for longer than might have been accidental. It sent a surge through him, which surprised him. He tried to concentrate.

Then Winnie placed her hand on his.

'You must have courage,' she said.

'I will, Winnie. I will.'

He was on the Ardnagréna Works with Gallagher when he saw Davitt riding towards him in the distance. He was followed by two carts carrying corn, and accompanied by six armed militia men on horses.

'Must have got knocked on the head once too often,' Gallagher commented. 'Needs his own army now.'

When the wages and back wages had been paid out in Ardnagréna, Luke went through the wage sheets to see who had not turned up. He worked out the wages still due and left money with Gallagher, with the request that he should pay out whatever was possible.

Two of the soldiers stayed with Gallagher. 'They can witness the payments,' Luke told him, unsure whether the Union would accept this or not. He rode towards Knocklenagh, accompanied by Davitt, one corn cart and four soldiers.

'What are you hearing, Martin?' Luke asked. 'What's happening everywhere else?'

'Just the usual,' Davitt said. 'There's been food carts attacked, that's the reason for the soldiers. There's a lot of talk about killing landlords, but I think there's nothing in it, they won't do it. Not that it'd do much good either. I reckon half the bastards are bankrupt anyhow.'

They rode on.

'This country is cursed,' Davitt said suddenly.

'I know,' Luke said.

'You know what, I'm going to get out. There's no point in staying here. Last time I was back in Straide, I was looking at little Michael. He's only a baby, but he'll grow up, and I started to think, this is no country for young men.'

'Where will ye go?'

'I'm thinking of Lancashire. Somewhere around Manchester. We've family somewhere there. But I don't know for certain, I'm only thinking about it. I haven't even mentioned it to my wife. I wouldn't want worrying her yet.'

They left the cart and two of the soldiers in Knocklenagh, and rode up towards Lisnadee. It was getting dark as they arrived. Durcan ran over.

'By God,' he said, 'I'm glad to see you. They were sure I wasn't going to pay them.'

'I wouldn't blame them for thinking that,' Luke said. 'It's late enough.'

He looked at the scene around him. There were far too few workers. Those he could see close up had lice crawling through their filthy blankets and coats.

'How many have you here today?' he asked Durcan.

'Thirty two by my count. Or at least we had. One died this morning.'

'We'll be a while getting to a hundred again.'

'We will,' Durcan said.

They paid off the workers. Then he closed the Works for the day. It was cold and dark enough already. They rode back to Knocklenagh again, Durcan carrying the corpse behind him on his horse. Neither of the remaining soldiers said anything. Luke and Durcan carried the corpse inside the graveyard. Then they rode to Durcan's house and brought the money and soldiers inside.

'You can stay with us,' Durcan said. 'We'll keep you warm anyhow.' Mrs. Durcan looked doubtful.

'That's good of you,' one of the soldiers said, 'but hadn't we better get some corn first.' They went to find the cart, and came back twenty minutes later with Indian corn and a small bag of rice.

Late that night Father Nugent came. He told Luke that he had been riding around the mountains, but said nothing of what he had seen, and Luke did not ask him. He agreed though to accompany him again the next day. Luke was depressed at the prospect, frightened again at what he knew they would encounter. But he knew too there was no other way. Another day or two of this, he thought, and I'll be back in Brockagh. Oh God, Winnie, how I miss you.

He lay on straw with Davitt, the priest and the soldiers. He pulled his coat over his head, and slept for a few hours. By morning, it was bitterly cold.

It was still early when they got up, and Davitt left. 'You'd better keep the militia fellows with you,' he told Luke. 'I'll leave the money here with you. You'll need it to pay everyone as soon as you can find them.'

'What about you?'

'I'll be fine. No one will attack me if I've no money.'

Luke counted the money and signed for it. Then he took the moneybags on his horse, and he and the priest set out. The two soldiers insisted on accompanying them, though Luke felt that with the present advanced state of hunger in the mountains, there was little risk involved. The morning was bright, and the mud on the road was frozen hard.

He paid out wages to men and women, including the widows and widowers; mothers and fathers; and even the children of those who had died over the Christmas.

By afternoon they were higher up the mountains, and the conditions worsened. They reached the huts and mud cabins scattered across Croghancoe.

In the first cabin, a dead man lay on the bed, a woman moaning beside him. Her legs were out of joint, and swollen at the ankles. One arm hung loose over the side of the bed. Luke left the money beside her, and signed her X himself before signing his own name. The priest counter-signed without comment.

At the next cabin, there was no answer to their knock. As Luke walked away, he noticed a hand protruding from a mound in a potato patch. The mound had been scrabbled away on one side, a part-eaten ribcage showing.

'The whole family?' one of the soldiers whispered.

'Yes,' Luke said, 'with foxes for company.' He had no wish to know how many bodies were underneath. From the edge of the mound the priest gave Extreme Unction. Luke turned away. There was no-one left to pay.

At the third cabin, there were six rat-eaten bodies, but again no living person. One of the soldiers vomited. The priest gave Extreme Unction from the door. Luke tied the door shut, and knotted it.

He saw similar scenes in other cabins, his brain hardly registering it all anymore. Hunger. Fever. And the snows, killing anyone spared till now. Whole families frozen to death. No turf, no wood and no chance of getting any. They left Croghancoe.

They rode past the old cottage by the Lisnadee Works.

'I saw ye got the bodies down,' Luke said.

'Whatever was left of them, we got down,' the priest replied.

Next day, they went back to the lower villages. He signed up new workers, and by the end of the day, he had thirty more. He explained the rules for Selection, and he asked people to notify others in the area of the positions available. There was a time when he would not have done this, since it would only have brought hundreds onto the Works all at once, but now it was different. He doubted if he could bring any of the Works back to a hundred.

When they reached Knocklenagh that night, the other militia men had already departed with the cart and driver. It was very late, and Luke still had money in his saddlebags, so it was decided that the soldiers would stay with him. They slept in Durcan's again.

The next morning was the first of 1847.

The priest started on sick calls around the lower parts of Knocklenagh. Luke hitched up his horse, and rode down to Brockagh with the soldiers.

They rode under Croghancoe, the mountain still white on the upper slopes. He stared at it, but there was no vastness now.

Only a deep and empty nothingness.

Chapter Eighteen

Mayo Constitution. January 1847:
We have been informed that a poor man at Mayo, near Balla, after having been reduced to the greatest destitution, was obliged to leave his home to beg, leaving his wife, a feeble old woman, after him. In a few days after his departure, some of the neighbours went to the wretched hovel of the old woman, and found her lying on a litter of straw in the corner, with the flesh of her shrivelled arms and face mangled and eat by rats. The wretched creature died in a short time after.

BLACK '47. The snow returned. For a few days, he was apprehensive as it continued falling. It was not as heavy as before though, and the people beat paths through it each morning and worked on. Every day, he visited Lisnadee and Ardnagrena. Every day, people died of the cold, but he knew he could not close the Works, and the bodies were deposited at the graveyards in Knocklenagh or Brockagh.

But it did not last. He woke one morning to a clear sky. It was still cold with frost, but as the day went on, the cold lessened. That evening there were rivulets of water running down the drains alongside the road.

He was at Ardnagrena when McKinnon arrived.

'I've been expecting you,' Luke said.

'Voisey told you, did he?'

'About the new Works? Yes. But where?'

McKinnon tied his horse's reins to a gatepost.

'He says that's up to you. Whatever you decide, they'll put it to Castlebar, and they'll tell Dublin.'

'What if they don't approve?'

'They'll approve.'

He took a map out of his saddlebag. He unfolded it, and put it over the saddle.

'Well,' Luke said, 'if you're asking me, I think the best would be Burrenabawn and Teenashilla. They're both up here.'

He pointed to a blank space on the map.

'Not even marked,' McKinnon said.

'Too small, I'd guess,' Luke said, 'but they're there alright. There's a track leading across from Lisnadee to both of them. It's solid enough, but could do with some widening. But there's another reason too.'

'What's that?'

Luke pointed at the Works in the distance. 'Look at them there. Do you know, half of them are from higher up the mountains. Every morning they tramp down here, and every night they tramp back, God only knows how they do it. I reckon these past weeks some of them haven't even made it back. I don't know what they'll think of that in Knockanure or Castlebar, but I'll tell you this – they need work up there, and they need roads.'

McKinnon folded his map.

'Burrenabawn and Teenashilla so. You just tell me what you want, and I'll see you get it.'

A week later, both sites were open. Luke asked Gallagher to take responsibility for them, while one of the gangers at Ardnagrena was promoted to take over Gallagher's position there. Father Nugent agreed to assist once again in locating the workers. As the snow cleared, and the bitter cold lessened, the numbers on all four Works started to climb.

Through it all, he was meeting Winnie. One day, they were spotted, and their friendship was a secret no more. Whenever they had met away from other people, Young John always came with them, but he was discreet. 'Near, but not too near,' as he had said. Luke was concerned about the consequences of all this, since Gallagher must now know of their relationship. Winnie was less concerned though.

'He's coming to accept you. I told you that before. He respects you now. Give him time, it won't be long, I promise you.'

'But if he knows we're meeting? Surely he knows that?'

'He does, but he knows too about Young John being with us. And Ma, she's on your side too. She'll convince him.'

He thought about that. Gallagher already knew they were meeting. But he had never mentioned it. Was that odd? Perhaps, or perhaps he had not yet made up his mind, and did not wish to discuss the matter with Luke until he had. But at least he had not decided against him. He was sure of that now.

But he still felt guilty about it all. He felt his own happiness when he was with Winnie was wrong in the middle of suffering. He mentioned this to her one night.

'But isn't that it?' she said. 'It's at a time like this we most need each other. It's the same with everyone. Family and friends. It's all that keeps us going.'

In the evenings, they spoke of many things. He found it healing, a way to deal with the shock of Croghancoe and the rest of it, a way to shun madness.

It eased too the pain of witnessing the suffering and misery every day on the Works. He wondered if it was right to burden Winnie with his pain. But she never objected, and when he arrived back at Gallaghers in the evenings, she always asked him what had happened that day.

And what she heard, horrified her. His description of people dying on the Works and in the cabins during the blizzard had shaken her, though she was strong enough not to allow him to see that. But even now, when the blizzard was over, the horror continued. She could see the skeletal people walking through Brockagh every day. One morning while Luke and Gallagher were away on the Works, she had to assist in removing the corpse of a woman she had known from the side of the street, and carry it down to the church.

Just as bad, was her growing isolation. Because she was Gallagher's daughter, and now known to be walking out with Luke, people were avoiding her. The desperate consequences of piecework were being blamed on Luke and on her father, and she was associated with them. Young women she had known all her life as friends now avoided her. In some ways, seeing their thin, pinched faces, she felt it was for the best. Family and friends – that was what she had told Luke. Family yes. Friends – no.

But who else was there? Perhaps her future lay in Kilduff and Carrigard. Perhaps it was her only future, the only place where Luke and Luke's wife would be accepted. Or perhaps not. What he had told her of Selection in Carrigard might mean that they would not be accepted there by anyone beyond Luke's own family. But it was all speculation. She would have to wait and see.

One afternoon, they went for a longer walk than usual. For some time, Young John chatted along with them. He already saw Luke as his elder brother, and a way into a wider world. He questioned him on England, the railways and the cities he had seen. But then, as always, he dropped back, and followed them at a distance.

'There's something worrying you,' Winnie said.

'Oh, I don't know. It's nothing. And everything.'

'Why don't you tell me?'

'It's like I said before. I just can't take this. You think I'm a tough fellow, but I'm not. During the day, I'm fine, I do what I have to do, but it's at night it all gets to me. I wake up, and I feel terrified. I just think of everything, and I can't sleep again. The fever, the hunger, the cold. Watching them dying on the Works.'

They walked along in silence for a while.

'You know,' he said, 'I was going to go back to England. There's a desperate shortage of good workers on the railways right now. Four shillings, even five shillings a day, no problem if a man can work. My cousin Danny, I told you about him.'

'Yes, I remember.'

'He's starting his own business contracting on the railways. He wanted me to come in as a partner. I never told you that.'

'You didn't.'

'Yes, he reckons that there would be good money to be made as a railway contractor, and do you know, I believe he can do it. He's very determined, is Danny.'

'So why didn't you go?'

He thought about that. He thought of mentioning Danny's intentions – making money from hungry Irish labour. But he no longer wished to explain it all.

'Father said I should stay on here,' he answered her. 'They hadn't enough people to work as clerks and supervisors on the Works around Carrigard. He told me it was my duty. Maybe he was right, but I'm earning two shillings a day. And people say I'm making too much, though I could do far better in England. No matter what I do, it's wrong.'

'If you'd gone back to England, we'd never have met, would we?'

He smiled at her. 'No, we wouldn't, would we? And God knows, you're worth more than five shillings a day! Or even a share of Danny's business.'

'Well, I hope I am.'

'You are. You know that too well for the teasing. And I don't want to lose you.'

'Why would you lose me?' she asked.

'It's all to do with Mayo, Winnie. It's a different place now. All the suffering, all the dying. But it's not just that. I've seen hunger before. I've seen family and friends dying of fever. But at least, through all that, I was always on their side.'

'And aren't you now?' she asked.

'No, I'm not, and you know that as well as I do. The hunger has changed everything. It all started months ago, the first time I started working on a Selection. Carrigard, that was the worst. My own friends, my own people, we had to refuse them. No, I had to refuse them. I'll never be forgiven for that.'

'But it wasn't your fault. You did what you had to.'

'I know, but nobody in Carrigard or Kilduff will ever see it that way. Nor Brockagh. I'm one of 'them' now – I'm the enemy. Just like Morton. I help him grinding people's faces into the mud. I could kill the bastard. They hate me here, they hate me in Carrigard. Mayo isn't my home anymore.'

'I don't hate you,' she whispered.

'I know that. You're all I have. I don't want to leave you, but I don't think I can stay in Mayo.'

'Where would you go? America?'

'I don't know. Danny, he says England. But maybe America would be better.'

'Yes,' she said. 'You've always said that.'

'Not always.'

'No?'

'Remember that first time we talked about it together. That was the first time I ever said about America to anyone. Even to myself. I'd never even thought about America. I was supposed to have the farm, I wasn't supposed to be going off to foreign places. But when you asked me, I just said it. And then I looked at you, God, I hardly knew you, and I thought – would she come too? But it was only a dream.'

'But now you know the answer.'

'Do I?' he asked.

'Yes you do, Luke. Yes, you do. Don't pretend.'

'You'd come to America?'

'Anywhere. So long as it's with you.'

'But...'

'Yes. We'd have to be married first.'

'But your father...'

'We'd have to ask him. Isn't that it?'

'And what would he say?'

'I don't know. He might still say no, but I know this for sure, his 'no' won't be as strong as before. And it's about time we got him used to the idea.'

They walked along for a few minutes more. He noticed that they were no longer accompanied.

'Where's Young John?'

'Oh, he said something about a rabbit burrow up the hill.'

They walked on until they came to a small shed with turf and hay in it. She went inside. He followed, his heart pounding.

For a few days, he said nothing to Gallagher, but Winnie was now his lover, and there was no way back. But was there a way forward? What would happen if Gallagher refused? Could she leave her own family, leave them forever?

In the end, he could no longer defer it. He was riding one morning with Gallagher to Ardnagrena. He decided to be straight.

'I must tell you, John, I want to marry your daughter.'

Gallagher spun around in the saddle.

'You what!'

'You heard. And yes, I know you've reason enough not to like me, Government man and all. But which or whether, that's what we're intending.'

'You're intending! Are you now?'

'We are, but it would be better with your blessing...'

'And if you don't have my blessing...'

'Then it will be worse for both of us, Winnie and me.'

They had halted. Gallagher turned his horse around to face Luke. 'You know, all this time I reckoned there was something between ye. But you told me there wasn't. You were lying to me.'

'I wasn't lying. When I told you that, there was nothing.'

'But from that time since, the pair of you have been going on and telling no one.'

Luke leant forward on his horse.

'Don't tell me you didn't know.'

'I'd heard stories.'

'Well, then?'

Gallagher shook his head, still angry.

'And at a time like this, with everyone dying.'

'I know, but the famine is the reason I'm here, so there couldn't have been any other time.'

He was beginning to feel he had the advantage, and decided to press it home.

'I know when I came here first, you didn't think much of me, and why should you? But we've been working together long enough, and you've had time to get to know the kind of man I am. Yes, there are hundreds here hate me. But the question is – do you? And before you say it, I reckon I know the answer to that. You might have once hated me, but you don't anymore. Now you know me, and if you know anyone better for Winnie, you can tell me. But if you don't...'

'You sure as hell think well of yourself.'

'Maybe I do, and maybe I shouldn't. But it's what your own family think. Young John. Una. Winnie for sure. But most of all it's what you think. Am I good enough for your daughter? That's the question, isn't it?'

He said nothing more. He knew Gallagher too well, and knew it was best to leave him talk and come to his own conclusions.

'But what would ye do if you were married?' Gallagher asked him. 'When all this is over, what then?'

Luke tried to hide his surprise. Gallagher was already looking to the future when he and Winnie were married. The answer was yes. Just like that.

'I'm supposed to be taking over the lease on the farm,' he said. 'We've a twenty one year lease, runs through to 1867, and my father, he wants me to take it over.'

'Forget your father. What about you? What are you really thinking?'

'I don't know,' Luke answered. 'My first plan is to get past the hunger, and then we'll see. There might be other chances outside of Mayo.'

'But where else is there?'

'God only knows. We'll see.'

'And if you leave – what about your lease then?'

'I've got a younger brother. And I know for certain he'd take it.'

'Aye,' Gallagher said. 'It might even be better that way. Before all this, I'd have advised ye to stay in Mayo, one way or the other. But now I don't know, I just don't know.'

They reached Ardnagrena and rode down through the lines of workers. The women's shifts were torn, many showing skeletal thighs. One old woman's shift was torn at the top, and through the side he could see shrivelled breasts hanging down, swinging backward and forward as she swung the pick.

That evening he wrote to his parents in Carrigard, informing them of his marriage plans. Early the next morning he rode down to Knockanure to post the letter. He thought of his letter to Danny. It was still in his coat pocket. Yes, it was the right decision not to go to England, and not just because of Danny's methods. Winnie was his future now, if not in Mayo, then in America. He posted both letters.

When he returned to Brockagh, things moved fast. In his letter to his father and mother, he had not mentioned anything about their attending, knowing how difficult it would be for them to come at such a time. He asked his mother to have the banns read from the church in Kilduff though, and waited for a response.

As soon as Mrs. Gallagher heard of Luke's proposal, she had Father Nugent read the banns from the altar in Brockagh, asking if any man knew a reason that Luke Ryan and Winifred Gallagher should not be wed. Luke was concerned about this. Again he wondered how wise it would be to celebrate a wedding in the middle of a famine. But Mrs. Gallagher insisted. No objections were heard in Brockagh Parish.

In the meantime, she had found a small cottage in the village whose owner had emigrated to Canada. She negotiated a small rent with the man's parents, who maintained their right to the cottage. She and Winnie scrubbed it from top to bottom, and lit a fire to warm it and dry out the damp.

When Luke received news from Carrigard and Kilduff, it arrived from a most unexpected source.

He was riding between Lisnadee and Ardnagrena when he saw McKinnon coming towards him.

'This is a surprise,' Luke said. 'I hadn't been expecting you.'

'I hadn't been expecting to be here myself,' McKinnon replied.

'Morton wants more inspections, I suppose.'

'Well, yes and no. That's my excuse anyhow, but it's not the real reason I'm here. It's about the banns.'

Luke froze in the saddle.

'Surely…'

'There's been an objection.'

He stared at McKinnon, unbelieving. He should have known. Seeking happiness in the middle of the horror, it was wrong, it always had been wrong.

'Who…?' he asked

'Fergus Brennan.'

'Fergus!'

It had started to rain. McKinnon dismounted, Luke following. They both sat hunched on the stone wall beside them, their coats pulled over their heads.

'Yes, Fergus,' McKinnon said. 'It seems that he's got your spiritual welfare at heart, the bastard. Your mother tried to get Father Reilly to read the banns, but Flynn insisted on reading them. Made sure to read them at every Mass too. But Fergus was the real problem. As soon as he heard, he started asking around Kilduff and up the Mountain. He spoke to as many of your mother's people as he could find. The Kellys. And the Brennans.'

'The Brennans?' Luke echoed.

'That was your grandmother's name.'

'Yes, I know.'

'Anyhow, it'd appear one of them – Una Brennan – married a fellow called John Gallagher from Brockagh.'

'Una! Una was a Brennan!'

'She was. And Fergus knew that.'

'But how in hell could Fergus have known about her?'

'Because she was a cousin of his mother's. And she was your mother's cousin too.'

'But that's impossible,' Luke said. 'I'd have known of her.'

'Why would you? She left the Mountain when she was only a child. She was brought up by an aunt of hers in Foxford.'

'But Mother never said a word about her.'

'She wouldn't remember. She was only a baby. And Una wasn't much older.'

Luke stared at him open-eyed.

'But Winnie. She's a cousin of mine, then?'

'Seems she is. A second cousin.'

McKinnon offered to accompany him back to Gallaghers, knowing how difficult it would be to explain everything, but Luke refused.

What he found most unbelievable was that Fergus had gone to all this trouble on a hunch. But for a man who wanted vengeance, it was a hunch worth checking, and it had turned out to be true.

So before he returned to Gallaghers, he questioned McKinnon about everything. Mrs. Gallagher had never mentioned anything to him about having relatives near Kilduff, but like McKinnon had said, this was not surprising if she had left the Mountain so many years before. Like Sorcha, she would not have kept contact after her parents died. Did she even know?

When he was sure of his facts, he left McKinnon, and rode back to Gallaghers.

He said nothing at first. He still found it almost impossible to believe what McKinnon had said, but now he knew it had to be true.

Over dinner he questioned Mrs. Gallagher. It was as McKinnon had said. Her maiden name was Brennan, and she had come from the Mountain. Her aunt, who she had always regarded as her true mother, had told her, but she had never thought it important. But she remembered now.

He asked her where. *Baile a' Cnoic.*

'*Baile a' Cnoic,*' he said. 'It's only a few miles from Carrigard and Kilduff.'

'I wouldn't know,' she said. 'It's all such a long time ago. I was only three when I left.'

'Maybe you knew the Brennans so?' Winnie said.

'Yes,' he said. 'I did.'

Yes, indeed I did. Kitty and Fergus. He would never have to explain that now. It was time to tell the rest of the story though, he could avoid it no longer.

'In fact, you know what, my mother was a Brennan. She came from *Baile a' Cnoic.*'

'So, your mother might be related to Ma then?' Winnie said, excited.

Luke saw Gallagher frowning in the background. Gallagher was always sharp. He knew what was coming.

'They're related sure enough,' Luke said. 'I know that for certain. Una's mother was a sister of my grandmother's.'

'Isn't that great!' Winnie said.

'No, it's not great,' he said. 'In fact it's terrible. Terrible news entirely.'

Mrs. Gallagher was staring at him now, shock spreading across her face. Now she knew too.

'You see, my love,' Luke said, 'that means that your mother and mine are first cousins, and you and me are second cousins. And that means we can't marry. The Church won't let us marry.'

There was a silence as the news sank in. Mrs. Gallagher had already come across the room, and was standing behind Winnie. Winnie's eyes opened, her lips trembling.

Gallagher asked him to tell what had happened. Mrs. Gallagher was sitting beside Winnie, hugging her into her shoulder. Luke explained it all, just as McKinnon had told him. When he finished, Gallagher said nothing.

'So that's the end,' Mrs. Gallagher said.

'It is,' Luke said.

He stayed in Gallaghers that night, but he knew it was impossible to stay longer. He could not live in the same house as Winnie. He would just have to let her mother take care of her, and he would have to go.

The next morning he paid Mrs. Gallagher for his board and lodgings. Then he slung his pack over his back, and walked down to the cottage that he had rented for himself and for Winnie. He threw himself on the bed, and stared at the rafters.

The next weeks were among the worst of his life, worse even than the end of the affair with Kitty. He was numb from the speed of it. Only a single week had passed. When he had first come to know Winnie, he reckoned he would never be able to persuade Gallagher. But Gallagher had agreed. They were to be married, and now, in a matter of days, it was all over.

Again he felt the pain of nothingness. He thought back to Kitty and all the pain and shock then. But that was different. She had been a married woman. He had deluded himself then, it could never have lasted. Now he was paying the price. Fergus had taken his revenge, and he could not blame him. If he had not been so embittered against Luke, he would not have gone to the Mountain and *Baile a' Cnoic*, and he would never have found out.

He thought of the morning in Knocklenagh during the snow, the priest telling him the meaning of God. What kind of God was this? The kind that allowed hunger and fever; let men and women and children die in pain and hunger. Yes, he had sinned with Kitty, and he had to suffer for it. He thought of the bruises on Kitty's face the last time he had seen her. She was suffering, she would suffer for the rest of her life. And so would he.

He had brought it all on himself. But it was not just Kitty. Winnie too, loving her, grasping for happiness when people were suffering and dying around him. That was wrong. It could never have lasted either.

The day after he left Gallagher's, he bought a bottle of *poitín* in the village. He started to drink, and by midnight it was gone. The next day, he suffered the worst hangover of his life. He lay in his bed all day, brooding.

What was left for him now? First Kitty, now Winnie. No woman to stand by him, no future, no hope. Yes, he could still take the farm. Michael was tough, but could he protect him against those who hated him. Luke Ryan, the man who brought Sorcha to the Workhouse, the man who refused so many the Works ticket that was their only chance of life.

What now? England?

Yes, and admit to Danny that he had been wrong. And the other men? Would they know stories from home? They surely would.

America then?

Yes, and all alone. No woman, no family, no friends.

America?

He went to the priest's house.

'I need confession.'

He knelt.

'There's no need to kneel. Sit up here at the table.'

The full story came out – Kitty, his father, Fergus, a long tale of pain that had once been joy. He told too of sinning with Winnie, but the priest dismissed that with a wave of his hand. At the end, they prayed. Five decades of the Rosary, something he had not done for many years.

Then he was absolved.

Chapter Nineteen

Liverpool Mail, January 1847:
The immense influx of Irish paupers into Liverpool, chiefly women and children, and the deplorable exhibition daily witnessed in front of the parish offices in Fenwick Street have excited very general disgust and alarm. The inhabitants of Liverpool, much as they had seen of Irish degradation in the close and crowded courts and cellars which are the resort of immigrants from the sister country, and much as they had heard of the destitution caused by the failure of the potato crop, had, comparatively, no previous knowledge of the lost state of the Irish peasantry, until the sickening and heart-rending spectacles had been presented to their view.

Danny had other matters on his mind, and food was not one of them.

Luke's refusal to join him had disappointed him at first, but the more he thought about it, the less important it seemed. If Luke had not the foresight to see the possibilities, then perhaps he was not the sort of partner that was needed in railway contracting. But that meant that he was now on his own, and he would have to rely on his own energy and capabilities, without anyone to share the workload.

The last few months had convinced him that his analysis of the situation and the opportunities were correct. Week after week, he saw the hungry Irish, thin and emaciated, desperate for work at any wage. He knew the English contractors found it difficult to deal with them. Few had the patience to wait for starving men to build up their rate of work, and fewer still had the patience with men who could not speak English. Yes, the opportunity was there, but only for a man who could bridge the divide between two cultures.

He himself was still a Mayo man in so many way. He spoke the language of the West of Ireland, and understood their way of thinking; not only from his childhood, but also from working with his own people on the railways. He was used to negotiations with Englishmen and English managers and contractors. He knew the way they thought, the way they spoke, the way that money was accounted for and profit made. He had anticipated that he would deal with the English side of the business, while Luke would help in bringing workers from Mayo. But Luke would not join him, so he would have to deal with the Mayo men in his own way, and he knew he could do it. It would involve more work, that was all.

He was thinking again about Stockport. From his previous visit he knew the names of the main contractors who were working on the line. He knew their requirements, and he knew what would be expected from any subcontractor working for them. He had already decided that he was going to revisit Stockport, but this time it would be with the set determination of negotiating a contract in any way possible. Before he left he wrote letters to banks in Manchester and Leeds.

Once again, he made his excuses to Farrelly, who was not suspicious. This time he mentioned cousins of his mother in Manchester. There were none that he knew of, but there was no reason to worry about that. He told Farrelly though that he would be gone for a longer period – a week or more perhaps. This all mystified Murtybeg even more, but again he could get no answers from Danny.

Danny walked into Leeds, and again he travelled to Sheffield and Manchester. But this time he did things different in Stockport. Rather than staying in a cheap lodging house, he found the best hotel in the centre of town. If he was going to be successful, he would have to act successful.

The next morning he left his hotel well before dawn and took a cab out of the town. Then he walked out along the Works on the Stockport & Warrington line. He had a small notebook with him. As he went, he noted all the different sections that were being worked on, the type of clay or shale or rock that was being moved, and the distance it was being moved between cuttings and embankments. Again and again he measured out distance by the simple expedient of walking and counting his steps. He had experimented many times in secret, and he knew that his own estimates were nearly as accurate as any tape measure. Sometimes he made rough sketches of the Works, sometimes he spoke to some of the navvies, enquiring into conditions on the Works. None of the foremen or gangmasters seemed to be very concerned.

That afternoon he had the luck to meet with one of the subcontractors. He pretended to be acting for a main contractor, and over the next half hour he found out the prices that were being bid in the area. They were very much as he had suspected, and he was certain that he could under-cut any other contractors on the railway.

It was late that evening when he got back to the hotel. He had walked over twenty miles, but his work was not over yet. In the light of a candle, he worked far into the night; calculating distances, tonnages, volumes, wages and costs. It was two in the morning before he slept.

He rose early again after only five hours sleep. His first task was to buy new clothes. He spared no expense. It cost him two pounds, but appearances were essential.

Then he visited the local branch of the Manchester & Salford Bank. As he had expected, cash had been transferred from his own bank in Leeds, and everything was in order.

He walked into the offices that the main contractor had rented in the town, and asked for one of the directors by name.

'And who should I say is calling, sir,' the clerk asked.

'Daniel Ryan,' he said. 'Managing Partner of Edwardes & Ryan.' Edwardes was a name he had once seen on a shop in Bristol.

'Yes sir,' the clerk said.

'That's spelt with '-es' at the end of Edwardes.'

'Yes, sir.'

A few moments later, he was ushered into the contractor's office.

'Edwardes & Ryan. Not a name I've known before,' the man said.

'No,' Danny said. 'We're not so well known in this area.'

'You've worked elsewhere then?'

'Indeed. We've handled many contracts in other parts of the country. At the moment, most are small. A year or so ago, we held a contract on the east side of the second Woodhead Tunnel, but that was minor. We've also been active near Carlisle. We've had some larger contracts on the Great Western around Box Tunnel too, though that was a few years ago.'

'Do you do tunnelling then?' the man asked.

'No, our speciality is in excavation and earthmoving. Cuttings and embankments represent most of what we do. Viaducts and tunnels we leave for the men who are professional in those areas.'

'Most sensible. As it happens, we're looking for sub-contractors in excavating, but only at sensible prices. Your speciality, you say.'

'Indeed. Both Mr. Edwardes and I have had considerable experience over the years.'

The man nodded.

'You're Irish, I would say, Mr. Ryan.'

'Yes. It is an advantage in certain ways. I handle the labour and operations. Mr. Edwardes works on the money and banking side.'

'An excellent combination. Just now, we have a small contract we are trying to let out at Gatley, about five or six miles from here.'

'The one just beyond the main line, isn't it?'

'That's right. You've seen it already?'

'I have,' Danny said. 'Mainly shale?'

'Yes, indeed. We reckon a total of ten thousand cubic yards to be moved.'

'I had reckoned on nine thousand, but that was by eye.' He said nothing for ten seconds. 'On the basis of ten thousand cubic yards and for the distance to be shifted, I would reckon a cost of two hundred and thirty pounds for labour at fivepence ha'penny the cubic yard.'

The contractor's eyebrows rose. That hit home, Danny thought, but this fellow is a professional. He won't comment on the price, he's too smart for that.

'You reckon fast, Mr. Ryan.'

'It's part of my business.'

'Of course.'

'But there would be additional for tools and moving spoil to the embankments. That would bring the full cost to no more than three hundred and seventy five pounds, all told.'

'Implements and carters at actual cost?'

'Yes. And completion would be within sixteen weeks from date of starting.'

'Sixteen weeks. That is fast.'

'It is. We are all under time pressure, and we aim to assist our customers through fast and accurate work. That way, we can handle more work, and both sides can make more profit.'

'There's just one final thing. Since we do not know your company, we may require a small performance bond.'

'Would ten per cent be sufficient for the main contract? Say thirty seven pounds?'

'That would be excellent.'

Tea had arrived. For half an hour they discussed more detailed aspects of the contract. Then Danny rose to go. The other man came around the desk to shake hands with him.

'It's always a pleasure to do business with a professional, Mr. Ryan.'

'Likewise.'

'Robert Anderson is the name. My friends call me Rob.'

'Danny so, Rob.'

Danny walked back to the Manchester & Salford Bank, arranged the bond, and left the details back to Anderson's office.

Then he wrote a letter to Farrelly, explaining that he would not be returning. He was committed now. There was no way back.

The only remaining detail was to find workers. The next day, he took a train to Liverpool.

Edwardes & Ryan was in business.

When he arrived in Liverpool, Danny found a different city to what he had known before. He saw at once that the city he had explored as a younger man had disappeared under an enormous flood of Irish immigration. He had expected this, but the extent of it still surprised him. England's second city – the world's greatest port – had become an Irish town.

He found Buckley's lodging house at the bottom of Scotland Road, but it was a busy evening, and it was impossible to get near the door.

'Two hundred's the limit,' a man beside him said. 'They won't take any more. The peelers would close them down if they did.'

'Two hundred!'

'They've them sleeping on the floor, under beds, hanging over ropes, every which way.'

He left. Two hundred! The house only had ten or twelve rooms. He walked back towards the centre of the city, and found a room more appropriate to the Managing Partner of Edwardes & Ryan.

He reconsidered his situation. It could be that the new situation in Liverpool could be turned to his advantage. Irishmen would be even more desperate for work than he had first thought. He decided to take one whole day to get to know Liverpool again.

The next morning he walked back by the bottom of Scotland Road, noting the packed tenements on either side. He walked into Buckley's, and explained his plans to Mrs. Buckley, leaving ten shillings with her as a deposit.

Then he walked back down the docks. There was still all the frantic activity that he had noted years ago; cargoes, sailors and passengers, coming and going without cease. He walked to the dock which specialised in the North American passenger trade. There seemed to be a constant flow of ships leaving – Charleston and Savannah; Philadelphia, New York and Boston; St. Johns, Quebec and Montreal. Long, long lines of humanity – groups of single men, groups of single women and large family groups with all their belongings beside them. He noticed that most of the accents were Irish.

He walked down the George's Dock, but he already knew what he would see. When he reached the dock, two ships had just arrived in, one from Waterford and one from Dublin. There were hundreds of people coming off among the cattle and pigs, many of them confused and frightened. He walked among them, questioning some about to their intentions. Some seemed to be going to America, but most had not got the fare, and intended to stay in England for some weeks or months. Many who were frightened of travelling too far intended on settling. That evening he ate on his own, considering his next move.

The following morning he was back at the George's Dock early. There was a ship in from Westport. He walked through fresh crowds of Irish, listening. He saw a group of eight or ten men and heard them speaking Irish. He recognised the accent as west Mayo.

He walked a few yards away and studied them. They were of varying ages. He guessed the youngest might have been fifteen, but most were in their twenties or thirties. One was much older, fifty or sixty, Danny guessed. If they had left families behind, they would be desperate to earn money fast to remit to Mayo.

The real problem though was the rate of work he could expect. They were far more emaciated than most on the quayside, the stark effects of hunger etched into their hollowed faces. He could see from the grime that they had not washed for many weeks. Their clothes, ragged and patched, hung loose about them, their trousers tied fast with rope. Their shoes were in tatters, though he knew they had been more expensive once, good shoes from Castlebar and Galway, sold cheap and second-hand along the west coast.

He walked across to talk to them in their own language.

'Just come in, have ye?' No one said anything. Then the older man came across to Danny.

'What's a man like you doing in English clothes?' Danny was surprised by the question, but decided to turn it to his advantage.

'We all dress like the English when we're here long enough.' He decided to raise the stakes. *'And feed like them too.'*

'We've little enough money to be feeding like Englishmen.'

'When you've enough money, you'll feed any way you want.'

One of the younger men came up to him, aggressive and angry.

'Aren't you the great fellow, mocking us because we have no money and no chance of getting it.'

'There's money enough for anyone who wants it,' Danny replied *'and I can tell ye how to get it.'*

'How's that?' one of the other men asked. *'How does a man make money so easy here that he cannot make at home?'*

'On the railways, that's how he does it. Aren't they just screaming out for men to build the railways? Anyone who can handle a shovel or use a pick, they'll pay money for that.'

'Where's that?'

'Over by Stockport.'

'Where?'

'Stockport. It's a long way from here, sixty miles or more.'

The men formed a huddle, and talked low among themselves. Danny walked away, knowing better than to press matters until they had a chance of thinking about things. At last the older man walked over to him.

'We don't know if you're here to help us or mock us, but if there's money we must follow it. God knows our families need it.'

'I know that,' Danny said.

'But this Stockport place, how can we get there? We lost two men getting

to Westport and another on the ship. We've no way of getting there. We have to go to the Workhouse first and get food inside us to give us the strength to walk.'

'There's no need to do that,' Danny said. 'If you're willing to work, I can get you to Stockport on the train. And if it's food you're looking for, I know where a man can eat.'

'And where would the money for all this come from?'

'You needn't worry about that. If you want to work with me, I'll pay for everything. And I'll pay you working on the railway too. There will be no need to go without food there either. I want strong men, and it's for me to give you the strength to work.'

The old man looked at him, still suspicious.

'So how much will you pay us?'

'Tenpence a day,' Danny said, 'and your food and lodgings with it. And more when you've the strength for it.'

The man nodded, thinking. Again Danny said nothing, waiting for him to draw his own conclusions.

'So how many do you want?' he asked at length.

'Twenty,' Danny said. 'Twenty men who are willing to work, and able to work hard when they've food inside them.'

The other man nodded. 'Twenty ye'll have so.'

He walked back to the other men. Danny was surprised by what happened next. Four of the younger men were despatched in various directions. Over the next few minutes, others came over to join them. Within a few minutes he had his first gang.

Danny would remember the next few weeks as the hardest he had ever worked. He had to deal with twenty hungry men, none of whom had ever been outside West Mayo in their lives.

He led them out and along the Docks. Their reaction to the enormous port with its incessant activity was not one of astonishment, but of fear. They clustered together, following him wherever he led. His first stop was the Public Baths. This caused confusion, but having explained the necessity of it and the procedures involved to the older man, they did what was expected of them, and shaved afterwards.

Then he brought them to a second-hand clothes dealer. There was protest now from the younger men, who wanted to know when they would be fed. 'I'd feed you at once,' Danny replied 'But I can't bring you anywhere, looking like that.'

Docile again, most changed their clothes. There were few enough who had any worth keeping. Danny paid the owner extra to have their own clothes burnt.

Back on the road, Danny had them gather around him. *'I know you're all tired and hungry now, so I'm going to bring you on to a place you can eat and rest. And then I'll give you money to send home to your families.'*

As they walked on towards Scotland Road, one of the men collapsed.

'What's wrong with him?' Danny asked.

'Fever.'

He called the old man over.

'We won't be allowed to go anywhere with him. You know that.'

'Must we wait till he dies?'

Danny thought fast. He knew the man was not in the final stages of fever, but it was clear he could not walk, and there was no question of him being allowed into Buckley's either. He turned back to the old man.

'We'll have to get him to hospital, but we can't do that unless he's standing.'

'For what reason?'

'Never mind.' Danny said.

With difficulty they got the man to stand. Then Danny stood out on the road and called a cab. He managed to get the sick man inside it, together with one of his friends. Then he pulled himself up front with the cab driver.

'What's wrong with him?' the cabby asked.

'Too much to drink, he's always at it.'

'Better not vomit in my cab.'

They continued the last few hundred yards towards Buckley's, the cab going at a walking pace, as the other men followed on the pavement.

'Can you just wait here a few minutes,' Danny said.

'I charge for waiting.'

Danny nodded. He brought the rest of the men inside. Mrs. Buckley led them into the rough dining room, where he addressed them all.

'Now I've got to take your friend to hospital, so I have to leave you here a while. Mrs. Buckley will feed you. But just remember, you haven't eaten well for many days, so eat slowly and not too much. I'll be back in an hour.'

Back outside, he joined the cab again.

'Where now?'

'The Workhouse.'

'I hope that fellow doesn't have fever.'

'Of course not.'

When they arrived at the Workhouse, he paid off the cabby. The man with fever was admitted to the fever hospital. Danny did not go in, not wanting to see it. The sick man's friend insisted on staying with him. He was concerned though that he could still join the rest when his friend died. Danny thought about that. If he stayed with his friend, he might contract fever, and that could be a problem later. He gave the man two shillings.

'*Here you are, this should get you to Stockport.*'

Then he scribbled out a non-existent address on a scrap of paper, and left him with his dying friend.

When he returned to Buckley's, the men had finished their breakfast – sausage, corn and cabbage, as much as Mrs. Buckley would allow them. Some of them were doubled over.

'I tried to stop them taking too much, but I couldn't,' Mrs. Buckley said.

'I know.'

Now he examined them all. There were no further signs of typhus, but he could see many were very weak. He told them they would all have a day and night to rest, while he arranged for money to be sent back to Mayo. Then he had a long discussion with the old man.

'*How do they call you?*'

'*Seán Donn O'Bhriain.*'

'*You can handle men it seems.*'

'*They respect the old in Baile Chruaich.*'

Danny decided to appoint him as a ganger, and, on his advice, a younger man as a second ganger. Then he wrote down all their names for the first roll call. Eighteen left.

He took his two new gangers down to the Post Office, warning the other men not to move. He organised four different postal orders, writing four letters to different addresses in Erris, explaining how the postal orders could be cashed, together with details of the families they were destined for.

That night he left the men in Buckley's sleeping on the floor and on ropes, while he again slept in the hotel. Next morning, he brought them to Lime Street and settled them all into a third class carriage. As soon as he did, a few English labourers who were already there got up, and left that carriage for the next. Danny himself travelled first class to Manchester. It was raining when they arrived.

He rented a cab for the weakest men. He himself travelled outside with the cabby, leading the men at a slow walking pace towards Stockport.

When they arrived at the cutting, he negotiated a cheap rent at some of the shacks nearby. Then he left them, and walked to a nearby boarding house where he fell into a deep sleep, and slept until dawn.

Next morning, Danny penned a quick note to Murtybeg in Leeds. Then he made his way back up to the shacks. His first shock was to discover that one of the weakest men had fever. He left him in the shack while he brought the others out along the line. That day he had to borrow picks and shovels from some of the other gangs. He explained his requirements to the two gangers, and watched as the work began. It was even slower than he had expected.

He took a cart back to the shack. He loaded the feverish man onto the cart, and brought him to the fever hospital in Stockport Workhouse. From there he went into the hardware store and bought all his requirements.

He went back to the Works. Seventeen left. He addressed them all.

'*You'll have to work faster than this. I'll be paying you tenpence a day, but at this rate, you're not worth it.*'

He called the two gangers to one side.

'*It will take time to work so fast,*' Seán Donn said.

'*I know that,*' Danny said, '*and I know it well. But I'm paying you fellows more so as to bring the work up to what we need. We'll feed them well over the next few days, and see how things turn out.*'

He had negotiated part payments with Anderson, but he did not dare to go to him until a reasonable amount of work had been completed, and a good work rate had been built up.

The next few weeks passed in hectic activity. One evening Danny was still working on accounts late in the evening. The landlady came up to his room.

'You'll kill yourself doing that, Mr. Ryan.'

'I've no choice.'

'Perhaps you need another assistant.'

He stopped, holding his pen up from the paper. 'And where do you think I'd find an assistant?' he asked, intrigued.

'There's a niece of mine working with a solicitor in Manchester. Her parents are only a half a mile from here. She'd rather be back working close to her family.'

A week later, Murtybeg arrived. He asked his way out along the cuttings and embankments until he found where Danny was working. As he walked, he was startled to see the gaunt appearance of the workmen and their sluggish pace.

Danny was standing at the end of the cutting, a notebook in his hand. He looked up in surprise. 'Well, by God,' he said, 'so you've arrived. You took long enough coming.'

'What did you expect?' Murtybeg said. 'You don't think I could walk out on the gang just like that.'

'Maybe not. But come on, anyhow. I'll show you the Works.'

Murtybeg followed him. They walked through a cutting.

'You're not paying them four shillings a day here,' Murtybeg said.

'No way. Ten pence more like it. A shilling if they're lucky.'

'They'll work for that!'

'What choice do they have? And anyhow, we feed them too. From all we hear they'd be dead of starvation if they'd stayed in Mayo.'

'Mayo! They're from Mayo?'

'Where else? But don't worry, Murteen, we're not taking the fellows from around Kilduff. Only from the sea coast. That's where they're really dying. Fever's the big killer.'

Murtybeg shook his head.

A few days later, Danny despatched him to Liverpool. He explained how to find the men. This might bring him beyond two gangs, but it would help in finalising the first part of the contract so he could claim his part payment. In addition, he knew he would soon start losing men to other gangs, or else have to pay them more. The new workers would help to keep wages down.

When Murtybeg arrived in Liverpool, he went straight to Buckley's, and spent the night with twenty men in a room, sleeping with his back to a wall. Early the following morning, he gulped down a bowl of hot porridge, and walked down towards the Docks. It was early in the day, and he reckoned he would have enough time to find men later in the morning. For now, he wanted to see Liverpool Port, see where the Irish were coming and going, and understand a city he knew he would see many times again. He walked north around the docks. Close up it was overwhelming. He could see dozens of ships, many more riding at anchor, waiting to come in. Cranes, funnels and masts. Flags of countries he had never seen. Chests of coffee and tea. Sacks of cane sugar. Thousands of tons of timber, some planed almost white, some dark and some almost black. Cattle, pigs and sheep. And cotton, hundreds of bales of it, whole warehouses of it.

Then, there were the girls. He could tell the difference between the accents of Liverpool, Wales and Scotland. But most were Irish. A young boy approached him, eyes down. Murtybeg reckoned he couldn't have been ten. 'Hey mister, I've got what you're looking for. My sister, very clean. Thruppence only, whole night. Best deal in Liverpool.'

Murtybeg turned on him in fury. 'Get lost, you little bastard.'

'Sorry mister, I was only trying to help.'

He went on, dodging between dockers and carts, threading his way between cargos being loaded and unloaded. Docks, more docks and docks within docks. Princes Dock, Trafalgar Dock and Clarence Dock. And then all the way back south again – the Canning Dock with the old dock of Liverpool inside it. The Albert Dock, the Duke's Dock, the King's, the Queen's, the Coburg, the Brunswick and the Toxteth.

He walked back to the George's Dock. As Danny had advised him, he made his way through lines of ragged Irish families, listening for groups of men speaking in Irish, listening to their accents, always listening. In a short time, he had six more Mayo men for Danny.

He led them north along Waterloo Road, east at Waterloo Dock and so to Scotland Road and into Buckley's.

The next morning he brought them down to the dirty dining room. He was surprised to hear his name called from the other side of the room. 'Murteen!'

He spun around. 'Mikey! Where the devil...'

That evening, he and Danny sat down to dinner.

'You've done well,' Danny said.

'I could have done better. We could have got twenty or fifty if you'd wanted them.'

'Give it time. There'll come a time when we might have call for them.'

'Oh, and there's something else I didn't tell you. I met a friend of yours in Buckley's.'

'Who's that?' Danny asked.

'Mikey Jordan.'

'Mikey! What was he doing in Liverpool. Going back to Mayo, was he?'

'Mayo? No way. He was heading for America.'

'America? What's he doing that for?'

'I think he got fed up of it all. Reckoned you left him in the lurch, and the money's better in America. He's going with Martin Farrelly.'

'Martin! Martin's going to America?'

'That's right. Mikey says Martin was mad at you.'

'I'm sure he was.'

'Says you ran off on them all.'

'Yes,' Danny said. 'I'm sure he'd think that. But if Martin's gone, who's running the gangs?'

'Bernie Lavan – he took over after you left. John Roughneen too.'

Danny shook his head. 'So Martin's gone to America. By God, I'd never have thought that would happen.'

'Neither did anyone else.'

'So damned fast too, and the pair of them not saying a word to any of us.'

'He's a deep fellow, Martin is.'

Danny turned back to his dinner. 'I wanted to talk to you about that cutting,' he said between mouthfuls.

'Forget that for a moment,' Murtybeg said. 'I've other news for you too. Jimmy Corrigan's in Liverpool.'

Danny took the fork from his mouth. 'He's what?'

'In Liverpool. Mikey met up with him only the day before he was talking to me.'

'But where...'

'Outside Buckley's. He wasn't staying there though, but it seems wherever he's living, it's not far.'

The news that Jimmy Corrigan was in Liverpool galvanised Danny. The next time Murtybeg was to go to Liverpool, he decided to accompany him.

When they arrived in Lime Street station, Danny stood before the train had even stopped. He brought down both packs, slung one over his shoulder, and threw the second to Murtybeg.

'Come on, time to go.'

Murtybeg followed.

'Where are we staying tonight? Buckley's?'

'Don't be silly. That's the last place I'd dream of staying.'

Murtybeg followed his brother across from the station into the foyer of a hotel close by. He grabbed Danny by the arm.

'Hey, hold on. Isn't this a bit beyond...'

Danny turned around, took his younger brother by the shoulders, and stared straight into his eyes.

'Now let's get this straight, for once and for all. Nothing is beyond us. Nothing. Do you understand?'

'Yes,' Murtybeg said.

Danny went over to the reception and booked a double room with single beds. Afterwards they sat in the restaurant, and Danny ordered dinner for both. Murtybeg stared at the chandeliers around him. Copying Danny, he unfolded the white linen napkin and spread it across his knees. As soon as the soup course had arrived, Danny took a spoonful. Then he leant across the table, gesturing with the spoon. 'Right, Murteen, here's our plan.'

The next morning they walked across the centre of Liverpool to Scotland Road. They stopped at a corner about fifty yards away from the boarding house.

'That's Buckley's over there,' Danny said.

'I know.'

'It looks quiet enough.'

'It should be, this time of the morning.'

'If you're lucky, everyone is out. Now go on.'

Murtybeg walked across the road, dodging carts and carriages ,and disappeared into the boarding house. Danny stood at the corner, watching. After a few minutes, Murtybeg came out again, forcing himself to walk rather than run.

'Well?' Danny said. 'How did you do?'

'Not a hope,' Murtybeg said. 'I asked the landlady. She asked four of the girls in the kitchens and two of the girls cleaning. Three fellows over their breakfast too. No one knew of Jimmy Corrigan.'

'Maybe they didn't want to know of him.'

'Maybe. But one way or another, they're not talking.'

'Damn,' Danny said.

'But I do have this,' Murtybeg said. He handed a sheet of paper to Danny.

'What's this?'

'A list of just about every boarding house along Scotland Road.'

'My God, there must be twenty. How did you get this?'

'I told them Jimmy was my long lost brother. The mammy said I couldn't go home to Mayo without him.'

'You know,' Danny said, 'there's times I think you're smarter than you let on.'

But it did not work. All that morning, afternoon and night, they followed the leads through boarding houses, bars, tenements and even two Workhouses. Every lead came to a dead end. They returned to their hotel. Once again, Murtybeg spread his white linen napkin across his knees.

'Maybe he's gone to America.'

'Maybe he has,' Danny replied. 'But there again, maybe he's not. No, I reckon Jimmy Corrigan is in this city, and someday I reckon we'll find him.'

Next day, when Danny returned from the Works, a young woman was waiting for him in the dining-room. She rose as he walked in.

'Irene Miller, Mr. Ryan,' she said, extending her hand. 'I understand you need an assistant.'

Chapter Twenty

Telegraph or Connaught Ranger, January 1847:
On Thursday a poor woman traversed our streets carrying a dead child in her arms, begging alms to enable her to buy a coffin wherein to bury her poor offspring, cut off by starvation.

Over the next few weeks, Luke threw himself into his work. It was a depressing time. Now he had all four Works running close to what they should have been. Nearly four hundred men, women and children working. Pain all around him and pain within him. But he tried to concentrate on his duties – filling in the wage sheets, paying out miserable wages to thin men and women, accompanying the priest around the mountains, paying more wages to the dead and dying.

At one cabin, they knocked on the door and waited, but there was no answer. Even through the door there was an overpowering smell, not of gangrene, but worse. Luke pushed the door open. On the bed, there was the decomposing corpse of a woman. Her face – cheeks, eyes and nose – had been eaten by rats. Three of them scurried away as he and the priest entered. The skull stared at the roof from empty sockets, the lips picked clean from the teeth. The last rites were administered from a distance. The two men looked at one another.

'We'll have to bury her,' the priest said.

They gripped the corpse by the wrists and ankles, and carried it out to the bog twenty yards from the cabin. Luke had noticed a *sleán* by the wall inside the cabin. He walked back, and brought it out. They dug a hole through soft slushy turf and moss, passing the *sleán* back and forward between them, black water seeping back in as they dug. They took off their boots, and dug on, sloshing through the mud. When they thought it was deep enough – less than two feet, Luke reckoned – they threw the corpse into it with a splash. They covered it in again, and washed their hands in a shallow bog-hole beside them. Then Luke tied on his boots, looking back to the rough grave. There was nothing showing, but the brown, black and green of the turf and moss.

They left.

'There's something I want to tell you,' the priest said. 'I've been arguing with myself, wondering if I should, or should I wait.'

'More bad news?'

'I don't know. It might be good news. In fact it might be very good news indeed.'

Luke looked at him in surprise. 'Good news?' he echoed.

'Maybe, though I don't know yet. I never told you, an old friend of mine at Maynooth, Eddie McQuillan, I wrote him a letter. He stayed on at the college after we all left, he's some sort of theologian now. He reckons it's a better sort of life than being a parish priest, from all I hear. But I wrote and told him about you and Winnie, and asked him his view about it. There was something I couldn't bring to mind about consanguinity and all that, so I asked him about it. I got a letter back from him yesterday, it took a few weeks in the coming. It seems there might be a way around it all.'

'There might?'

'We'll have to ask for an Episcopal Dispensation.'

'A what?'

'An Episcopal Dispensation. If you're only a second cousin of Winnie's, the bishop can let you marry. He's the only one can do it.'

Luke stared at him, unable to speak.

'Go on,' he said at last, 'go on, go on.'

'I've already written to the bishop in Achonry, and now I'm waiting to hear back. It could be a while though.'

'And what if he refuses?'

'If he refuses, just move to another diocese. Ask another bishop, and get married there.'

They had come to the next house, the familiar stink of typhus and gangrene. The priest put his hands on Luke's shoulder.

'Just one thing. Don't tell Winnie yet. We wouldn't want to raise her hopes.'

'No, Father,' Luke said.

He spent the next week in feverish activity, alternating between hope, impatience and fear.

He rode between Ardnagrena, Benstreeva, Burrenabawn and Lisnadee, and up across the mud villages higher up the mountains, looking for new workers and searching out people to pay. He knew Winnie, and he knew the thought of her was the only thing that would keep him going. He tried to put it out of his mind, not daring to hope.

At Mass the next Sunday, the Gallaghers were at the top of the church, only a few yards away. He stared at the back of Winnie's head, unable to concentrate on anything else. He made his way out at the end of the Mass, not wishing to be seen by them. He walked back to the cottage, trying to put her out of his mind. He started to prepare corn for breakfast. There was a knock on the door. The priest was outside, holding a letter with the insignia of the Diocese of Achonry.

The two men walked up to Gallaghers, and the priest explained everything that had happened. Gallagher was the only one who responded, questioning the priest about the dispensation. Winnie hugged her mother, tears in her eyes. Then she threw her arms around Luke.

'I knew it. I knew it. I knew you'd never leave me.'

Early one morning, she came to him. He grasped her, and kissed her. Then he led her to the bed. They made love with an urgency that he had never known, an urgency that came from pain and loss and sudden salvation. Afterwards they lay on the old bed, gasping.

'Does anyone know you're here?' he asked.

'Maybe.'

'Like who?'

'Ma. She sent me to McIlhenny's to buy corn, but I think she knew I wouldn't be back any time soon.'

Then he told her about Kitty. She had known of this, ever since he had alluded to it the day he had come back to Brockagh after the snows. Since then though, she had never dared to ask more. Perhaps, she reflected, she did not want to know. But she knew now that he wanted to tell her, and she would have to know. And she listened as he told her about the brief affair and the long heartbreak that followed. He told her too how Fergus had taken his revenge, and come close to breaking his heart again. And hers.

She had said nothing.

'Maybe I shouldn't have told you all that,' he said.

'No, it's not that. I want to know all about you, and isn't she part of you? Oh, Luke.' She hugged him. 'Having your heart broken like that. And her too. No life left for her, her husband beating her and her only love off to America.'

'If we go. I never said we would.'

She released him, and lay back on the bed.

'That's true,' she said. 'But it's what you want, isn't it?'

'Maybe it is.'

'Well then?'

'If we go, we make do with it.'

'But I keep thinking, what kind of place is it? It frightens me.'

'*Arra*, don't be worrying about it,' he said. 'Lots of the lads from around

Kilduff have gone, and from all we hear, they're having a great time.'

'But I've been hearing other stories. They say it's hard enough crossing the ocean, but to get there, and to find they hate you. That's what I've been hearing. How different is that from here?'

'Will you not be listening to nonsense like that. Sure, it's hard at the start, but there's work aplenty.'

'But what kind of work?'

'Railways, and isn't that what I'm used to? They're building railways every which way they can. They say there's more work on American railways than in England. God knows, it's a huge country. And if it's not the railways it'll be something else – working the harvests, loading boats, out cutting trees in the forest. Isn't that it?'

'It is, and it isn't. There's people starving in the towns. Families pushed into a room, dying of fever.'

'But sure that's no different to anywhere. Didn't I see enough of that in England? Liverpool, Manchester and the rest of them. But that's not for the likes of us. There's work enough for any fellow strong enough to take it, and money enough to pay him. No, it isn't places like that we'd be staying. The railways, that's the thing. I'm sure of it.'

'Maybe you're right' she said.

'I am right. Now you just let me do the worrying, and you believe what I'm telling you.'

Time was passing. They dressed, and Winnie walked over towards McIlhenny's. After a few minutes, Luke rode up to Gallaghers, and he and John Gallagher rode on to Ardnagrena, passing silent people walking towards the Works. Sometimes Gallagher greeted those he knew, but no one returned his greeting, and he too sank into silence.

A few days later, Luke was going through the worksheets on the Burrenabawn Works when McKinnon arrived to continue surveying the site.

'I'm sorry how everything turned out with Winnie,' he said. 'It was a desperate business.'

'Well, there's no need to be sorry anymore. Everything is going ahead.'

'What!'

'Yes, Father Nugent here, he wrote to the bishop, and we got a dispensation from him. It seems it's something the bishops can do. So we're getting married after all.'

'The bishops...I never knew about that.'

'Neither did I.'

'Oh, but Luke, that's great news. Are you sure?'

'Certain.'

McKinnon laid his pack on the ground.

'A dispensation, eh. From the bishop too! When I was courting Sabina, the only man I had to ask was your father.'

He opened the pack and took out a tape.

'So when...?'

'Three days' time.'

'Three days?'

'Any chance you could stay over?'

McKinnon shook his head. 'Not a hope in hell. I'd love to, but I've work to do. I'm headed for the Union. Then Castlebar and on out to Bellacorick, Belmullet and Louisburgh, and then out the Killeries.'

'Sounds a lot of travel.'

'It is. Maybe you'd introduce me to your bride before I leave so. Here, take the end of this tape. God, I still can't believe it.'

'It's true,' Luke said. 'No going back this time.' He took the tape. 'Remember the first time we did this together?'

'Aye. A long time ago. Eight years, isn't it? You never thought I'd end up as your uncle?'

'I did not.'

They carried out a few more measurements. McKinnon started reeling the tape in. 'I'm sure you've plenty to do,' he said, 'but I have to tell you our friend Mr. Morton wants to see you again tomorrow.'

'God damn him to hell.'

They both rode back towards Brockagh. Dead eyes watched them, not even caring enough to hate.

When they arrived at Gallaghers, Luke dismounted and knocked on the door. Winnie answered and looked at McKinnon in surprise.

'It's alright,' Luke said, 'we're not coming in. I just wanted you to meet my uncle.'

McKinnon held out a hand. 'Ian McKinnon. I'm honoured to meet you.'

Winnie, recovering her composure, smiled at him. 'So this is the great Ian McKinnon,' she said. 'Luke has told me all about you.'

'Some of it good, I hope.'

Mrs. Gallagher had appeared at the door, curious.

'This is Luke's uncle, Ma.'

'Luke's uncle! Come on in out of that, would ye.'

McKinnon shook his head. 'I'll not bother ye. Luke said I was to meet his bride, that was all. I'll be on my way now.'

'Indeed you will not. You'll come on in, and that's all about it.'

McKinnon followed her into the kitchen, as Winnie produced the *poitín*.

The younger boys stared at McKinnon, just as curious as their mother. He had taken everything in at once. The house, better than most in Brockagh, and the family, better fed than most too.

'Luke told me the news. I still can't believe it.'

'Aye,' Mrs. Gallagher said, 'we couldn't believe it either. And poor Winnie here, she near passed out.'

'Enough of that out of you, Ma,' Winnie said.

McKinnon sipped the *poitín*. 'How is it with ye here?' he asked. 'How are you doing through all this?'

'Alright,' Mrs. Gallagher replied. 'Though God knows it was looking awful bad after the summer. We didn't know what was going to happen, until Luke arrived with the Works. So at least we've got money, though it doesn't go as far as it did.'

'No?'

'No,' Mrs. Gallagher, said. 'Not with the merchants around here. They know how much we need the corn, and by God, they're determined to get every last penny out of us. Damned bastards!'

Winnie looked at her mother in surprise. She decided to change the subject.

'We hear you're from Scotland,' she said. 'What decided you to come over here?'

'Oh, it wasn't me decided,' McKinnon replied. 'I was working for the Ordnance Survey up the north of Scotland. They told me they needed me more in Ireland, so there wasn't much deciding in it. It was that or nothing. But it was only supposed to be for a year. I'd be well back in Scotland by now, if it wasn't for meeting up with Luke and his aunt.'

'Leave me out of it,' Luke said, laughing. 'It was Sabina, that's who kept you here.'

Mrs. Gallagher fed them with corn and cabbage.

'So you've you been working on the Survey ever since?' she asked.

'No,' McKinnon said, 'that all finished in '39. I've done the odd bit of work surveying for the County Council in Castlebar, and sometimes for the Unions. So when they started on the Relief, they asked me back to work at surveying again. It's the longest time I've had at surveying since '39.'

'Hard work I'd say,' Winnie said.

'Hard enough,' McKinnon said, 'but it's much worse now with this bloody piecework. You know, I started back on surveying to help out with the Relief, but by God, I never thought it'd end like this. The people in Castlebar won't have a penny out of place. We were paying out little enough, but now it's even less, and the people on the Works, they're all blaming it on me. I know how they feel, I can't blame them, it's no way to treat people. It's fine for those fellows back in their offices, but it's us here that have to measure it all out and give them the few pennies that Castlebar will let them have.'

'Don't we know it,' Mrs. Gallagher said. 'My John, he thought the same as yourself, that he'd be helping out by helping Luke here. Now no one will talk to him, his friends pass him in the street without as much as a nod.'

Luke held up his hand. 'Now hold on there. We didn't bring Ian in to be talking about piecework.'

'God, no,' McKinnon said. 'I came in to see Luke's bride, and here we are, talking like this.' He walked to where Winnie was sitting.

'Now let's have a closer look,' he said. 'Let's see those teeth. Close your mouth, girl, and open your lips.'

'Indeed I will not.'

'But how can I tell the condition of you if I can't examine your teeth? Have you seen her fetlocks Luke?'

Luke laughed. 'Not too close. She wouldn't let me do that.'

'Are ye no good at all? Surely you've given her a run around the yard, see what the chest is like.'

'I wouldn't worry,' Luke said. 'Her condition is fine.'

Winnie stood up, and gave him a sharp slap on the ear. 'If ye're both quite finished...'

'She's spirited anyhow,' McKinnon said.

'She is that,' Luke said.

'You'll be staying for the wedding,' Mrs. Gallagher asked.

'I wish to God I could,' McKinnon replied, 'but I'm afraid I have to go down to the Union in Knockanure, and I'm taking Luke with me. He's to make a report to the Committee tomorrow, and after that I'm heading off to the West of the county. So I can't come, but I'll make sure Luke is back in time, don't worry about that.'

'You'll stay tonight though?'

'Of course you will,' Winnie said.

He relented. A few hours later, Gallagher arrived back. They spoke far into the night. First the wedding, then famine and fever. It was impossible to get away from it.

Next morning, Mrs. Gallagher served them corn and cabbage again. Winnie was morose, disturbed by the previous night's discussion.

'Do you think it's right,' she asked. 'Do you think we should be getting married at a time like this when there's people dying.'

'I'll tell you this,' McKinnon answered, 'as long as people like you can keep your spirits up, and marry at a time like this, then there's hope for this country yet.'

'And amen to that,' Mrs. Gallagher said.

McKinnon raised his mug.

'So here's to the pair of ye. Long life and happiness.'

'Long life and happiness,' Mrs. Gallagher repeated.

They were riding back in the direction of Knockanure.

'You'll do well with her,' McKinnon said. 'Very well.'

'I know.'

'If she stands by you now, she'll do it forever.'

They rode on through lines of workers on the Ardnagrena Works. A boy's body lay on the grass beside the road, but they did not stop to ask about it.

'You've been doing a lot of travelling?' Luke asked.

'Far too much.'

'What's the rest of Mayo like?'

McKinnon let the reins go slack, allowing his horse to eat the grass on the verge. 'In one word – savage. I heard all that you told Pat about Lisnadee and the mountains. You won't believe it, but I think Erris is worse.'

Luke leant back as his own horse started to graze the verge. 'Nothing could be worse.'

'Do you know,' McKinnon said, 'there are people out Erris who don't even exist. They don't rent any land, they don't even have cabins to live in. They just dig in under the hags of turf and cover it up with a few branches.'

'What do they live on?'

'Potatoes. When there are any.'

'But what about the landlord?'

'No one knows who owns the half of it. The land is so miserable, nobody even claims it. And with the rates as high as they are, I don't think anyone ever will. There's thousands of them out there, dying like flies. Fever and outright starvation.'

'What about Relief Works?'

'Who'd pay for them? It's like I said, there's no ratepayers. No money. No one to apply for help. No, there's no Relief in Erris, no question of it.'

Luke whipped his horse with his reins, and they rode on again.

'Surely it's not like that all over?'

'That's what it's like right along the west of the county,' McKinnon replied. 'Bogs and mountains and the wind straight off the ocean. A desperate place. Achill is the same, but there's strange things happening there.'

'Like what?'

'The Mission. Nangle's Mission. They're well able to get food. Their friends in England, they send it over through Westport. So his people have enough to eat.'

'His people?' Luke asked.

'The ones who are working on the Mission, and the ones who've converted. They're the only ones Nangle is feeding. Some would say you can't blame him, he feeds his own first. Still, I'm not sure he's right in what he's doing. The rest of Achill, it's as bad as Erris. But the people know that if they join the Mission, they'll be fed. They're saying you have to convert first, become a Protestant before they'll feed you. It's the wrong way to do things, but Nangle and his fellows, they can't see that. Damned fools.'

'Isn't it what you'd expect, though?'

'No,' McKinnon responded angrily, 'it's not what I'd expect. The Quakers, they don't do it that way. They'll feed a man because he needs food, not because he's one of theirs.'

'I never heard about Quakers feeding people,' Luke said.

'You mightn't have heard about it yet, but by God, you will. Those fellows, they're shaming everyone. And that includes the Government. Damn it, if the Quakers can feed people direct, why can't Dublin Castle do it? They've been talking about it for months. That's all they ever do – talk, talk, talk.'

Chapter Twenty One

Telegraph or Connaught Ranger, January 1847:
I did go down, and such a deplorable sight I never witnessed.
He was lying upon a pallet of straw, and the poor wife beside
him, with her thigh bone out of joint, and her leg much swollen. The man's face was fearful to look at, the rats having
disfigured it much during the night.

Sarah's father was dead, and the Workhouse had no Master. The last days of
her father's life had been horrifying. She was well used to the black fever in
the sheds, but to see it in her own father had been beyond bearing.

Sarah's mother carried on as Matron. She told Sarah that the patients
in the fever sheds needed her, and she could not abandon them. She insisted
that she was alright, that she could cope. Sarah knew different. Often in
the bedroom they now shared, she would hear her mother sobbing. She
was afraid for her too. Watching her in the sheds every day, she thought she
would surely be infected as well, and the thought terrified her.

Her father was buried in the graveyard in the church in Knockanure,
but the inmates were not so fortunate. They were buried in the mass grave
behind the main block. Every day, more of the pit was dug, as the last part
was back-filled. She wondered where it would stop, and what would happen
when it reached the wall.

She could see the gaunt crowds at the gate, calling for admission, the
women holding up famished babies. Even though she had no official position
in the Union, she worked through the day on administration and accounts.
But she also spent time in the refectory and in the dormitories, helping out
and always observing. She went into the fever sheds against her mother's
objections, mopping the faces of those raving with typhus, cleaning out the
foul straw, bringing in fresh and talking to those still able to talk.

As she dressed, she thought back over the years of her childhood. There
had been hard times before, but nothing ever like this. Most years – the years
when there was little hunger – she had accepted the Workhouses as normal.
As a child, she had known no different. To her, Asylums or Workhouses had
always been her home.

Her parents had first worked in the new Asylums in the 1830s. There was the huge Lunatic Asylum in Dublin with its thousands of inmates, that was where she had her first memories. Then there was the new Clonmel Lunatic Asylum for South Tipperary. Her father had been assistant to the Superintendent, and her mother assistant to the Matron. Here she wandered through the grounds of the Asylum at will. Reflecting back now, she found this almost impossible to believe. Her own friends were frightened of the inmates – terrified even. They called them loonies and told her they did all sorts of terrible things. She wondered why she had seen none of these terrible things.

There was old Paddy, a patient, who worked as their unpaid gardener in the little house behind the Asylum. He was a small man, hardly her own height. He always had stories to tell her. And there was Eileen, another patient, who worked in the kitchen in their house. She never spoke, not once that Sarah could remember. She shuffled around the kitchen, and when she was finished, she shuffled back to the women's ward.

The Asylum had been built beside the Workhouse – the South Tipperary Union. It was here that her father had transferred to the Poor Law. He became Master of the Workhouse, but they did not have to move house, and Sarah was not even aware of her father's rise in the world.

Later they moved to County Cork. Dunmanway Workhouse was different. There was no Asylum there. Her father was Master of the Workhouse again, and her mother was promoted to Matron. It was far smaller than Clonmel though, and the area around was poorer. Even in the good years, she saw more hunger; more emaciated men and women. They never had enough potatoes to last the full year. In the month before the harvest, the numbers in the Workhouse doubled, and sometimes doubled again, emptying just as quickly as the time for digging arrived.

Her mother was from Mayo though, and when Sarah's aunt in Westport had written to tell them of vacancies in the Workhouse in Knockanure, they had applied at once. At first Knockanure had been no different to Dunmanway. The blight on the potatoes in 1845 had changed all that, and by the middle of 1846 the Workhouse was full. They had waited for the new crop when the inmates would be able to go back to their homes again. Then the rumours started coming in from the surrounding countryside, unbelievable at first, but confirmed every day, as more and more desperate people arrived at the Workhouse, until it was full far beyond its capacity, and her father was turning hungry people away. Outside the Workhouse, she had seen the gangs on the Famine Relief Works. She knew that there were thousands of them – tens of thousands according to some. Now, even with all the extra inmates, the Workhouse was unnaturally quiet.

Her parents had been working without a break, and she had helped her father in the office, transcribing letters for him. He wrote to the Poor Law

Guardians, begging for more money, more Indian meal, more provisions of any kind. He wrote to Lord Clanowen, Lord Lucan and the Marquis of Sligo; he wrote to Sir Roger Palmer, and on one occasion to the Viceroy. He begged for permission to operate Outdoor Relief and feed the people directly, without working. He had been doing this with Voisey at the end of 1846, against all the regulations. Dublin Castle would have to allow Outdoor Relief in the West, but Sarah thought it would have little effect in Knockanure. If they hadn't enough meal to feed the Workhouse inmates, how could they feed the entire countryside?

Now her father was dead. Apart from the horror and heartbreak, this had stunned her further, since he did not work in the fever sheds. Her mother had been much more likely to catch the fever, even Sarah herself had been in greater danger. But it was her father who had died. Now the Workhouse had no Master, and her mother spent many anxious hours in her father's office trying to understand everything, but her year or two of schooling had given her very little ability with numbers.

When Sarah was dressed, she ate a little meal for breakfast, and went across to the administration building. Pat was there already.

'I'm terribly sorry,' he said. 'I've only just heard.'

'It's kind of you to say so. It was a terrible shock to my mother.'

'I'm sure it was. But what about you?'

'I'll be fine.' Her voice was crisp, cutting off further discussion – or pity. She glanced at the papers, scattered all across the desk. 'Working early, I see.'

'I have to,' Pat replied. 'Things have been getting a little beyond us since your father got sick and old Donegan died. It'll take me a few days to sort this out.'

They worked together for some hours. Then Sarah left to help her mother in the fever sheds. Some of the inmates helped too, but in the past week, three of these had become patients. Again she thought of her mother; looking at her, wondering.

When they arrived at the Union in Knockanure, McKinnon went to one of the offices, while Luke walked across to the main committee room. There were six other men waiting ahead of him. There was a clerk on the other side of the corridor.

'Papers.'

'What?'

'Your work sheets.'

'Sorry,' Luke said, and handed them over.

Just as he sat down to wait, he saw the Master's daughter passing by. She stopped.

'We've met before, haven't we?'

'We have. Luke Ryan. Just down from Brockagh. '

'Yes. I remember.'

She walked away. She stopped again, and came back .

'You'll be a while waiting. Would you like a look around?'

Luke hesitated. 'I'm not sure that I would, but I will anyhow.' There were a few hollow laughs from the other men. He followed her.

'Aren't you a brother of Pat Ryan's?' she asked.

'That's right,' he replied. 'And you're the Master's daughter?'

'You've a good memory. I was the Master's daughter. Sarah Cronin. Miss Cronin to you.'

'You were? You're not now?'

'Never mind.'

They walked past a long line of inmates snaking down the stairs to the refectory. Inside, no one was sitting. There were only two small tables, both just inside the door. One of the inmates was handing out plates, most chipped. On the floor, there were two enormous pots – one with corn, one with cabbage. As he watched, two more pots of corn and cabbage were dragged in on a low wagon, and the two men drawing it waited for the other pots to empty. A woman was stirring the cabbage with a farmyard fork.

The inmates shuffled past each of the two pots as the pot-women ladled food onto the plates. Then they shuffled in single file, pushing their plates along the shelves by the walls and eating with their fingers. Some of the younger children were barely able to reach the shelf. The line was moving at a good speed. Where it came to the end of the shelves, a woman on the second table was taking plates to a tank in the centre of the room, where they were rinsed in grey, greasy water and brought back to the start of the line. Some of the older people, who could not eat their meal in time, stood in the centre of the room, chewing as fast as they could, before returning the plates. Any plates with unfinished food were being sent back to the start of the line and given to other inmates.

'My God. What's this?'

'This is how we feed them. We tried using tables, but we couldn't feed them all.'

'And this all works?'

'It's the only way. Father started it. This way we can cook enough, and still get the pots over to the fever sheds in the afternoon.'

They walked across the lawn.

'What's going on here?' he asked. 'I just don't understand.'

'It's only the numbers of people. The Workhouse was built for five hundred.'

'And how many now?'

'Over twelve hundred the last time we counted. Now – I don't know. Pat might.'

She opened the door of the first shed. He stepped back and whipped his hand to his mouth, dry retching.

'Are you alright?'

He shook his head. 'Yes, yes. I'm fine.' He followed her inside, trying to breathe through his mouth to avoid the overwhelming stink of gangrene. On either side were fever patients at different stages of disease. All the beds had two or three patients in them, more lying on the floor between them.

A man dressed in better clothes was trying to feed one of the patients. The girl tapped him on the shoulder.

'This is Luke Ryan from Brockagh, Mr. Yardley.' The man stood.

'Edward Yardley. Originally from Staffordshire.'

'You're not supposed to be in here,' Sarah said. 'You know that.'

'I know, I know. I'm just trying to help out.'

'You're a long way from Staffordshire,' Luke said.

'Yes, yes. I'm from the Society of Friends, you see. We're trying to set up a Soup Kitchen here in Knockanure, like we have in Castlebar.'

'Where will you get the money for that?'

'Mainly from the Friends in England and Dublin. And there's some question we might get funds from the British Association. We'll see.'

The Quakers! It was just like McKinnon had said. They were the first to feed the people. He wondered when – or whether – they would come to Brockagh. Or Kilduff.

Sarah led him to the other side of the yard. He could see a heap of clay, inmates shovelling from it into a wide pit. He could smell it before he got to it. They stood at the edge.

Beneath him was a scene from hell. Bodies lay piled on top on of one another; legs, arms and heads at every angle. Parts of bodies protruded from where the inmates had already shovelled clay on top of them, the yellow of their bodies mingling with the brown of the clay. All the bodies were skeletal, many showing the advanced stages of typhus. Through the stink, he could recognise the familiar sweet stench of gangrene, mixing with the sour smell of decomposition and faeces. The heap seemed to be moving. Rats, dozens of them, gnawing at limbs, faces and eyes.

At the edge, half buried under the other bodies, he could see the corpse of a child, head and shoulders protruding. The eye sockets were open and eyeless. The head was skull-like, the skin pulled taut into the teeth and the eye-sockets. The hair on the top of the child's head had disappeared, and there was the familiar fur-like hair growing down the side of its cheeks.

The face of a fox. The face of death.

He could feel his hands shaking.

'Are you alright?' Sarah shouted.

He wiped his brow.

'Yes, I'm fine,' he said. He followed her back to the administration block.

Twenty minutes later, he was sitting with the Board of Guardians. This time it looked like the full Board. Lord Clanowen was at the top of the table. Morton and Voisey were both there, though Luke noted the Workhouse Master was absent.

'Your results are impressive as always,' Morton said.

'Yes, Mr. Morton.'

'All four Works are running very well.'

'Yes, Mr. Morton.'

'Your next duty will be to shut them down.'

'What?'

'Shut them down. All four.'

'But we can't do that?'

'It's not as bad as it sounds,' Voisey said from the other side of the table. 'We're going to replace them with Soup Kitchens. Our brethren from the Society of Friends have shown us the way in other counties, and we think we will follow. It will give the people the chance to return to their own farms and grow the little they can. God willing, we may be able to stop the fever and hunger that way.'

Morton gathered up the worksheets, and handed them back to him. 'Your responsibility will be to close all the Works around Brockagh, by Saturday fortnight at the latest. After that, you will remain in Brockagh, and be responsible for opening and supervising the Kitchens.'

'And when will the Kitchens open?'

'We will notify you of that when we consider it appropriate,' Morton said. 'Next.'

He found his way into the office where Pat was working. Sarah was working alongside him.

'I'd heard you were here,' Pat said. 'Sarah said she'd met you.'

'That's right,' Luke said. 'She was showing me around. I knew it was bad here, but I never knew it was like this.'

'And it shouldn't be either,' Pat replied. 'It's a matter of money – always money, money, money. We're doing our best. We're working all the hours God sent. But without money, there's a limit. We can't buy enough food. We can't stop the fever.'

'I showed him the fever sheds,' Sarah said.

Luke grimaced.

'That's the way it is,' Pat said, 'and from what Ian tells us, that's the way it is right across the county. There's nothing else we can do, just put them in the sheds and leave them to die.'

'I know,' Luke said. 'Sarah showed me the way you're burying them too.'

Pat threw an angry glance at Sarah. 'I don't go up there anymore,' he said. 'I've a job to do, and there's no point in upsetting myself. If I go over there, I can't work for the rest of the day.'

'Yes,' Luke said. 'I can understand that.'

'I'll just be going on,' Sarah said. 'I'll leave you two to talk, I'm sure you have enough to talk about.'

'Yes,' Pat said. 'Thanks for everything.'

He waited until the door had closed.

'Poor girl, her father just died.'

'What? The Master?'

'That's right,' Pat said. 'It's taken her badly, I'd say.'

'I'm sorry to hear that,' Luke said. 'Would you tell her how sorry I am?'

'Of course.'

'I wonder why she didn't tell me?'

'She's like that.'

Luke stared out the window. He could just see the edge of the trench in the dusk.

'I don't understand it anymore,' he whispered. 'All this dying.'

'What's there not to understand?'

'Aren't you feeding them?'

Pat put down his pen. 'True enough,' he said, 'and you're not the only one that doesn't understand. But it's not the hunger that's the problem. The fever's worse than the hunger. Much worse. Ten times worse.'

'So much?'

'Yes, the fever's the killer in the workhouses. They're all running from the hunger, coming in to where we feed them. And what are we doing? Crowding them together in the kitchens and the dormitories. Packed like pigs they are, and if any man jack of them has black fever, in a few weeks most all of them have. We think we're doing good, we think we're feeding them, when all we're doing in the end is killing them with fever instead.'

He took two candles from the drawer of the desk, and placed them in the candle stands on the desk.

'Is it that bad?' Luke asked.

'I'll tell you how bad it is,' Pat said, 'I've been going through the numbers myself, and this is the way I reckon it. The fever is enough to kill the whole workhouse every second month.' He took a scrap of paper from the floor and lit the candles from the flames in the turf fire. They flared.

'Every second month?'

'Isn't that what I'm telling you? It's a killing engine, this place, that's all it is. One giant killing engine.'

The trench was nearly invisible now. Luke shook his head in bewilderment, saying nothing.

'I'm sorry,' Pat said. 'I shouldn't have told you any of this.'

'*Arra* hell,' Luke answered. 'It's as well to know.'

'At least it's not as bad with ye in the mountains.'

'Maybe, maybe not. Or maybe I don't know. But there's fever on the mountains too. And for every hundred workers you have down here, there's a thousand up there, and I reckon the lesson's the same, even if the fever's slower spreading. The more work we give them, the more we bring them together, and the more we're killing them, if the cold or hunger doesn't get them first.'

'Yes,' Pat replied, 'and that's what they can't see in the Union. The hunger started the fever right enough, but now it's the fever that's the worse, and all we're doing is feeding it. The fever will kill far more than hunger ever will. And it's a savage way to die.'

Luke thought about that. The screams. The rotten stench of dying flesh, gorging on itself. He felt his stomach heaving, but controlled the urge.

When he spoke at last, it was with resignation. 'To hell with it all,' he said, 'we're not going to sort it out, you and me, that's for certain. It's our own people we should be worried about. How's things in Carrigard?'

'As good as can be. Father and Mother are fine, Murty and Aileen too. Father is over the fever, like I told you. From all we hear, the price of corn in Kilduff is as high as it is here, but with the money we're sending over, they've enough to eat.'

'Thank God for that. At least that's one thing off my mind for now.' He looked at the papers scattered all over the desk. 'I suppose I'd better help you with this.'

Pat passed a pile of paper across to him.

'Here, start adding this lot.'

After an hour, they stopped.

'Look,' Pat said, 'I was awful sorry to hear about that business about your wedding. It was a desperate thing to happen.'

'There's no need to be sorry anymore. The wedding is going ahead.'

'Going ahead!'

'Yes, going ahead.'

'But, but…why the devil didn't you tell me?'

'I wasn't thinking of it just now.'

'God, but you're the queer one. But how…'

'Father Nugent, the priest up in Brockagh, he wrote to the bishop in Achonry. Got an Episcopal Dispensation.'

'Now what in hell is that?'

'It just means that the bishop can allow second cousins to marry if he wants to.'

Pat stared at him, still unbelieving. 'You mean…?'

'Yes, it's going ahead in two days' time. We're not taking any chances this time. We can't let Fergus wreck things again. By the time he hears about it, it'll be too late for him, the bastard.'

'And what about Mother and Father?'

'I wrote to them, but I doubt they'll know yet.'

'Then they won't be able to come.'

'They weren't able to come the last time, and we can't wait. You'll have to explain it all to them after.'

'Oh, thanks!'

'After all, you're the only one in the family who's going to be there.'

'I'll try my damnedest. Though with the amount of work going on here, I don't know.'

'Well, I hope you can. There won't be anyone else from Carrigard, that's for sure.'

'Fine so,' Pat said. 'But tell me about Winnie. Is she better than Kitty?'

'I'll kill you for that.'

'Only teasing. Go on.'

'Yes, well, she's the Gallaghers' daughter.'

'They're the people you're staying with in Brockagh?'

'That's right. She was the first of them I met. She opened the door when I knocked on it. I fell for her straight away.'

'*Arra*, go on out of that!'

'No, it's true,' Luke said. 'I never believed in that kind of thing myself. But it happened, it did happen. Still, it took an awful long time to come together. And it wasn't just that business about second cousins, we didn't know about that then. Her father didn't like me. He was a proud man, didn't like working under a younger man like myself. It took a long time for him to come around and get to like me. I only asked him months later, when I was sure of his answer. He said yes at once.'

'But Winnie! What's she like?'

'There's only one way to find out. Come to Brockagh and see.'

'I don't know. We'll see.'

They turned back to the accounts and worksheets. They worked a while, then Luke leant back, restless.

'Do you think I'm mad?' he asked.

'Why would I think that?'

'It's just seeing all that's happening, all that's going on around us. Sometimes I reckon it wrong to get married at a time like this.'

'Don't be silly,' Pat said. 'Life goes on, and we have to keep going with it. Isn't that the way of it?'

Luke shook his head. The door opened before he could reply.

'Come on, you two,' Sarah shouted at them. 'Time for dinner, you're holding everyone up.'

She closed the door. Luke put his pen down, and stood.

'I've told you about Winnie. Now you tell me about Sarah.'

Pat looked at him in surprise. 'Now why would you ask me a question like that? Why would you think I'd know more about her than anyone else?' He made for the door, avoiding Luke's eyes.

'Oh, I don't know,' Luke said, 'I just thought you might.' He followed his brother to the dining room, wondering.

The next morning, he spoke to Voisey and McKinnon. Then McKinnon left for Kilduff and Castlebar, and Luke started back towards Brockagh.

He thought back on the last few days. So much had happened, it was almost impossible to take it all in. Thin men and women working at Lisnadee, starving and feverish. The Workhouse.

A killing engine?

The countryside was quiet. He rode past starving people at the edge of the road. He could not get the vision of the pit out of his mind. Corpses, dozens of them, the eyeless children. Rats. He thought about Winnie, trying to escape from the nightmare.

The night before the wedding, the Gallagher family were sitting around the table, as Mrs. Gallagher and Winnie finished the cooking.

'You're looking awful gloomy there, Luke,' Mrs. Gallagher said. 'You've got the look of a condemned man.'

'Dead right too,' Gallagher said. 'Just wait till Winnie gets her clutches into him.'

Winnie gave her father a slap on the back of the head. Gallagher laughed. 'There you are. Assault and battery. Now you know what's coming!'

Luke smiled. Winnie held her hand over him. 'And don't you say a word, husband-to-be, or you'll get the same!'

'Would I dare?'

'But why so gloomy?' Mrs. Gallagher asked. 'Is it the hunger?'

'No, it's nothing. I'm very happy. It's just I don't look that way.'

'God help us, I wouldn't like to see you when you're sad.'

She put a plate out in front of him. 'I know what's wrong with you. You're thinking it's wrong to be happy at a time like this. Isn't that it?'

'That's right, Una,' he said. 'How could anyone be happy, the times that are in it?'

'Well, let me tell you something. You're wrong. It's at times like this we need to have people marrying. All the fever and hunger this past year – we've taken a terrible beating. People are giving up – dying or leaving. If we don't have young people like you marrying and rearing families, Mayo is finished.'

Luke said nothing. He looked across the table towards Winnie.

'We're thinking of America, Ma,' she whispered.

'America?'

'Did I hear you right?' asked Gallagher. 'You're thinking of America.'

'But I told you.'

'You said about going, but you never said about America. Not for certain.'

'I'm sorry,' Luke said. 'We should have said it earlier. We haven't decided yet though. We're only thinking of it.'

'What would you want going to America for? Isn't England closer?' Gallagher asked.

'That's as may be, but America is where the best chances are. '

'But where would you go?'

'I don't rightly know yet. The fellows back home go to Philadelphia. New York too, it's said to be a good town. No end of work for a man who wants it.'

'What would you do there?'

'I don't know yet. They say there's work on the docks loading boats. Building railways too, and God knows, I'm used to that.'

'But why would you want to go at all?' asked Mrs. Gallagher. 'Surely it's not hunger that's driving you.'

'No, it's not that,' Luke said. 'I told Winnie already, it's the Works. It's turned people against me, in Carrigard as well as here. John knows what I mean.'

'I know right enough,' Gallagher said. 'But the bad times will pass. Come Christmas, we'll all see things different.'

'Maybe we will,' Luke said.

'And don't you have Carrigard,' Mrs. Gallagher said. 'Isn't the farm going to be yours? What would your mother and father do if you left?'

'They've still got Pat. He'll take it if I don't. If I take it, he's the one who'll have to go.'

'Would you not give it a try though? God knows, Carrigard is a lot nearer than America.'

'I'll think about it,' Luke said.

'No,' Winnie said. 'We'll think about it. There's two of us now.'

There was a knock on the door. Winnie went to answer it. She came back with the caller.

'A Mr. Pat Ryan, looking for his brother!'

Gallagher stood up. 'So this is Pat,' he said, 'and we just talking about you. By God, we never expected you here tonight. You're most welcome.'

'Aye,' Pat said, 'and I never expected to be here either.' Luke, still sitting, was smiling. Pat walked over to the table, looking into Luke's eyes.

'Aren't you the cute one?'

'Who, me?'

'That was a smart move, getting Ian to talk to Voisey for you.'

'Yes...well...I reckoned Ian would be more persuasive than me or you.'

'Damned right he was. Voisey told me I had a Christian duty to be at my brother's wedding. Not that I could go, mind you. That I had to go.'

'Well, wasn't he right.'

'*Arra*, hell...'

Gallagher stood up. 'Would you stop arguing the pair of you. Come on there, let's get your horse settled for the night.'

'Horse!' Pat said, nearly shouting. 'What horse?'

'You mean you walked?' Mrs. Gallagher said.

'Walked' is right. All the damned way, every single mile of it.'

Luke laughed. 'Isn't it good for you, doing a bit of walking for a change. Now quit whinging, and say hello to your new sister-in-law.'

The next morning, he walked over to the priest-house. 'I nearly forgot, Father, I'm going to need confession.'

'Again?'

'Yes, Father. There's something I forgot to tell you before.'

'Kneel here, and tell me.'

He knelt.

'I attacked a man. Destroyed his business.'

'We won't worry about that. Any others?'

'Yes, Father.' He hesitated, and said nothing.

'Sins of the flesh?'

'Yes, Father.'

'Christ admonishes us against sins of the flesh. You know that.'

'Yes, Father.'

'But that's perfection, and nobody's perfect.' He raised his hand and

275

made the sign of the cross. 'I absolve thee in the name of the Lord.'

'What penance, Father.'

'What penance! Haven't you done enough penance these months past?' Luke rose from his knees.

'There's something else I wanted to mention, Father.'

'Not another sin surely.'

'Worse than that. They're closing the Works.'

'They're what!'

'Yes, they're replacing them with Soup Kitchens, but I'm afraid they're not going to do it fast enough. I have my orders. The Works close on Saturday fortnight. Morton says so, and there's no way Morton will ever go back on a decision.'

The priest shook his head. 'What does John Gallagher think?'

'I haven't told him yet. I haven't told anyone.'

The priest was staring into the fire. 'Let's leave it that way. Today is a day to celebrate. We'll worry about it all tomorrow.'

That afternoon, Luke Ryan and Winifred Gallagher were married by Father Nugent in the little church in Brockagh. A few of the Gallaghers' relatives attended and only one of the Ryans. After the ceremony, they returned to Gallagher's for a few drinks. It was a quiet affair.

Luke and Winnie left early, and walked back to the old cottage. For many years, Winnie thought of that night as one of the most ecstatic of her life.

It was followed by one of the most terrible.

Chapter Twenty Two

Telegraph or Connaught Ranger, February 1847:
Another wretched woman died in Stabball last week, and for
want of a coffin she lay on the damp floor of a hut for some
days. A plate was laid on her face to keep the soot drops from
it. In Gallowshill, another poor woman died from want. She
remained from Sunday morning until Wednesday evening
unburied for want of a coffin, which was at length procured by
the subscriptions of a few individuals. Last week, a female men-
dicant died at Coursepark, near Rathbane, in a house where
she got shelter for the night. All efforts to procure a coffin for
her proved fruitless, and a few days after her decease, far gone
in decomposition, the body was tied on some wattles, tied with
hay ropes, and in this horrible state was borne through the
streets of our town to the old churchyard for interment.

They lay together, bare legs touching, her head cradled on his shoulder.
During the night, he had thrown some more turf on the fire, and the house
was warm. The old bed had been well dried. Two of Mrs. Gallagher's
blankets covered them.

'Your mother was right,' he said. 'This was the right time to marry. If we
gave up now, we'd be finished. Besides, I think I'd go mad. Sometimes I think
I'm halfway there already. You really are all I've got.'

'Don't be silly. Think of your own family. Pat worships you, he told me
so. Young John too. And as for Ma!'

'Perhaps,' he said. 'But tell me, what do you think about America now?'

'I'd put it out of my mind for now. We should see how the next few
months turn out. Wait till harvest maybe.'

'Yes, I think you're right. We'll see how it all turns out.'

He watched the shadows and the play of light from the fire on the rafters.
He turned to face her, kissing her forehead and stroking the side of her cheek.

'Yesterday was the greatest day of my life.'

'Mine too,' she said.

'I didn't want to spoil it with talk of Relief, but I've an awful lot of work
to do today, and I have to do it.'

'I understand.'

'No you don't. There's one thing I haven't told you. They're closing the Works. Now.'

'Oh God…But they can't.'

'They can though. They're going to run them down, and start Soup Kitchens.'

'But – when? When?'

'God knows. That'll be part of my job now. I have to close the Works, and start the Kitchens running. But Morton wants all the Works shut on Saturday fortnight, no argument. Voisey's doing his best to get corn to Brockagh as soon as he can, but it'll be well after we close the Works.'

Winnie turned her face away, trying to hold back the tears.

'This is a great start to our marriage.'

'Isn't it. But remember what you said. Courage.'

They dressed and walked to Gallagher's, Luke leading his horse. Pat had slept at Gallaghers' and was preparing to leave. He winked at Luke when he saw him. Luke playfully tried to hit him, but Pat stepped back, laughing. But Luke was no longer in the mood for horseplay.

When Pat had left, Young John was sent to fetch the priest. When he arrived, the three men discussed the situation. Father Nugent had already decided to ride up to Burrenabawn and Teenashilla, asking his way to those dying or dead.

Luke thought of asking the priest to make the announcements about the ending of the Works, but then he decided it would be unfair. He did ask him though to take note of all the workers who would not be returning. He suspected it would be a large number.

Then another problem arose. It was Gallagher who brought it up. 'We can't just leave all the Works unfinished.'

'I know,' Luke said. 'There's months of work on every site. There's no way on God's earth we could finish them all that fast.'

'So what can we do?' the priest asked.

'I've been thinking about that' Luke said. 'Ardnagrena – that's where we'll start. We'll close it over the next few days…'

'But we can't do that. There's weeks of work left.'

'There is,' Luke said, 'but the base of the road is laid. We can finish off the hard-core – that'll only take a few days. It will leave a damned rough top for anyone walking or riding on it, but it'll have to do. And if the road is there, then sometime they'll put a proper top on it.'

'Will they?'

'They will, because they'll have to,' Luke said. 'It mightn't be soon, but it will be done. Lisnadee – that's the one we must do, and we've got to do it right too. The fellows on the Sligo side are near finished. Once we're done, there'll be a direct road from this part of Mayo, straight through to Sligo Town.'

'So ye'd use the workers from Ardnagrena?'

'We'd have to,' Luke said.

'But to bring them all the way up to Lisnadee – it's a long way for them.'

'I know.'

'And it's worse than that,' Gallagher said. 'Even with the extra gangs, it won't be enough. We still couldn't reach the Sligo side in time.'

'I know that too,' Luke said. 'So the next question is Burrenabawn and Teenashilla.'

'What are ye saying?' the priest asked. 'Ye'd abandon them? Is that it?'

'It's the only way, Father,' Luke said. 'I've been going through all the figures. We'll need all the workers at Lisnadee. There's no other way we'll finish it in time.'

'And anyhow, the Works above are only started,' Gallagher said. 'There's not much to abandon.'

'But what about the Union?' the priest asked. 'What will Morton say?'

'Morton can go to hell,' Luke answered. 'If he doesn't agree with it, he can finish Lisnadee on his own. We'll give the bastard a pick and a shovel, and see how he likes it.'

'But…'

'Don't worry about it, Father,' Gallagher said. 'They'll see the sense of it.'

'And anyhow, we'll have Voisey on our side,' Luke said. 'Davitt and McKinnon too.'

'But to just abandon two roads…'

'What else can we do?' Luke asked. 'We've few enough to finish any road in the time we've left.'

Afterwards he and Gallagher rode over to Ardnagrena.

The announcement that the Works were to be terminated caused panic. Luke's reference to the Soup Kitchens did little to allay it. Within a few seconds, he and Gallagher were being jostled by a crowd of angry men and women, pulling at them, pushing them, shouting at them.

'You're trying to kill us all.'

'Murderers, murderers.'

'You don't care.'

'Hang them.'

There was a shout from the rear of the crowd, this time in Irish. *'Leave them be!'*

The crowd separated as a tall, gaunt man came up to Gallagher. Luke had noticed him before, both because of his great height and his advanced age. He had never heard him speak though, not even when he had been given his wages.

'*Explain this to us, Seán,*' the man said, addressing Gallagher only. '*Is this stranger to be trusted?*'

'*He is, Cairbre-Mór. He is of Kilduff. His people are respected. He is a man to trust.*'

'*Yet he started the new way of working. The* piecework.' The last word was in English, spat out with contempt.

'*He did, but it was not of his doing. The Government men in Castlebar, they would have no other way.*'

'*He says we will work until Saturday.*'

'*Until Saturday is all the time the Government men will give us.*'

'*Then they will feed us?*'

'*After that, yes.*'

'*But on what day?*'

'*That is not known to us. We wait to be told.*'

'*The Black Fever is killing us. The hunger kills our young.*'

'*That I know. We do what we can, but it is never enough.*'

The man said nothing for a few seconds. Then he addressed the crowd around him. '*These men we can trust. Seán Gallachóir I have known for many years. If Seán says the outsider is also to be trusted, then he is right. Your anger is not for them. These men will fight for food.*'

'*But will they, Cairbre-Mór? Is this certain?*'

'*It is certain. Go back to your work now. We work until the Saturday ahead of us.*'

The crowd dispersed.

'That's the first time I've had anyone threaten to hang me,' Luke said.

'They wouldn't have done it.'

'I know, but they were damned angry.'

'Worse than that, they were terrified.'

He left Gallagher at Ardnagrena and rode to Lisnadee on his own. Durcan gathered the workers together. When he spoke, he was answered with complete silence. Luke rode back to Brockagh.

The three men met again in the priest-house that evening. Father Nugent was looking a little shaken, though he had not been threatened. They spent hours bringing all the calculations up to date, and assessing which workers were unlikely to return.

It was decided that Luke would accompany the priest towards Burrena-bawn and Teenashilla the next day, paying out wages where due. The day after, he would do the same with Gallagher's assistance at Ardnagrena and Lisnadee, though he knew he had not enough money to finish the payments.

As they worked on, they heard a murmur of voices outside. They went out. There were hundreds of people there. It seemed as if they were praying, but these were no prayers, only begging. Most was in Irish, repeated quietly again and again.

'*Tá an gealar againn.*' The fever is with us.

'*Tá an ocras orainn.*' The hunger is on us.

'*Tabhair bia duinn.*' Give us food.

The priest held out his hands.

'*I have no food to give you,*' he said.

No one answered.

He raised his hand in blessing. No one knelt.

The murmuring went on.

'*Give us food.*'

Later, when the work was finished, Luke walked through the crowd back to the old cottage. There was a group of about fifty women outside, the same murmuring. They wore black shawls against the cold drizzle, pulled down halfway over their eyes, giving them a sinister and threatening look. But they parted to let him pass. He opened the door. Winnie was huddled by the fire. She was crying. He put his arms around her. 'I'm sorry, *a ghrá*. I didn't know.'

She grasped his hand, saying nothing.

'I didn't even know you were here,' he said.

'I came down to prepare dinner,' she whispered. 'There was no one else here then.'

'Why didn't you go back up to your mother?'

'I couldn't. Every time I tried, the women were all around me. They wouldn't let me through. Eileen Dunne, she had a dead baby. She kept holding it up to me.'

'Oh God.'

That night, they both tried to sleep, but the low murmuring outside made it impossible.

'*Tá an bás againn.*' Death is with us.

'*Give us food.*'

Early the next morning, Luke took his bride of two days back to her mother with her mother's blankets. Then he and Gallagher hitched up a cart, and drove to the cottage. They manhandled the old bed into the cart, and took it back. An hour later, the old cottage was in flames.

Every evening, the wage sheets were updated, and plans made. Luke checked and re-checked figures, Gallagher and the priest helping as best they could.

Every night the murmuring voices went on, now outside Gallagher's.
'*Food…food…food…*'
'*Give us food.*'

Pat had left Brockagh after the wedding, walking rapidly. He reached Ardnagrena where a tall, gaunt man, stood in front of him, transfixing him with his eyes. Then he shook his head, and walked away. Pat went on. He reached the main road and turned towards Knockanure.

From time to time he passed other gangs, still working too. Along the side roads he could see more, but he knew most would be closing in the next few days.

As he walked, he saw something else that he had not noticed before. The potato fields along the side of the road were no different to what they had been in December. Many of them had not even been dug the previous autumn, and the lazy-bed ridges were still there, some with long pools of rainwater lying between them. What was most disturbing was the absence of an early planting. The crop had been destroyed twice. The people no longer believed in it.

Where anything was planted, it was corn. He wondered about that. Corn to pay the rent. Corn to stop them being evicted. Or corn to eat? But he knew they could never grow enough corn in Mayo to feed everyone. He wondered when the Kitchens would open? He wondered too where the Kitchens would get the food to feed thousands of starving men and women.

He slept soundly that night, a deep, deep sleep with no dreams. He rose early, dressed himself and walked back to his office. Sarah was there before him.

'What are you doing here so early?' he asked.

'Just working.' She threw a sheet across to him. 'Here, check this.'

He scanned the long column of pounds, shillings and pence.

'Correct to the farthing,' he said. 'As always.'

'Of course,' she said. 'Didn't you know it would be. Try another.' She waited as he checked it.

'Correct again,' he said.

She grasped his pen. 'Enough of that,' she said. 'Did it go ahead this time? Was everything alright?'

'What?'

'The wedding, you fool.'

'Oh, the wedding,' he replied. 'Yes, it went ahead alright. There's many a girl in Mayo will have cause to regret that.' He winked at her. She blushed.

'And tell me, how do you find his new wife?' she asked, trying to hide her confusion.

'She's a good woman. Gentle, very gentle, but do you know, beneath it all, I think she's even tougher than Luke.'

Winnie recovered. Being back among the familiar surroundings of her father's house helped. Mrs. Gallagher understood all too well what had happened and was able to console her daughter while Luke and Gallagher were out.

But it was a strange situation for them. Now they were married, but it was as if their marriage was delayed again. There was no privacy in the Gallagher house, nor any chance of it. Luke took to sleeping in the back room with the boys once more. In the early morning, he would dress and go to where Winnie was sleeping. He would lie down on top of the blanket beside her, kissing her on the forehead. When she woke, she put her arms around him, drawing him close, the blanket still separating them. It was at times like this that they talked; whispering, wondering about the future.

They could not stay in Brockagh, that was clear. Once the Works were over, he and Gallagher would be dismissed, and he could not expect to stay with the Gallaghers.

'So what do we do now?' she asked him one morning, as they lay shivering in the early cold. 'When do we go to America? Or do we go at all?'

'I've been thinking about that. We can't go at once, that's for sure. Father wouldn't be able for the farm and the quarry on his own.'

'But what about Pat?'

'Pat? Yes, he'll be the one will take the farm. But when? He's always wanted it but right now he has a good job with the Union, and we'll be needing his money to buy corn.'

'But for how long?' she asked.

'I don't rightly know the answer to that, my love. There's been no question of him being given the sack yet, and as long as he's not, he'll have to stay working in Knockanure. God knows, they need him there, and they'll need him for a while yet.'

'So what are you saying? How long should we stay?'

'I don't know for sure. We'll have to talk it through with Father and Mother, and it depends on the harvest too. If it's a good one, they'll have less to worry about, Pat'll have less work in the Union, and we'd have less need for his money anyhow.'

'But if he stays at the Union?' she asked.

'He won't.'

'But supposing he did. From all I'm hearing, it sounds as if they'll need him.'

'We might still go to America, though we'd have to be sending some money home. With that and what Pat might earn in the Union, they'd have plenty enough to live, and Father wouldn't have any call to be working in the quarry. And in any case, there mightn't be too much work in the quarry if they're ending the road building around Carrigard.'

'But if Pat wasn't there, ye'd lose the quarry. And if ye lost it, ye'd lose it forever.'

'You're right though. And what's worse, we might lose the whole farm.'

'Well then?'

'They might get him to sign the lease instead of me.'

'And if they don't.'

'We'd be trapped. And one more thing – we haven't enough money to get to America either. We'll have to think about that too.'

'But how could we go then?'

'England, that might be the only way. Go back and work on the railways until we'd have enough to buy the tickets out of Liverpool.'

'And work with your cousin?'

'Maybe, maybe not. But no matter which way, I think it's best to wait until the harvest. We'll decide then. By then, we'll know whether to stay or leave, and where we might have to go.'

They continued winding down the Works. The Ardnagrena road was left with a rough finish. There were protests about being transferred to the more distant Lisnadee Works, and Luke noticed the next day that not all the Ardnagrena workers had turned up at Lisnadee.

The same happened at Burrenabawn and Teenashilla. What now, he thought. If they were too weak to walk and earning no wages, how long could they live?

But the Works at Lisnadee went on. In the end, they finished it as planned, all the way to the Sligo county boundary, but as McKinnon later commented, 'it was a damned close run thing.'

As the Works were coming to an end, Luke was working from early morning to late at night, going through the worksheets, checking figures again and again.

The situation was becoming urgent now. When Davitt arrived, it would be the last time. Not only would it be essential to have all the piecework calculations complete by Friday night, but it would also be necessary to know what was owed to workers who had not returned to the Works. There would be no further chance of payment.

Luke had already written to the Pay Office in Castlebar and given the letter to Pat to post in Knockanure. He had heard from Voisey that they had almost no money at the Union in Knockanure. It was seen as far too dangerous to keep large amounts of cash in outlying areas without the militia. And having militia all over the county cost money.

In his letter, he had guaranteed that he would be in Castlebar at dawn on the Saturday morning, so that the total amount due could be collected before Davitt left. He also requested a fresh horse to be available so as to accompany Davitt back.

On the Friday, he finished all the calculations with no time to spare.

It was near midnight, when he left. He kissed Winnie, holding her close. Then he mounted his horse and started towards Castlebar.

He rode through the night, meeting no one. The weather had cleared. It was a bright night with stars. He wondered why he had never seen them so brilliant before.

The stars faded. The country was still and silent, no one moving. He saw a body lying by the side of the road. He knocked on the door of a cabin. Silence. At the next cabin, he was met with a scream, but the door remained shut. He rode on.

As dawn broke, he passed other people on the road, but no one said anything. He helped an older woman carry two pails of water from the well, and left them at her door. She said nothing.

At Castlebar, the sun was rising behind him. Davitt met him at the door of the Pay Office.

'We got your message. Just tell me the amount, and we should be ready to leave in a few minutes.'

'That's fine,' Luke replied, 'but aren't I supposed to report to Morton first.'

'I don't think he's here just now, I haven't seen him for a few days. He must be out and about.'

Davitt went in to collect the money, while Luke went to the stables to saddle a fresh mount. Twenty minutes later, they were riding back to Brockagh, accompanied by six militia.

'When are they going to open the Kitchens, Martin?'

'Might be another week or two. It's you fellows in Brockagh are going to have it hardest though.'

'Why's that?'

'They're only closing the Works slowly. Brockagh is one of the first – seems Morton doesn't like you. Some of the others will run a few weeks longer. Like Castlebar.'

'Damn it, if he doesn't like me, that's between him and me. Why punish everyone else?'

'That's Morton. Ours is not to reason why.'

Luke shook his head.

'Heard anything about the Works around Kilduff?' he asked.

'Nothing about closing them yet, that's for sure.'

Now they had no difficulty at the Works. The workers were paid off in total silence. Luke signed off on all the payments and took a further advance from Davitt to cover the remaining amounts due to those who had not turned up.

For the next week, he continued making payments in the outlying areas of Brockagh parish, sometimes accompanied by Father Nugent, sometimes by Gallagher or Durcan. It had been a wet winter, and the mountain tracks were deep in mire. As always, the most difficult area was the high ground around Lisnadee – through the mud *clocháns* of Benstreeva and Croghancoe overlooking the lake, where the boreens and tracks were almost impassable.

Tillage had been pushed high up the mountain, the lazy beds with their withered stalks stretching into areas which had been bog. Much of it was still bog with no roads. Yet potatoes had been grown here, and mud cabins had been built on land with almost no foundation.

Still, the people were dying, many were already dead. Sometimes they buried corpses, since their families were too weak to dig. There was no question of bringing the bodies back to Knocklenagh now. In any case, he now knew for certain that the bodies of fever victims spread fever. Often they found a corpses in abandoned cabins with no family at all. No wages were paid; there was no one alive to take them. Sometimes they buried the bodies. Sometimes they didn't.

One day, McKinnon arrived. The Works having been finished, a final report had to be made to Knockanure. He and Luke spent the next two days riding around the Works measuring out the work done. At each, McKinnon signed off Luke's worksheets. He checked all the payments required, but they were correct, all the calculations done, so there was nothing owing either way.

McKinnon also confirmed that Luke was to stay on and administer the Soup Kitchens. Luke asked when these would be opened, and McKinnon told him he would be informed by letter in the next few days.

As McKinnon left, Luke gave him three pounds.

'If you're going over near Kilduff, would you drop this into Father and Mother.'

When he arrived back in Brockagh, he discussed everything with Winnie. Now there was no decision to be made about their future, at least for a few weeks or months.

All week he waited for the letter from Knockanure, but it did not arrive. Before the end of the week, all the Works payments were finished.

The Relief Works were over.

It was snowing again.

A week later, he had still not received any notification from Knockanure. He had been anxious, now he was becoming alarmed.

'I don't know what's happening,' he told Winnie one morning. 'I'll just have to go over to Knockanure and find out.'

He left Brockagh and rode down towards Ardnagrena. The snow had been well trampled into the road, and it was bitterly cold. Heaps of rock and stone lay on the side of the roads, abandoned as the Works had come to an end. As he came closer to Knockanure, he saw Relief Works still in operation. On the hills to the side, he could see many more. Davitt had been right. The Brockagh Works had been the first to close.

When he arrived in Knockanure, a group of women surrounded him in a sea of leering faces. He urged his horse on, but one grasped the bridle. He lashed at her with his reins, harder and harder, until red welts showed on her sunken cheeks. She dropped to the ground screaming, and he rode through, and on to the back-gate of the Union. He went to Voisey's office in the administration building. Yardley was there too.

'I don't have to ask why you're here,' Voisey said as he waved Luke to a seat.

'No, I suppose not,' Luke said. 'It's just that Ian said to me that we should hear from you within a day or two. It's two weeks now. No Works, no Kitchens. Everybody keeps asking me, and I don't know what to tell them.'

'I don't know either,' Voisey said. 'I know there's Government corn coming through Ballina and Westport. Little enough, mind you, and it's all accounted for. There's only a few places have supplies.'

'But if there's no corn for Brockagh, why did they insist on closing the Works.'

'I don't know the answer to that either. All I know is Morton wanted it.'

'Morton, Morton,' Luke said. 'Always bloody Morton.'

Afterwards he went down the corridor to Pat's office. Sarah was sitting alongside him. Pat looked up in surprise. 'We weren't expecting you.'

'And I shouldn't be here either,' Luke said. 'Just give me something to work on.'

Pat and Sarah looked at each other. Pat handed him a sheet.

'Here, add these.'

They worked silently for an hour. Sarah was the first to notice the heavy creaking sound. She went to the window.

'Pat! Luke!' They both rushed to the window.

'Corn,' Luke exclaimed. 'Corn at last.'

It was carried by six large freight wagons, each drawn by two horses. The consignment was accompanied by military, twelve soldiers in all, one sitting on each of the carts with guns; six more with sabres, riding along the flanks, lashing at the hungry crowd around them with their whips and boots, sometimes threatening them with their sabres.

All three left the office and walked out into the street. Voisey and Yardley were there already. The convoy had stopped.

An officer dismounted. 'I'm looking for Mr. Edward Yardley.'

Yardley stood forward.

'You're Edward Yardley?'

'I am.'

'You're the Quaker representative in Knockanure, are you?'

'I am.'

'Six wagons of Indian corn for you. Eighty sacks in each, four hundred and eighty in total. I want you to sign here and here. You may, of course, want to check them first.'

Yardley shook his head in disbelief.

'I wasn't expecting the military!'

'You're all the same, you Quaker fellows. You think it all turns up by magic. Let me tell you, Mr. Yardley, if we had not come, it would never have got out of Westport.'

Yardley went to start counting the sacks, as the soldiers started to unload.

'We'll help you,' Sarah said.

A few minutes later, they had found that the officer's count was precise.

'One thing I didn't mention,' the officer said, 'You've more coming – should be here in a few hours. Six Workhouse type pots. There's no escort on those – they won't be stolen. Now, if you could just sign here.'

Yardley signed as instructed.

'I wasn't expecting this amount of protection,' he said to Voisey.

'I'm not surprised,' Voisey replied. 'I understand it's becoming normal. It used be that the RIC would accompany the carts, but the people are becoming desperate.'

'So how do we protect the corn now.'

'Don't worry,' the officer said. 'I would suggest that six of my men should stay here with you. They'll be needed here next week in any case when the corn arrives for the Workhouse.'

'Thank you, lieutenant. Most kind.'

The pots arrived. The Union had already been buying turnips in from the merchants, and cabbage and turnips from some of the surrounding demesne farms. A few hours later, using labour rounded up by Voisey, Yardley had all six pots in operation. Sarah, Luke and Pat each stood over one of the pots, ladling out the contents as fast as bowls or rough plates were presented to them. The soldiers and the local police kept the six long lines in order.

The system here was different from the Relief Works – there was no system. No announcement had been made. No Selection was necessary – all were fed. But it was very little.

Sarah's mother stayed working in the fever sheds.

That evening Luke stayed in Knockanure. He joined the others for dinner in the administration block. The fare was not very different to what they had been ladling out. The Workhouse had not seen meat in weeks. There were eight at dinner – Luke and Pat; Sarah and her mother; Voisey and Yardley; the local RIC sergeant and the young corporal commanding the troops who remained.

'Up from Claremorris, Corporal?' the sergeant asked.

'Yes sir. Though I haven't been there since two weeks back.'

'What's it like down there?'

'Terrible, sir. They had to close the Workhouse for a few days, but I hear they managed to open it again. What's worst though is the fever. They're dying everywhere. It's the same in Westport and Castlebar and Foxford. You just can't get away from it.'

Yes, thought Luke, he's right. All you have to do is look at the Workhouse. They die from hunger in the first week. If they live that long, it's fever. Will it never end?

Yardley was talking. 'What do you think?' he asked Voisey. 'How many did we feed today?'

'I was trying to reckon that. Two thousand is my guess.'

'I was reckoning even more,' the sergeant said.

'One way or another, we're going to have a bigger number tomorrow,' Yardley said. 'If this is what we get without even telling anyone, we'll have an awful lot more when word gets around.'

'I wonder how long your supplies will last?' asked Voisey.

'God only knows.'

Early the next morning, Luke left the Union in Knockanure and rode back along the frozen road to Brockagh. As he passed through Lisnadee, he could see the slopes of Croghancoe. Again he felt the terror. He shook his head, and rode on.

Sarah spent the next day at the Soup Kitchen. For security, Voisey had it taken inside the walls of the Union. A crowd of thousands formed outside the gates, but the militia kept order, and only a hundred were admitted at a time. Behind them, the Workhouse was still operating in its own way; a different world again. Sarah worked on, not even stopping when it started to rain. Rain at last. The last of the snow was melting.

For hours, she ladled the soup into the bowls held up to her. The rain got heavier, but no one left the lines, they just kept shuffling on through the slush towards the soup. Her only rest came as they finished feeding each group, and they were hustled out through the gates again, before the next group were admitted. On one occasion, she saw a woman lying on the ground, an infant crying alongside. She walked over, but two militiamen came through the gates and pulled the woman standing, an arm over each shoulder. One of the militiamen grasped the baby's hand, and they dragged mother and child towards the fever sheds.

As darkness fell, she walked back to the administration block. There were still hundreds of people outside the gate, but she was far too tired to continue, and drenched through. She went to her own room, stripped and rubbed herself down before dressing in dry clothes. As she went back past the offices, she saw a door ajar at the end of the corridor. There was still a single candle burning. She went in.

'Pat,' she said, 'you'll ruin your eyes doing that. You've been working far too long already.'

'You're right. I'm just finishing for the night – a few last columns to add.'

When he had finished one, he turned to her. 'Things are getting worse here. Even with the Quaker corn.'

'They sound worse in Brockagh, from all Luke says.'

'I know. He's told me so often. There's times I wish to God he wouldn't.'

'All the men and women freezing to death on the Works. It must have been terrible for him. '

'Yes. But Luke's tough. A lot tougher than I am.'

'I don't believe that,' she said.

'It's true though. And he needs to be tough. I'm only helping out with the accounts here. Luke, he's the one who has to deal with the people. They were in a dreadful state when they heard about the Works being ended.'

'I'm sure they were.'

He checked what he had added. 'I know it all makes sense. I know there's no point having sick and starving people working on the roads. Brockagh showed us that. It's much better to feed the people and let them work on their own plots to grow next year's crop. God knows, I never thought they'd allow Outdoor Relief.'

'Remember Morton?' asked Sarah. 'I wonder what he'd have thought.'

'That bastard! Who cares?'

'Well, he doesn't anymore.'

'No?'

'Not much. He's dead.'

'What! Who told you that?'

'That corporal fellow. He told me.'

'What happened?'

'Got the fever in Castlebar. Died screaming, that's what he said.'

'Good enough for him,' Pat said.

'Now isn't that a terrible thing to say?'

'Sorry so. But he was a right bas...I'm sorry.'

'You don't have to be sorry.'

'Sorry – I'll stop it now. Still, I'll tell you this. Things could have been better handled at Brockagh. Morton – he had this thing against Luke – thought he was trying to get above his station. The Works were closed – Morton insisted on it, and they still haven't opened the Kitchens. There was damned little Luke could do about it, but the people blamed him anyhow.'

Chapter Twenty Three

Telegraph or Connaught Ranger, April 1847:
Death from Want. On Wednesday last the body of a poor woman was found dead in a field adjoining this town. A child belonging to the deceased had piled some stones around the body to protect it from the dogs and the pigs.

When Luke returned to Brockagh, the situation was worsening. The Works had closed, the people had no money, and there were no Soup Kitchens. Starvation was etched deeper on every face. There was still no outright hunger in Gallaghers' though. Luke was still being paid, and he could afford to buy corn for the family, though it was very little. He was sending little money back to Carrigard, but he knew Pat was doing so.

Any time he went out, gaunt, starving people followed him everywhere, begging for food that he could not give them. Now he no longer went out unless it was essential, and neither did anyone else except Gallagher. The murmuring continued outside their house.

'Food, food, food.'

He became more desperate. He thought of the Quaker supplies arriving in Knockanure, but he reckoned there was little chance of that in Brockagh. He would just have to wait out until the Government supplies arrived. As at Durcans at Christmas, he tried to stop eating, but Winnie would not allow it. He no longer felt hungry, but he knew she was right.

In the mornings, he still rose early. He would go out to the other room, and lie on the bed beside Winnie, though they said little.

Late one evening, they were sitting around the table, the younger boys already asleep in the back room.

There was a knock at the door. A young boy stood outside.

'Message for Luke Ryan. Father Nugent wants him up at the priest-house.'

Luke took his jacket, and walked out.

'What's this about?' he asked.

'Don't know. There's some other fellow there. He looks like Quality.'

Luke walked over, and entered the priest-house without knocking. The room was dark, the two men sitting around the table in the light of a single candle. The flame threw light and shadow across the priest's face, more hollowed than before. Luke sat.

'This is Edward Yardley, ' the priest said. 'I believe you've already met?'

'Yes. Down at Knockanure.'

'Indeed,' Yardley said. 'Good to meet you again, Luke.'

'I don't know if you are aware,' the priest went on, 'but Edward is one of the Quakers.'

'Yes, I remember that.'

'But you go on Edward. You tell him.'

'Yes, yes,' Yardley said. 'As you know from Knockanure, we've been organising our own relief efforts independently of the Union and the Government. We're going to open our own Soup Kitchen right here in Brockagh...'

'WHEN?' The question was loud and abrupt.

Yardley looked at him in surprise. 'The day after tomorrow,' he said.

Luke put his head in his hands. 'Thank God...,' he said. 'Thank God... Thank God for that.'

He worked frantically over the next few days. Winnie felt concerned, until she realised that he was only working out the frustration and hurt of the days since the Works had closed. She began to realise how tense she had been herself. She decided then that she would have to work outside the home. There was little enough work cooking and cleaning, where Mrs. Gallagher already did it all.

As soon as the Quaker supplies arrived from Westport, she threw herself into hectic activity, cooking corn and cabbage and organising other women to do the same. This time only three soldiers were left to guard the supplies, which were stored in another derelict cottage just beside the Gallaghers. Brockagh was tiny compared to Knockanure, though the population of the surrounding parishes was considerable.

At first they operated three pots in the centre of Brockagh. Luke recognised that while these might be enough for the area around Ardnagrena and Brockagh, it would be impossible to expect people from the mountains to come in every day. He suggested an alternative to Yardley. They organised two carts, which were despatched to the mountains, carrying one of the large pots with sacks of corn and loose cabbage. The travelling Kitchen spent a day each in Knocklenagh and Lisnadee, always accompanied by Timothy Durcan and one soldier. Each person was given one hot ration every third day, together with two cooked rations for reheating. Durcan kept a watchful eye out for desperate people trying to double-claim. Often he stood on the side, watching the lines of ragged people with the dull expressions in their eyes. No-one looked at him.

The crowds outside Gallaghers and the church dwindled away. Luke and Winnie stayed with her parents. There were other abandoned cottages nearby, but Winnie could not face the isolation during the day.

The turn of events had surprised him. As the old man in Ardnagrena had said, he had fought for food. He had tried everything to get food from the Union. In the end, it had arrived from the Quakers.

It also struck him as odd that Yardley was a Quaker. As he came to know Yardley better, he realised that he was a religious man, and he began to understand the deeper sources of his charity. Yardley was no missionary. Through all the time he was in Brockagh, Luke never heard him referring to his own faith. He worked closely too with Father Nugent, who had never objected to his presence.

One day, Luke stood with Yardley, watching the lines.

'You know,' Yardley said, 'James Voisey told me that we could only do our best, and that men could not perform miracles.'

'Yes, he once said that to me too.'

'We're feeding as many as we can and giving them as much as we can. God knows, it's little enough.'

'Can you go on with this, though?'

'That's the question, isn't it! When do you think the Government's supplies will arrive?'

'Soon, I hope,' Luke answered without conviction.

'I hope so. But you know, I think fever is going to be worse than hunger. An awful lot worse. And we've no fever hospital in Brockagh.'

'I doubt the Union would have the money to build one.'

'We'll have to do it ourselves.'

'How could we do that?' Luke asked. 'Just how in hell could we do that?'

'There's a lot of empty cottages around. Maybe we could use some of those.'

'I think most of them carry fever though. I wouldn't like to stay in a house where anyone has died of fever.'

'No. But it mightn't matter much to a man who already has fever.'

'I suppose not.'

'You know, we've lost Doctor Short to fever now. Doctor Connolly and Mr. Cronin before that – same thing. And Mr. Morton – I hear he's dead too.'

Luke stopped still. Morton's dead, he thought. Perhaps there's some justice in the world after all.

He helped Yardley with the fever cottages. There was little they could do for the patients, but there were other reasons.

One was quarantine. This was a word Luke had never heard before Yardley mentioned it. It was essential to isolate the patients to stop them infecting their own families. Having seen many who had been abandoned by their own families, Luke understood.

A second reason was to feed the patients. At the Soup Kitchens, it was necessary to be strict about the limited rations given out. No one was given rations for anyone else – only those who could walk were fed. But now they arranged food deliveries to the fever cottages. Luke knew though that after a few days of fever this no longer mattered, since the patients could not eat.

A third reason was heat. Many times they went up and down the lines of patients, mopping their faces and bodies with cooling water.

The last reason was hygiene. Every day, they had to clean the patients. Luke found this duty the most nauseating of all. They had no beds, they used straw as bedding, taken from the roofs of derelict cabins. Every morning they washed the patients, and then pitched out the foul straw, stinking with rice water diarrhoea, faeces and urine. Then all the floors were scrubbed, and fresh straw brought in. Fresh corpses were buried within an hour of death. To Luke's horror, a common pit was opened in the little graveyard beside Brockagh Church, and back-filled in the same way as in Knockanure Union, as the rats gnawed at the dead bodies.

Within a few days, Yardley had four cottages operating as fever wards near Brockagh, and another four in the outlying areas. Men and women, often weak themselves, were organised as nurses and cleaners.

Winnie worked in the Brockagh fever cottages. This worried Luke – he tried to forbid her, but she would not have it.

'You might die,' he said.

'So might you.'

'Don't worry about me. I just don't want you going into the wards again.'

'But I must. If I didn't, I wouldn't be the woman you married, would I?'

He could think of no answer to that.

A few days later, Yardley became ill. He insisted on moving to the fever cottages himself. Quarantine had to be maintained. As he weakened, Winnie took care of him, mopping his hot brow and cleaning him. Luke too continued working in the fever cottages. He knew it was at the risk of his own life, but in spite of the pain of fever, he no longer cared about it. He was terrified though that Winnie would die, and he felt that if she did, he would have been responsible for it.

And he had other worries too. Day by day, the Quaker supplies were running lower. The price of corn was rising to impossible heights, and he knew there were no cheaper supplies anywhere else in the county. He tried not to think about that. They would feed the people while they could, and after that they would just have to see what developed.

In the end, it too was very close.

The Quaker supplies were down to the last sacks of corn when the Government supplies arrived. Winnie came out of one of the fever cottages as the convoy stopped. Luke was there already, talking to one of the cart men. A crowd had gathered around the carts. The six soldiers were looking very nervous, but the people watching were quiet. Very quiet.

Luke left the soldiers with the cart and walked with Winnie back towards the house. Gallagher rose as they walked in.

'It's arrived,' Luke said. 'The corn is here.'

'It's come?'

'It has. I think the worst is over.'

'Just so long as the early potato crop is a good one.'

'Yes,' Luke said, 'that would help.'

Gallagher poured out four mugs of *poitín*. They all sat down at the table.

'What was that cart man saying to you?' Winnie asked.

'Telling me about Ballina,' Luke replied. 'He says there's ships lining up, coming in with corn.'

Gallagher shook his head in amazement.

'Where's it all coming from?'

'England. France. Even America.'

'But – didn't the Government stop bringing ships in?'

'I don't know,' Luke said, 'but from all I hear it's the big merchants buying it in now. Castlebar is buying it off them.'

'At these prices!' Mrs. Gallagher exclaimed.

'Not anymore. The price of corn is dropping fast. '

'That'll give McIlhenny something to think about,' she commented.

'Aye,' Gallagher said, 'and bankrupt the bastard.'

'Bad cess to him too,' Winnie added, with vehemence.

The changeover to the Government supplies went smoothly. The system was already up and running alongside Yardley's supplies, and within a day Gallagher, Durcan and all the rest were running each of the four Kitchens with little difficulty. After two days, the six militia men left, and rode back towards Castlebar.

Mrs. Caroline Yardley,   Brockagh,
Shirecliffe House,   County Mayo
Tamworth,
Staffordshire   27th April 1847

Dear Mrs. Yardley

It is my sad duty to tell you that your husband, Edward Yardley, has died here in Brockagh.

Mr. Yardley had been working these months past at Knockanure Union, where I first came to know him. He then came to Brockagh to set up a Soup Kitchen for the feeding of the starving, and he started fever sheds for the sick. But then he sickened and died yesterday. He has been buried here in Brockagh. There were none of his own faith here, so our priest, Fr. Nugent, read a Christian blessing over his grave.

Should you wish to know more you can write either to the Poor Law Commissioner, Mr. James Voisey, at Knockanure Union, Co. Mayo, or direct to Fr. Nugent here in Brockagh.

With sympathy,

Luke Ryan

As he was supervising the Kitchen in the centre of Brockagh, he saw a horseman coming towards him. It was Voisey. Luke showed him the Kitchen in operation, quiet lines of people moving to the pots. He explained about the other Kitchens at Ardnagrena, Lisnadee, Burrenabawn and Teenashilla. He also showed Voisey the fever cottages in Brockagh.

They went into the first cottage. The women were washing down the patients. Fresh straw was being spread on the floor, and in one corner a stinking heap of straw and excrement was being shovelled into a barrow. Luke saw the look in Voisey's eyes.

'It's the best we can do.'

'I know, I know,' Voisey replied. 'It's no worse than Knockanure.'

At that moment, a second barrow was wheeled in. A corpse was lifted into it, and wheeled out again. The two men glanced at each other.

'They're dying like flies,' Voisey said.

'Not like it used to be,' Luke said. 'It's better since we opened the Kitchens.'

'Where are you burying them?'

'In the graveyards. Pits. One in Knocklenagh, one here in Brockagh. Father Nugent is arranging all that.'

'We should thank the Lord for that. And for Father Nugent too, he's a good man.'

'You're right. I don't know what I'd have done here without him.'

'And Edward Yardley too. We need men like them.'

Luke stopped. 'I'm sorry, I should have told you. Yardley's dead. He got the fever, and died yesterday.'

Voisey looked at him in horror. 'Edward is dead?'

'He is.'

'We must write to his widow.'

'I've already done that.'

Voisey had a shaken, half-defeated look in his eyes.

'This fever spares no one. Edward too, on top of all the others. Will it never end?'

Afterwards Voisey explained that the Union was instituting a new

297

policy for Brockagh. It had been decided to ask Father Nugent to supervise the Soup Kitchens in Brockagh and the outlying districts on behalf of the Union. Corn and other food was now arriving in Ballina, and another consignment was to be sent in the next few days. In addition, Brockagh was to have a doctor. As a result, the Union had decided that it was no longer necessary to have any other clerks around Brockagh. Luke's work with the Union at Brockagh was to be terminated in two weeks. It had been decided that he should report back to Gaffney in Kilduff.

Luke thought about that. It all came flooding back to him, the Selections at Carrigard, turning away his own people. No, he had no interest in that. Carrigard, yes. But he would never work for the Union again.

That evening they discussed it all at Gallagher's. The time had come for definite decisions. Clearly Luke would have to leave Brockagh and take over the running of the farm with his father in Carrigard. Next day, he wrote a letter to his father and mother, saying he would return, bringing his bride with him.

Early next morning he lay beside Winnie on the bed.

'It seems the time has come.'

'It has, Luke. Time to start our real married life. And I'm looking forward to meeting all your family, after all you've told me about them. But still...'

'Yes. You'll be sorry to leave Brockagh.'

In many ways, he was relieved. Father Nugent was well regarded in the parish, and had the moral authority to run the Kitchens without question.

As promised, the supplies from Ballina arrived a few days later. Luke had not been requested to travel to Ballina. Corn was being imported in large quantities now, and the distribution system around the county was working well.

He was relieved too when the doctor arrived from Castlebar. He brought a young nurse with him. Luke showed them through the fever cottages in Brockagh, and then brought them around the outlying ones too. What he saw nauseated him again. He wondered whether he would ever harden up to it. But it would not be necessary anymore. He insisted now that Winnie stop working in the cottages.

When they left Brockagh, Gallagher insisted that he would bring them to Knockanure in the wagon. As they drove, Luke noticed that most of the Relief Works were still in operation. Only a few had closed since he had last been down to Knockanure. Davitt had been right. The Works around Brockagh had been closed well ahead of the rest of the county.

As they came close to the Union, a woman came up to the cart, one arm extended, a dead baby in the other.

'Please sirs, a penny for a coffin and a grave. I don't want the trench in the Union for the child.'

Winnie whipped the shawl across her own face. Luke took a few coins, and handed them to the woman, but her hands were shaking, and the coins dropped. When the wagon had passed, she scrabbled for them in the mud.

'How much did you give her,' Winnie asked.

'I don't know,' Luke said. 'I didn't look.' Gallagher glanced at him, but said nothing.

When they arrived, they left the wagon in the yard behind the administration block and went to Pat's office. Sarah was there too. This time, she did not leave the office.

Pat jumped up at once. 'By God, it's great to see you. Mr. Gallagher, I wasn't expecting you.'

'How else do you think they would have got here?' Gallagher asked. 'You don't think I'd leave my daughter to walk all the way?'

'Of course not.'

'Seems like you were expecting us,' Luke said.

'Expecting you!' Pat exclaimed. 'We've been expecting you for two weeks. Mother wrote to me at once, she was so delighted. And she's just dying to meet her new daughter-in-law. It seems I have to drive you over, not keep her waiting.'

'I was going to go on over,' Gallagher said.

'There's no need,' Pat said. 'I'll be able to borrow a Union wagon and take them over.'

'Fine so,' Luke said.

Pat sat, and waved Luke to the other seat. 'You know the other news?'

'What's that?' Luke asked.

'Morton's dead.'

'Yes. So I'd heard.'

'Isn't it great?'

'Now that's a terrible thing to say,' Sarah said. 'I told you before.'

'No, it's not,' Pat said. 'I've no pity for the bastard. May he rot in hell.'

'Be that as it may, you shouldn't talk like that about the dead.' She stood, and walked across to Winnie. 'You'll have to forgive them,' she said. 'No manners, these fellows. They haven't even offered you a seat.'

'Oh, my God,' Pat said, 'here, Winnie, sit down here.'

'It's a bit late now,' Sarah said, 'and you haven't introduced us either.' She took Winnie's hand. 'I'm delighted to meet you. I'm Sarah Cronin. I'm working here with Pat, trying to help him out. Not that I get much thanks for it.'

'Would you listen to her,' Pat said. 'Always complaining, never stops.'

Luke and Gallagher went to the next office to collect their wages. All the barony wages were now being paid out of Knockanure.

An hour later, Winnie hugged her father. Then Luke held out his hand as she mounted the wagon to drive to Carrigard.

Chapter Twenty Four

Tyrawly Herald, May 1847:

In some of the remote parts of this Union, particularly in the Barony of Erris, disease is committing serious havoc. On Monday, the 17th inst., in the townland in Inver in the Barony referred to, there were no less than 32 human beings dead – dead of famine – dead of pestilence produced and propagated by want. The deaths in this district arising from destitution and its consequences are awfully numerous and of daily occurrence.

When they were within a mile of Carrigard, he saw another Relief Works. As the existing road turned to the right, a new road was being built straight ahead. He noticed one difference from the ones he had already seen – the workers were wearing a uniform. The uniform of the Workhouse.

'What's this?' he asked his brother.

'Oh, this is the New Line too. It's running down to the bridge on the river. Meets up with the New Line from Carrigard.'

'They're still using gangs from the Workhouse?'

'That's right.'

Luke stood in the wagon, still observing. 'How many are there, Pat?'

'Three hundred anyhow.'

'They're very slow.'

'That's why they're so many.'

As they crossed the ford, he could see the new bridge, already half built, a hundred yards up the river.

'They're not using the Union fellows on that.'

'No. They need masons for that.'

'Stones from the quarry?'

'That's right. Ours and Benson's.'

As they came close to the house, the old road came closer to the New Line again. They drove past many people Luke knew, but no one acknowledged him.

Pat stopped the wagon by the entrance to the quarry.

'Father,' he shouted. Michael looked up from where he was watching a cart being loaded. Then he ran over.

'Well, by God. So this is Winnie.'

He came up to the front of the wagon, and grasped the bridle, leading the horse the last few yards to the house. He held out his hand for Winnie to get down. Then he did something that Luke had never expected. He hugged her and kissed her on the cheek. Then he led her into the house.

'Come on in, girl. Elly just can't wait to meet you.'

Luke held his breath as his mother ran across the kitchen.

'Winnie,' she cried as she threw her arms around her. She stood back. 'Now let's see you. Ian tells us all you're a fine class of a girl.'

'Oh, don't be silly.'

'No, no. That's what he said. You shouldn't be so shy about it neither.'

'But...'

'But sure enough of that. Come here now, I've something to show you.' She beckoned Winnie over to the cradle. Brigid was asleep.

'Shhh,' she said to Winnie, 'don't wake her.'

Winnie looked closely at the sleeping child. 'What age is she? A year perhaps?'

'A little over,' Eleanor said.

'Isn't she beautiful. Luke told me all about her. The poor little mite, with no mother.'

'I don't think I'd worry about that,' Luke said from the table. 'Little Brigid has more mothers than any girl in Mayo.'

And one more now, he thought.

He had noticed a change in the kitchen. There was a new wall to one end of it. His father saw him staring.

'Oh, you haven't seen this, of course. Your mother insisted, said you'd have to have a room to yourselves, the pair of you.'

Luke looked up at the wall, all the way to the apex at the rafters.

'It's well built.'

'Of course. Come on, I'll show you.'

They left the women in the kitchen, and his father brought him into the new bedroom. There was a solid wooden bed at one end.

'Where did this come from?' he asked.

'Where do you think,' his father replied. 'Your mother insisted I make this too. Good seasoned timber.'

Luke felt the headboard. 'By God, this will last for generations.'

'And so will we,' Michael said.

They walked out into the haggard.

'Now tell me, what about the potatoes?' Michael asked. 'What was the condition of them coming down from Brockagh?'

'Good enough. There was no sign of blight anyhow.'

'No, we seem to be lucky enough with the early crop. We won't have any difficulty here.'

'You're ahead of the rest of the county so. From what we saw, the spring planting is well down. I'd say there's only a quarter the normal amount.'

'A quarter!'

'Could be less.'

'What are they going to live on? The Kitchens?'

'The Kitchens for now at least,' Luke said. 'And with any luck, they'll have planted more potatoes, and we'll have a better crop in the autumn. And there's always the Workhouse.'

'There is,' Michael said. 'But what about Pat? What do you think – will he stay in Knockanure?'

'I was thinking about that. They've no Master, and the accounts are in a terrible way. I'm sure they'll keep him until they appoint a new Master. After that, I don't know.'

'Your mother is hoping they'll keep him. A good job as a clerk – he wouldn't have to go on the railways.'

'I doubt it'd happen. If they get a new Master, I can't see they could afford the expense of a new clerk as well.'

'A pity,' Michael said. 'And talking of clerks, there's a message for you from Gaffney. He wants to see you the minute you're back.'

'Gaffney?'

'You'll have to go tomorrow. He'll be in Carrigard for the morning.'

'What in hell does he want?'

'Seems they're a bit short again. Says he'll need you a lot over the next few weeks.'

Luke shook his head.

A room of their own. That night they made love, relaxed and easy for the first time since they had to leave the old cottage. Afterwards they lay back, talking quietly.

'I think I'm going to like your mother,' Winnie said.

'I knew you would. She's very like you.'

'Is that why you married me?'

'*Arra*, what. Would you stop annoying me.'

'Annoying you, is it? Isn't it the only way to get you to talk?'

'Don't I talk enough?'

'You never told me much about Nessy.'

'I know, *a ghrá*. It's just how I found it so hard to talk about.'

'Your mother told me more about her. It was a terrible thing.'

'I know. I was there when she died. It was awful. Did she tell you about everyone else though – Sabina, Aileen?'

'Yes,' Winnie said. 'And Kitty.'

'Who?'

'Who indeed? Kitty, and stop pretending you didn't hear.'

'I'd hoped she wouldn't tell you about that.'

'You'd told me already. And any way you look at it, there's Brigid. Kitty will want to see her, won't she?'

'I don't know what's going to happen now. I just don't know.'

'Don't worry. I'll do my best by her, I promise you, Luke.'

'I'm sure you will.'

'I will. And while we're talking of other girls, what about Sarah?'

'What about her?'

'I think you'll be seeing a lot more of her.'

'Why's that?'

'Oh, I don't know,' she replied. 'It's just her and Pat, the way they talk. There's something between them, I'm sure of it.'

'Would you have a bit of sense. He's only a young fellow, hardly nineteen. And she's older than him. Anyhow, she's from a different class, what could she see in Pat?'

'You might be right. But I still think there's something there.'

The next morning, after Pat had left, Eleanor took Brigid out of her bed and set her on the floor. The child ran across the floor towards the table. She threw her hands onto Winnie's knees. Then she looked into her face.

'*Not Kitty,*' she cried.

There was a silence. Luke was the first to speak.

'*You'd better be careful, little Brigid. A girl could get into trouble saying things like that.*'

Winnie had taken Brigid up, and was holding her on her lap, facing her. Brigid put her hand up, feeling Winnie's mouth and nose.

'*Not Kitty,*' she repeated.

Eleanor walked around the table. She picked Brigid up. Holding the child in one arm, she pointed to Winnie with the other.

'*Of course she's not Kitty, muttonhead. That's Winnie.*'

'*Winnie?*' the child asked.

'*Your new aunty. Aunty Winnie.*'

'*Aunty Winnie?*'

Luke was looking out the window.

'It's going to be a grand day by the look of it.'

'Aye,' Michael said, 'and there's no point in wasting it while there's work to be done. And don't forget, you've got to see Gaffney.'

The men left.

An hour later, Aileen came in. Winnie noticed the craven look in her eyes. But she greeted her warmly, and Aileen's mood began to change.

Then Sabina came. 'So this is Winnie. I've heard all about you.'

'I'm sure you have. I hope at least the half of it was good.'

'All of it was, at least what Ian told me. In fact, you know what? If he was a younger man, I'd be getting worried about him and you.'

Brigid ran across the room again to where Sabina sat on a stool beside the fire. She pulled again and again at Sabina's hand until Sabina stood, and followed her across the room. She brought her to Winnie, and pointed up.

'Winnie is Kitty now. New Kitty.'

'The notions they get,' Eleanor exclaimed. *''New Kitty' indeed.'*

Luke walked past the quarry and out where the New Line of road towards Knockanure was being completed. Thin skeletons of men and women were still working, levelling off the surface and tamping it down. He thought of Lisnadee, but in some ways this was worse. These were his own people. He knew many of them, but he did not greet any of them. They were starving, and he was not.

When he arrived at the old cottage, Gaffney was there.

'Glad to see you again. Did they work you hard?'

'No harder than here, Mr. Gaffney.'

'You look tired.'

'I haven't been sleeping well.'

'How's it in Brockagh?'

'Quieter than it was.'

'Any trouble?'

'We had a little at one of the sites. It quietened down fast enough though. The real trouble was people looking for food. No violence, no nothing, they were just always there. Following us everywhere, asking for food.'

'What about the Soup Kitchens?'

'Fine now, though they took long enough in the coming. They could have kept the Works open longer. We paid off everyone though, and closed them all down.'

'What? The Works are shut.'

'Weeks back.'

'You closed the Works before the Kitchens opened?'

'Not me, Mr. Gaffney. Castlebar. They opened the Kitchens weeks later. Lucky we had a Quaker Kitchen before that.'

Gaffney shook his head. 'And you let this happen?'

'I had no choice. I just wasn't given any supplies.'

'What! Why?'

There was nothing in Knockanure, and Castlebar wouldn't supply us.'

'But couldn't you have kept the Works open.'

'Strict instructions. Morton told me to shut down; wouldn't hear any objections.'

'Damn it, Luke, you should have written to me. We'd soon have sorted Morton out.'

Luke looked up in surprise, hardly able to think of what to say next. 'I didn't think of that,' he said at last. 'I wouldn't have thought you could.'

'No,' Gaffney said. 'I suppose you wouldn't. A pity.' He smiled. 'Not that it'll matter to poor Morton now. Seems the Almighty got to him first.'

'Yes,' Luke said. 'I'd heard that.'

Gaffney looked out the door, drumming his fingers on the table. Outside the gangs were assembling for the Works.

'Well, it seems like Morton had his way in Brockagh. But it isn't going to happen that way here. If Castlebar try anything like that on us, there'll be hell to pay.'

'Yes, Mr. Gaffney.'

Gaffney stood. 'By God, I'm glad you're back. There's a hell of a lot to be doing here.'

'But I'm not coming back,' Luke said.

Gaffney stopped dead, and looked at him, unbelieving. Then he walked back from the door, and sat on the corner of the desk.

'You're not coming back?'

'That's right. I've had too much of it. It's bad enough the way they hate me in Brockagh, and it's happened here too.'

'They hate you?'

'They do,' Luke replied. 'It's easier for you. You don't have to live here, but I do.'

Gaffney looked at him in amazement. 'But why would they hate you? You're helping them, aren't you? If you're fair, why should they hate you?'

'Nobody else sees it that way. Have you ever tried telling your own friends about fairness when you have to refuse them a ticket? And as for piecework – that's just cruel, and I won't have anything more to do with it.'

Gaffney stood up again. 'Look, you're tired; we're both tired. We'll talk again.'

One morning, when the men had gone out, Winnie and Eleanor were working alone.

'This will be a new life for you,' Eleanor said.

'I know it will, Mother, I've a lot to learn.'

'You don't have to call me Mother.'

'*Why not? That's what Luke calls you, and you are my mother now.*'

Eleanor thought about it for a while. '*Well, if I'm going to be your mother, I'll have to be a good one. Many mothers don't get on with their sons' wives. They think they've stolen their sons from them. They hate them.*'

'*But we're not going to be like that,*' Winnie said.

'*No, we're too much alike, you and me. And we've too much to be doing to be bothered hating one another.*'

'*Keeping our men happy.*'

'*Keeping them strong too. And they'll need to be strong, the times that are in it.*'

They took their pails down to the well. Brigid came with them, holding Winnie's hand.

There were already six women at the well. Two of the older ones sat on the wall, the other four gathered around them, all talking in Irish. As Eleanor and Winnie approached, a silence descended. Eleanor said nothing either. She and Winnie passed between the women, filled their pails, and walked back to the road.

'*They don't have much to say for themselves,*' Winnie said.

'*Indeed they don't. Eileen Walsh, she's Eamonn Walsh's widow. Luke had to refuse him a place on the Works. Gaffney had a rule about needing four children, and Luke couldn't take him on. The other one beside her, that's her sister. They're always going on about how Luke and Pat could get jobs, even though they didn't have any children at all.*'

As they started walking home, Winnie was surprised by the weight of the pails. After a hundred yards, she had to stop. Each of her palms had an angry red weal where the wire of the pail had cut into it.

'*I should have thought of that, alanna,*' Eleanor said. '*Tomorrow we'll take some rags to hold around the wire, though your hands will get used to it soon enough.*'

When they arrived home, Eleanor handed Winnie a clay pipe, and took another herself. Winnie was surprised. '*I wouldn't have thought you'd be able to buy tobacco.*'

'*We're not. But we've still a little bit left, hidden away where the fellows won't find it.*'

They sat on the stools beside the fire. Eleanor took a twig, put it into the flames, and then held it across to Winnie.

'*Now, tell me this child, what happened up the mountains with Luke? Why will he not talk about it?*'

'*I think it was too awful for him,*' Winnie replied. '*We saw it bad enough in Brockagh, and I'll tell you, that scared me. All the people, they were like skeletons, they were; begging us for food we couldn't give them. But up the*

306

mountains, when the snows came, they weren't just starving to death, they were freezing too. He was doing all he could, but what can you do when people drop dead right in front of you. They used to put the bodies over the horses every night, and bring them back to Knocklenagh for burying.'

'I see,' Eleanor said.

'But it wasn't only that, I think. There's other things too, but he won't tell me about them. He thought he was going mad, I don't know.'

Eleanor thought back to the time she had found him after Fergus's attack. What was it then? Was it the same now? She decided to put it out of her mind.

'So what now? What do ye think ye'll do now?'

Winnie sucked at the pipe, staring into the flames. 'I don't know,' she said. 'Luke is thinking of all sorts of things. Even America.'

'America!'

'Yes. And please, don't say that to anyone.'

'Of course not, child. But why?'

'It might be the only way. I don't know.'

America, Eleanor thought. She had always reckoned it was going to be America. Winnie was talking as if there was still a choice, but what choice was there? Luke would leave the farm and take Winnie with him. But what of Carrigard? Pat would have what he always wanted. If he still wanted it. She wondered about that.

And Kitty. What about Kitty? Kitty did not come. She did not come that day, nor the following week. Many evenings, Eleanor thought about it. In some ways, it was just as well. Introducing Winnie to Kitty could be difficult, and she had no idea how it would turn out. Again she began to miss Kitty and her fund of stories. She thought of going over to Brennans' to see if she could talk to her, but on reflection, she reckoned that might cause more trouble. She wondered if perhaps she would have to consider Kitty as belonging to the past, but this made her sad. She did not know what to do. In the end, she would be overtaken by events.

Luke walked up to the rath one evening, and sat on a rock, looking out on all the settlements he knew, stretching out the Knockanure Road and behind that up to the Mountain. *Gort mór, Abhann an Rí, Lios Cregain, Cnoc rua, Currach an Dúin, Áth na mBó, Craobhaín, Gort na Móna, Árd na gCaiseal, Sliabh Meán, Baile a' Cnoic.*

Most of the cabins had thatched roofs, but here and there he could see black gaps like rotten teeth, where the thatch had collapsed. Many cabins had smoke coming from rough chimneys, or streaming out through the doors. Many more had no smoke and no sign of life.

'What did Gaffney want?'

Luke spun around, surprised. 'You shouldn't have come up on me like that, Father. I wasn't expecting it.'

Michael sat down beside him.

'Well, go on.'

'He wanted me to work with him again. Help him with piecework, and closing the Works down, I think. After that, God knows.'

Michael took up a twig, and idly twisted it in his fingers. 'We should be able to do it well enough. I worked the farm on my own for long enough, I'll do it again.'

'There's no need. I'm not joining him.'

Michael broke the twig between his fingers. 'You're not!'

'I've had enough of it – here and in Brockagh. I'll be damned before I start forcing piecework on our own people and starving them when the Works close.'

For a long time, Michael said nothing. Then he pointed to a cottage a hundred yards away. 'You heard about old Roughneen, died of fever a few days back. His wife's got it now.' He pointed to the cottage beside it. 'The McGlinns, dead of hunger and fever, all except Matt. He's gone to America now.'

Luke looked at his father in horror. But Michael went on. He pointed further down the Knockanure road. 'Liscreggan over. Hunger and fever, they died like flies. It's better now, but they took a terrible beating.' He nodded towards the Mountain. 'Árd na gCaiseal, the half of them died of hunger. They didn't wait around for it in Sliabh Meán though, they took themselves off, every single one of them together, walking to Dublin and Liverpool and God knows where, there's not one of them left. Baile a' Cnoic, that's where your mother's people came from...'

'STOP IT.'

Michael turned around, and stared at him in surprise.

Luke stood up. 'I've had enough,' he whispered.

He started to walk down towards the house. Michael followed, breaking the twig into smaller and smaller pieces.

Next day, after the Works had closed, Gaffney came to the Ryan house carrying a brown leather satchel. Michael brought him in, and the three men sat around the table.

'I was thinking of what you were saying the other day,' Gaffney said to Luke. 'I can understand it too. Piecework is tough. Selection too. That can't be easy for any man who has family and friends around. But we've no choice. We have to get the work done.'

'Then let other people do it,' Luke said.

Winnie and Eleanor, both of whom were sitting by the fire, looked across in surprise. There was a silence.

'I will,' Gaffney said at length. 'I'll let other people deal with matters like that, but I still need you. So I've a suggestion to put to you. You can take it or leave it, but I'd ask you at least to listen.'

He leant down to the satchel, took out all the papers, and passed them across to Luke.

'You told me about Brockagh yourself, and how they closed the Works before the Kitchens opened. Well, I told you it wasn't going to happen like that here, and I am determined it will not. You know yourself what it's like dealing with Castlebar. Fine, Morton is gone, but even so we have to fight them every inch of the way. It's not just for badness, it's that they have far too much to be doing, and there's not enough food anyhow. So who is going to get that food? He who shouts the loudest. We have to have all the requisitions ready, we've got to have our arguments ready, we've got to be able to go and pick up the supplies when they're available. I'm responsible for it all now. Kilduff, Carrigard, the Mountain, the whole damned lot. It's going to be a rough summer. Have you seen how few potatoes are planted? Even without the blight, there's not going to be enough, and the Works are going to be over. What's going to happen then? People have to be fed, one way or the other. That's my responsibility now.'

He stood up, and pointed across the table to Luke.

'And yours.'

Luke said nothing.

'Fine,' Gaffney went on, 'I'm going to make it easy for you. I'm not asking you to supervise the Works, I'll handle that. As you said yourself, they can hate me, but I'm not worried about it. When this is all over, I'll be back in Dublin. So I'm prepared to protect you here, not have you doing the nasty work. But I'm not prepared to do everything myself. I need you too. I need you to help me to feed the people. Your own people.'

'Go on,' Luke said.

'Two things. First, we have to have all the requisitions done. What I want you to do is to work out what's needed for the Kitchens, do the requisitions, and make sure they're right. I don't want to have to check them, and I know with you I won't have to. Then when you're finished, take them over to Castlebar, and argue our corner with them. I need someone for that who's able to think on his feet. If there's one kind of food they don't have, we'll take another, whatever they've got. But we've got to get it. And don't take any excuses from them. Demand what's yours by right. The price of corn is way down, and it's pouring into Westport. But if we don't get it, there'll be no Kitchens here, and the people will starve.'

'I thought you said it was going to be easy, Mr. Gaffney.'

'Easy in not having to face the people on the Works, that was all I said. But by God, it's going to be hard work, and I know I can depend on you for that.'

Luke thought back to closing the Works at Ardnagrena. Men and women, frightened and angry. The old man calming his people. '*Your anger is not for them. These men will fight for food.*'

But would they see it like that in Carrigard? Or Kilduff? Would they believe that he was fighting for them, or that he was just another Government man?

Gaffney was leaning across the table.

'Well, Luke, what's it to be – yes or no?'

'Yes, damn it, yes.'

Michael saw Gaffney to the door. He came back to the table and stood staring at Luke. 'By God, aren't you the hard man, talking to Gaffney like that.'

'Talking to him,' Eleanor exclaimed. 'Sure, he hardly said a word.'

'Isn't that what I'm saying? I never thought I'd see Gaffney like that. Begging, he was. If he'd gone down on his knees, I wouldn't have been surprised. You're one tough fellow.'

'Tough, bedamned,' Luke said. 'He got his way in the end, didn't he. I was the one who gave in.'

'And why wouldn't you?' Eleanor said. 'Isn't he right. We'll still need the money. And the poor fellow needs your help, everyone does.'

He thought back to Ardnagrena and Lisnadee. The pit beside the Workhouse. He said nothing. Winnie came over from the fire, and took his hand.

'Remember what we agreed. Courage.'

'Yes,' he said. He gathered the papers, and put them into the satchel.

Next morning, he spread the papers across the kitchen table. There were many requisitions and worksheets, none of them totalled.

'Is there much work in it?' Winnie asked him.

'I reckon a few hours anyway.'

When he had finished adding and cross-checking, he walked up to Kilduff.

'I've gone as far as I can, Mr. Gaffney.'

'George,' Gaffney said

'What?'

'George is my name. There's no need to be officious, we're in this together now.'

'Fine,' Luke said, and placed the worksheets on the table. 'I think you'll find these are right, but you can check them if you like.'

'If you've done them, there's no need to check them. What about the rest?'

'These I'm concerned about,' Luke said, putting the requisition forms down. 'You're looking for an awful lot of corn. It's much more than we got in Brockagh.'

'Two reasons for that. One, we're going to need it around here. Don't forget, we have to feed the Mountain too. And two, no matter what we ask for, they're going to cut us back. If we ask for twice what we want, we might at least get the half of it. I doubt that will last us more than a few weeks, but we should be able to get something from the Quakers too.'

'Which Quakers?'

'That Yardley fellow over in Brockagh. I sent a message across. They might bring in some more through Ballina, but we don't know yet. Haven't had a reply from him yet.'

'Yardley is dead.'

'What!'

'Got the fever up in Brockagh. Dead in two days.'

Gaffney looked at him. 'Damn it, he was our only Quaker contact. We don't know anyone else.'

'So it's back to Castlebar, isn't it?'

'It is. Perhaps it's best if I can finish out these requisitions, I'll show you how. Then you can go over to Castlebar tomorrow and see how much they'll give you. The only problem is I don't have a horse to spare. I'll need my own.'

'I'll walk.'

An hour later, he was leaving the office.

'Haven't you forgotten something?' Gaffney asked him.

'What's that?'

'Your wages.'

'To be honest, I never even thought of them.'

'Two shillings thruppence a day. That's all Castlebar will allow.

'It'll be enough.'

'I hope so. Though with the hours you're going to be working, you'll be earning it.'

He set out well before dawn, walking towards Castlebar. The sun rose. Mayo was devastated. Few potato fields had been planted, most had only weeds growing. Sometimes he passed hungry people, but they ignored him. He saw a man's body slumped at the side of the road. Moving closer, he knelt beside it. He picked up the familiar smells of gangrene and decomposition. He stood and walked on.

What kind of country was this? Could he stay here, raise a family in

311

such a place? If it was only for Winnie and himself, he would say 'no, forget Mayo, let's go to America,' but what of his father and mother? And what about the farm?

It was still morning when he arrived. Castlebar was no different to the countryside, except the hungry were gathered in clusters. The town was silent, and it had started to rain. The Soup Kitchen was already open, six giant pots, lines of hundreds extending from each. They stretched across the street and down the Green, blocking his way. He forced his way through each line. People shuffled back, but no one said anything.

When he came to the administration block, he thought of calling in to see if either McKinnon or Davitt were there, but he decided against it. He asked his way to the requisitions office. There were already five men waiting outside. One was from the north west of the county. 'I don't know why I'm here,' he said to Luke. 'There's been no rates paid, I doubt they'll give much corn.'

The man went in. A few minutes later, he pushed his way out past Luke, but said nothing. Luke entered. He handed the requisitions to the clerk. As Gaffney had expected, they were cut back, but not as much as Luke had feared.

'When can we expect it?' he asked the clerk.

'As soon as ye get it. That's up to you.'

'I don't understand.'

'Look,' the clerk said, 'it's in Westport, and we've no way of getting it to you.'

He stamped the requisitions, and handed them back to him.

'McMahon's, they're the corn factors, it's all paid for. Second warehouse on the quays in Westport. All you have to do is bring your wagons and collect it.'

'Wagons. We don't have wagons.'

'Neither do we.'

Chapter Twenty Five

Tyrawly Herald, May 1847:
Even sudden deaths are now of almost momentary frequen-
cy so worn and exhausted are the physical energies of the
people. On Tuesday last a wretched man dropped dead at
Crosspatrick, near Killala, from mere destitution. This is a
fearful state of things, and what renders it doubly so is its
pervading generality.

He walked back towards Kilduff. As he passed the cottage, he saw the body again. A dog was sniffing at it. He took a stick and drove the animal away, but when he looked back from the next corner, he could see the dog returning. He went on, but the distance was beginning to tell on him. He found a shed and slept, slumped sideways across the turf. It was dark when he woke, and he walked on through the night to Carrigard.

Next morning, he went to Gaffney's office.

'How did it go?' Gaffney asked him.

'Good and bad. They only cut us back a quarter, but we have to collect it ourselves.'

'Collect it!'

'They've no wagons,' Luke said.

'No wagons! Do they think we have wagons?'

'What they think doesn't matter, they're leaving it to us.'

'But we don't have any.'

'I know. And damned few horses either. We're going to have to use carts. Donkey-and-carts.'

Gaffney stared at him unbelieving. 'Donkey-and-carts! How many do you think we'll need of those?'

'I don't know. If we can't get enough, we'll just have to do the trip twice.'

'Twice? To Castlebar?'

'Westport, George.'

'Westport! That's twice the distance. Why in hell Westport?'

'They've no supplies in Castlebar. It's still in the warehouses in Westport.'

'And how the devil are we going to get it all here on time?' He threw a letter onto the table. 'This came in from Castlebar this morning. They want the Works closed on Saturday.'

Luke read through the letter. 'They seem pretty definite about it.'

'I wouldn't worry about it yet. I'm intending to ride over to Castlebar, kick up hell about it. I might be able to get an extension, but not for long. But we're going to have to get that corn, one way or the other.'

'So what now?'

Gaffney stood up and walked to the window. After a few moments, he turned back towards Luke. 'There are three things we have to do, and every one of them is damned near impossible. First, we get an extension to the Works. Second, we find as many donkeys as we can, if they haven't all been eaten. And third, we pay the men to drive the carts to Westport.'

'Pay them!' Luke exclaimed.

'Pay them, and keep our mouths shut. Pretend it's all part of the Works. Morton's dead, the bastard, no one is going to be checking whether we're paying them to swing a pick or drive a donkey. Except McKinnon, and he'll keep his mouth shut.'

'He will.'

'Now here's our plan. I'm going over to Castlebar in the morning to get an extension on the Works. I'll have a word with McKinnon when I get back. And you,' – he pointed at Luke – 'you find those bloody donkeys.'

Luke spent the next day walking the farms around Kilduff. Even though he knew some of the farms that had donkeys before the blight, it was a hard search now. He did not want to say what he was looking for. In some farms, he saw donkeys tethered or out in the fields. Many were emaciated. He ignored those. As he had expected, many farms had no donkeys at all. He walked to the Mountain and found almost none.

What he found was starving people – and worse. In one cabin, there were three children sitting on the floor across from the dead body of a woman lying on a bed of heather and straw. In another, he found the corpse of a man, clearly dead for some time, the face and finger-tips gnawed away. He noted down the locations of both cabins to tell the priest later.

Where he found any donkeys that were strong enough, he noted their owners on a scrap of paper. That evening he returned to Gaffney's office. McKinnon was there.

'Well, Luke?' Gaffney asked.

'I reckon we might get them. Twenty anyhow, maybe more.'

'We might be able to work it so. We've got an extension on the Works, though it's only a week. And Ian is willing to turn a blind eye.'

'What about the piecework?' Luke asked.

'I wouldn't worry,' McKinnon said. 'They've no spare surveyors in Castlebar. If I say the work's been done, it's been done, and that's all about it.'

'And what happens if Castlebar finds out?'

'Then I'll go over and raise hell with them again,' Gaffney answered. 'They're asking us to do the impossible, so what do they expect? Now stop worrying.'

He took Luke's list and glanced through it. 'How many of these people are on the Works?'

'I don't know, but I'm reckoning the most of them.'

He took out the worksheets. 'Let's work through them. See how many are on the list here, and we'll have a word with them all tomorrow.'

Two days later, the convoy left Kilduff. Sixteen carts, some with horses, most with donkeys. Michael led the way, driving their cart along, out the road towards Castlebar.

An hour from Kilduff they fell in with a group of young men and women walking. Each had a pack slung over their shoulders, and they were clearly tired. One asked if they could sit on the carts. Michael was doubtful, but they were all taken on board, two or three on each cart. The couple sitting with Michael were carrying a baby. Luke followed behind, walking.

'*Where are you all heading?*' he asked.

'*Westport,*' the man replied '*and after that, America, God willing. There's no future for us here. We're reckoning we might as well go while we're still strong. Another blight, and we'll have neither strength nor money.*'

They were passing a small mud cabin. A woman stood outside, holding a baby, two more in the doorway behind her.

'*Food...*' the woman asked, holding her hand out. Luke knew his father was carrying hard boiled corn in the cart, but he said nothing, and walked on.

'*Where would ye go in America,*' Luke asked the couple.

'*We don't rightly know. There's talk of work on the railways, they're building any god's amount of them.*'

When they reached Castlebar, the Kitchens were already open. Once again it was necessary to cross through the lines, but this time it was more difficult than it had been for Luke walking on his own. Michael was leading the first cart. He came up to the edge of the first line, and stopped. The line kept shuffling forward, but no one looked towards Michael. It was as if he did not exist.

'Can you make way there?' he asked.

Still they dragged themselves forward, each following close behind the one in front.

'*Come on, come on, move back there. We've got to get through.*'

Luke could see his father was getting angry. Michael tried to force his way through the crowd, but his horse shied back.

Luke walked back along the line of carts.

'*We're going to need your help here,*' he said to the three young men in one of the carts. '*We're not going to get to Westport otherwise.*'

When a dozen of the younger men had joined him, they made their way to the top again. Pushing through, they forced a way through the first of the lines. Michael led the horse forward, the other carts following in close order. The crowd was no longer silent. There was much swearing and pushing as the convoy forced its way through each of the lines, and broke clear.

'Damned bastards,' a man shouted after them. 'You just wait till you're coming back.'

Outside the town, they saw an over-turned wagon by the road. There were empty sacks strewn across the road. Many had burst, and a few women were picking the last grains from the mud.

A few miles further, they met a convoy coming towards them – three corn carts, accompanied by militia. They each stopped.

'Where are you headed?' Luke asked one driver.

'Castlebar. And I can tell you we're going to need the soldiers. There'd be riots in the town otherwise.'

'I'd say you're right,' he said, and they drove on.

When they reached Westport, the convoy halted outside the docks, and Michael stayed with the carts. Luke walked down the quays towards the warehouses. He could see four ships unloading. Outside he could see the sails of more ships riding at anchor, waiting to unload. At the end of the docks though, he could see that one was being loaded, live cattle being driven in at one end, barrels rolled in at the other. Closer in there were three more ships tied up. The docks beside them were crowded with hundreds of people.

The woman handed Luke a baby out of a cart. Her man jumped down, and helped her out.

'*Good luck in America,*' Luke said as he handed the baby back.

He went into the warehouse, where he was directed upstairs to a young clerk in a rough office overlooking the corn. He presented the stamped requisition forms.

'Ah yes, Mr. Ryan. We've been expecting you. We should have this consignment loaded up for you in an hour or so, all ready to roll.'

'I believe I have to see it weighed,' Luke said.

'That's right. In case you're concerned, the Weights & Measures fellow was around just two days ago.'

'I'm happy to hear that.'

'Not that we'd dare to do anything. They'd hang us out of the rafters here, if they even thought we were trying short-measure.'

Luke looked down through the warehouse. Beneath him were mountains of loose corn. In the centre, sacks of corn were built high in stacks, men on the ground unloading them from the carts onto pallets to be hoisted to the men on top, still building them higher. Idly he counted down one of the stacks and along each side, multiplying it all out. He shook his head at his own answer. He looked back to the clerk.

'Just one thing I'm puzzled about. I saw a ship down the end. It seems to be loading up.'

'Ah yes, that's right,' the clerk said. 'Cattle and butter going over to England. Does it surprise you?'

'Just a little. I didn't think we'd be sending food out at a time like this.'

'Yes, I suppose it is surprising. And there'll be more to come after harvest. We send a lot of grain from here to Dublin. Including barley for Guinness – most important.'

'But isn't it a bit odd? Bringing corn all the way in from America, while we're sending food out?'

The clerk pressed his fingers together, looking out the barred window. 'Yes, in ways you're right. But you see, Indian corn is cheap food. Butter and beef, they're far too expensive. It's better to supply ten pounds of corn than one pound of beef, don't you think?'

'But why not just keep it all here in Mayo – corn and beef?'

'How would you pay for the Soup Kitchens then?'

'I thought the Government was paying for them?'

'Not quite,' the clerk said. 'It's not like with the Relief Works. It's the ratepayers that are paying for the Soup Kitchens. Alright, the Government is lending them most of the money, but in the end, it's out of their pockets. If there's no money from beef, there's no money to pay the rates, and no money for corn.'

'I'm damned sure there's many of them that could well afford to pay the rates. Lucan and Clanowen, for example.'

'True enough, but there's many that can't. I reckon half the landlords in Mayo are bankrupt already.'

Luke walked back past the line of carts and wagons towards where his father was waiting. They brought their own convoy forward, and joined the line. As they came closer, the clerk came out.

'I was looking for you. We want you to witness the weighing.'

Luke followed the clerk back inside. A bare pallet was weighed, and then each pallet load was weighed separately and brought down to their allocated loading bay. All through the loading, groups of emigrants passed alongside the carts, heading for the end of the docks.

'How many militia men are coming with us?' Luke asked the clerk.

The clerk looked at him in astonishment. 'Militia men? Where the devil do you think we'd get militia men.'

'We had militia before, up in Brockagh.'

'Ah yes,' the clerk said. 'But that was then. With this amount of corn coming in, there's no chance. They only go with the big convoys – Castlebar, Claremorris and the like. Can't be wasting militia men on small loads.'

When Luke had signed for everything, and the carts were loaded, Michael started to turn the convoy around and led the carts back towards Castlebar and Kilduff. It was getting dark. Luke kept thinking of what the clerk had told him of food leaving Mayo. For a long time, he could not shake the lines of cattle and barrels of butter out of his mind. Nor could he stop thinking of the gangs of emigrants walking past and the increasing crowds at the end of the pier. Food out, food in. People out, but sure as hell, none coming in.

Michael interrupted his thoughts. 'We're not going to make Kilduff tonight. And you know what, I don't think we should even try. We should stay this side of Castlebar for the night. If we've no militia men, we'd be risking everything trying to run through the town. '

'We could just as easy be attacked out here, Father.'

'We could, but there'd be less of them. We'd be better able to protect ourselves. Then we can make our way through Castlebar early in the morning when everyone is asleep.'

An hour later, they stopped beside a high wall.

'That would be the side of Lord Sligo's estate,' Michael said.

'I'd guess you're right, Father.'

'The wall will protect us. We'll stay here.'

With much cursing and swearing, they backed the horses and donkeys off the road so as to push the end of the carts up against the wall, axle to axle beside each other. Then they released the donkeys, tying them under a few trees beside the carts. It was drizzling. Some of the men crept under their carts to shelter. Luke stood with Michael at one end of the line of carts.

'What do you think, Father? Will we get through?'

'I think we will. Though if I thought we'd have no soldiers, I'd have brought another dozen or twenty men with us. We might have need for them.'

'You think we'll have to fight?'

'We might, and if we do, we'll fight like hell. Castlebar town has already got its own supplies. We've no need to feel sorry for anyone. These are our supplies, and we've got every right to them.'

They stood under a tree for another hour, rain dripping from the branches.

'It's quiet enough now,' Michael said. 'No one's going to come tonight. You go to sleep.'

'No Father, I'll stay on watch.'

'No, you sleep for now. I'll wake you in a few hours, and you can take over the watch.'

Luke crept under the cart. Again he started thinking of cattle and butter going out of Westport. At last he decided to stop worrying about it and think of his own immediate duties. And Winnie.

He was asleep when the shouting woke him. Through the noise, he heard his father's voice – 'Get up, get up. We're being attacked.'

He came out, rubbing his eyes in the half light of early dawn. The other men were already crawling out from under the carts. There was a crowd of twenty or thirty men and women trying to surround the carts at the back of the convoy.

Already two men were on top of the last wagon, passing out sacks of corn. The women were throwing stones and rocks at the Kilduff men, who had little to defend themselves apart from a few whips and the long sticks they used for the donkeys. The animals were braying in fright.

They were outnumbered, but he saw that half the crowd were women. While the men fought, the women were grabbing sacks of corn from the carts and trying to run away, staggering under the weight. Some had children, screaming with fright as they grasped their mothers' skirts. On the edge he saw a woman holding a baby, standing and watching the scene, directing the women to where the carts were least defended.

Luke raced to where the sacks were being passed down, and lashed a woman across her arms. She screamed in pain and fell back. Two other women attacked him, but his father lashed one of them with his whip, and Luke lashed the second one across the mouth, drawing blood. Two men came at them in fury, one swung out at him with his fist, but Luke seized his fist, twisted his arm around, and dropped him heavily on the ground. His father was down, but again Luke grasped the assailant by one arm, jerked it behind his back, and twisted hard. The man screamed in pain, and rolled off Michael.

Another attacker rushed at Michael, who was still on the ground. He was brandishing a rock over Michael's head. Luke grabbed a stone, and smashed it into the man's head. He stared at Luke with a look of childish surprise. Then he dropped silently to the ground.

The fight became more bloody, as both sides used stones and rocks. The tide of the battle was turning, as the advantage of the stronger Kilduff men started to tell against the half-starved mob. A few more minutes, and some of them started to fall back, dragging their injured with them. They were pursued by the Kilduff men until Michael called them off.

Luke returned from the chase. The man he had hit was still lying where he had fallen, a shallow bloodied depression in the side of his forehead. Luke knelt beside him. Carefully he felt through his protruding ribs for breathing or heartbeat.

There was none.

'Luke, what are you doing? Come on.'

Impatiently, he waved his hand at his father, still watching for any movement in the man's chest. None. He leant over the man, holding his ear over the man's mouth, listening for breathing and the feel of it on his ear.

None.

He stood up. There were bags on the road, including some that had burst.

'Leave the burst ones,' Michael shouted. 'We've no time.'

They loaded the rest into the carts, together with four injured men. Then the convoy started off towards Castlebar, Luke and Michael each leading two carts. Already the starving people were creeping back to pick up the corn lying on the ground. In the convoy, the injured men groaned as the carts jolted along. The rain had stopped.

The sun was rising as they reached Castlebar, but as Michael had anticipated, there was no one in the streets, and they passed through unscathed. For the rest of the journey they were watched from cottages and fields by skeletal men and women, but no one attacked them.

Late that afternoon they arrived in Kilduff. The carts were unloaded, and the sacks were carried into one of the houses on the main street. Four men were put on guard, two on the front and two on the back.

'Ye're both very quiet,' Eleanor said.

'You tell her, Luke.'

'We were attacked coming out of Westport.'

'Attacked? But who attacked ye?'

'A crowd of hungry people, that's who,' Luke replied. 'They wanted our corn, and we wouldn't give it to them.'

'Damned right, we wouldn't,' Michael said. 'And by God, we had a hell of a fight to keep it. One fellow, he was going to kill me with a rock when I was down. I'd be dead now if it wasn't for Luke. Gave him a belt of a stone, that sorted him out.'

'He was going to kill you?' Eleanor exclaimed. 'But why...?'

'They're desperate, that's why,' Luke said. 'There's other places around where the Works closed early. Most of the loads going from Westport have militia men going with them, but they're only taking them to the big towns first. It's a terrible thing, taking corn past starving people.'

'Aye,' Michael said, 'and taking cattle and butter the other way too.'

'The other way?'

'That's right,' Luke said. 'They're sending cattle and butter to England to pay for corn from everywhere else.'

'But why?' Winnie asked. 'I don't understand.'

'Corn's cheaper, so we get more of it. At least that's what the fellow told me.'

'But that's mad,' Eleanor said.

'I don't know if it is or it isn't. But I'll tell you this, Mother, Westport is like nothing on earth. The ships are lining up to come in. The warehouses are stuffed with corn and all sorts of things. Flour, wheat, rice, beans – you can't imagine it. It's getting enough of it out of Westport, that's the thing.'

He found it impossible to sleep that night. Gaunt scarecrows, walking skeletons. He had not started working with Gaffney to be fighting desperate men and starving women. But if they hadn't fought, the supplies would never have got through to Kilduff. The rest of Mayo would have their corn soon enough.

But it was worse than that. He had killed a man. No matter which way he looked at it, no matter how much they were protecting their own corn and their own people, there was a man dead, and he had done it. But if he hadn't, Michael would be dead. Maybe, maybe not.

He could not get away from the corpse lying on the ground. Feeling for any sign of life through the man's ribs, no flesh between them. Perhaps there was a heartbeat, perhaps he just hadn't felt it. Maybe the man was still alive. Did he believe that? No.

What now? He had told no one, not even his father, and it was not that Michael would ever talk. Winnie neither. But if the secret ever got out, he would hang for it.

Did their attackers know where they were from, though? Probably not. And even if they did, no one could identify who had killed the man. The battle had been savage and confused. No one would be able to trace it back to him.

But still, however it had happened, however good the reason for it, he had killed a starving man. He kept trying to sleep, but his dreams were troubled, and he awoke again and again.

'What's wrong?'

'Nothing. I just can't sleep.'

'Was it the fight?'

'Yes, yes. It was a desperate thing.'

'Tell me about it.'

'Not now, pet. Some other time. Go back to sleep.'

He slept a little, but when he woke he was still tired. Winnie was asleep, and he did not disturb her. He dressed, ate a little bread with buttermilk, and left the house.

When he arrived in the office, Gaffney was already there.

'You're in early.'

'I couldn't sleep,' Luke said.

'Wasn't it worth it?'

'What?'

'What?' Gaffney repeated, eyebrows raised. 'You brought the corn back from Westport, you did the impossible, and you say 'what?''

'Oh sorry, I wasn't thinking about that. We had to fight for it, you heard about that?'

'Heard about it! Everyone has heard about it. I knew I could depend on you. Come hell or high water, I knew you'd bring the corn home.'

Over the next few weeks, he stayed in Gaffney's office, going through the lists of people on the Works and deciding who should have food tickets for the Kitchens. Then he sent a message to Father Reilly, who joined him, filling in the blanks – the families who had never been on the Works and perhaps needed food even more. In the evenings, he would go down to the house they were using as a warehouse to check the allocation of sacks of corn and rice for each of the Kitchens and decide which men from the Works would accompany the carts up to the feeding points. He continued working on the worksheets too, calculating daily rates and piecework for each of the workers. Often he took papers home at night and worked till late in the light of a candle that he had taken from the office.

'Will it be enough, George?' he asked Gaffney one night.

'What? The Kitchens?'

'Yes. Can they feed them all?'

'Damned if I know,' Gaffney said, 'but I'll tell you, Luke, Ireland has never seen anything like this. You know, the last time I was over with Andy Irvine he told me they were feeding hundreds of thousands of people in Mayo alone.'

'Hundreds of thousands?'

'One, two, three hundred thousand, he had no idea. But whatever it is, it's a very big number, and if they're doing this in one county, can you think what it's like right across the country.'

Luke shook his head. 'Sure don't I know? Didn't I see it in Westport myself? Ships lining up, bringing the corn in. But will it be enough? That's the question, isn't it?'

'God only knows the answer to that,' Gaffney said. 'But I just hope to God they keep the Kitchens running. If they close them early, there'll be a famine the likes of which this country has never seen.'

As Gaffney had promised, he was not asked to involve himself in the day to day operation of the Kitchens. In spite of the worst famine in memory, the people still felt humiliated to have to queue for food. Michael refused to join any queue, paying or otherwise. Instead, Eleanor visited the corn merchant every week and bought the corn. Sometimes Luke would accompany her, and was amazed to note that his mother was a very good negotiator. The price of corn was dropping, and Eleanor was always the first to know about it.

Still he could not sleep. Always he saw the look of surprise on his victim's face as the stone smashed the side of his skull, turning into a look of emptiness as he slumped to the ground. No-one else seemed to be worried though. Stories of the battle by Lord Sligo's wall had circulated in the entire district, and all the men involved were proud of their role in it. The more he thought of it though, the worse he felt. Fighting hungry women, killing a hungry man. Pride never came into it.

Once again, he was torn both ways. He discussed everything with Winnie. The daily evidence of fever still horrified him, but they had potatoes again, even if many did not. In addition, he had his work, and he felt he could not abandon it. Perhaps things would improve across the summer. Perhaps the harvest in autumn would be a good one, and his responsibilities would be less. In any case, this would give him time to consider where he should go and what he should do.

Gaffney had fever sheds constructed in all the townlands around Kilduff. On Luke's advice, these were built a distance from the villages, and in many areas they used abandoned cottages. For fever-ridden people, there was no shame in accepting food, and Luke organised the feeding of the patients. Not that they could eat very much. In the final stages of fever, they ate nothing at all.

Winnie wanted to work in the fever sheds on the Carrigard side of Kilduff, but this time, Luke forbade it. She protested, but this was one point on which he would not be moved.

Gaffney kept his word. He waited until the Soup Kitchens were fully working before the Relief Works were closed.

Luke knew the day on which the Works would be closed. It was a Saturday, and he made sure to stay in Gaffney's office that day, working through the final calculations on the worksheets. He had no desire to see what was happening on the Works – he had seen it enough already. He prepared the calculations and the cash for the final payments. The gangers came to his office to collect the cash, but he did not accompany them back to the Works, nor on their journeys around Kilduff and the Mountain the next week, paying the dying and the dead.

But he still had to supply food to the fever sheds. As he accompanied the carts, he saw the results of the Works closures. Some roads were complete. The New Line from Carrigard running out to the Knockanure road had been finished some weeks before, as the last stones were laid on the bridge. But up the Mountain, some roads were incomplete. He saw abandoned quarries and water-logged trenches where roads had been cut through the turf, but never reached anywhere.

He had avoided the worst. He had kept far distant from the Kitchens; avoided seeing the humiliation in his own people. But the fever sheds brought him back to the horror. One night he twisted and turned until Winnie woke, and held him tight.

'Don't worry,' she whispered. 'It'll be over soon. All bad things come to an end.'

Late one night, Eleanor answered a knock on the door. One of the constables from Kilduff Barracks was outside. He lived close by Carrigard.

He held one finger to his lips. 'There's evictions tomorrow.'

She stared at him.

'Over at Clanowen's land at *Gort na Móna*. They're sending a crowbar brigade down from Claremorris. They're intent on levelling forty houses.' He held his finger to his lips again. 'I'm not telling anyone else. And you never saw me here tonight.'

'I never heard anything,' Eleanor replied. 'I never saw anyone.'

Then he was gone. She walked back into the room.

'Who was there?' asked Michael.

'No-one important,' Eleanor said.

'What did he say?'

'He said there's evictions tomorrow at *Gort na Móna*. Seems Clanowen is sending in a crowbar gang. They're levelling forty houses.'

'Who was it though?' Luke asked.

'Never you mind.'

'We'll have to tell them,' Winnie said.

'It'll cause a riot if we tell them,' Michael said.

'But we can't not tell them,' Eleanor said. 'It'll be terrible if they're taken by surprise. What's the worse? Do we tell them or not?'

'I don't know,' Michael said. 'We'll be damned if we do, and damned if we don't.'

'I think we'll have to,' Winnie said. 'There'll have to be houses arranged for them to go to. The sooner the better for that.'

'You're right, but we'll still be blamed for any trouble.'

'It'll wait till the morning,' Eleanor said. 'We'll do it at sunrise.'

Before dawn, they went in different directions to raise the alarm, and to see which houses might be willing to take in evicted families. Eleanor walked down to Kilduff to notify Father Reilly and Doctor Stone. As she passed the RIC barracks, she noticed the activity inside, many men in rough civilian clothes eating an early breakfast. Sergeant Kavanagh was supervising, as his own men seated the others and brought out the food. There were military uniforms too. And sabres. Now she knew for certain.

Luke and Winnie had been up before dawn and cut across directly to *Gort na Móna* without taking the main road to Kilduff. Their arrival caused panic. Within twenty minutes, the whole district was awake.

'*How do we know it's true?*' asked one woman.

'We don't,' Winnie said. '*We only have it on what we were told. It could be wrong.*'

'*It's as well to be prepared,*' one said. '*Bad news has an awful habit of being true.*'

'*We'll fight the bastards,*' one of the younger men said.

'*Have care,*' another said. '*Eviction is bad, but transportation is worse. No one comes back from Van Diemen's Land.*'

Father Reilly arrived.

'*How many of you here are behind with your rent?*' he asked.

'*Most all of us, Father,*' one of the men replied. '*And those of us that aren't are only tenants at his lordship's pleasure.*'

'*But even tenants-at-will, they wouldn't take their growing crops,*' another said.

'*Clanowen would,*' an old woman said. '*He's done it before, he'll do it again.*'

By now, a crowd of fifty men had formed at the front.

'*We're going to fight them, Father.*'

'*I would advise you against that. They've got military with them.*'

'*But we can't just let them walk in and destroy our houses.*'

'*There's nothing else we can do. Fight to win – perhaps. Fight to die – why would you want to do that?*'

'*You're a coward,*' a voice shouted from the back. The priest turned in the direction from which the shout had come. No one spoke. '*If there's killing to be done here today, I will put my own neck forward first. Will that make you happy?*'

Still, no one spoke. Then a man at the front broke the silence. '*We must try, Father. Perhaps we do not fight, but why make it easy? If we stand in their way without moving, they're the ones that must attack, not us.*'

'*If that's what you want, I can't stop you.*'

A young woman came over to the priest, and clutched his sleeve. '*If they evict us, what will happen to us?*'

'*Yes, Father,*' asked an older woman. '*Where will we sleep tonight.*'

'*I'm hoping tonight will be alright. We're sending messages to whoever might be willing to take you, and of course the church remains open.*'

'*And after that, Father?*'

'*I don't know,*' Father Reilly said. '*I just don't know.*'

They waited another hour. The crowd of men at the front had grown to nearly a hundred, and the tension mounted. Luke reckoned few were fit enough to fight anyone, armed or otherwise. If there was to be a battle, it would be a massacre.

There was a shout from one of the men on the corner. Ten cavalry men appeared, followed by a gang of twenty or thirty men, with four carts carrying battering rams and crowbars. On the flanks there were eight constables, including four from the Kilduff RIC barracks. They came closer, a steady tramp of hooves and boots, bridles rattling.

Many of the younger men at the front were armed with pitchforks. The six cavalrymen came right up to them, and halted. The officer, a pitchfork at his horse and another at his chest, took a piece of paper from his pocket.

'SILENCE,' he roared.

The noise subsided. He started to read from the paper.

'Our Sovereign Lady the Queen, charges and commands that all persons being assembled immediately do disperse themselves, and peaceably do depart to their habitations or their lawful business upon the pains contained in the Act made in the first year of King George the First for preventing tumultuous and riotous assemblies. God save the Queen.'

For a few seconds, nobody moved. Then a stone came from the back of the crowd, and hit one of the cavalrymen in the face, drawing blood. The officer looked to all the soldiers, their hands on the hilts of their sabres, and shouted an order. The sabres were drawn.

'*Stop,*' shouted Father Reilly. He walked down between the sabres and the pitchforks. Both sides shuffled a few steps back to let him pass. He addressed the crowd. '*We have no chance. What you have heard is the Riot Act. If there's a battle now, they'll call it a riot, and all involved will be transported. And if anyone is killed, men here will be hung.*'

He stopped for a few seconds. No one spoke.

'*It's the work of the Devil,*' he went on, '*but this time we must turn our cheeks. Start getting your things together, and we'll arrange where everyone will sleep tonight.'*

The crowd started to disperse. But it was not finished yet.

'I want the man who threw that stone found and arrested,' the officer shouted.

The priest turned back and walked up to the horse. He looked the officer straight in the eyes. 'You've had your way,' he whispered in English. 'It could have been worse. Just let things be.'

The officer dropped his eyes.

Over the next hour, the eviction proceeded without violence. From time to time, curses were shouted at the tumblers, and at the soldiers and police protecting them. The soldiers were from the Claremorris barracks, far enough away to know no one. But a few of the RIC men from Kilduff looked unhappy.

Carts had arrived in from the surrounding area, and household goods and possessions were being loaded up, and taken away. Luke and Winnie both helped in emptying the houses and loading the carts. He saw his father's horse and cart half way down the line, waiting to be loaded.

'Hold on a moment, Winnie,' he said, and walked down towards his father. Just as he got to the cart, the priest came. 'I was wondering if you could manage four tonight.'

'Of course, Father,' Michael answered him.

'Ellen Morrisroe and her three children. She's a widow.'

The priest led them to one of the cabins that had not yet been tumbled. There was a woman inside with three children around her, all under ten.

'Luke Ryan,' she said, almost whispering. *'You killed my man.'*

No one moved. *'Their father,'* she said, pointing at the children. *'You killed him. You wouldn't let him on the Works.'*

'Leave this to me,' Winnie said, her hand on his shoulder. He hesitated. The priest took his arm. 'Come on.' The two men walked out.

He went to where his father was waiting with the cart, and the two men led it back to the widow's house. Already other carts were moving down the rough road towards Kilduff. Soldiers stood in groups, sometimes talking among themselves, mostly saying nothing. At the back of the village, the tumblers had already started their work and were prising stones from the apex of a roof. One of the cross-beams collapsed, bringing the roof down at one end. A minute later, the other end collapsed too, and the roof disintegrated into a heap of thatch.

Tumbling cabins. He thought of bringing Sorcha to the Workhouse. Tumbling her cabin, burning the thatch. The work of the Devil? No, not possible. Not us.

A few minutes later, Winnie came out again with the widow and her children. The woman was crying. Luke and his father started to load her possessions onto the cart. The tumblers had started on the house across from them. Again the roof collapsed at one gable. Luke passed his father a hessian sack of turnips, and they unloaded it into the cart before he went back for more. Three sackfuls of turnips, a small flitch of beef and buttermilk.

The cabin beside them was proving more difficult. Every time the tumblers knocked stones or mud from its crossbeam, it fell down to the next level, but would not collapse. Two of the tumblers were working with a crowbar and a heavy hammer. They were sweating heavily, even though it was not yet warm.

'Not used to heavy work, those fellows,' Luke said.

'Or maybe just frightened,' his father answered. 'God knows, they've enough to be frightened about, soldiers or not.'

They continued the loading. The roof across from them was now on the ground, but it would not flatten. It formed a long tent, from the ground at one end to half way up the gable at the other. The two tumblers were jumping up and down on it, but making little impression. One of the others came over.

'Can you not do better than that?' he shouted at them.

'We're trying, sir.'

'Well, try harder. They'll come back, and live in that.'

'We'll strip it, sir.'

'Don't be a fool. That'll take all day, and they'll re-thatch it anyhow.'

'What else can we do sir?'

'Burn the damned thing.' He took a box of lucifer matches from his pocket, and threw it to the two men.

One tried to ignite the thatch. It sputtered, and the flame died. He tried another. This time, it took.

Luke and his father had finished loading a rough table and four chairs on the cart. He knew Ellen Morrisroe had no use for them where she was going, but he did as she asked. By now the fire in the thatch had taken well and was roaring up towards the remaining apex of the roof. Luke still stood in the street, watching the flames and smoke.

'What are you looking at, you bastard,' shouted one of the men.

He did not reply. He stared through the soaring flames towards the Mountain, thinking of Croghancoe. Then he turned away.

His father walked to the cart, helping the widow and her children into it. Luke went over and grasped the bridle. He walked in front, leading the horse.

High over the Mountain, black smoke scarred a blue and white sky.

Chapter Twenty Six

Telegraph or Connaught Ranger, May 1847:
In the Westport Union, the test of outdoor relief has be put in operation were no less than 30,000 human beings are now receiving gratuitous relief at a weekly outlay of £1,200! Thus, while the poor of Westport are fed and cared for, those in and around Castlebar are left to die, and after death to be buried without coffins. What a curse hangs over our town and its poor mendicants.

That night, Ellen Morrisroe had their bed, and shared it with her three children. Luke and Winnie slept on straw, both wrapped in blankets beside the fire.

'What did you say to her?' he asked.

'I only spoke to her as woman to woman. I told her I understood her sorrow and her anger. I told her to direct her anger at those who never tried and never cared, and to see you and Father Reilly as the men you are.'

'What did she say?'

'She heard what I said. She accepted it because I'm a woman, and you're my man. But deep down, the anger is still there.'

'It's what I told you before, Winnie. I'm a stranger here now. I wish to God I'd stayed in England.'

'No, you don't.'

'I know, I know. If I'd stayed in England, I'd never have met you. But still we'll have to do something, and if it's not England it's going to have to be America. And how we can get to America without going to England first, I just do not know. Isn't that it?'

'We said we'd wait and see.'

'Fine so,' Luke said.

The next few days were tense ones for Luke. Every morning, he left the house early so as to avoid meeting Ellen Morrisroe. Eleanor was resentful of having to share the limited food with another family, even though the arrangement was to be temporary. In the end, the woman herself decided that enough was enough, and suggested she would go to a cousin in Knockanure.

Luke loaded her furniture on the cart and drove the family to Knockanure. No one said a word. As they entered the town, they could see two crowds. As always, there was a large one outside the Workhouse, clamouring for admission. He recognised families he knew from the Mountain, the pitiful results of the Clanowen evictions.

The second crowd was around the Soup Kitchen pots. There had been fighting, and the men and women who had come down from the Mountain stood apart, waiting to be fed if there was anything left over.

Luke found the house. A man came to the door, and responded angrily to Luke's explanation.

'This is nothing to do with me. I don't have to take them.'

'Neither do we,' Luke said. 'They're your family.' He began to unload the furniture.

'What are you doing?' the man shouted at him. 'What do you expect me to do with that?'

'Do what you like. I'm going home.'

One morning, Winnie went down to the well on her own. Over the weeks she had discovered which of the women were well disposed towards the Ryans, and which were not.

On this morning, she exchanged a few words with some of the younger women as she filled her two pails. As she started back up the path towards the road, she saw another young woman coming towards her. She stood aside to let Winnie pass.

'Nice morning,' Winnie said.

'Indeed it is,' the other said.

Winnie was at the gate when she heard the women greet the stranger. Kitty! She stopped to open the gate, thinking. Kitty was a common enough name. But she was curious, very curious.

She hefted the pails out, and closed the gate. Then she carried them a few yards down, and stopped beside a blackthorn bush, where she could not be seen from the well. The women were talkative, and it was ten minutes before the other came out.

Winnie waited until she drew level. For a moment she thought she was mistaken. From all she had known of Kitty, she had expected more than this thin, haggard woman. Her cheeks were sunken, one scarred red, the other marked by a bruised puffiness beneath the eye. Her shift was ragged and torn.

'Kitty?' Winnie whispered. 'Kitty Brennan?'

The other woman looked at her, surprised. 'Yes.'

'I've got a message for you from Brigid.'

'Brigid who?'

'Brigid Ryan, you eejit.'

'Brigid…?

'She says she's missing you. She wants to know when she'll be seeing you again?'

Kitty stared at her. 'Brigid? So you…you're…?'

'Winnie, Kitty. Winnie Ryan. Brigid's new aunty. Among other things.'

She held out her hand. Kitty stared at her, holding her own hand out, before Winnie grasped it, and squeezed it tightly.

That night, when they were in bed and the house was silent, she told him about the meeting. He seemed quite unperturbed about it all.

'Well, ye had to meet some time. Sure, I suppose there's no harm in it, so long as ye weren't tearing each other's hair out.'

'Haven't you the right opinion of yourself, Luke Ryan, to think we'd be fighting over the likes of you.'

'So you're going to tell me you're the best of friends. Is that it?'

'Maybe we are.'

'I don't believe it.'

'Well, you'd better believe it. In fact, I even told her what an *amadán* she was staying away from little Brigid.'

'You didn't!'

'I did. So there.'

A few days later, Kitty joined the other women in Carrigard. Brigid ran across the room, her arms held high. *'Kitty,'* she cried.

Kitty took the child, and rocked her in her arms. *'I've been missing you, alanna.'*

Now the tension in the house lessened. The women resumed their old friendship. Once again though, Eleanor could see though that Aileen had fallen into her old depression. Carrigard School was coming to an end, and she knew it.

The relationship between Winnie and Kitty was a strange one. Winnie felt she should have disliked her, but she could not. In many ways, she admired Kitty. She had a spirit that would not be beaten. They could all see that the bruises on her face had resumed, but in spite of the beatings and the hunger, her wit always came through.

It was more than a matter of wit though. When the women talked about the *Gort na Móna* evictions, Kitty became angry, denouncing not only Clanowen and the evictors, but Father Reilly too. The other women said nothing in reply. Winnie felt that she should have defended the priest, but she too said nothing. She thought it was better not to provoke an argument with Kitty, especially because of Luke's previous relationship with her.

But it was Kitty's feelings for Brigid that surprised Winnie more than anything else. She suspected that Kitty herself would not have children. Brigid was now over a year old, and well able to play up to the affections of all her mothers. As Luke had anticipated, Winnie too had been drawn in by her charm. She too wanted the best for Brigid.

When the other women told her of their ambitions for Brigid, she found it hard to believe at first. But she became accustomed to the idea, though she never mentioned it to Luke. She knew the other women were determined about it, and she was surprised to see that Kitty's determination was perhaps the strongest of all. In this way too, she came to respect Kitty, and even develop an affection and a sympathy for her.

But still she knew how hard it would be for Luke to meet with Kitty. Often she sat at the end of the table, looking through the window for the men returning so that Kitty could get out in time. At times she thought this was childish, but she could think of no better way, and like Eleanor, she did not want Kitty to stop coming.

One evening, as Luke came in for dinner, his mother told him that McKinnon had fever.

'Who told you?' he asked.

'One of the fellows coming out of town. I haven't been down yet.'

'I'll go.'

'Would you not wait for your dinner?'

'I won't be long.'

He walked to Kilduff. Sabina was not in the bar. He went upstairs and knocked on the bedroom door. She was sitting in a chair beside the bed. Even from the door, he could see the rash on McKinnon's face.

'How is he?'

'Complaining of headaches all the time,' Sabina said.

McKinnon interrupted. 'There's no need to ask about me like that. I can still speak, you know.'

'Sorry.'

'Anyhow, in answer to your question – I'm not great, but I'll live.'

'Are you sure it's fever?'

'It's the fever alright. But I wouldn't worry. I had it before, back in Scotland when I was a child. It didn't kill me then, and it won't kill me now.'

'I suppose you're right,' Luke said.

Pat and Sarah were in the office, Pat at the main desk, Sarah at the table in the corner. He tried to work, but he was watching her too, thinking. After an hour, he put his pen down.

'Sarah.'

'Yes,' said Sarah, without looking up.

'There's something I wanted to ask you.'

'What's that?'

'Will you marry me?'

'What!'

'You heard.'

She stared at him. 'You asked me to marry you?'

'I did.' His heart was pounding. He felt a rush of blood to his face and hoped it was not obvious.

'But we hardly know each other.'

'You don't even believe that yourself.'

He was beginning to feel more confident. She had not refused. If she had wanted to refuse, she would have said it at once. Still she said nothing. She was playing for time, he was sure of that. He decided to press on.

'You haven't answered.'

'I just don't know what to say. A young fellow like you, haven't you got the right cheek.'

'Have I? Maybe I have. But you still haven't given me an answer.'

'Let me ask you one thing,' she said. 'What age are you?'

'What difference does that make?'

'It makes a big difference. Now it's you who can't do the answering.'

'Nineteen.'

'What!'

'Nineteen I said. And what's wrong with that. There's fellows around our place get married at sixteen.'

His heart was still pounding, but it was calming now. She still had not refused.

'Do you know how old I am?' she asked.

'I don't. Does it matter?'

'I think it does.'

'Go on so. What age are you?'

'Twenty-one. I'm two years older than you. Two full years.'

'That's not much.'

'You never give up, do you?'

'Not till I get an answer. You can say 'no' if you want. If you do, I'll never ask you again.'

Damn it, he thought, that was stupid. All on one card now. If she says no, it's over.

She was silent. He knew better than to say anything, and waited. At last she spoke.

'Well, I'm not going to say no. But I'm not going to say yes either, because I still think you're too young. So I'll make you a deal. You can ask me again when you're old enough. The day you're twenty-one, you can ask me then. That's if you still want to.'

'Of course I'll still want to. But what will your answer be?'

'Never mind.'

One afternoon Voisey came into the office. There had been a meeting of the Guardians all morning. He took the chair across from Pat, and sat down.

'There's two things I want to discuss with you,' he said to Pat. 'The first concerns you. The Guardians have decided that we need an additional clerk here in the Union. They are advertising for a new Master – we had been intending that you stay on until then in any case, but they now feel, even after that appointment is made, that another permanent clerical position will be required. This will be at a remuneration of thirty five pounds annually. I took the liberty of putting your name forward, and should you be minded to accept, the position will be yours as and from next Monday.'

Pat and Sarah glanced at each other. He did not hesitate.

'Of course. I'd be delighted to accept.'

'I hope it doesn't interfere with any other plans you might have had.'

'Not at all. As you might know, Luke has gone back to Carrigard to take over the farm. My only other option would be emigration, and I don't want that if I can avoid it.'

'Very well. I'll notify the Guardians of your acceptance. But before I do, there is another matter I'd like to discuss.'

'Yes, Mr. Voisey.'

'I'm sure you're well aware from working on the accounts that the Union cannot go on like this. Rates are uncollected all over the county, and even if we brought the Military in to enforce collection, our opinion is that little more could be raised in this way. The rates have increased four times over in this barony, and most of the landlords would be bankrupted if we tried to enforce payment.'

'Yes, I can see that,' Pat said. 'But what else can we do?'

'We've decided on another approach. The stronger sort, both in the Workhouse and those who are on relief in the Kitchens, will be given the opportunity for emigration.'

'But they can't afford it, Mr. Voisey. Where would they get the money from?'

'That's the point, Pat. We are going to pay them to leave. The Union has agreed with Lord Lucan and Lord Clanowen to put a fund together for anyone who wants to go. We've already chartered a ship to carry them from Westport to British America.'

'British America!' Pat echoed.

'Canada. Quebec to be exact. You may be aware that many of the American ports have not been allowing Irish ships to land their passengers. So it seems to us the only destination that is open is Canada, and Quebec will be the main destination. The first ship will be in Westport in two weeks, and God willing, she'll make Quebec in six weeks. And this is where you come in.'

'Yes, Mr. Voisey?'

'I want you to start arranging who will go. We're offering each person one pound to leave and families no more than three pounds in total. This should be sufficient to assist them once they reach Quebec. There's any amount of work in the forests of Canada for a man who wants it.'

Pat soon discovered that his new task was not as difficult as he had anticipated. Almost all the younger men in the Workhouse volunteered at once. America was seen as the land of opportunity, and few had the knowledge to distinguish 'British America' from the United States. Not that it seemed to matter. Pat had heard stories of Irishmen landing in Canada and making their way to the United States across the long, unguarded border between the two countries.

At the Soup Kitchens, there was a different kind of problem in that too many families volunteered, families that Pat knew well could not make the voyage. He was also concerned about fever. He decided that any family with any member showing signs of fever would not be permitted to join.

Two weeks later, Winnie was cooking with Eleanor in the kitchen. It was a warm day.

'*Look, Mother!*' Outside the door, a long ragged procession of people were walking. Between them, wagons and carts creaked towards Kilduff.

They both ran outside.

'*There must be hundreds,*' Eleanor said.

'*Water?*' asked one of the women. '*Do ye have water?*

Winnie and Eleanor brought out all the mugs they had, as well as all the jars of water. Each mug was swallowed, and passed back until there was no water left.

'*Where in the name of God are ye all going?*' Eleanor asked one woman.

'*America,*' she replied, and walked on.

McKinnon did not improve. Every day now, Luke dropped by to see the old warrior. Often McKinnon would only speak in Scots Gaelic, the same rough northern dialect that he had tried to teach Sabina. Luke could just about understand enough to hold a conversation, speaking himself in the dialect his mother had used when he was a baby – the language of the Mountain. Sometimes McKinnon spoke of the crofts and fishing villages of the Hebrides and Sutherland. Sometimes he talked of the days when he had first come to Kilduff with the Survey, of meeting Sabina, of the different languages and cultures. Sometimes Luke asked him about the Peninsular Wars, it brought back old memories and friendships. But to the end, he would never talk of Waterloo.

But then the full horror of black fever became more evident. McKinnon's memory lapsed into ravings, and Luke spoke to him no more. Every day, he called around. Gangrene was well advanced by now, but Luke was well used to the stench of it. Sometimes he told Sabina to rest, while he mopped McKinnon's face with cold water.

The fever was coming to its climax. One evening, Luke and Winnie walked down to the bar. Sabina met them. 'He's much worse. I don't think he'll live.'

Winnie put her arm around her.

'That's right,' Luke said. 'You stay here.'

He went upstairs on his own, and sat in silence beside the bed. Then Winnie and Sabina came up with Eleanor. Luke went to find the priest, but he was already out on a sick call. He returned to the bedside, and waited with the women.

An hour later, Father Reilly arrived.

McKinnon's breathing was shallower now, and his face was pale. For an hour past he had been shouting strange words, but even this had stopped. Sabina cradled his head, sobbing. There was no response.

The priest started 'I anoint thee with the chrism of salvation...' dubbing McKinnon on the forehead, lips and heart. The women were silent.

The priest turned to them. 'Let us pray,' he said. They went to their knees. The priest led the prayer –

'Our Father, Who art in heaven, hallowed be Thy name, Thy kingdom come, Thy will be done on earth as it is in heaven...'

They gave the response –

'...Give us this day our daily bread, and forgive us our trespasses as we forgive those who trespass against us, and lead us not into temptation, but deliver us from evil.'

Suddenly McKinnon moaned, his eyes open, the eyeballs rolling wildly, but unseeing.

The priest continued –

'Hail Mary, full of grace, the Lord is with thee, blessed art thou amongst women, and blessed is the fruit of thy womb, Jesus...'

Again they answered –

'...Holy Mary, Mother of God, pray for us sinners, now and at the hour of our death.'

They repeated the prayer –

'Hail Mary, full of grace…

Ostende!

…the Lord is with thee…

Bruges!

…blessed art thou amongst women…

Ghent!

…and blessed is the fruit of thy womb, Jesus…

Aalst!

…Holy Mary, Mother of God…

Brussels!

For the past hour, the carriages had been rolling in to the sound of the music. Another carriage passed.

'The Iron Duke,' McNulty exclaimed.

'Another Irishman,' Geraghty said.

'He never thought so,' McKinnon said.

'Who cares what he thought,' Geraghty said. 'He can't stop being Irish just by not thinking it.'

'That's right,' McNulty said. 'And anyhow, isn't half the army Irish.'

'Might be,' McKinnon said, 'but don't forget, you fellows, this is a Scottish regiment. Some of us here might even be Scots.'

'Scots be damned. There's more Irish than Scots. Where are the Highlanders when they're needed.'

'Shut your mouth, or you might find out.'

…pray for us sinners…

Quatres Bras!

Ney's cavalry had lined up.

'Oh God,' McNulty said. 'They'll ride right over us. They'll kill us all.'

'Charge,' Henderson screamed.

'Charge? Charge what – cavalry?'

'Charge, or by God, I'll have you all flogged.'

The battalion started to move forward. 'Oh Jesus,' cried McNulty, 'we're charging cavalry. Oh Mary, oh Mother of God.' A few of the horses facing them pawed at the ground.

There was a shout of 'Remember Badajoz,' and a wild screaming as the entire division ran forward, bayonets fixed. The French cavalry wavered…

…now and at the hour of our death.'

WATERLOO, 1815. They had been standing on the ridge for four hours, watching the battle below. They had already been in action earlier in the afternoon when their desperate bayonet charge against overwhelming odds had brought the French infantry advance to a halt. Since then they had suffered no direct attack. It was hot though, and still there was no water.

'We've nothing behind us,' McNulty said. 'No reserves, no water, no nothing.'

'Maybe we are the reserves,' Geraghty said.

'The French are beaten anyway,' McKinnon said. 'They've done their damnedest, their bolt is shot.'

For twenty minutes no one spoke. Then they saw more troops moving into position below them.

'If the French are beaten,' McNulty said, 'what's this?'

'Oh Christ Almighty,' Geraghty said, 'the *Garde*.'

'The *Garde*?' McNulty echoed.

'The *Garde Imperiale*,' Geraghty repeated, pronouncing it as if in English. 'We're finished now. They've never retreated. Never.'

'Aye, and cavalry never retreated before infantry either,' McKinnon said. 'But we showed them...'

'You don't understand,' Geraghty said. 'These damned bastards are the worst. They don't retreat. They've no signal for it. They don't even know how.'

'I know,' McKinnon said. 'You don't have to tell me.'

They watched, almost in terror, as the *Garde* started to assemble.

'I don't think we're going to have to fight them,' McKinnon said after a few minutes. 'They're not facing in our direction. They're going to hit the right.'

A single horseman rode to the front of the *Garde*. There was a roar from the French troops – '*Vive l'Empereur!*'

'Napoleon!' exclaimed McNulty.

'By God,' McKinnon said. 'After all these years. That's him, that's the man.'

'Doesn't look much from here,' Geraghty said. 'Bit of a small fellow.'

'Aye,' McNulty said, 'a bit small alright.'

Napoleon started to lead the *Garde* forward to screams of '*Vive l'Empereur! Vive Napoleon!*' After a few hundred yards, he retired, passing command to Ney, now leading the attack. Then the entire French line was moving forward alongside the *Garde*.

'Oh Jesus,' Geraghty said, 'Oh Jesus Christ.'

'My God,' McNulty muttered, 'there's thousands of them.'

McKinnon said nothing. The division was stood to attention in three ranks.

'Ready,' roared Henderson. The first rank moved forward.

'Aim.'

At the same moment, the leading French officer pointed his sabre forward, screaming – '*Pour la Gloire de la…*'

'FIRE.'

'Glory be to the Father, and to the Son, and to the Holy Ghost…

The officer and many other figures in the French front line dropped, but the rest reformed, filled the gaps, and came on. Another French officer barked an order, and the French muskets came up. There was a fusillade.

McNulty slumped forward, a small hole in his forehead, the back of his head a shattered mass of brains. McKinnon stepped forward with Geraghty, flicked brain off his sleeve, and aimed as commanded. The British ranks fired again, more Frenchmen fell, they reformed again, and fired again.

Geraghty fell back with a cry. The side of his throat had been torn asunder. He made a strangled choking sound, his legs kicking as he inhaled his own blood, suffocating. McKinnon knelt over him.

'Stand up you bastard, and face the foe,' shouted Henderson. 'Stand up, or by God, I'll kill you myself.'

McKinnon stood, and reloaded. Geraghty's choking went on, his face purple, his spasms fouling him, his legs still thrashing.

…as it was in the beginning, is now, and ever shall be…

The French had halted. Now they fixed bayonets, and charged. When they were only yards away, McKinnon saw a French giant coming straight at him, bayonet forward. With no time to spare, McKinnon raised his gun, and fired. The Frenchman's face exploded in blood and brain and bone. His bayonet fell at McKinnon's feet.

McKinnon was powerless now, but the next Frenchman stopped, looked in horror at his companion, and then directly at McKinnon, his bayonet shaking. For a few seconds, both men stared into each other's eyes.

A scream came through the din – '*le Garde recule!*' To the right, Napoleon's Imperial Guard had broken.

The Frenchman dropped the bayonet and fled, vomiting as he ran. Around him, other Frenchmen were already running.

The cry became general – '*le Garde recule, le Garde recule!*'

Geraghty was dead, but from time to time an eyeball flickered, and one of his legs still quivered in spasm.

…world without end, amen.'

Chapter Twenty Seven

Liverpool Mercury, June 1847:
We were assured yesterday by a medical gentleman that the fever that now rages is the most malignant with which our town has been visited, and that at least 10,000 persons are now labouring. He stated that it is now spreading amongst small shopkeepers, bread bakers, publicans, and others who come more immediately in contact with the poorer classes. It is to be hoped that the operation of the act for the removal of the Irish poor to their own country and the exertions now making by the parish authorities, will soon produce a favourable change in the health of the town.

Danny had the Works running well. He had a Works office built at the site. He shared it only with Irene Miller, except when he was out on the Works. His landlady had been right – Irene was a fast and accurate worker. Good looking too! But what Danny liked most about her was that she did not always bend to his will. She could spot better and faster ways of working, and was prepared to fight her corner, even when Danny disagreed. After a while he came to understand that her suggestions were well thought out, and that there was little point in arguing with her. More and more, he left the administration to her.

This resulted in something else he had not expected. She understood the methods he was using, and wanted to apply them even more rigorously than he would himself. One morning they argued about it all.

'You're paying these people too much,' she said.

'What!'

'You're paying them too much. No need for that when they start.'

'What else can we do? They have to eat.'

'They do. And isn't that all they get in Mayo? They don't pay them in the Soup Kitchens.'

'Soup Kitchens!' He wondered where she had heard about that.

'Yes, Soup Kitchens. Isn't that all we have to do here? Pay them less, but feed them better. It would cost far less. Harden them up faster, without any being wasted on drink.'

'But they'd leave,' Danny said.

'And go where? They're too hungry, they need the food. And no one else would take them. They're too slow, they can't make themselves understood in English. Who would have them?'

He thought about that.

'Go on. What would you do then?'

'Raise their wages slowly. They'd stay long enough.'

'And then?'

'Then it doesn't matter. There's thousands of them coming in to Liverpool every day. Just keep getting more as we need them.'

'We?'

'You. We. Does it matter?'

'Maybe, maybe not.'

'So stop interrupting, I'm trying to help you. Have you thought out these accounts yet?'

'I have,' Danny said, 'but let's hear your side of the story.'

'Look – I reckon you're making sixpence a day out of each of them. That's gross after all the labour and materials. Three shillings a week is not enough. If you cut their wages and started a Soup Kitchen, you should be able to get five shillings a week, six even. Thirty workers – seven, eight, nine pounds a week. You should be able to keep five pounds, maybe six per week after feeding them. Say twenty or twenty five a month.'

Danny whistled. 'Not bad.'

'No, not bad. At least for those who might be satisfied with it.'

'What do you mean?' asked Danny, startled.

'Look, you're employing thirty men. Why?'

'To finish the contract, why else?'

'If you employed sixty, you'd be clearing a forty or fifty pounds a month, and finish the contract in half the time.'

'And what then?'

'Go back to Anderson, go for a bigger contract. Double the size, ten times the size. Why not? You've already shown you can do it cheaper than anyone else. And faster. If you show him you can do it faster again, he's yours for as long as they're building the line.'

'God, you are ambitious,' Danny said.

'Don't be silly. Brassey did it, why can't we?'

'We?'

'Yes, Mr. Ryan. We.'

For the first time in his life Danny found that there was someone prepared to be tougher than him – and a woman too. Not that it was that straightforward.

Murtybeg spent most of the time out on the Works. While the men were

341

silent enough, he became aware of their unhappiness at the rates they were being paid. Stories of higher wages filtered through from the other gangs. In the evenings, when he came back to the office, arguments developed between the three of them.

'You can't go on like this, Danny,' he said one night. 'It's cruel.'

'Cruel to who?' Irene responded, not even waiting for Danny to reply. 'Isn't it better than what they're used to. They've got work and food and a roof over their heads. You tell me what they've got in Mayo.'

'Not much,' Murtybeg said, shaking his head. Danny said nothing.

'What game is she playing at,' Murtybeg asked as they walked back to their lodgings that night.

'Damned if I know.'

'She seems more concerned about you than anyone. I wonder why?'

Yes, Danny thought. I wonder why? She might have her own reasons, that's what Murteen is getting at. Maybe he's right, and maybe it wouldn't be a bad idea. He decided to change the subject.

'I want you to go to Liverpool, Murteen.'

'Liverpool? Why?'

'We're going to need more workers, a lot more.'

Danny opened his Soup Kitchen. On Irene's advice, he had her aunt tender for the contract, though he checked the prices with other caterers. With few potatoes available even in Britain, he had corn and rice bought in, together with barley, turnips, carrots and cabbage. To build up the strength of starving men, it was essential to have meat as well, though he saw no point in over-paying for that. Instead they used the cheaper cuts of meat and offal – liver, kidneys, heart and tongue. Oxtails and sheep's heads were thrown in for flavour.

Danny found the stew revolting and never touched it. But he knew it was nutritious, and reckoned it was better than anything they could get in west Mayo. They could complain if they liked, but they would know the consequences.

As he slashed their wages, they started to drift away. Some joined other gangs, and some took to the roads. He was no longer concerned about this. He had found another means of keeping men in place. When they first arrived on the Works, he offered to send money back to the families. The first payment was made on arrival on the Works, but afterwards it was done a month in arrears. This meant that the men were even more reliant on the Kitchens for survival since they had no money themselves – it had already gone to Mayo. Also, as soon as anyone left, Danny had the payment cut off, and kept it himself. He knew the men could not afford this. He knew too that as the famine tightened its grip through the summer of 1847 their families in Erris and Achill could not afford the loss of their only income.

Every week too, he sent Murtybeg to Liverpool, and within a few weeks he had fifty men working on the line. On Murtybeg's insistence, they never employed anyone from east Mayo. He had no wish that family or friends around Kilduff and Carrigard should hear of the means that they were using to run the business. Not that Danny was concerned though.

This all resulted in a heavy increase in administration and supervision. As he himself was becoming more involved in financial and contractual negotiations, it was necessary to bring Murtybeg back into the office when he was not in Liverpool. He needed foremen on the line, and he needed them fast. One evening he wrote a letter to Leeds. A week later, he had Bernie Lavan, Jamesy McManus and John Roughneen working on the line as foremen, all at wages far higher than they had ever expected. He no longer even thought of asking Luke.

As time went on, Murtybeg was becoming more morose. Liverpool depressed him. Every time he walked down the docks, he could see the results of starvation and the signs of fever in desperate people coming off the Irish boats. He told Danny about it all, but Danny was not worried. He could only see opportunity.

One day, on the Liverpool Docks, Murtybeg saw something that surprised him. There was a group of people, a hundred or so, dressed in the uniform of the Liverpool Workhouse. He wondered what they were doing there, and his bafflement increased when he heard them speaking in Irish, but the idiom and accent were unfamiliar to him. When he spoke to them, he discovered they were from West Cork – the area around Skibbereen. But what he heard next astonished him. The Liverpool Union was chartering ships to send their inmates back to Ireland. They saw no reason that thousands of Irish beggars should be a charge on Liverpool ratepayers, and this group was being sent home to West Cork, where most of the Workhouses were already bankrupt.

He found a bar along the docks, and went in, ordering sausage and a pint of ale. The bar was crowded with dockers and sailors, but he sat at the back, trying to concentrate. If the Union was sending people back to Ireland, they would be really desperate. Also, as in any Workhouse, such people would be used to working for nothing at all beyond board and lodgings. Faced with the alternative of starvation in Ireland they would be delighted with the prospect of working for food and a little cash. He gulped down the rest of his pint, walked up to the Union building, and asked for the administration block.

When he returned to Gatley, he had fifteen men with him. They were still dressed in the uniform of the Workhouse. Danny looked at him in surprise.

'What's this, Murteen? Are they on contract from the Union?'

'They're on contract from no one,' Murtybeg said. 'They're ours to keep. But I told them the first thing we'd do is to get them new rig-outs, they don't want to be seen like this all the time.'

That evening, after they had squeezed the men into the existing shacks, sleeping on the floor for the night, Murtybeg explained it all to Danny. He told him of the Union repatriating Irish inmates. He told him of the fear in people's eyes along the docks, knowing that they were being sent home to hunger and fever. But best of all, the men he had brought – young single men from the West of Ireland – were no longer starving or weak. A few weeks in the Workhouse had fed them well, and strengthened them with hard work.

'And even if they only stay a few weeks,' he went on, 'we'll get the work out of them, and there are hundreds – thousands – more waiting where they came from.'

Danny clapped him on the shoulder.

'By God, Murteen, I never knew you had it in you.'

Neither did Murtybeg. He was finding ways now of salving his conscience, convincing himself that he was giving the men a better alternative than being sent back to die in Cork or Kerry or Mayo or Donegal; giving them an alternative which would give them a little money to feed their families in Ireland or Liverpool. The difference between life and death.

But Danny did not need to salve his conscience. Murtybeg had provided the final piece of the jigsaw. He would have as many men as he wanted, paying them as little as he wanted. The future was open.

He rode into Stockport. His first call was the Manchester & Salford Bank, where he asked for the Manager.

'We are hoping to negotiate on new contracts very shortly,' he explained. 'We're going to need a loan from you, and we may need it fast.'

'A loan!' the Manager exclaimed. 'We don't lend to labour contractors. It's a matter of policy. Head Office won't allow it.'

'Then I will need your support in arranging the loan, and I am sure you will give me support once you understand the figures.'

He laid out some sheets of accounts on the desk.

'These are our accounts to date since we started the business.'

For the next hour, the man examined the figures, as Danny explained them. Finally they sat down again. 'These are impressive figures, Mr. Ryan.'

'I know,' Danny said. 'Can I count on your support though?'

'I don't know. First I must have details of your lending requirements.'

'As you will understand, that depends on the contracts I can negotiate. Once that's complete, I will be able to come back to you with the projections, and we can take it from there.'

'Very well. But I warn you – it's against policy.'

His second call was on Rob Anderson. He rose from behind his desk as Danny came in.

'Well, well. I've been waiting for you.'

'I didn't like burdening you,' Danny said, 'until I knew where we were with the Gatley contract.'

'Well ahead of schedule, from what my surveyors tell me.'

'We're reckoning we're two weeks ahead, and we might even be able to improve on that.'

'I don't know how you do it.'

'We have our methods,' Danny said. 'But that's not what I came here to talk about. I understand you've a new contract beyond Timperley.'

'We have. I was intending to talk to you about that. Fifty thousand cubic yards, though you probably know that already. Perhaps you can give me a quotation, but the first question is – can you handle it?'

'In principle, yes,' Danny replied.

'In principle?'

'I don't have to tell you, Edwardes & Ryan will need financial assistance for a contract of that size. I'm talking to the Manchester & Salford Bank already, and I'm going to need your support for that.'

'What sort of support?'

'Just this. Once we have the contractual terms agreed, and before we sign off on it, I'll have to organise the loan through the Head Office in Manchester. I'm sure if they understand Anderson & Son are our customers, there should be no problem there, but it might be better if I had you with me at the negotiations.'

'By God, you are ambitious.'

When Danny arrived back at the office that evening, Irene was hunched over the accounts by the light of a candle.

'Where's Murteen?' Danny asked.

'He's just gone to Liverpool again. Don't you remember?'

'Oh yes, yes.'

'So where have you been?'

'Just in with Anderson.

'You didn't tell me that.'

'We're negotiating a new contract up beyond Timperley. If we get it, it'll be for fifty thousand cubic yards. We'll need a lot more men. We'll need to get up to a hundred at least.'

'A hundred!'

'Maybe more. But there's two other things I have to arrange before I go ahead. We're going to need a loan from the Manchester & Salford Bank, though I have that under way.'

'And what's the second thing?'

'I'm going to need a wife.'

She turned from the accounts and looked him in the eyes.

'Yes, you are,' she said. 'And how long it's taken you to work that out.'

She moved closer to him, and began to unbutton his shirt.

Murtybeg arrived back from Liverpool with more workers. That evening he went through the projections with Danny and Irene, checking the work to be done against the number of workers they had and the cost of it all. When they had finished, Irene left them.

'I thought you should know,' Murtybeg said, 'Jimmy Corrigan is still in Liverpool.'

'Well, that's no surprise,' Danny said. 'Did you think he'd gone to America or what?'

'No, but I think we'll find him this time. He's working on the docks.'

'Who told you that?'

'Mrs. Buckley.'

Danny whistled. 'This could be very interesting.'

'Couldn't it just.'

On the Sunday, they were both on a train to Liverpool. Danny had decided Sunday was best since a docker would be less likely to be working. If Jimmy was staying in Buckley's, they would find him easy enough.

Again, Murtybeg went into Buckley's on his own. A few minutes later, he came out again.

'We have him. He's down at the Albert Dock. They're offloading the Rachel. They say it's an American ship, just in last night.'

'Working on a Sunday, eh?'

'Offering double time, it seems.'

'And who told you? Mrs. Buckley?'

'Not this time. I asked an old fellow who was still at his breakfast. Thought it was safer.'

'Did he recognise you?'

'Hardly. He was English.'

'Excellent.'

They walked towards the docks.

'We're just about there,' Danny said after a few minutes. 'That's the Albert Dock.'

'And there's the ship,' Murtybeg said.

'Yes. I see it.'

'So what do we do now?'

'Let's just sit here a while and watch. Be patient.'

A hundred yards away bales of cotton were being unloaded from the ship.

'How many fellows are there?' Murtybeg asked.

'I'm not certain. Twenty, twenty-five maybe.'

'We can't risk that.'

'No,' Danny said. 'We've got to get him on his own.'

'So how do we do that?'

'Wait till he needs a piss.'

'What!'

'I've been watching. Every so often, one of them goes around the back of that wall. Now why do you think they'd do that?'

Murtybeg whistled. 'Of course.'

'Come on.'

They walked rapidly through the gang of dockers, not looking to left or right. They continued around to the back of the wall.

'He didn't see us,' Murtybeg said.

'No. But we saw him. Now this is what we're going to do.'

For an hour they waited, watching other men relieving themselves against the wall. Murtybeg was beginning to doubt that Corrigan would come at all. Then they saw him.

He walked around to the back of the wall, faced it, and started undoing his buttons.

Danny walked up beside him.

'Well, Jimmy...'

Corrigan turned around to face him. A look of horror spread across his face. He was in the most vulnerable position that a man could be. Murtybeg stepped forward on the other side, seized one of Corrigan's arms, and twisted it high behind his back. Danny stepped forward, and hit Corrigan hard, below and into the ribs. Corrigan doubled forward, retching.

'Hold him back again, Murteen.' Murtybeg jerked him back.

Danny punched Corrigan's nose and mouth. Corrigan's head fell forward, blood streaming. Murtybeg grasped him by the hair with one hand, and pulled his head back.

Danny stood back and smashed his right fist up into Corrigan's chin.

'Good night, Jimmy,' he whispered, as Corrigan slumped to the ground, a yellow pool spreading down to his knees.

They turned him onto his back. Danny took out the rock hammer which he had been carrying in the deep pocket inside his overcoat. Murtybeg looked away as Danny smashed both of Corrigan's knees, twice each for certainty. One by one he smashed his fingers. Then he hammered his elbows, and twisted each back over his own knee.

Corrigan's fly was still unbuttoned. Danny took a knife from his inner pocket.

'A surgical one, Murteen. Quicker. Less of a mess too.'

Murtybeg stared at him in horror.

'No, Danny,' he screamed. 'Don't...for God's sake, Danny...NO.'

They walked back along the ship where the cotton was being unloaded. No one even looked at them. They stopped at a drawbridge. Danny took out the hammer and the knife, and dropped them over, watching them disappear into the black waters of the Mersey.

'Where did you learn fighting like that?' Murtybeg asked.

'Oh, all along the Great Western. Those Welsh fellows were a rough lot. A man had to be able to protect himself.'

'Seems like you learnt well.'

'Luke did too, though he'd never admit it.'

'And Jimmy'll never forget it.'

'Not when he tries to stand, he won't.'

'I couldn't watch.'

'No, but it was necessary. He'll never work on the docks again, the bastard. Nor on the rails.'

'What'll he do, so?'

'Beg, if he wants. Who cares?'

Chapter Twenty Eight

The Nation, Dublin, June 1847:
On my way on this day to attend a call, I witnessed a most appalling sight – a dead body thrown one side of a ditch with a child in her arms – and upon enquiring the cause I was told by a bystander that she was found dead in the street this morning from actual starvation.
Rev. John Brennan, parish priest of Killedan.

McKinnon's burial was rapid. A rough built coffin was used, and within a few hours his corpse was interred in Kilduff graveyard. Even as the clods and clay were being thrown on the coffin, Luke could still smell the gangrene. At least McKinnon had his own coffin and his own grave. In time, he would have a headstone.

Later that morning he walked across to Knockanure. As always, there was a large crowd at the front gate close to the admissions unit. For fear of fever, he went no further. He went around the back of the Union, and was admitted at the back gate. As he walked to the administration building, he saw the corpses being thrown into the pit, and clay shovelled over them. This time he went no nearer. He went straight to Pat's office.

'I wasn't expecting you,' Pat said.

'It's as well you weren't. It's no good news I'm bringing. Ian is dead.'

'Ian! But…'

'Died last night. Black fever. We buried him this morning.'

'But I never knew. Why didn't you tell me?'

'We didn't want worrying you. There was nothing we could do. We had to bury him fast. Didn't want to be spreading fever.'

'You should have warned me. I'd liked to have seen him before he went.'

'There wasn't much point, he was only raving. But don't worry, you'll be in time for the funeral.'

'I thought you said…'

'Yes, we buried him this morning because we had to. But there's a Mass tomorrow morning, and we'll all walk to the grave after. Can you make it?'

'I don't know. There's a lot to do here.'

A bell rang.

'Time to eat,' Sarah said from the corner. 'I'm sure you'll join us.'

Luke followed them down to the small dining room. Voisey was there with another man. 'It's good to see you again,' Voisey said.

'And you, Mr. Voisey.'

'I'd like you to meet Cecil Trinder. Cecil is to be our new Master. Just appointed yesterday.'

They sat as one of the inmates started to serve the meal.

Sarah's mother arrived. 'Luke Ryan, is it? What brings you here?'

'I only came over to tell Pat that our uncle had died.'

'What! Mr. McKinnon? He's dead?'

'He is,' Luke said.

'But what happened to him? It's not that long since we saw him last.'

'Fever,' Luke said. 'He died yesterday.'

'Fever,' Voisey echoed. 'God! This damned fever doesn't spare any of us. I'm truly sorry to hear that. He will be a sore loss to the county.'

Luke started to eat. Even here, even in such a room with schooled people, he could not get away from fever. He glanced at Mrs. Cronin again. Perhaps she had fever, and didn't know it yet. Perhaps it was in the clothes she was wearing. To hell with it, forget fever.

Pat interrupted his thoughts. 'I never told you, Ellen Morrisroe, she died yesterday too.'

He looked up in surprise. 'I thought she was with her cousin.'

'She thought she was too. But he wouldn't have her. He drove her off. She was lucky to get into the Workhouse. She wouldn't have, only she sent a message to me, and I got her in.'

'A message?'

'She said she knew you.'

'Aye,' Luke said. 'She did too.'

'You knew her?' Voisey asked.

'Only for a few weeks. She stayed with us for a while after the evictions on the Mountain.'

'Lord Clanowen's, was it?' Voisey asked.

'That's right. You knew about it?'

'By God we did. We'd hundreds of them here, all trying to get in. I don't know what happened to most of them. We couldn't even take the half of them.'

'Clanowen is an evil man,' Luke said.

'I shouldn't comment on that.'

'No, you shouldn't,' Mrs. Cronin said. 'You don't talk about the Guardians in front of anyone else.'

They ate in silence for a while. Voisey spoke again.

'Will there be a service for Mr. McKinnon?'

'Tomorrow morning,' Pat answered.

'You'll go, surely?'

'I don't know.'

'Of course you will. He was your uncle, you must show respect. He will have our prayers too.'

After Luke had left, Pat sat for a long time staring out the window. Sarah came across, and stood beside him, putting her hand on his shoulder.

'I'm sorry.'

'*Arra*, it's fine Sarah. It's not as if it was Father.'

'Still, we'll all miss him. And the county can't afford to lose surveyors either.'

'I'll have to go over.'

'I know that. And so does Voisey. You must go.'

'But look at this lot. I haven't the time. I've too much to finish. I'll just have to work through the night and go over then.'

'I'd come with you if I could.'

Pat turned around for the first time, and looked at her in surprise. 'You'd what?'

'I'd come with you. Only to represent the Union. Your uncle was well known here.'

'I wonder what your mother would think of that?'

'Why should she think anything?'

'I don't know. It's just that...'

'I told her there isn't anything between us.'

He looked at her startled. 'You did?'

'I did. And there isn't. At least for the next two years, there isn't.'

'You shouldn't say things like that, Sarah. You had me worried.'

'You're easy worried. It's two years' time you should be worrying. You've two years to prove yourself. Voisey has given you the chance. It's up to you now.'

Pat worked through half the night. Then he took his coat, and left the office. As he walked out, he noticed there was already activity in the dormitories. At the end of the yard, horses were being yoked up to carts, a dozen or more. Another ship's charter – he had worked on the papers himself only a few days before. Westport or Ballina, he could not remember. In the door leading to the dormitories, a frightened family clung to each other in the cold.

He left the Workhouse by the back gate. He thought at that time there would be no one waiting for admission, but already there were people asleep by the wall.

He walked through a grey dawn towards Carrigard. As he got closer, the sun was rising. He saw men and women he knew working in the fields or walking the road. He called out to them, but they ignored him. Perhaps they were frightened of fever. Or Government men.

He reached Carrigard and went into the house. Eleanor was preparing meal for the hens.

She looked up in surprise. 'Pat.' She ran, and threw her arms around him. 'You must be hungry.'

'Tired more like. I've been working and walking all night.'

'Well, sit down there and rest.'

He sat at the table. 'No one up, Mother?'

'At this time of the morning. I'm only just up myself.'

'Where's Luke? Isn't he up?'

'He's down with Sabina, Winnie too. She's taken it very badly, Sabina has, so they stayed there last night. I just don't know what's going to happen. Someone has to run the bar, I suppose. Not that there's many have money for drink.'

She put the bucket of feed by the back door. 'So how's Knockanure?'

'It's a bit better than it was a few months back, but they're still dying at an awful rate. The Master's dead, they've only just got a new one. We've had two doctors – both dead. We've none now. But we're hoping it'll get better. The numbers in the Workhouse keep dropping. The Guardians are hiring boats and sending them all off to America.'

'I know, we'd heard about that.'

'It's the only thing they can do. There's no room in the Workhouse, they'd only die of fever.'

'Yes, I suppose you're right.' She swung a pot of oatmeal back off the fire. 'Your father's not getting any younger.'

'I know.'

'He was well able for things before Luke came home from England. Thought he could outwork any of the young lads. But that was then, and he's not up to it now. I think the quarry knocked it out of him. Pretends he can keep up with the young fellows, but he knows he can't.'

'What is he now – he must be sixty four?'

'Sixty four he is. Who'd have thought it? Young girls never think of things like that. You know, I was so flattered when he started courting me. Only eighteen I was then, and a big strong fellow like him, over twice my age. But you forget, if he's older than you then, he'll always be older than you. Good God, where have the years gone.'

'He's plenty more years in him yet. All of us lot, we seem to go on forever.'

'True enough,' she said, 'true enough. But to be honest, it's not that that's worrying me.'

'What then?'

Eleanor came over to the table, and sat across from him. 'I want to tell you something. And you're to promise not to tell a soul.'

'What's that?'

'I think Luke is going to leave.'

'Leave? But sure why would he leave?'

'He hasn't said anything yet. But I reckon he's thinking of it.'

'Where would they go?'

'America, I think.'

'America! But how do you know this?'

'I don't know it for certain.'

'But why America? Why not England?'

'And join Danny, is it? Working men into the ground. No, I reckon he won't do that.'

'But why not join Farrelly?' he asked. 'Wouldn't that be the thing to do?'

'It surely would. It's what I reckon he will do.'

'Well then?'

'Martin's in America.'

'He's what!' Pat exclaimed.

'In America.'

'That can't be true.'

'Oh, it's true right enough. I've only just heard it myself from Katie Jordan. Mikey's gone with Martin.'

'Mikey too?'

'Yes.'

'Does Luke know?'

'He does.'

'But...but if Luke goes to America...'

'The farm will be yours. Isn't it what you've always wanted?'

'Well, yes, but...'

'But what?'

'I don't know. Let's wait, and see.'

He thought of telling his mother about his promotion, but decided not to. Thirty five pounds a year, he had been so proud of it, so anxious to tell the family about it. But there was no point in upsetting everyone. No point in saying anything about Sarah either.

A moment later, Michael came into the kitchen. 'Well, look who's arrived now,' he said. 'We didn't know if you'd be able to come.'

'I reckoned I had to come when I heard it.'

But Pat's mind was not on McKinnon anymore. He looked at his father, wondering if he had he come to the same conclusions as his mother? How long could he continue working the farm like he did? Would Luke go? How

353

long until he himself would be expected to return to Carrigard?

They walked to Kilduff. The church was crowded. Sabina was at the front, a line of women shaking her hands, then hugging her. Luke and Winnie were there already. Michael, Eleanor and Pat sat beside them. The line of women started to move away, and behind Pat people left their pews, and shuffled back. The stigma of the Workhouse still clung to him. The Government man. After the Mass, they went to the graveyard where the priest intoned the Sorrowful Mysteries of the Rosary over McKinnon's grave. Then they walked back to the bar for a wake without a corpse. It was well past midnight when Pat left again for Knockanure. No-one else had mentioned America or Farrelly.

Two nights later, there was a knock at the door. Luke answered it. Owen Corrigan was standing outside.

'Owen, by God. What brings you here?'

'Business.'

Luke thought at once that there was something strange about Corrigan's manner. He led him inside. Corrigan shook hands with Michael, and nodded to Eleanor.

'You're in bad form,' Luke said.

'Haven't I every right to be,' Corrigan replied.

Luke was puzzled, but on his guard. 'What's troubling you?'

'Jimmy.'

'Jimmy? What about Jimmy?'

'You know well what I mean. And don't pretend you don't.'

'I don't,' Luke said. 'I don't know what you're talking about.'

'If you don't know, you bloody well should. Go and ask your cousins. Ask them what happened to Jimmy.'

'Who, Danny?'

'Aye,' Corrigan said, 'and his little brother too.'

'What! Murtybeg?'

'Murtybeg too.'

Michael stood, and walked to the fire, looking into it. 'There's no one here that knows what you're talking about, but if you would let us know, then we could see what we can do about it.'

Corrigan looked at the three of them. 'Do you have any drink?'

Eleanor went over the cupboard, took out a bottle, and poured a mug of *poitín*.

'Go on,' Michael said.

'Yes. Well, we hear Jimmy is in the Workhouse Infirmary in Liverpool. Your two cousins, Luke – they cornered him, and beat him until he screamed for mercy. They did things to him that should never be done to any man. And from all we hear, he'll never work again.'

Michael sat at the table again.

'Have you told Aileen and Murty anything of this?'

'Not yet. I thought I'd tell Luke here first, seeing as we once knew each other.'

'Well, perhaps you could leave it that way,' Eleanor said. 'You know the way Aileen is. If there's any telling to be done, I'll do it.'

'Fair enough,' Corrigan said. 'But what are we going to do about Jimmy? I'll have to get him, isn't that it? I'll have to go over to Liverpool, find him, and bring him home.'

Liverpool, Luke was thinking. Maybe I should go to Liverpool too. Forget Mayo, just go, take Winnie with me, and stay there. Yes, go over to Stockport, and have a word with Danny while I'm about it.

Danny?

What kind of animal is he? Is he mad or what?

Oh to hell with all that, there's better places than Liverpool or Stockport. But where? New York? Philadelphia? Boston? Somewhere.

Anywhere.

The women met a few days after the funeral. Eleanor led Sabina into the kitchen. Kitty was there already. She rose, and hugged her.

'I'm sorry,' she said.

'It's good of you to say it,' Sabina answered. 'But in one way I'm happy it's over. It was a terrible few weeks.'

'It was,' Kitty said. 'I'd have come to the funeral, but...*well, you know.*'

'*Yes, alanna, I understand.*'

Brigid ran into the room, and threw her arms around Sabina's knees. Sabina lifted her into her lap. The child saw the tears in her eyes, and started to cry.

'*There, there, there's no need for you to cry.*' She hugged the child close into her bosom.

'*So what are you going to do now?*' Eleanor asked.

'*What can I do?*' Sabina said. '*Just keep running the bar, that's all. Mind you, that's been hard enough the past few nights, what with everyone saying they're sorry. But it's settled down, and there's even the odd bit of laughter in the bar, though there's few enough there. At night it's harder, it's awful lonesome in a big house.*'

'*You'll be less lonesome when you have Brigid,*' Kitty said.

Eleanor looked across at her in alarm. '*Brigid...*'

'*Sure she'll have to be in Kilduff. Four nights a week perhaps. How else will she get her schooling. It's there or Liscreggan.*'

'*Don't let Aileen hear you saying that.*'

'*I won't, but it's the way it's going to be. Isn't it?*'

'Yes,' Eleanor said. She sat on a stool by the hearth. '*Yes, that's the way it will have to be. But when? That's the question.*'

'*As soon as she's three,*' Kitty said.

'*She'll be three the year after next,*' Sabina said.

'*She will,*' Eleanor said. She was staring into the flames, thinking.

Alicia dead and Brigid going. Stop being silly. It's only Kilduff, it's only a mile away, I can walk up whenever I like. She'll be here three nights a week anyhow. And all the summer. But what when she gets beyond the school in Kilduff. Castlebar? She won't be back on weekends then. Six years till then, they'll only teach her four years in Kilduff. And then what? Oh, what's wrong with me, I knew all that already.

Eleanor and Michael did not speak about Farrelly. She wanted to keep her thoughts to herself for now. She knew how restless Luke was, and how much Ellen Morrisroe had unsettled him. Perhaps England had been as much on his mind as America at that time, but the news of Farrelly's emigration had focussed everything, made America real.

But she decided to wait and see what would develop. Someday more news would arrive from America, either through Mikey Jordan's family or Farrelly's. She never anticipated that the contact might be much more direct than that.

But what about Pat? She had accepted for many years that Luke would emigrate, and when he did, Pat would take over. He was still young, but Mr. Burke would have no interest in evicting the family as long as they worked the quarry and paid their rent.

But Pat's lack of enthusiasm when he realised that the farm might be his had disturbed her. She had no idea what was behind it. The answer was not long in coming.

One morning, while the men were out, she and Winnie were making brown bread. '*What do you think?*' she said. '*Isn't it time we found a young girl for Pat.*'

'Aye,' Winnie replied. '*That might not be a bad idea at all. Though mind you, he might have some ideas of his own. There's girls in Knockanure, and you know Pat, he's a nice young fellow.*'

'*Indeed he is,*' Eleanor said. '*There's many a girl would be happy to have him.*'

'*There are. In fact, I think there's already one who'd be interested, and I think he's eyeing her up too.*'

'*And who might that be?*'

'*Sarah. Sarah Cronin. She's over in the Workhouse!*'

'She's in the Workhouse!'

Winnie laughed. 'Oh, no, not in that way. She's the Matron's daughter. Her father was the old Master – he died. She's a lovely girl, sharp too.'

'The Matron's daughter! But that's impossible. How do you know this?'

'Well, I don't. I only met her for five or ten minutes the time we came through Knockanure. She and Pat are working together on the books in the Workhouse. It was just the way they were talking and eyeing each other. I'm only guessing, mind you, but I think there's something between them.'

Eleanor returned to her work. The Matron's daughter? She would be used to better things than Carrigard. And Pat was working as a clerk already. If there was anything between them, he would want to stay on in Knockanure. The look in his eyes when she mentioned the farm – perhaps that explained it all. He wanted to stay with the Union, if they would keep him. How likely was that? She had no idea. It was ironic though. It was what she had always hoped for, but never expected, a good clerical position for Pat. But if Luke left, what then?

A few days later, a letter arrived.

'There's a letter there for you, Luke.'

'Who is it from, Mother?'

'How would I know? Winnie says it's from America.' Eleanor knew well who it was from.

Luke sat down at the table, slitting it open with his knife. He felt all eyes on him as he glanced through it.

'Well, who is it from? You can tell us surely.'

'Farrelly.'

'Farrelly,' Michael exclaimed. 'What does he have to say?' Luke saw the look of alarm on his father's face.

'Seems he's working on some railroad near Philadelphia.'

'Philadelphia,' Winnie echoed. 'So why's he writing to you?'

'He wants me to join him. Says the money's great, and he wants me to head up another gang.'

That afternoon he worked with his father in the bog. Michael had said nothing all morning, and Luke was worried. The silence was ominous.

They leant on their *sleáns* as a long line of carts and people streamed past. Most were in rags. The carts held high mounds of packs. On top, old men and women clung to the bags and the sides of the carts.

'More from the Workhouse,' Michael said.

'I'd say you're right.'

When the convoy had passed, they took their *sleáns* and coats, and walked along the road towards the house. There were two men and a woman lying at the edge. Luke could smell the gangrene. Fever! He looked closely at all three. 'They're dead,' he said.

'I know,' Michael said. 'They must have thrown them off the carts, the bastards. Didn't want burying them.'

'Damn it, why should we let them get away with that? I'll go after them, you stay here.'

He ran after the convoy. By the time he overtook the carts they were already entering Kilduff. He made his way to the front of the convoy. The leading cart was being driven by a man in the official uniform of the Workhouse. Luke ran up to him.

'*You've left some behind.*'

'*The devil we have,*' the man said, aggression in his voice.

'*You have. Three dead. And they're yours.*'

'*It's nothing to do with us,*' the man responded and whipped the horse on. Luke grasped the bridle and stopped the horse. The other carts were stopping behind, dozens of eyes on Luke.

'*Let go, you bastard.*' the man shouted.

'*Not until you've buried them.*'

Abruptly the man lashed him across the cheek. Luke fell to the ground, writhing with the pain of it. The convoy trundled on.

He got up and ran after the convoy. When he reached to top, the man lashed at him again, but Luke stepped back and caught the whip. The man tried to hold as Luke pulled back, but he could not. Luke stood holding the whip until the man jumped down, and swung at him. He grasped the man's arm and twisted it sharply behind his back. The man screamed in pain. Luke swung him around and punched him on the nose, drawing blood. As he staggered back, Luke hit him harder, into the stomach and up towards the ribcage. The man fell to the ground, gasping. Luke stood over him.

'*You don't ever attack people in this town again,*' he shouted. '*Now go on, get moving.*'

The man clambered back on the cart, still gasping. Luke lashed at the horse with the whip. Then he stood at the side of the street, still holding the whip, as the convoy started forward again. He walked to the church and knocked on the door beside it. Father Reilly answered his knock.

'We've got a dead woman and two dead men out the road.'

'You don't look too well yourself. What happened to your face?'

Luke felt the weal. It was bleeding. 'Oh, some fellow whipped me.' He held up the whip. 'He won't do it again.'

The priest went in to collect his holy oils. As they walked out towards Carrigard, Luke explained what had happened.

'You're a tough man,' the priest said.

'No tougher than a man has to be.'

When they arrived at the bodies, the priest administered the Last Rites. 'We're going to have to bury them,' he said.

'I know,' Luke said.

'You'd better go back and get the cart,' Michael said. 'We wouldn't want carrying them the way they are.'

Luke left. When he arrived back, he and Michael manhandled the corpses into the cart. Then he knelt beside the ditch, washing his hands.

He and the priest mounted the cart and started back towards Kilduff graveyard, as Michael walked back towards the house.

Some time later, Luke arrived back.

'Well, did you get them buried?' Michael asked.

'Not yet. Fr. Reilly is going to organise a few fellows from the town. I think we've done enough.'

'Dead right, we have. But if they lose three just coming from Knockanure, God knows how many more they'll throw off before they get to Westport.'

'That's someone else's worry.'

Eleanor served up the dinner. Cabbage and corn.

'It shows you what I've always said,' Michael said. 'It's only the beggars go. The best people, they stay at home.'

'Yes, Father.'

Only the beggars go? That was only because the Union was paying to get rid of them. He thought about Farrelly. The best went too. The only difference was that they paid for themselves.

That night he lay on the bed beside Winnie, reading the letter again and again in the weak candlelight.

Mr. Luke Ryan	C/o Pennsylvania Railroad
Carrigard	Market Street
Kilduff	Harrisburg
Co. Mayo	Pennsylvania
Ireland	United States of America

May 1, 1847

My Dear Luke,

You will be surprised to note the above address. I must confess I am no less surprised myself. In any case, I must tell you that I decided some time back to leave Leeds and travel to America with Mikey Jordan. I had written to a cousin of mine in Philadelphia about this, and from what he said the money is better over here. He was surely right.

The journey was a terrible one, but we were better off than most. We slept on the upper deck together with some young farming men from the country around Frankfurt, but they only spoke Dutch, so we kept pretty much to ourselves. The lower deck was packed with hundreds of Irish, many from Mayo, I am sure. Big numbers of them died on the passage.

When we arrived in Philadelphia, my cousin met us, and we stayed with him for some nights. But from all we heard, it appeared that the best chances were with the PRR who are presently building a railroad from Philadelphia to Pittsburgh, which is in the western part of the State of Pennsylvania. So without wishing to impose further on my cousin, we travelled to Harrisburg with some other fellows from Mayo and Donegal. Harrisburg is a small town, perhaps a hundred miles west of Philadelphia. The line here is just starting, and we are working very hard. We have no settled lodgings, but a letter to the above address will find me, as one of our fellows goes there to collect the mail every week.

Perhaps you will stay in Mayo, and that is your own choice. But there are great chances in this country to work hard, and earn better money than you have ever earned, even in England.

Either way, we all look forward to hearing from you again.

Your old friend,

Martin Farrelly

What now? He could not put his thoughts in order. He blew out the candle.

'What are you thinking?' Winnie whispered beside him.

'I don't know, my love. He's as bad as Danny, Martin is. Just as soon as we're settled down, he writes and tells us how great things are everywhere else. Everywhere but Mayo.'

'We said we'd wait.'

'I know we did. But what are we going to do about Martin? He'll be waiting for an answer, one way or another.'

'Well, you don't have to write back yet.'

He lay awake thinking. America? It was going to be America, but still the question was when. The real problem was the hunger. There were ships from Westport to America, but they cost money, and that kind of money could not be spared now. But if they waited for the hunger to be over, they could be waiting for ever.

The only way he could see to make money fast was to join Danny again, but the talk with Corrigan had upset him. He had already known that

Danny was ruthless. Exploiting helpless people was bad enough. But he had never suspected that Danny had such a savage streak of cruelty. Oh, to hell with all that.

No one referred to Farrelly's letter again. Luke walked down to Sabina. He swore her to secrecy and asked her opinion.

'You'll consider it, so,' she said.

'I will, and seriously,' he said. 'But I don't even have an idea where Harrisburg is.'

'Ian used to have maps of America.'

'What? I never heard that.'

'I don't think he wanted encouraging you.'

A few minutes later, they were poring over a map of the eastern United States.

'Well, we've got Philadelphia,' Luke said. 'And we've got Pittsburgh, but there's no sign of Harrisburg.'

'It must be somewhere,' Sabina said. 'Martin wouldn't lie, would he.'

'I suppose not. Still, it must be one tiny place if they don't even reckon it important enough to be marked. Not that it'll matter much one way or another. The railway will have moved on before I get anywhere near Harrisburg.'

'Why so?' Sabina asked.

"The first thing will be to get there, and given I'll have to go over to England first, I sure as hell won't be in Harrisburg any time soon.'

'Why England?'

'Where do you think the money for all this is going to come from? The damned hunger isn't over and might never be. We're surely not starving, but we're not in the way of putting up cash for a ticket. And since we don't have it here, I'll have to go over to England to find it. Work with Danny again, maybe?'

'Danny!'

'Why not? It's the fastest way I know of getting money on the railways. He's always been asking me to join him.'

Sabina looked doubtful. 'But then you might stay in England, would you?'

'Doubt it. And I wouldn't want working for Danny forever.'

'You've heard about what happened Jimmy Corrigan then?'

'I have,' Luke said.

'It's all over Kilduff, and I'd reckon the fellows in America will hear of it soon. A savage business, by all accounts. No, Luke, working with Danny? You'd never be able to show your face around here again. Nor with any of the Kilduff lads in America.'

He placed a coin on the counter, shaking his head.

'So what can I do?'

She was silent as she drew a pint of Guinness and watched it settle.

'I don't know,' she said at last. 'There might be other ways of doing it.'

'Like what? Like bloody what?'

Sabina placed the beer in front of him. 'Tell me Luke, have you ever thought of the rest of the family. Even when the hunger ends – if it ends – we should be thinking of new chances. Not just the desperate need in the here and now. Mayo is finished, you know.'

Luke sipped his beer thoughtfully. 'That's rough coming from you.'

'It's not a matter of being rough, it's facing facts. If we want to break the hunger, we have to look much further than farming in County Mayo.'

'But how...?'

'America is half of the answer, Luke. We've got to get at least one of the family properly settled there, and able to bring others out when times are better.'

'And that'll cost money.

'It will, Luke. It will.'

'And what's the other half the answer? '

'Education.'

'Education!'

'Yes. For the whole family. And it'll cost far more than we can ever afford here. So we've got to get you and Winnie to America, and the sooner the better. But it won't be done through England. You'll have to go direct. New York or Philadelphia if possible, otherwise Canada.'

'Canada!'

'Quebec is cheaper, from all I hear.'

'But I've no money either way.'

'No? But I might.'

'You...?'

'Not much, maybe. I can easy get more, though. Screw a bit more credit from the brewers. Tighten up what the cattle dealers owe. And the bank likes me too. It'll all add up. Not a lot, but it should cover your tickets, and a bit more for when you reach Quebec or wherever.'

'You really believe you could do all that?'

'I'm sure I can.'

'But you'll have to be repaid.'

'Now don't be worrying your head about that. The first thing to remember is this, we're all family. Even when you do have the money, there's better things to do with it than repaying me. If ye're all well set up in America in ten years' time, then would be the time of thinking of settling up, and perhaps not even then. Who cares.'

'But...'

362

'No more 'buts' out of you, Luke. You and Winnie are the future of this family. I know that, your mother knows it. Even Aileen knows, and – dare I say it – so does Kitty.'

'Kitty. What in hell does she have to do with this?'

'Never mind.'

In bed that night Luke told Winnie about Sabina's offer. She was surprised.

'You really think she could get the money?' she asked.

'She's certain she can.'

'But would you take it?'

'What choice do we have, my love? We don't have the money to spare here, that's for sure and certain. My only other chance would be to work with Danny.'

'No way should you do that,' she said with force.

'Well, then.'

The battle of Lord Sligo's wall was not repeated. More militiamen were recruited from Claremorris and accompanied the convoys of wagons out of Westport and through Castlebar. Three more consignments of corn arrived in Kilduff, and they were all stored under guard. But then one brought a shock to Luke and Gaffney.

'That's the last one you'll be getting,' the militia captain said, as the convoy started to pull out towards Ballaghaderreen.

'It's what?'

'The last. They're reckoning the harvest is looking good. There's no need for hunger now.'

They went back into the office.

'What now? Luke asked.

'Only one thing I can think of,' Gaffney said. 'We'll go over to Castlebar and see Andy Irvine.'

Next morning, he and Gaffney were riding towards Castlebar.

'Damn it to hell, – no need for hunger! Are they all mad?'

'I don't know,' Gaffney said. 'Maybe they want to believe good news.'

'Good news is right. Sure, the crop is better, no arguing that. But can't they see the amount that's been planted. How much is it? Half a normal year? A quarter? What do you think?'

Gaffney reined in his horse, looking at the fields around him.

'I think you're right,' he said at length. 'A quarter, no more. I wonder why? No seed potatoes? Or maybe they don't believe in it anymore. They reckon they'll have enough with oats. But there won't be enough.'

'Damned right, there won't.'

An hour later, they were sitting in Irvine's office in Castlebar.

'There's no point in thumping the table,' Irvine said. 'You've had your way long enough, George. But there's damned little coming into Westport. I can't sign requisitions for what I don't have, and that's an end to it.'

They left. When they arrived back in Gaffney's office, Luke started to tear up the requisition forms.

'For God's sake, calm down,' Gaffney said.

'But what are we going to tell them?'

'I told you, I'll do the telling. Then they can't blame you.'

'Oh, can't they?'

A few days later, he was accompanying a final consignment of carts up the Mountain. In spite of two donkeys on each, they were creaking slowly, urged on by the men. Luke noticed another man walking behind, and pulled the cart over to let him go. It was Father Reilly.

'What way are you going?' Luke asked him.

'Up towards *Baile a' Cnoic.*'

'Someone dying?'

'Everyone is dying. I don't bother waiting anymore. I just do my rounds every day, call in everywhere at least once a week.'

'And what about the church?'

'Oh, I let Father Flynn take care of that. He's good with buildings.'

Luke pulled the donkey forward again. 'You'll be busy so.'

'I will. But it's not just that today. I'd heard ye were taking the corn up. I'm supposed to be looking after the Kitchens on the Mountain.'

'I didn't know that.'

'No? I've been doing it this long time. The Union has been demanding it, they've had enough problems with Nangle and the like with their conversions, so they prefer using priests now.'

'I see,' Luke said. 'But you know this is the last load?'

'Yes, I do know. And I'm the one who's going to have to tell them.'

'I don't suppose Flynn would have the guts to do that.'

'No,' Father Reilly said. 'Not his line of country.'

They went through what was left of *Gort na Móna.* Blackened ground, gaunt gables still standing.

'You know they still blame me for this,' the priest said.

'Why you?'

'They reckon I shouldn't have stopped them fighting the militia.'

'It's easy saying that now. I wonder what they would have said after the militia sabering them.'

'I don't know. It's just I don't like taking the side of the militia either. It's an evil thing, an eviction.'

'It is.'

They walked out of the village, leading the donkeys up towards *Baile a' Cnoic*. He was depressed and frightened, remembering that day at *Gort na Móna*. The woman and her family too. The priest had entrusted them to him, and he had brought them to Knockanure. He had never expected that her relatives would have brought her to the Workhouse. Or maybe he had, maybe he was just trying to hide it from himself. He felt the need to tell the priest about it, almost as if seeking absolution for his sins.

'You'll remember Ellen Morrisroe? You asked us to take her and her children.'

'I remember.'

'She's dead. Died in the Workhouse.'

'Dead?' the priest exclaimed. 'What about her children?'

He thought back to the pit in Knockanure and the faces of dead children. 'I'm sorry. What did you say?' he asked.

'Her children. What happened to them?' the priest asked again. He was staring at Luke, slightly puzzled.

'I don't know. I just don't know,' Luke said.

When they reached *Baile a' Cnoic*, the priest went from house to house giving the Last Rites to the dying and the dead. Luke thought back to Brockagh. Long days riding around the mountains with another priest.

Lisnadee. Benstreeva. Teenashilla. Burrenabawn. And Croghancoe.

Another place. No different to here though.

Some of the women helped the priest to prepare the food for the Soup Kitchen. A crowd was gathering already. To Luke, there seemed to be less than before. He thought of what his father had told him at the rath. Long days of famine and fever?

The Workhouse? England? America?

He had some of the women bring small bowls of soup into the fever shed. As he had half expected, few of the patients took any of the food. He went out again and stood beside the pot where the soup was being ladled out. The priest was talking to the crowd.

'I've got to tell you – this is the end of the food.'

No one said anything.

'We've no more left in Kilduff. The Kitchens are closing everywhere.'

Still no one responded. Grey faces watched them. Grey clothes, frayed shifts and trousers, broken boots. Thin, gaunt, dying people. Broken men and women, staring in silence at a priest who could not stop an eviction nor feed his people. And what was he? Luke Ryan – a Government man.

By rights he should not be here. Gaffney had said he was not required to be at the Kitchens. But he wasn't working the pots, he was only delivering supplies. They were still watching him though – another man who could not feed them, a man who was holding the food back from them. Guilty. Guilty as charged.

He went over to the carts and waited there with the cart men. After a few minutes, the priest came and joined them, and they drove the donkeys back towards Kilduff.

Chapter Twenty Nine

Telegraph or Connaught Ranger, June 1847:
This town and the country westward to the Killeries is one
charnel emporium of disease, and the number of deaths in
the villages along the sea coast is incredible.

He lay awake past midnight, watching the flickering shadows from the fire
playing on the rafters. Every time he tried to sleep, nightmare images came
back to him. The man in the battle outside Westport, the look on his face as
the rock smashed his head in. Sorcha, the look on her face too as he turned
and left her in the Workhouse. Ellen Morrisroe, dead of fever; surely he had
known her cousin would not keep them.

Her children too, what happened to them? And the pit, the stench of
gangrene, the children with the fox faces. He tried to think. There was no
point in feeling guilty. He had done what he had to do. But still it gnawed at
him. Deliberate or otherwise, he was a killer.

Was it any wonder people hated him? Refusing work tickets to desperate
men. Closing the Works in Brockagh. Closing the Kitchens around Kilduff.
Yes, Gaffney had kept his promise. He had not had to be present when the
people were told the Kitchens were closing, except at *Baile a' Cnoic,* and that
hardly counted. But still they blamed him for it. Every time he had refused a
ticket on the Works, every time a Kitchen closed, he was seen as responsible
for the deaths that would follow.

'What's wrong?' Winnie whispered.

'I just can't sleep. I'm sorry. You go back to sleep.'

'But tell me. Tell me. What's wrong?'

'There's no hope now. We'll have to go, and soon.'

'I know. I'm trying not to think about it, but we'll have to do something.'

'I think Danny was right all along. There's no future in farming in Mayo.
We'll never be able to depend on the potato again.'

'But what will your mother and father do?'

'There's only one chance for them. We'll have to send money. Pat will
too. At least they'd buy corn.'

'And what about us then?' she asked.

'America is best. It might have been better if I'd stayed in England anyhow.'

'But…'

'I know, I know. But I'd never have killed anyone either.'

'You'd never have…what?'

'Keep your voice down.'

'But what…Who?' He could hear the shock in her voice. He waited, while she understood the full meaning of what he had said. Then he went on.

'From now on,' he said, 'my life is in your hands. I can tell you what happened, and I think you'll understand. But other people mightn't, or might not want to. And if any of this gets out, they'll hang me for it.'

She said nothing, waiting.

'Remember about the attack…'

'At Lord Sligo's wall?'

'Yes,' he said, 'the Battle of Lord Sligo's Wall, as they all call it. But I'll tell you this, it was nothing to be proud of. Fighting starving women. Great fellows, weren't we?'

'Is that why you never talked about it.'

'That, and other reasons. Remember about the fellow who was just about to kill Father with the rock?'

'But you hit him first.'

'I did. But I didn't just hit him. The stone smashed his head in. I killed him.'

'Killed…you…you killed him.'

'Killed him. Dead.'

'But no-one ever said…'

'No-one ever knew.'

'Then how…?'

'I felt for his heart. Listened for his breathing. No-one else saw. But he was dead alright. I've seen enough dead men to know.'

'But it could have been anyone. How would they know it was you? Weren't there hundreds of stones thrown.'

'There were. I don't think anyone will ever be able to point the finger at me. At least I hope not, but I can never be sure. I know I killed a man, though. Now you do too. And you know the kind of man you married.'

'Don't say that,' she said.

'It's up to you now. I'll have to go to America, it's safer for me there, safer even than England, I don't want to hang. You can follow me. But only if that's what you want.'

'Don't be silly. Of course it's what I want. This changes nothing. I'd follow you anywhere.'

'I know you would. It's just you and me now, *a ghrá*. Wherever we go, we go together.'

He slept. For a long time she lay thinking. Hanging. Why had he said that? Perhaps someone had seen him. Perhaps someone knew who he was. Even one of their own people might have seen him and known that the man had died. Would such a man be able to keep his mouth shut, or would he see it as a great thing, and tell everyone when he had enough beer inside him.

Hanging? Once in Ballina her father had pointed out a beggar woman whose husband had been hung for murder. Now she thought of herself, avoided by everyone, a widow reduced to begging. No. Still, she would not rest unless Luke went to America. Their last and only chance.

Winnie and Eleanor were out feeding the hens with left-over potato skins. They threw the mashed skins on the ground, and the hens came, pecking at the food and pecking at each other.

'Poor fellows,' Eleanor said. '*They're getting scrawnier and scrawnier.*'

'*Aren't they just*' Winnie said. '*The peelings are getting thinner and thinner, and they know it.*'

'*One thing's for certain,*' Eleanor said. '*When the time comes for strangling them, there'll be little enough meat left.*' A hen pecked at her leg. '*Get down, you devil,*' she said, flicking her hand at it.

They walked back towards the house.

'*There's something I wanted to say to you, Mother*' Winnie said.

'*What's that, child.*'

'*It's going to have to be America. There's no other way.*'

Eleanor stopped dead. '*Ye've decided so.*'

'*We have.*'

'*But why? What decided ye?*'

Winnie thought of what Luke had told her, but she knew she could not say anything of this to Eleanor.

'*At least we'd be able to earn money,*' she said at last. '*Send it back to you here.*'

'*You'll have to send money to your family too,*' Eleanor said.

'*I know.*'

'*But the ticket money? We'd never spare that. Not now.*'

'*Sabina will lend it to us.*'

'*Sabina!*'

'*She promised it to Luke. Reckons it's best for all the family.*'

'*But she never said...*'

'*She's still waiting for our answer.*'

Eleanor was thinking, but hardly knew what to say.

'*And what about the farm here?*' she asked.

'*I don't know. One thing is certain, we can't depend on potatoes now.*'

They'll feed you one year, and kill you the next.'

'You have the right of it,' Eleanor said. 'And it's not worth farming without potatoes. The grain will only pay the rent, and we can't live on anything else we'd grow.'

'That's it, isn't it.'

'But leaving the farm? I don't know. Michael's getting too old for farming, even if he won't say it. And what about me – I'm young yet. Pat's always wanted the farm. But he's doing well in Knockanure, he might stay on. Why would he come back here?'

'I don't know that he would.'

'I wonder what he'd do if he thought ye might go to America, though. What do you think? Would he stay, or come home?'

'That might be different,' Winnie said. 'If he knew for certain the farm was his, he might come home. Who knows? A lot depends on Sarah Cronin.'

Michael and Luke were working in the bog, throwing sods of turf from the small ricks up onto the cart. Then Luke led the horse out along the narrow boreen, and stopped.

'Fordes,' he said. 'I never knew they had a cart.' He tied the horse to a blackthorn bush, and he and his father walked over.

'Good morning to you, Eileen,' Michael called out. 'Are you going far?'

'Far enough.' There were three packs on the cart. She walked into the house and brought out another, her two children following.

'There's little enough for us here,' she said. 'Ever since Mark caught the fever, we've had no way of working the farm. So we're going to America – Westport, Liverpool and America.'

'It's a long way to be going on your own.'

'I won't be going on my own. There's twenty of us going.'

'Twenty!' Luke exclaimed. 'Surely not from Carrigard?'

'Some from Carrigard. More from Cnoc rua.'

'But who?'

'John Carney with his two sons and the wife of the oldest. Bernie Murtagh's son with his wife and children. Matt and Mary Grogan.'

'Matt? But hasn't he a good lease. Why would he have to go?'

'He doesn't have to go. He just reckons there's better chances in America.'

'But their farm?'

'O'Brien's are taking it, the bastards.'

Luke had seen another cart coming down from the boreen across from them. There were two men and a woman in it. One of the men jumped down, and walked up to them. It was John Carney.

'Johnny! What's this I hear?' Michael asked.

370

'We're going to America. There's nothing for us here.'

Carney helped Eileen Forde out with two more packs and then carefully locked the door with an old rusty key. He helped the widow up into the cart and jumped up beside her. He whipped the animals, and the carts started to move. No one spoke to Luke.

A hundred yards away, on the Knockanure road, Luke could see four other carts waiting for them. The convoy started to move towards Kilduff.

Over the next few days, they saw many convoys. Some were the familiar ones coming from Knockanure Workhouse, broken people fleeing hunger and fever. Paid to go by the Union, clearing out the Workhouse and indirectly clearing out the Mountain. The barony of Clanowen was sending its people to America.

But what Luke also found disturbing were the other lines of carts, less in numbers, but carrying people who were not starving. Families who no longer believed in Ireland or Mayo.

Through all this time, Michael had said nothing. But then one morning when they were working in the haggard, he brought the subject up, taking Luke by surprise.

'So you'll go, will you? Join Farrelly in America?'

Luke was quick with his response. 'Let me ask you one thing first, Father. What would you do if you were me?'

Michael thought back to the years when he was little older than Luke. The bitter years waiting for his father, a man he no longer respected, to die. Wasted years. And the blight. Would it come back? Were they all fooling themselves that they could farm in Mayo?

'I'd go,' he said.

'Well then?'

'But it's not as simple as that. There's still the lease.'

'There is,' Luke said. 'But Pat's the one who really wants it.'

'True enough,' Michael said, 'but he's still not twenty-one.'

'What is he? Nineteen? And you're saying Burke wouldn't accept that, or that he'd throw ye out for the sake of two years?

'No,' Michael said. 'I'm not saying that. But if...'

'If what? If he evicted ye, who else could take it? There's no-one else around here with the money anymore. And even if there was, they wouldn't touch a farm where there'd been an eviction, not now. He'll know all that, and he'll know I'll be sending money back from America. No, the lease will be safe enough.'

'But we need to get that in writing.'

'Fair enough,' Luke said. 'I'll write to Burke tonight. If he says no, I'll

371

stay, but I reckon after all that's happened in the last year, there's no way on God's earth he'd say that.'

When they came in, Winnie was making up the bed. Luke went in, and closed the door.

'I told him,' Luke said.

'What? About America?'

'Yes. About America.'

'What did he say?'

'Nothing much. He doesn't like it, but he sees the sense of it. No, he won't stand in our way.'

'I'm glad so,' she said. 'All that talk about hanging, you had me worried.'

'*Arra* hell...'

'No, it's no little thing. You might say that no one saw you, but there's no way you could be sure of that. And if anyone did see you, they'd not be able to keep their mouth shut. No, there's no 'buts' about it. We're going to America, and the sooner the better.'

They went out to the table where Eleanor was serving. Luke noticed his mother was crying. He thought back to the first day he had come home. '*You're not to go away again,*' she had said. Yes, if she had reason to cry when he came home, she would have more reason for it when he was leaving.

'I've told your mother,' Michael said, 'though I think she knew already. But which or whether, she knows it's the only way.'

Eleanor nodded her head. She sat down.

'I'm sorry. It'll be hard on ye,' Luke said.

'Sure it's the way it has to be,' Michael said. 'But I'm well able for the farm, and Pat will be coming home soon enough.'

'And if he doesn't...' Eleanor said.

That evening, Luke wrote the letter to Mr. Burke. He pointed out that the work on the Relief Works and on the Soup Kitchens had come to an end, and while they were hopeful they could continue to pay the rent, there could be no guarantee of this if the blight returned. The best way therefore was for Luke to work in America where he had a job arranged, and he could pay the rent from there.

A few days later, they received a letter from Edmond White. He stated that Mr. Burke would accept this arrangement but only for a maximum of one year.

'But it wouldn't be worth going to America for only a year,' Winnie said.

'No,' Luke said, 'but we'll ask for two. By then Pat will be twenty-one, and he'll be able to sign it.'

'Yes,' Michael said. 'That's it. Then, one way or the other, we can keep the lease.'

Luke wrote a second letter, this time directly to Edmond White, pointing out that Pat would be twenty-one in two years, and asking for an extension. They received a reply stating that Mr. Burke would accept either arrangement, so long as one of Michael's sons, of legal age, would be living on the farm and acting as co-lessee within two years.

'And that means Pat,' Luke said to Winnie that night. 'And we're going to America.'

Mr. Patrick Ryan	Carrigard
Knockanure Union	Sunday
Knockanure	
Co. Mayo	

My Dear Pat,

I am writing to tell you that the farm will now be yours. I am sure you will be happy to hear this, since it is something that has been dear to your heart for many years.

After much thinking about it, Winnie and me have decided that our future is in America. As you may know, Martin Farrelly is working in Pennsylvania, and he has invited me to join him there.

Mr. Burke has already agreed that when you are twenty-one you will sign the lease along with Father, and so the lease will stay in the family even when I'm gone to America. He would not have agreed to my going otherwise. But that will not be for some time yet, so I am sure we will meet before I go, either here or in Knockanure.

Luke

There were reports and rumours filtering back to Kilduff from the seaports of the West – Sligo, Westport and Galway. The most disturbing rumours concerned the United States.

One morning, as Winnie walked towards Kilduff, she met a group of twenty men and women walking towards Carrigard and Knockanure.

'Is there water near?' a woman asked her.

'You'll find water at the well, over where the women are standing.'

She was desperately thin. She made to walk on, but Winnie stopped her.

'Have ye been travelling?'

The woman glanced at her, her eyes rolling, but she said did not reply. The group was still walking, following Winnie's directions to the well, and the woman followed them. Winnie walked back with them.

'Where have ye been?' she asked.

'We have been away.'

'*But where?*'

'*America.*'

'*America!*'

'Yes,' she said, '*it was to America we went. One day we spent in America.*'

'*One day! But how long have you been away?*'

'*Two months on the Great Sea. One day in America. The soldiers came, the men of the Crown, so all the people, they had to walk to Westport. We went from Westport with the ship they called the Arcturus. I went with my sister. But many joined us in Westport. There were many hundreds of them. And hundreds of us. So we all went to America for a day. There were not a hundred when we returned. The people who came with us, they had the Black Fever, they brought it on the ship with them. At first it was only their own, but then many more became sick. That was when my sister died. They threw her into the sea. Four weeks travelling, and we came to their great city, Boston. But other ships found us, and they would not allow us to stop.*'

'*They would not allow it? But everyone goes to Boston.*'

'*Not us. The ships of the Americans stopped us. They had guns.*'

'*Guns!*' Winnie wondered if she should believe what she was being told.

'*Guns,*' the woman repeated. '*And so we had to leave their harbour. Our ship carried us three days more until we found a quiet place. But when most were off, the soldiers came. The soldiers of the Americans. They would not let us stay. They caught the captain, and with a pistol to his head, they told him to leave. We all had to go. Five weeks more we spent on the Great Sea, but we were not so many, and the fever became less. And so we came to Westport, where we had left.*'

'*And the money. Did they give you back your money?*'

The woman stopped, and looked at Winnie, but said nothing more.

When Winnie returned, she told Luke of all she had learnt. That afternoon he walked into Kilduff, asking who knew more. In the bar, only one elderly man knew of the voyage of the Arcturus. He gave Luke two names in *Baile a' Cnoic*. Luke walked through the broken remains of Lord Clanowen's burnt village and the silent village of *Sliabh Meán*. He walked on, higher up the Mountain. Up here, everyone knew the story, and he spoke with two men and an old woman who had survived the journey. They all confirmed what Winnie had heard.

They heard many more rumours, and listened to what advice they could, though much was contradictory. People still spoke of travelling through Liverpool to America, but there were reports that many Liverpool ships had also been barred from American ports. So it would have to be Quebec. Sabina had been right on that. But it was getting late in the year, and they would have to decide soon.

'I don't like this,' Luke said to Winnie one evening. 'I don't want you dying on me before we even get to America.'

'But what else can we do?'

'Go on the upper deck. We'd be away from the fever there.'

'But we'd only have enough money for one...'

'True enough.'

She stared at him. 'No,' she shouted. 'If we go, we go together, and that's an end to it.'

But already she knew that there might be no other way. As time passed, she began to suspect she was pregnant. She discussed it with Eleanor one morning.

'I've missed my bleeding, Mother.'

'But, what? Are you sure? For how long?'

'Long enough. I haven't been counting days, but it's too long, that's for sure and certain.'

'But what about America?'

'I don't know,' Winnie replied. She thought again of telling Eleanor about the man Luke had killed, but once more she decided it would only worry Eleanor and would not help.

'I don't know,' she repeated, *'and God knows, we don't want to be separated. But Luke – I think he has to go.'*

'And you'll have to stay, child. There's no way you could travel on those ships with a baby or expecting one.'

'But we swore we'd never be apart,' Winnie said.

'I know, child, I know,' Eleanor said. *'God knows, you haven't been long married. But the sea travel will be rough, and things in Quebec aren't much better by all accounts.'*

Winnie had tears in her eyes. *'You're right,'* she said. *'Not long married, and now to be apart again.'*

'Yes, alanna, it's cruel. But sure you'll have us, won't you. Sabina too, and little Brigid, won't she be delighted to have a new little friend.'

Winnie looked at the child.

'Are you sure she wouldn't be jealous of another baby. All the attention she gets now, aren't we spoiling her.'

'Arra no, there's no reason for her to be jealous. Aren't there enough of us to give her and the new baby all the kindness they want.'

'I suppose there are.'

Yes, Eleanor thought to herself, there are. *She'll get all the attention she wants, little Brigid. And the new baby too. But there's one thing you didn't say, Winnie. You never said it would be more sensible to go back to Brockagh. You didn't, did you? My first grandchild, born in this house. Won't that be something?*

Kitty and Sabina came down to the house that afternoon. When Eleanor told them about the pregnancy, she saw the look of sadness in Kitty's eyes. Wishing it was hers, she thought. She'll never forget, poor girl.

'*But what can ye do?*' Kitty asked Winnie. '*Will ye stay then?*'

Eleanor answered for her. '*Would that they could. Sure isn't it what we'd all like, but there's no way it can be done. Luke will have to go, but Winnie will have to stay until the child is born.*'

'*And give the little thing chance to get enough strength to travel,*' Sabina said. '*Isn't that it?*'

'*Yes*' Kitty said. '*And give Brigid a brother or sister to play with.*'

'*But not for long,*' Winnie said.

Kitty kissed Brigid on the forehead. '*Does Luke know about this?*'

'*Not yet.*'

'*You'll have to tell him, won't you? He'll have to have a say in all this.*'

She told him that night.

'Are you sure?' he asked.

'As sure as any woman can be. No, my love, the baby's there, and there's no way we can give it back.'

'But – what now?'

'Isn't it what we were thinking all along? You'll have to go, and I'll have to stay.'

'But we said…'

'Yes, my love. It'll break my heart too. But there's no other way, *a ghrá*.'

'But when would you come?'

'That I don't know. As soon as the little one is fit for it, then I'll follow you. There's one good thing though. You'll be able to go on the upper deck, with only the one of us travelling. And with Sabina's money, you won't have to work in England to earn the money.'

He did not answer.

One morning they walked down to Sabina. The bar was deserted. Sabina took down Ian's maps, and they studied them closely. 'Where's Harrisburg?' Winnie asked.

'We're reckoning about a hundred miles west of Philadelphia. Just about – there.' He pointed at a blank space in the middle.

'I don't see a town.'

'Oh, it's there alright.'

'And what about Quebec?'

'Up, around here.' He pointed to a beer stain above the map.

'How would you get between the two?'

'There shouldn't be too much trouble, from all I hear. Work a while, get a bit of money, then sail down to New York and Philadelphia.'

'Is it far?'

'Far enough.'

When all had been agreed, he and Sabina met with the shipping agent as he came through on his weekly visit to Kilduff. They bought a ticket for a boat leaving Liverpool for Quebec. The last of the season, the agent told them.

'You got the ticket, did you?' Winnie asked as he returned.

'I did. By Liverpool. Going out of Westport costs too much.'

'The upper deck?'

'No. Steerage.'

Winnie looked at him, too stunned to speak. Eleanor left down the dishcloth she had been using, and walked across the room to him. 'You're going steerage?'

'I am. There's no choice in the matter. The upper deck is all booked out. It's steerage or nothing. And even that I'm lucky to get. There's few enough places left. The boat's the last of the season from Liverpool, August the eleventh. After that there's not enough sailing time before the river to Quebec freezes.'

Winnie had started to cry. 'But you'll die.'

'Me? I'm not going to die, my love. All these months in the mountains I've been with fevered people and people dead of it. If I was going to die of fever, it's there I'd have died, not on some ship going to America.'

'You're taking a terrible chance,' Eleanor said.

'The chance is little enough, Mother. And anyhow, it's the way it has to be, so that's an end to it.'

That night she woke from a nightmare of hanging and death. Luke was still beside her, snoring gently.

It had taken her long enough to accept that no one had seen what had happened at Lord Sligo's wall, but now there was another danger. Fever. Yes, he was strong, and if he was going to die of fever, it would have been in the fever sheds at Brockagh. But was she certain? She thought again of the woman's story of crossing the *Great Ocean* and all who had died on it. She could not rest until Luke wrote to her from America. How long would that take? Five weeks to get there. Five more for a letter to come.

And what if it never came? It will come. It will come.

Mr. Martin Farrelly   Carrigard
C/o Pennsylvania Railroad   Kilduff
Market Street   Co. Mayo
Harrisburg   Ireland
Pennsylvania
United States of America   24th June 1847

Dear Martin,

All here were surprised to hear that you had gone to America. I can
understand your thinking though, and there are many men around Kilduff
and Carrigard who would think the same, but they do not have the money
to hand that would bring them to America. I too had been thinking of
America for a long time, and your letter was the last push.

I am sorry for the delay in writing to you. Even when I got your letter,
I was not sure what to do. God knows there are enough things to sort
out here on the farm. Also, I had been thinking of going back to the rails
in England to earn money, and perhaps travel to America in a few years,
though where I did not know. But now my plan is to go to America right
away. As it happens, I will not be going direct though. I do not know how
much ye know in Harrisburg about what is happening between here and
Pennsylvania, but from all we hear, many of the American ports are closed
to Irish ships.

The other thing I must tell you is that I am married, and my wife is
now expecting a baby, which will make it difficult for her to travel. I have
therefore bought a ticket to travel to Quebec by Liverpool, and this will
be for me alone in the first place. My intention is to then cross the border
into the United States, and meet with you as soon as possible. When I have
earned enough money, I will bring my wife and baby out.

While Quebec remains open to us though, the story on the ships is
a terrible one, with many dying of fever on the crossing, but I have little
choice about that. My ship leaves Liverpool on the eleventh of August, and
I am told it might take four or five weeks to reach Quebec, if the ice does
not stop it. In any case, I will write you another letter as soon as I land in
Canada, and tell you of my plans.

I look forward to seeing you and Mikey as soon as I can.

Your old friend,

Luke Ryan

That Sunday, Pat walked over to Carrigard. The family were at their mid-day
meal.

'I just wish to God you'd have told me what ye were planning earlier,' he said, brushing aside Eleanor's greeting. 'America, is it? Why all the secrecy?'

'But we did tell you,' Luke said. 'I wrote last week. Did you not get it?'

'Oh, I got it right enough, and a hell of a shock it gave me. I'd have come over that very night, except for the way the Union is. Could ye not have warned me?'

'There was no point,' Winnie said. 'We were only thinking about it till now.'

'And anyhow,' Luke said, 'isn't this what you wanted. The farm will be yours now.'

Pat glared at his brother. 'Well, no one asked me. What if I want to stay on with the Union?'

'The Union! Why the devil would you want to stay there?'

'Maybe because I like it. There's not many places would give you thirty five pounds a year, all found. A good position for life.'

Eleanor glanced at Michael.

'What's that you say?' he asked. 'Thirty five pounds per year. Where did you get that from?'

'The Union is offering it to me. Voisey said it was mine for the taking.'

'Why didn't you tell us?'

'I hadn't decided to accept. But the more I thought about it, the better it seemed. Thirty five pounds a year, you don't get that everywhere.'

There was a silence around the table. Then Eleanor spoke.

'But if you don't sign for the farm in two years, Luke will have to come back from America.'

'Then let him come back.'

'Come back?' Luke said. 'That's easy for you to say. Sure why bother going if I'm to come back after two years?'

'Because we'd all be together,' Eleanor answered him. 'One family – Carrigard or Knockanure.'

'And what if the blight returns?'

'But the blight's gone, can't you see it with your own eyes. It won't come back.'

'You've no way of knowing that.'

'Maybe not,' Eleanor said. 'But if it stays away two years, would you come back then?'

Luke hesitated.

Winnie put her hand on his arm. 'She's right, *a ghrá*. We'd all be together.'

He looked from Winnie to Eleanor, bewildered.

'Fine so,' he said at last. 'If there's no blight for two years, I'll come back.'

'Promise,' Eleanor said.

'I'll do my damnedest, but I can't promise.'

That night Pat stayed in Carrigard. He lay awake in his bed, thinking. In spite of everything, he was still uncertain.

Luke would come back, and he himself would stay in Knockanure. Did he believe that? And even if it turned out that way, it would mean abandoning the farm which he had wanted for so many years. Blight or no blight, he wanted to keep some sort of claim to it. But how?

If he returned to Carrigard, Luke and Winnie would stay away, and he would have to give up his position in the Union. And with it, thirty five pounds a year and any chance of promotion. Why would he do that? What future had the farm anyhow? Did he really want it?

And Sarah? Two years she had asked. A few years, his own mother had asked. He would have to be twenty-one years old to co-sign for the farm. And twenty-one to propose to Sarah. What if Luke stayed away though, and he had to farm in Carrigard – no choice? What kind of future could he offer her then?

He rose before dawn, and walked back to Knockanure. He avoided the crowd at the front gate, and went around the back instead. There were a few families there, but one of the inmates opened the gate a few inches, and he squeezed in. He walked along the edge of the trench. For a few moments he stopped there, staring at the corpses below. The scene no longer upset him, as it once did. It was as if it was unreal, not of this world.

He walked on to the administration block.

'So what now?' Sarah asked.

'I don't know. '

'What happens if you don't take it?'

'Luke has to come home, and farm it.'

'Will he though?'

'I don't know that neither. He says he will, but I don't know that I'd believe him. America's a long way away, and I've not heard of many returning. And if he doesn't come back I'd be trapped.'

'Maybe you could sign the lease, and rent out the farm.'

'No chance of that. There's a nasty little clause in the lease about no sub-letting. No, if the farm wasn't being worked, the agent would want to let it to someone else. And there's only one house.'

'So if ye both stayed away, they'd be evicted.'

'That's the way it's looking. They could move in with Sabina though.'

'Who?' she asked.

'My aunt. Ian McKinnon's widow. She runs a bar in Kilduff. She'll be lonely enough as it is.'

Sarah worked on for a few minutes, writing out a requisition form. Then she put her pen in the inkpot.

'Well, you've two years to think about it.'

'If Father lasts out that long.'

'What do you mean?'

'Look, he's an old man. I'm not sure that he could keep the farm and the quarry running with Luke gone. In fact, I'm sure he couldn't.'

He totted another column. 'Isn't it strange. All these years I've wanted the farm, thinking Luke had it. And now that I can have it, I don't know if I want it or not.'

'But at the same time, it mightn't be a bad idea,' Sarah said.

He looked at her in surprise. 'Do you really think that?'

'Maybe, maybe not. It's just that I'm sick of the Workhouse and the fever sheds. All these years living in Workhouses, I usen't mind it when I was a child. It's only as you get older you can see how hard it is. Maybe like Voisey says it's getting better. This thing of shipping people off to America though – I don't know. But one way or another, money or no money, we've done our share.'

'But you'd never settle in to Carrigard. You've never worked on a farm in your life.'

'You're right,' she said. 'I haven't. But all I know is this – your mother, she's a strong woman, from all you tell me. We'd get on well, your mother and me, I'm sure of it. And that would make it all possible. Maybe we should give it a try.'

'But it's not possible. It's not my mother's the problem – it's yours. She would never agree to it, you know that. And she'd be right. She'd only agree to us marrying if she thought I'd a chance of making Master. She'd never agree to you marrying a farmer.'

'Maybe she would, maybe she wouldn't.'

'I know she wouldn't. And even supposing we defied her, you'd never go from this to a small farm and the chance of another hunger hanging over you. There's no future in it, you know that as well as I do.'

They both turned back to their work. Then Pat stopped again. 'You know what...'

'Wait till I finish this.'

A moment later, she looked up. 'Well, what were you going to say?'

'I was just thinking. Either way we're talking about marriage. Aren't we?'

She threw the pen at him.

The building of Kilduff School was finished before the summer. It opened before the harvest, and attendance was compulsory. Because the school could not take every child in the area, compulsion was only applied to Kilduff and a radius of one mile from it, until the school in Liscreggan could be opened. As it happened, the one-mile radius included Carrigard.

In spite of the hunger, it worked. Every morning, Murty sat alone in his school, watching the ragged children making their way to the school in Kilduff. He knew there was no chance of opening Carrigard School again. His time as a teacher was finished.

For weeks he had been having nightmares. His fevered brain kept going back to his childhood and the horrors of 1798, dreaming of a one-eyed giant chasing him into the haggard, rebels hanging out of every branch around him. In the early hours of the morning, he would wake up, watching the dawn, thinking of the future, not knowing which way to turn.

One evening he wrote a letter to Danny.

When Danny received Murty's letter, he sat staring at it for a long time. Then he stood up, and left the office, walking out along the Works.

'Murteen.'

Murtybeg ran over. He guessed from the tone of his brother's voice that there was something serious afoot.

'What is it?'

'I want you to go somewhere for me.'

'Liverpool?'

'A bit further than that. Mayo. Carrigard.'

'Carrigard...' Now he knew there was something wrong. Someone had died perhaps?

'But...'

'Here, read this,' Danny said, thrusting the letter at him.

Murtybeg glanced through it. 'Closing. I can't believe it.'

'Not closing. Closed.'

'But what will he do? And Mother, how will she take it?'

'God only knows. That's why I want you to go to Mayo. Go over, and bring them back here.'

'What!'

'Damn it, I know. I don't want it any more than you do. But we've no choice now. I told Luke, I told them all, they all knew this was going to happen, but they didn't want to think about it, and now it has. Now they're going to be begging for more and more money, sitting out the rest of their lives in Carrigard, frittering it all away. And I'm not going to have that. Pa has a brain in his head, we can use him for many years yet. He doesn't need to understand it all, he only needs to be able to add and subtract, that's all we need. Make him earn his keep.'

Murtybeg thought about that. He could see that the plan had its benefits.

His father had a certain pride and would wish to work. But what would his reaction be if he saw what he and Danny were doing; how railway contractors made their money. And his mother, she had never been outside Mayo in her life. She would be terrified.

'But what about Ma, she'll go to pieces.'

'That's where you come in,' Danny said. 'You'll take care of her, at least while you're not out working.'

'Me!'

'Yes, you. I've been thinking it's about time you had a house anyhow, a nice little cottage. If we can't find one here, we'll build one. You can't be in lodgings for the rest of your life. A house with two bedrooms and a kitchen. Let Ma make her brown bread as much as she wants. She'll be happy with that.'

'I suppose it's an idea.'

'It is, and anyhow it won't be a problem for you for long. Isn't it about time you found yourself some girl? She'd help too.'

'Perhaps. Seems you've found one for yourself anyhow.'

'Well, you'd better get to work on it, and find one too.'

'Maybe I should have a word with Irene's aunt, see if she has any more nieces.'

'I doubt it,' Danny said. 'They don't make them like that anymore.'

And just as well too.

But he ran into an unexpected problem. Irene was violently against the idea of bringing his parents from Mayo. Now, for the first time, there was a battle of wills between them. She threatened to stop working for him and go back to her old employment with the solicitors, she threatened everything she could think of, but Danny held tight. He knew if he was to marry Irene, there could only be one boss, and she would have to understand who that would be.

In the end, she relented, but conditionally. Her first condition was a ring – she would not continue living with Danny without a commitment to marriage. Danny agreed. After all, it was what he had proposed right from the start. Her second condition took him aback though.

She wanted them to move out of the lodgings into a house of their own. If a cottage had to be found for her in-laws, then she and Danny could not continue to live in lodgings, no matter how good. Their house would have to be appropriate to the Managing Partner of Edwardes & Ryan, and even more so, to his wife. Danny agreed to this too, but the scale of her plans stunned him. She had clearly been thinking about it for many weeks, and she already had a site in mind, out near Newton on the junction of the Liverpool & Manchester Railway and the Grand Trunk Railway. The house would be built new, and would be designed to include reception rooms, four bedrooms, a bathroom, a kitchen and a stables.

He had won, but at what a price!

The next week he walked into the Stockport branch of the Manchester & Salford Bank, accompanied by Rob Anderson. They laid out a copy of the proposed contract, together with the financial projections.

'As you can see, we have the support of Anderson & Son, so I presume you'll have no difficulty in supporting our application,' Danny said.

The manager cast his eyes down the projections. 'These are impressive, Mr. Ryan. Can they be achieved though?'

Anderson answered. 'Mr. Ryan has done it before, I see no reason why he can't do it again.'

'The question is, do we have your support or not?' Danny said.

'On these figures, yes. But it's still...'

'Yes,' Danny interrupted, 'a matter of policy – I know. But what is your opinion.'

'It's a good proposal.'

'Good. We'll leave these with you.'

'Can I have another copy to send to Head Office.'

'That's already been done. All we need is your support – a letter in writing.'

'I'll send it tomorrow.'

'No,' Anderson said, 'you'll give it to us today. We're meeting with your board in Manchester this afternoon.'

'But...'

'If you can't do it, Anderson & Son will have to change its account to another branch.'

Ten minutes later, they left the bank with the letter of recommendation. They walked to Stockport station and caught the train into Manchester.

Danny was startled when they entered the Head Office of the Manchester & Salford Bank. The reception hall was done out in marble, with crystal chandeliers hanging from a ceiling three floors above.

A few minutes later, they were in the board room, again going through accounts, projections and contracts.

'So, what's the full amount,' the Chairman asked. 'How much are we lending you?'

'Twelve hundred and fifty pounds to start,' responded Danny. 'And a facility for a further twelve hundred and fifty over the coming year.'

One of the directors raised his eyebrows. 'What if we have another railway panic?'

'I doubt we will,' Anderson said. 'There's a heavy demand for railways up and down the country. People must travel.'

'You might be right, I don't know.'

'There is one other minor matter,' Danny said, anxious to change the subject. 'It's more of a personal nature in fact. My fiancée and I are intending to build a house out by Newton. We will of course be looking for a loan. Three hundred pounds should be enough. And a further fifty pounds for a house for two of our senior supervisors.'

'Can you wait outside, gentlemen,' the Chairman said.

Twenty minutes later, he came out.

'All approved,' he said. 'Though we will require mortgages on the houses.'

'Of course,' Danny said.

He and Anderson walked out on to Mosley Street and across Peter's Square.

'A whiskey, Danny?'

'Why not?'

They continued to the Midland Hotel on Peter Street, and went into the lounge bar. The barman came over to take their order.

'Glen Fiddich, no water.'

'I'll have a Jameson,' Danny said.

'You'll never go to Scotch, Danny?'

'Never. I always remember my roots. I'm proud to be Irish, I'm proud of my country.'

'I'm sure you are. It's made you what you are.'

The barman came back, carrying two whiskies in crystal glasses on a silver tray.

'To success, Rob.'

'Success, Danny.'

They drank.

'I didn't know you were getting married.'

'Sorry. I should have told you. You're invited of course, Mrs. Anderson too.'

Anderson raised his glass. 'Long life and happiness.'

They drank again. Then Anderson put his glass down, staring Danny in the eyes.

'One other thing I meant to ask you. Tell me about Neville Edwardes.'

'Oh, the very best.'

'I'm sure he is. Seems he's a very shy fellow. Or he would be, if he even existed.'

'What do you mean?'

'Come, come. You wouldn't fool a friend, would you?'

Danny smiled. The candelabras in the foyer sparkled their reflections through the bevelled mirrors in the lounge. 'You think Neville doesn't exist, do you?'

'I know he doesn't.'

'And when did you come to that conclusion?'

'That first morning back in Stockport. 'Edwardes & Ryan' you said. I knew it straight away.'

'I don't believe you,' Danny said.

'Yes, it's true. And I thought to myself 'God, this is one sharp fellow. Cheeky bastard too.' I decided there and then that you and I were going to work together.'

Danny lifted his glass. He stared into a rainbow of colours in the deep crystal cuts.

'I don't know what to say.'

'Just what you said,' Anderson said. 'Success.'

That night Danny replied to his father's letter.

Chapter Thirty

Telegraph or Connaught Ranger, June 1847:
From Erris the accounts are most dreadful, and should the
fever and other diseases now raging there continue as at
present, we must fear that there will not be sufficient left to
gather in the scanty crops which some of the inhabitants had
put in the ground. We have talked with a trustworthy gentleman for some time located there. He says it is not unusual
to see in some villages from 10 to 20 dead in a day; that he
himself saw the cabins pulled down to cover the remains of
a family of 6 or 7 dead inside, and that the dead bodies of
many persons had been buried in cabbage plots and beside
the hedges, without coffins!

In Carrigard, the plans for America continued. Pat had not returned from Knockanure for some time. From the single letter they received, it appeared he was working every day.

Then, one morning, he walked across to Carrigard. He had attended Mass in the church in the Workhouse with all the inmates, and the stink still clung to his nostrils. But his mother gave him a plate of cabbage and potatoes, and he began to feel better.

That afternoon Edmond White came to visit. Eleanor was a little surprised and apprehensive when she saw him, but brought him in. Michael took out a bottle of whiskey, and White joined everyone around the table.

'So what have you decided?' he asked them.

'Luke will still go to America,' Michael answered, 'but he's coming back in two years, just as ye asked.'

'So what will he be doing in America.'

'Working on the railways,' Luke answered.

'Hard work, I'd say.'

'I've done it before.'

'In America?'

'No. In England.'

'So why not go there instead of America?'

'There wouldn't be a chance of getting work. There's thousands of fellows looking for work there.'

'There are,' White said, 'and the most of them Irish too. But wouldn't it be the same in America?'

'It would,' Luke said, 'but I've already work set up. Martin Farrelly – he's an old friend of mine from the railways in England. He's working on the rails in Pennsylvania, along with a lot of other Mayo lads. There's a job there for me.'

'Martin Farrelly? He wouldn't be one of the Farrellys of Liscreggan?'

'That's right,' Luke said. 'John Farrelly's son. He's been on the rails in England for twenty years. Went over to America a few months back.

'Did he now?' White said. He took out a notebook, and scribbled in it. 'They should be well able to pay the rent so.'

'They should, I suppose,' Michael said.

White sipped at his whiskey. 'A good whiskey, I'd say, Mr. Ryan.'

'It is,' Michael replied. 'All the way from Dublin. And it's not every day we'd have it out.'

'Indeed not,' White said. 'But now, there's one other matter I wanted to discuss with you. All the land that was used up by the roadworks – we had promised to make it up to you.'

'Yes,' Michael said, 'I remember.'

'It must have been a fair amount.'

'Extending the quarry – I reckon that took half an acre,' Michael said. 'Putting the road across the land – I haven't measured that. Must have taken an acre anyhow, more perhaps.'

'Yes,' White said, 'I'd been meaning to talk to you about a rent reduction, but we feel now there might be a better solution. You'll know that Fordes have gone to Boston.'

'Of course,' Michael said.

'We're looking for someone to take over the tenancy. Someone reliable.'

Eleanor glanced across to Michael and Luke and Pat. 'No,' she whispered. 'We can't.'

'You shouldn't feel bad about it,' White continued. 'They're in America now. They weren't evicted. The farm is there and available for anyone who wants to rent it. The Fordes will have a better life now, they're not concerned about the farm.'

'But there's growing crops on it,' Eleanor said.

'We won't insist that you pay for what's there already,' White said.

'But they're not our crops. They belong to the Fordes.'

'I don't think they'd be too worried about them now.'

The room went silent.

'But you can think about the matter,' White said. I'll be back in the morning. I'll need your answer then.'

Eleanor saw White out. She came back to the table.

'What do we do now?' she asked.

'Well, it's going to be your choice too,' Michael said.

'But it's land grabbing,' Eleanor said.

'No it's not,' Michael said. 'It's just as he said. Fordes are gone. It's not their concern. And just like he said, they've taken two acres of our land. They have to make up to us for it.'

'It's not just that, though,' Eleanor said. 'It's taking advantage of the famine. All that suffering, and now we profit out of it.'

'But the O'Briens are taking the Grogan farm,' Michael said. 'They didn't feel guilty about it. There's no need to worry yourself about it.'

'Father is right,' Pat said. 'We'll take it.'

His father looked up sharply. 'What did you say?'

'I said we'll take it.'

'I didn't think you'd have an interest in it,' Luke said.

'I didn't say either way. And anyhow, what business is it of yours?'

'Shush now,' Eleanor said. 'There's no call for that.'

'Sorry,' Pat said. 'But one way or another, he's off to America for two years, and we've got to decide now. And like I say, I think we should take Forde's. If we don't, someone else will.'

'That's it so,' Michael said. 'We'll take it.'

An hour before dusk, Pat left to return to Knockanure.

Afterwards Luke drove the cow down to the cowshed for milking. As he followed the cow inside, there was a movement in the shadows.

'Who's there.'

'*Whisht, we mean you no harm.*'

'*Who are you? What are you doing here?*'

'*We're walking to Westport,*' the voice replied.

'For America?'

'*Yes, America. America it is.*'

Even in the remaining light, Luke could see how thin they were. There was a man with a woman, two children and a baby. He heard a moan behind him. He turned and saw a youth lying on the hay. He was not moving.

'*Is he alright?*'

'*It's just how he couldn't keep walking. He'll be better in the morning.*'

Luke milked the cow. Then he went to take the milk to his mother.

'*Hold on here, I'll be back.*'

He told his mother and father what had happened.

'Perhaps we should ask them over,' Eleanor said.

'We'll do no such thing,' Michael said. 'They might have fever.'

'We can feed them at least.'

'Haven't we little enough for ourselves.'

'Maybe so,' Eleanor said, 'but we must try to help.'

She gave Luke half a brown loaf and buttermilk. He brought the food across to the cowshed.

'*God bless you,*' the woman said. '*We'll not be troubling you beyond the night.*'

When Luke returned to the cowshed the next morning, the youth was dead. The woman was keening, the two children looking on, wide-eyed. Luke knelt, and examined the body. There was no sign of fever. He had been killed by hunger only.

'*We didn't want to be bothering you,*' the man said, '*but we'll have to bury him. Perhaps you could help us with that. Ye have a cart?*'

'*We do.*'

He went back to the house, and explained the situation to his father and mother.

'God, is there no end to it,' Michael exclaimed. 'We'll be carrying bodies for the whole county.'

Luke hitched up the horse and cart, and brought it to the cowshed. They lifted the corpse inside, and the rest of the family climbed up. Luke drove the horse towards Kilduff.

'*Where are ye from?*' he asked the man.

'*Baile a' Cnoic,*' he answered. He nodded towards the corpse. '*We could not travel so far with him the way he was.*'

Luke was going to mention about his mother coming from the Mountain, but decided not to.

'*What family are ye?*' he asked.

'*O'Ceallaigh,*' the man replied.

Luke was startled. *O'Ceallaigh* – O'Kelly – his mother's name. He knew that all of Eleanor's family had left the Mountain, but it could well be that this man was a cousin, or at least a second cousin of hers. He decided not to pursue the matter. If it turned out this family was related, he would have to drive them all the way to Westport, and that he did not want.

When they arrived at Kilduff, he drove straight to the graveyard. There were two men inside, digging a trench. At the side, four decomposing corpses were laid in line.

One of the gravediggers looked up from the trench as Luke and the man took the corpse down from the cart.

'Just leave him there beside the others,' he shouted.

They did as they were told. The woman vomited.

'*Will he not get a blessing*,' the man asked. '*He needs the priest.*'

'*The priest will be along, don't worry*,' the gravedigger replied.

They stayed on, the woman keening over the corpse while holding the baby close to her breast. Then her husband took her by the arm, and pulled her up.

'*Come on, Máire. 'Tis time to go.*'

Luke watched as they started to walk out the Castlebar road. Then he led the horse and cart out of the graveyard, and drove back towards Carrigard.

On the few occasions that all the women met together, Brigid's future education was a matter they always discussed. The suffering all around them only increased their determination that one at least would be able to escape hunger and fever.

It was a matter that Winnie and Eleanor talked about every day when the men were out working. Eleanor foresaw a time when Brigid would return to Mayo from wherever she might have been trained. Maybe she could teach in Kilduff school or Liscreggan. By that time Father Flynn might be dead, and Father Reilly might have taken over. To have one of their own teaching would be a matter of intense pride, but Eleanor knew that this was not the only reason. It was for Brigid too, and for the future.

One evening as the men returned from the fields, Luke sensed there was something in the air. He sat down at the table with his father, and waited as Winnie laid the table.

Eleanor ladled out the cabbage. She leant over Michael's shoulder as she spooned it onto his plate. 'We've decided that Brigid is going to go on to teacher training college,' she said.

Michael looked around abruptly.

'What are you on about, woman?'

'Teacher training. She's going to be a teacher.'

'*Arra*, will you stop being stupid. Pass the potatoes along, would you,' he said to Winnie.

Luke was staring at his mother. So that was why Sabina had talked about education. It was all beginning to make sense. He remembered how Sabina had spoken of Kitty, and how quickly she had backed away from it. Training colleges! Could it have been Kitty's idea? Perhaps, perhaps not, but she certainly would have known of it.

Winnie laid the bowl of potatoes in front of Michael. He took one, and cut into it, looking for rot. There was none. Without further comment he began to eat.

'We're serious, Michael,' Eleanor said.

'Serious!' Michael said, spluttering. He gulped down the potato. 'We can hardly put a bite into our mouths, and now you want us to have teachers. '

'That's right. So as we'll never face hunger again.'

'Never face hunger, is it? Would you have a bit of sense, woman.'

'No,' Eleanor said, 'it's you who'll have to have sense now. We'll do it with you or we'll do it without you. Brigid will be a teacher. And it's best you're with us. Murty too, though it'll be harder on him.'

Michael took another potato, and cut into it. It was clean.

'Has Sabina been giving you ideas.'

'It wasn't her idea,' Eleanor said. 'But whoever thought of them, they're the right ideas.'

She had no desire to say whose idea it had been. If Michael knew Kitty had first said it, Brigid would have no further education, that was certain.

Michael took a forkful of cabbage with the potato. He started on a third potato, examining it as if to find wisdom there.

'Are you in on this?' he asked Winnie.

'Of course. I married into this family, didn't I? I always believed the Ryans could do great things.'

Luke was holding a forkful of bacon in the air. He put it back on the plate, and waited for his father to speak.

'Great things, you say?' asked Michael. The potato was sound.

'Great things,' Winnie repeated. 'Brigid can do it. We can all help her do it.'

'Murty was a teacher. Look what happened to him.'

'Yes,' Winnie said, 'but he was the wrong kind of teacher. He wasn't trained their way.'

Luke was looking at her in surprise. 'You never said anything of this to me before.'

'You never asked me,' Winnie said.

'And it's just as Winnie says,' Eleanor said, before Luke could reply. 'The old ways are gone. They beat Murty. But they're not going to beat us.'

'By God, that's fighting talk,' Michael said.

'It's fighting talk alright,' Luke echoed. 'All this time, the women are talking among themselves and never telling us a word. And now we're going to take on the whole damned world.'

'And we're going to win too,' Winnie said. 'Don't forget that.'

Michael put a large forkful of potato and cabbage into his mouth, and chewed it in silence. He looked at everyone, holding their eyes, Winnie's longest of all. When he was ready, he spoke.

'Where's all the money going to come from for this?'

'Everyone,' Eleanor said. 'Luke is going to send us money when he gets to America.'

'Am I?' Luke asked, feigning ignorance. 'For schooling?'

'Yes you are, and if you don't, Winnie will do it for you. And Sabina will pay too. We'll write and tell Danny what we're doing, he'll be sure to help. Murtybeg too. They have the money, from all accounts, and it might help them with their consciences too. The pennies will soon mount up.'

'That's begging,' Michael shouted. 'I won't do it.'

'No, Michael. It's pride. Pride in Brigid. And pride in our family.'

Again he ate, chewing with deliberation. He took another potato and cut it.

'How are you planning to do all this, even if you get the money?'

'There's only one way it can be done to start, and that's through the school in Kilduff, Liscreggan's too far. She'll have to stay four nights a week with Sabina, but that's no matter. Then it'll have to be the school in Castlebar. She has to get a higher class of schooling than Kilduff is able to give her. That might take three or four years more. After that, it's a secondary school and then one of the training colleges – Galway, Belfast, Dublin, I don't know. Glasgow even.'

'Glasgow!'

'Wherever. Believe me, Michael, this thing is going to be done, and we are going to do it.'

Michael shook his head. 'You're mad.'

'No, *a ghrá*. We might be women, but we're not stupid, and we're surely not mad.'

'And when is this all going to start?'

'Two years' time. She'll be three by then, well old enough for it.'

Michael went back to his meal. Luke held his breath, not knowing what to say.

'And what will Murty think?' Michael asked at length. 'It'll be a right slap in the face for him.'

'It will,' Eleanor said, 'and we'll all have to do the best we can for him. But his school is gone, and there's nothing we can do about that.'

Michael finished his meal without a word. Then he turned to face the baby. 'Well, by God, little Brigid,' he whispered. He stood up from the table, shaking his head. 'By God Almighty.'

Aileen became more and more morose and lapsed into silence. Eleanor did what she could. She went up every day, she brought Aileen down to meet the other women – Winnie, Sabina and Kitty. But even Kitty was quieter than normal, and Aileen rarely said a word.

Then Danny's letter arrived. Murty sat at his table, and read it again and again, disbelieving.

'What does he say?' Aileen asked.

'He wants us to go to England.'

Aileen's jaw dropped, and he saw the fear returning to her eyes.

'It's not as bad as it seems. He's offering me a job, a good one too, some kind of supervisor. Contracts Manager, he calls it. He reckons with my knowledge and experience, I should be able to help him with the contracts on the railways. Wage sheets, requisitions, bids and contracts, that kind of thing. And he'll have a house ready for us, Murteen will be living with us. And talking of Murteen, Danny's sending him over here to take us back.'

'But we'd have to leave Mayo.'

Murty looked at his wife, remembering the old days when he first courted her, all the joy and laughter. The happiness too when her babies arrived – Nessa, Danny and little Murteen.

'Yes,' he said. 'We'd have to go to England. But we'll be a family again. You and me, Danny and Murteen. Isn't it what you always wanted?'

'Yes, but...I don't know.'

Murty replied to Danny's letter, accepting his offer. Four days later, Danny's reply came, together with two pounds in cash. Transport would be arranged for them, and they were advised to be ready to travel at any time.

'There's a coach outside,' Winnie said one afternoon.

'I wonder who it is,' Eleanor said, walking over to the window. 'Whoever it is, he must be quality.'

'Lord Clanowen, no doubt,' Luke said from the table. 'Decided he'd drop in for a chat.'

'We'll have none of that nonsense out of you,' Michael said. 'Just go outside, and see who it is.'

Luke walked out, just as the coachman opened the door of the coach. Murtybeg stepped out.

'Murteen, what the devil...'

Murtybeg strode over, and shook Luke's hand. 'God, it's great to see you again.'

'But...!'

'Didn't you know I was coming? It's all been arranged.'

He took a pack that the coachman was handing down.

'But...in a coach! We weren't expecting that.'

'Why not?'

'Well, I don't know. And aren't you a few days early?'

Murtybeg put down his pack. 'Early bedamned. You should know all about it, and you the cause of it.'

'Me! Why me?'

'Danny reckoned one of us should come over and see you before you went to America, and since he wasn't going to come, that only left me.'

'But how…?'

'Like a bat out of hell. Express to Liverpool, steamer to Dublin, the Castlebar mail coach, and I hired this fellow to get here in time. It might have helped if you'd told us the date you were going, we had no idea.'

'I'm sorry,' Luke said.' You're right, I should have told you.'

'I was coming over for Ma and Pa anyhow, so Danny said I should come over in time to see you. That was the rush.'

'Well, I'm sorry. But anyhow you're here now, come on in and see everyone.'

'Hold on a second. I've got to pay this fellow first.'

He took coins out of his pocket, and counted them carefully into the coachman's hand. 'Friday,' he said.

The man nodded. He grasped the horses by the reins, backed the coach into the gateway, and swung it back into the road. Then he climbed up, shaking the reins on the horses flanks. Luke was still staring at the coach, noticing the well-sprung axles. Must be comfortable to ride in that. His mother was right. Quality indeed.

The rest of the family had come outside, and Murtybeg strode over to them. Eleanor threw her arms around him. 'Murteen, it's great to see you back. Are you staying for long?'

'The end of the week at least. Not that Danny liked that, but I told him I was, and that was all about it. And now, if you'll stop being so rude, perhaps you'd be so good as to introduce me.'

'Oh God, yes,' Luke said. 'Winnie, this is Murtybeg, you've heard all about him. My cousin, a decent fellow even so.'

'I'm happy to meet you,' Winnie said, taking him by the hand. Then she hugged him, and kissed him on the cheek. 'In fact, I'm delighted to meet you.'

Murtybeg looked at her in surprise. 'Well, I'm delighted I got the chance. I reckoned if I didn't get here before you went to America, I'd never have the chance of meeting you at all.'

'Oh, you've plenty of time for that,' Winnie said. 'Sure I'm not going for another six or eight months.'

'You're not?'

'No, not until after the baby has come.'

'Baby! What baby?'

'Luke's. Who else's?'

'I didn't mean it that way,' Murtybeg said. 'It's just this husband of yours, he never tells us anything in his letters. Always whinging, never tells us the important things.'

'*Arra*, don't worry about it,' Luke said. 'If you're here till Friday, you'll have plenty of time to catch up with everything.'

'I will,' Murtybeg said. 'Now, if you'll all be excusing me, I've got to go up and see Ma and Pa, and start telling them about their trip.'

'Yes,' Eleanor said, 'you go, and do that. Sure we'll see ye all tonight.'

That evening, Murty, Aileen and Murtybeg came down to the house. Luke thought Aileen looked more withdrawn than ever.

'Did you hear about Danny?' Murty asked. 'He's getting married.'

'He's what!' Michael exclaimed.

'Getting married. Murteen has just told us.'

'Getting married,' Eleanor echoed. 'Isn't that wonderful.'

Isn't it, Luke was thinking. I wonder what class of a woman caught Danny. She'll need to be one tough lady to deal with the likes of him.

Eleanor had taken out a bottle of *poitín*. 'And when is the wedding to be?' she asked.

'Three weeks' time,' Murty said. 'And it's going to be a big one, by all accounts.'

'So what about ye,' Michael asked. 'What are your plans now.'

'We'll stay some days yet,' Murty said. 'Murteen here will help us getting everything together, then it's going to be the coach to Castlebar, and the mail coach to Dublin.'

'More coaches,' Luke said. 'That costs money.'

'So it does,' Murty said, 'but it seems that Danny has a good amount of that. What between that and a good position working with Danny, we'll manage well. We'll get used to England soon enough.'

Luke thought he saw a flicker of doubt in Murtybeg's eyes. He didn't comment though. Murty was talking to him.

'Nervous about America?' he asked.

'I'd be a fool to deny it,' Luke said. He glanced across to Winnie. 'Sad too. I won't see the baby when it's born. We'll meet again in America, though, won't we, my love?'

'Yes,' Winnie said, 'we will.'

'What do you think of it all?' she asked as they lay in bed that night. 'Is it all as good as Murtybeg says?'

'I don't know, my love. There's something he's not saying, and I'm not sure what it is.'

It was a dry day. He was out cutting hay early, not wanting to waste sunshine. He was surprised when he saw Murtybeg coming across towards him.

'God, you're up early.'

'No more than yourself.'

'I've work to be doing,' Luke said. 'What's your reason?'

'*Arra*, I just couldn't sleep,' Murtybeg said.

'Restless, are you? What's troubling you? Go on, tell me about it.' He could see the look in Murtybeg's face. Fearful of being trapped perhaps? Or just wanting to talk, confess it all, share his worries?

'Tell you about what?'

'Everything. But you could start with Jimmy Corrigan.'

Luke noticed the sharp intake of breath.

'Well,' Murtybeg said, 'you seem to know about it. Danny wanted his revenge, and he was going to get it.'

'So you had nothing to do with it?'

'I only held him for Danny to punch him.'

'No one else is going to believe that.'

'I didn't know that Danny was going to smash his hands and legs.'

'He did what?'

'You heard. And anyhow, it could have been worse.'

Luke stared in disbelief. 'Worse! How in hell could it have been worse?'

'Well, when Jimmy was on the ground – his trousers open – Danny took out a knife. He was going to cut it off.'

Luke gasped. 'He was going to what!'

'Cut it off. Make sure no one else ended up like Nessy. But I stopped him.'

'You stopped him?'

'I did. I grabbed his arm, and held it back, knife and all.'

'*Arra*, he didn't mean it,' Luke said, unimpressed. 'He was just trying to frighten you.'

'Oh, he meant it alright,' Murtybeg said.

Luke grabbed him by the collar. 'I don't know if he did or he didn't. But either way, you don't ever tell that story again. Do you hear me?'

'No,' Murtybeg said, taken aback by the violence of Luke's voice.

Luke released his grip on the collar. 'Now, tell me the rest of it. What's happening now? What's going to happen to Murty and Aileen once they get to England?'

Murtybeg jerked the collar back from his throat. 'Well, it's like this,' he said. 'Sure, Danny is becoming a rich man, and he's getting married, building a house for himself. And like he promised in his letter, he'll be taking on Pa, giving him a job, and all in all, it'll be much better than doing nothing in Carrigard. But Pa's going to get some shocks, Ma too. Irene is one hell of a tough lady, rough too, no less than Danny. They'll make a great pair, and I'm sure they'll go far. But it's the ways they're making their money, that's what worries me, and once Pa finds out about it, there'll be hell to pay. But he'll be trapped by then, and there'll be no way back to Mayo for either of them.'

Luke walked over towards the wall and sat down. He took some brown bread and buttermilk out of his pack.

'Maybe you should take it easy while you're here. Just look around you. The sun is shining. Have you ever seen Nephin so clear. And look over there – there's the Reek. We might as well enjoy it all while we can.'

'Enjoy it, is it,' Murtybeg said, 'after you near strangling me.'

'Sorry. I won't do it again.'

'Oh, thanks. But do you not know what I'm telling you, do you not understand? Danny is a hell of a bastard when it comes to employing men. You've never seen anything like it.'

Luke started munching on the bread, but continued talking. 'I might know more than you think,' he said. 'There's two things you might forget. First, Danny invited me to join him as a partner, but now he has you instead. He wrote to me, told me how he was intending making money, using poor fellows from the West of Mayo who knew no better. Isn't that what you're doing now?'

'It is, but...'

'And I'll tell you the second thing. I've worked on the railways.'

'But you were with Farrelly. That was different.'

'True enough, but I saw what was going on with other gangs. The English gangers were bad, the Welsh were worse. But the worst of all were the Irish fellows. Men from the West – Mayo men, Donegal too, they were damned bastards. I saw what they did to their own. Money was the only god they ever had, never thought of anything else. And sure as hell, they never thought of the men working for them, and the most of them coming from their own villages.'

Murtybeg took a slice of bread, ate it and washed it down with buttermilk. He was half thinking how long it was since he had ever tasted either, but he had other matters on his mind.

'You might be right in all that. But it's different now.'

'How is it different now?' Luke asked.

'It's worse. It's all to do with the hunger. The fellows from out beyond Bellacorick, Crossmolina and Belmullet; down Erris and all over that way. They'll work for nothing at all. And they're pouring into Liverpool in their thousands, dreaming of America, but not a penny in their pockets to get there. They're trying to get into the Workhouse, but the Union won't have them, they send them back to Dublin as soon as they get the chance. So they're squeezing into cellars, tiny rooms, anything they can get, all along Scotland Road.'

'Scotland Road? That's where Buckley's is.'

'Buckley's! You should see Buckley's now, you wouldn't know it. Forty in a room, families and all, sleeping in shifts around the clock, and then walking the streets begging for food.'

'So what about Danny?' Luke asked.

'Danny just stays over on the railway, himself and Irene, sorting out the books and making sure everything is running right. They've got Bernie Lavan working as a ganger...'

'Bernie Lavan!'

'Yes, Bernie. Jamesy McManus and Johnny Roughneen too. Bernie and Johnny were running the gang in Leeds after Martin left. Danny reckoned they'd have enough practice to run his gangs for him.'

'God, I never knew that. But...'

'But what?'

'But if they're all gone, who's running the gangs in Leeds?'

'Damned if I know,' Murtybeg said. 'It's no concern of mine.'

'I just thought you'd be interested, that's all.'

'Haven't I got enough to do as it is, without worrying about them fellows. I spend half my time in Liverpool, finding the men for Danny, bringing them over as fast as I can, it seems now it's never enough. He's looking for a hundred.'

'A hundred!' Luke exclaimed.

'Does that surprise you?'

'Well, yes. In so little time.'

'But how many were working for you back in the winter.'

Luke thought about that. Four Works, three gangs on each. Near enough four hundred. When they could get them. When they weren't dying too fast to be replaced.

'Yes,' he said, 'but that was different. I wasn't making money out of them, was I?'

'Not like Danny. But weren't you able to make enough to feed yourself, the family too. And there's many enough around here that didn't, from all I hear.'

Gaunt figures, dying in the snow. Yes, they had lived, and lived better than most. Himself working as a supervisor, Pat as a clerk, and even his father running the quarry. Yes, they had fed themselves, but many others had died, lost everything, even life itself. Sure, Danny had money, but how different was he himself?

'Who told you about that?' he asked sharply.

'Pa was on about it last night. He told me what was happening here and up the mountains.'

'He what?'

'You didn't tell us any of that in your letters,' Murtybeg said. 'And whatever you might think about Danny, he feeds them, keeps them alive. Which is more than you could ever do.'

Luke stood, and made as if to strike Murtybeg, but Murtybeg caught his arm, and held it tight. 'Sit down, there's no merit in hitting me. It won't change anything.'

Luke stared at him, angry, but shamed too. He sat. 'So what's going to happen now?' he asked.

'I'm going to bring Ma and Pa back. Like I said, we'll have Pa working on the books. But when he works out what Danny is doing, there's going to be one hell of a row. By then it'll be too late for him though, he'll have no way back to Mayo, no schools that'll take him. And what other kind of jobs could he get around Stockport and Manchester at his age. And Ma? Sure, she could work in the mills, but how much could she earn? No, they'll be caught, they'll have their nice little house and good money, but he'll have sold out, thrown away everything he believes in, and he'll know it.'

'And what about you?'

'Me, is it?' Murtybeg said. 'I've sold out this long time.'

A letter arrived from Knockanure. Luke took it up to Murty's house.

'Pat's coming over on Sunday,' he told them.

'That'll be too late,' Murtybeg said. 'We're leaving tomorrow.'

'Could you not wait over?' Luke asked.

'I've got the coachman coming over tomorrow, and there's no way I can change that. Nor would I want to.'

'Why didn't you walk over to see him?'

Murtybeg took him by the arm, and led him outside. 'Listen, I see enough of Workhouses as it is. I know every damned inch of the Liverpool Union, and I don't want to see Knockanure. Now when Pat comes over, just give him my regards, and tell him how sorry I was to miss him.'

The next morning they left. The coach arrived early, glistening in the sunlight. Luke helped to heft the packs into it, all Murty and Aileen's possessions, or at least those that were worth taking. He noticed the fresh smell of leather from the inside. Leather seats, even leather sides to the inside of the cab. Tooled leather around the bevelled glass windows.

A group of twenty emaciated people passed by, eyeing the coach and the black horses; horses that would never pull a plough. Luke watched the group. They'll never make Westport, he thought, let alone America.

Murtybeg saw none of this though. He held his hand out to help his mother into the coach, and his father followed. Murty shook his head when he saw the interior.

'You can't say Danny isn't thinking of you,' Murtybeg said, seeing his father's reaction. 'We'll be travelling in comfort, all the way to Stockport.' Then he sat inside, and closed the door.

As the coach pulled off, Eleanor stood on the road, one arm around her husband's shoulders, the other waving. Winnie waved too, but Luke just stood in the road.

He was walking back from the bog when he saw her coming out the road from Kilduff. They both stopped. Her appearance startled him. Bare feet yes, that was no surprise, but she was desperately thin, her high cheekbones showing prominent above sunken cheeks, with the purple-yellow signs of bruising. Her hair was longer, but lank. The shift she was wearing was more frayed than ever. He saw too the look in her eyes, half startled, half defeated.

She stood, staring at him. 'Luke,' she murmured. *'It's been so long.'*

'Yes, Kitty. A lot of things have happened since then. But what of ye? How have ye been taking it?'

'Not good. Mr. Brennan's dead, got the fever. I'm living with old Mrs. Brennan now.' She seemed distracted. *'Fergus too,'* she added, as if she had only just remembered. Or perhaps no longer cared.

'Yes, I'd heard he'd stayed back. I'd have thought he'd have gone to England for the harvest.'

'And maybe he should have. But we wouldn't let him go, Mrs. Brennan nor me. We reckoned that if he went to England, he'd never come back, and then it would be like half the other families around, a year of money coming back, then nothing. So we kept him here, digging rotten potatoes and drinking himself to sleep every night.'

He saw the bruises and thought of Fergus, picturing him that night in the field, angry and vengeful. But now – drinking himself to sleep. All the hurt and pain of a man with no pride left, taking it out on a woman who could no longer defend herself.

She threw her arms around him, and squeezed him tight. *'And wherever you are in America, just think of me, and I'll think of you.'*

Then she released him and walked on. For a long time, he stood in the road, watching her. Then he turned back to Carrigard.

That night, he told Winnie. He was surprised by how accepting she was.

'These things are never easy,' she said. 'You'll miss her now, you'll miss her for the rest of your life. And do you know, when I go to join you in America, I'll miss her too.'

Chapter Thirty One

Tyrawly Herald, July 1847:
Belmullet it would appear is a doomed town. As matters stand at present, fever is committing dreadful havoc amongst the inhabitants of this small town, and the fame of its diseased state is quite sufficient to deter strangers from entering within its dread precincts. Remote and isolated to a certain extent as this town is, we cannot but apprehend that the most fearful consequences must have to be recorded in that locality.

Mr. Luke Ryan   C/o Pennsylvania Railroad
Carrigard   Market Street
Kilduff   Harrisburg
Co. Mayo   Pennsylvania
Ireland   United States of America

June 21, 1847

My Dear Luke,

I thought it better to write to you again following my last letter, though I have received no answer from you since. I know the post takes long enough though. Since I wrote, we have received further news from fellows coming here from Ireland, and I felt I had to pass it on to you, should you decide to come to America.

It now appears that many of the American ports are closed to ships coming from Ireland. This has made things harder for families crossing the Atlantic. Many ships sail direct to Canadian ports, the most for Quebec. We have all heard terrible stories of Quebec, and all here would like to see you arrive alive. I understand that fever rages in that city, and so my advice would be to get out of it as soon as you can.

It may be hard for you to travel down to the United States in the winter though. There are some fellows from Crossmolina here working with us who travelled down that way. They reckon your best plan would be to work some months in the Canadian forests.

The winter is the season for cutting, and if you are still as strong as

I remember you, you will be able to make good money there. They tell me there are many logging camps on the Bonnechere river, and there is good employment to be had there. The Bonnechere forests are owned by a Galway man of the name of John Egan. Many of the fellows here worked for him before they came down to Pennsylvania. From all we hear, he is a tough man. He is held to be the richest man in Canada, and he did not come to that through being easy on his workers. You will find though that by working in the forests you will make enough money to come south, since you will have nothing to spend it on all winter.

In the spring or summer, they say you should be able to travel down the Champlain river, perhaps travelling with the logs to earn pay. Lake Champlain is where the border with the United States lies. Then you will follow the Champlain canal to the Hudson river and so down to New York. From there you can take a train down to Philadelphia and on out to Harrisburg.

You may already have decided not to come to America, and if not, you might pass this letter on to anyone else who may be thinking of it,

Your old friend,

Martin Farrelly

'Isn't it great that he can tell you everything,' Eleanor said over dinner.

'It is,' Luke said, 'and he not even knowing whether I was coming or not.'

'He'll know soon enough,' Michael said. 'Your letter will be there by now, I'd say.'

'He didn't know which way I was going to go either. But he tells us all about Quebec in the letter. It was as if he knew what we were thinking.'

'It only says what we know already,' Michael said. 'Quebec is the only way in. He knows that as well as we do.'

Winnie glanced up from her plate, concerned. 'But working the winter in Canada,' she said. 'It's awful cold, from what I hear.'

Luke winced, thinking of other cold places. Lisnadee, Croghancoe. Don't be silly, he told himself. That was hunger, this is about tough men working hard in logging camps. Not the same thing.

'*Arra*, he'll have no problem,' Michael said. 'He's a tough fellow, and hard work never killed any man. It'll keep him warm too.'

'But he's talking about months,' Eleanor said.

'Yes,' Luke said, 'but what of it? In fact, the timing might be very nice. When is our baby to be born?'

'Sometime in the Spring,' Winnie answered. 'It's hard to say.'

'Aye, and you'll need another month or two to settle down. By then the winter storms will be over, and I'll be well down to Pennsylvania and working hard for good money. June or July will be the time to travel. Don't worry about it my love, it will all work out.'

Yes, he thought. If Philadelphia is letting in the Irish ships by then. What if they don't? Bring Winnie and the baby in by Quebec and down the logging rivers? To hell with it, we'll think about that when we have to.

'How will we stand it,' she asked him that night. 'We said we'd never be apart, and now...'

'It's like we said, *a ghrá*. There's no other way.'

'I know, I know, but I still won't be able to rest easy until we're together again.'

'Don't worry. That day will be soon enough coming.'

It was late morning on Sunday when Pat arrived. He had come from Knockanure with a horse and cart, and Eleanor was startled to see that there was someone else in the cart.

'Sarah!' Winnie said. 'It's Sarah.' She turned to Eleanor, whispering. *'Didn't I tell you there was something between them.'*

Pat jumped down from the cart. He led the horse into the haggard, and tied it to the wooden bar outside the cowshed. He held his hand out for Sarah. They both walked into the kitchen.

'I'm sorry taking you by surprise like this, Mother.'

'And so you should be,' Winnie said. 'If we had known there was quality coming, we'd have been more prepared.'

'Would you go on out of that,' Pat said. 'Quality indeed. I'd like you to meet Sarah. She works with me in the office. She knows Luke, she wanted to meet him again before he goes.'

Eleanor was recovering her composure. 'And that's the only reason you brought her over, I suppose?'

'Well, yes, I mean no. I thought you'd like to meet her anyhow.'

'Of course I would,' Eleanor said. 'You're very welcome to our little cottage,' she said to Sarah. 'Not quite what you're used to, I'm sure, but we do the best we can.'

'I'm happy to meet you,' Sarah said.

'Yes, yes. Well, sit down here, and we'll see what we can get you. Winnie – do we have any of that tea left?'

As Winnie started to busy herself with brown bread and very expensive tea, Eleanor went behind the blanket, and led Brigid in by the hand. The child looked into Sarah's face, puzzled at first.

'That's Sarah, *Brigid,'* Winnie said. Eleanor waited. Then Brigid held her arms up.

Sarah lifted her onto her knee. 'My goodness, aren't you the big girl.'

Brigid put her hand up to Sarah's face, feeling her nose and cheek and mouth.

'Sarah,' she said.

Eleanor was pouring the tea. 'Come on now,' she said to Pat. 'Aren't you going to tell us about Sarah.'

'Oh yes...Sarah here knew Luke well, she used to meet him whenever he came through Knockanure. She'd heard about him going to America, so when I told her I was going over, she wanted to come too.'

Eleanor glanced over at Winnie, who winked back at her.

'Isn't it very kind of her,' Eleanor said. 'I'm sure Luke would be delighted to see you.'

'And talking of Luke, where is he?' Pat asked.

'They're up the top field,' Winnie answered. 'Good drying, they've been out since early.'

'Hadn't you better go up and see them,' Eleanor said.

'I thought I'd better stay here with Sarah.'

'Would you go on out of that,' Eleanor said. 'What are you worried about, do you think we're going to eat her?'

'Well, no, but...'

'Go on, and stop worrying.'

He left.

Sarah was not worried. She was still playing with the child in her lap. One thing that was clear was that Brigid was well fed and well dressed. It was clear too that no-one else in the room had eaten enough over the past year, but Brigid had. This was something she had seen in children before, even in the Workhouse. Especially in the Workhouse. Parents coming in, half-starved themselves, brought in children who were far better fed than themselves. Not that that lasted very long once they were inside.

She remembered that Pat had mentioned about a cousin of his dying in childbirth, and that his mother was rearing the child. But as they told her about Sabina and Kitty too, she was beginning to realise that it was not only Eleanor who was rearing Brigid.

Later, when they told her of their plans for Brigid, she was taken aback. Neither her mother or father had any such ambitions for her. Yet here she was in a tiny cottage, in the midst of the worst famine the country had ever known, and these women were talking about education, teaching colleges and other ambitions for a child who was not two years old.

'But how will ye do this?' she asked. 'Where will all the money come from? Most people have enough trouble feeding, let alone be thinking of teaching girls to be teachers.'

Eleanor changed the subject. The subject of money was something Sarah could work out herself.

'What do you think of Luke going?' she asked. 'Did it surprise you?'

'It did,' Sarah answered. 'I could never understand it, I still can't. I thought he was going to be a farmer. What reason would he have for leaving?'

'There were a lot of reasons,' Eleanor replied. 'In one way, Luke was lucky enough. He didn't have to work here for very long before he went to Knockanure and Brockagh. Mind you, the few days he worked on the Works here – from here to the bridge below – were long enough. He was working on the Selection for the first day, taking on some people, refusing others, his own friends and cousins. It was a very bitter time. So when he was told he was needed in Knockanure, it was a relief to him, he thought he would be better getting out of the way for a while.'

'I can understand that,' Sarah said.

'Yes,' Eleanor said. 'But from all we hear, it was worse around Brockagh. Winnie has been telling us all about it. Luke won't say a word, I don't know why, but the winter must have been terrible.'

'It was,' Sarah said. 'It was bad in the Workhouse, but Pat – he told me what Luke had told him about the mountains – I couldn't believe it at first.'

Eleanor started taking potatoes over to the basin and washing them. Sarah joined her.

'There's no need for that, child.'

'Sure I'm well used to it in the Workhouse.'

Winnie went out for water, filled the pot, and swung it out over the fire to boil.

'So tell me the rest of it,' Sarah asked. 'What happened when he came home?'

'Well, it all seemed alright for a while after. There were a lot of people around that wouldn't speak to him nor to Winnie neither. But then, there were the Clanowen evictions in *Gort na Móna*, you knew about that?'

'Of course I did,' Sarah replied. 'Didn't I see it in the Workhouse myself. Hundreds of them. It was a terrible thing.'

'It was,' Winnie said. 'There was a lot of bitterness about *Gort na Móna*. It was the one of the main things that decided Luke to go to America.'

'But why? Surely he wasn't afraid of being evicted?'

'No, no, it wasn't that at all,' Winnie said. 'You see, we had Ellen Morrisroe and her three children staying with us, after they'd all been evicted. Then Luke took her to Knockanure, and afterwards she went to the Workhouse. She's dead now, I believe. But while she was staying with us, she wouldn't even talk to him. She held that he had killed her husband.'

'How could he have done that?'

'Well, he didn't, of course,' Eleanor said, before Winnie could reply. 'What he did do was to refuse her husband for the Relief Works. There was a rule that a man had to have four children before he could work on Relief around Carrigard. Luke had to refuse him. He had no choice, but Ellen could never see it that way. All she saw was that her man had been refused, and when he went home, he'd caught the fever.'

'But that was fever, not hunger. Wouldn't he have got fever anyhow.'

'I don't know about that,' Eleanor said. 'Some say the hunger brings the fever, I just don't know.'

'But to blame Luke...'

'Yes, it's unfair. But we never know how people think. You see, we're proud people here. Too proud. A man is ashamed if he can't feed his own children. And to have to beg, whether for work or for soup, that's worse, much worse. But to stoop to begging and to be refused, that's enough to break any man. No, I understand the bitterness, I understand it too well.'

'And what do you think?' Sarah asked. 'Was Luke right in what he did?'

'Like I say, the decision wasn't his. There just wasn't the work or the food for everyone. But Luke was always a good lad. He didn't have to stay back – he could have earned three times the wages on the railways in England, but he wouldn't do that. He wanted to stay here in Mayo. They needed men like him on the Works. He reckoned it was his duty, and now he's paying the price for it.'

'Yes,' Sarah said, thoughtfully. 'And he won't be the only one. Most of the people who helped on Relief or the Soup Kitchens, they're going now. The clerks, the gangers, the supervisors, the women cooking the soup. They couldn't do enough, no one could, but they're being blamed for what they couldn't do. I'm not saying they're all saints, but one way or another they'll all be blamed for the sins of the few – the preachers and the gombeen men. And all because they couldn't get the food to feed the people.'

Winnie had been thinking of what Luke had told her about the Battle of Lord Sligo's wall. Glorious for some, shaming for others. Killing a man. There were other reasons why Luke wanted to leave, and neither Eleanor nor Sarah knew about them. It was as well to leave it that way.

'If the Government had spent enough on food, there'd have been no need for hunger,' she said. 'Or emigration. Or evictions.'

'That's true,' Eleanor said, surprised at the anger in Winnie's voice.

'And what about Father Reilly,' Winnie said. 'Many say he was wrong in what he did that day in *Gort na Móna*.'

'He might have been,' Eleanor said, 'though it took courage to walk down between lines of pitchforks and sabres.'

'But there were only six sabres,' Winnie said. 'They could have set them running soon enough.'

'That's as may be,' Eleanor said, 'but if they did, there'd be a hundred sabres back the next day. No, for me, what Father Reilly did was right. There's no point in bloodshed when there's nothing we can do about it. It's not just a matter of right and wrong. It's a matter of power and weakness too. When we can't win, we have to wait. The law had its way that day, next time we'll see justice instead.'

'But when?' asked Winnie.

'You're young yet. Be patient. The time will come.'

They said nothing for some time. Sarah was thinking of Winnie. Tougher than Luke, Pat had said. Perhaps.

Winnie put the potatoes into the pot. She took the turnips off the boil, and started to mash them. 'You didn't come over for no reason,' she said to Sarah.

'I came to see Luke off. Or don't you believe me?'

'Or perhaps Pat asked you, was that it?'

'Maybe.'

'It's that he wanted you to meet all of us, isn't that it?'

Eleanor was washing the cabbage, saying nothing.

'Yes,' Sarah said at length. 'He wanted me to meet you all. And you especially,' she said to Eleanor. 'He wanted to see how the two of us would get on. He reckoned it important now that Luke is leaving.'

Eleanor turned around. 'But – you and Pat? Is that it?'

'It is,' Sarah said. 'Or at least it will be. Give it a year or two, but yes, it will be the two of us then. Did Pat not tell you?'

'Pat never tells us anything.' She took the cabbage out of the basin, and put it in the pot beside her.

'But the question is where? Isn't that it?' Winnie asked.

Eleanor looked across at her, surprised again.

'Surely there's no doubt about that,' she said. 'Hasn't he got a good job in the Union?'

'He has,' Sarah said. 'At least for now. But how long it will last, I don't know. It hasn't been confirmed yet, and even if it is, I'm not sure that he wants to stay working in the Workhouse. Me neither.'

'But isn't it your home,' Eleanor asked.

'It is for now. But I don't think I can put up with that for the rest of my life.'

'Why not, child?'

'Never mind.'

'You can tell us, surely.'

'Later. I'll tell you later.'

Eleanor said nothing. *So that's it*, she thought. *It's just as Winnie told me. Pat and Sarah. So what now? Danny and Murtybeg gone. Murty and Aileen gone. Luke going, Winnie and her baby too, and they won't be coming back, whatever Luke might think or promise. And Pat? She thought he would come back to the farm. But thirty five pounds a year. Now Sarah too. A grand girl, but you could never expect her to live the life of a farmer's wife, whatever she might say about the Workhouse. So what about us? Two old people, getting older, waiting for the letters with the money every month. And what of the farm? Two farms now with Forde's, and no-one to farm either of them. Oh God.*

The men came in.

'Ye took your time,' Eleanor said.

'We did,' Michael said. 'We thought we might as well make use of Pat here while we had him. We brought him back down by the bog – wouldn't want him to forget how to use a *sleán*.'

'Indeed,' Eleanor said. 'Now enough of that. This is Sarah, she came over from Knockanure to see us all.'

Sarah rose to greet Michael. 'Mr. Ryan…'

'Sarah – you're most welcome. I just hope the ladies here have been treating you well.'

'They have indeed. And here's someone else I'm happy to meet again,'

'And I'm happy you could come,' Luke answered. 'Pat says you only came to see me off. No other reason in the world.'

'Would you not be minding him,' Eleanor said. 'Pat says more than his prayers.'

'What do you mean?' Pat asked.

'Never mind,' Eleanor said.

'God you're a silent lot, keeping everything to yourselves. And ye never told me anything in your letters about Murtybeg being over and they're all gone now.'

'I'm sorry, *alanna*,' Eleanor said. 'We could have told you, but we reckoned you had enough to be worrying about over in Knockanure. And sure they'll be back often enough. Murtybeg says they'll visit once a year.'

Yes, thought Luke. I'm sure they will. I wonder does she even believe that herself.

The men sat for their dinner. Eleanor ladled potatoes, turnip and cabbage onto their plates.

'Sit down there,' she said to Sarah.

'I ate this morning.'

'Would you sit down there, like a good girl, and hold your *whisht*.'

She put a plate in front of Sarah and a mug of buttermilk alongside. As Sarah started to eat, Brigid came around to her, shyly, holding a small bowl of mashed potato and cabbage with a small spoon. She handed it up to Sarah. Idly, without even thinking about it, Sarah took the child on her knee, and started to feed her.

'Well, tell us this Sarah,' Michael said, 'how are things in Knockanure? How's the Workhouse now?'

'Would you stop it,' Eleanor said. 'Can't you leave the poor girl alone, and let her have a bite to eat.'

'No, Elly, let's hear what she has to say. Any time we ask anyone else about it, they never say a word, Luke here just looks all strange if we ask him, and as for Pat – or even Ian – you might as well have been speaking to a stone. Come on girl, what's happening at Knockanure?'

Sarah looked from Pat to Luke. Neither said anything. She took another spoonful from the bowl, and held it out for Brigid.

'Terrible things,' she said. 'You're better not knowing about them.'

'Let me be the judge of that,' Michael said.

'We're all doing all we can, but it's impossible. We've a new Master. My father was Master, but he died.'

'Yes,' Eleanor said, 'we'd heard. I'm sorry.'

Sarah looked uncertain, but went on.

'My mother, she's the Matron, she's working all the hours God sent in the fever sheds. I'm terrified she'll get it too and follow my father. We've lost two doctors to fever already, and they hardly ever visited the sheds, The rest of us, we're working from dark to dark, but it's never enough. The ratepayers, the most of them are bankrupt, the only one with any money is Lord Clanowen.'

'That bastard,' Eleanor said.

Sarah looked at her in surprise. She had already been taken by Eleanor's strong opinions, and she was beginning to understand that there was a lot more to Pat's mother than Pat had ever told her.

'Yes,' she said. 'The *Gort na Móna* evictions were a terrible thing. We saw all of that in the Workhouse, took them in as fast as we could, but as fast as they came in to work, they went out the other end to the fever sheds. I reckon most of them are dead.'

Michael looked up. He dropped his fork to the plate. 'What's that you say?'

Sarah held her breath for a moment, and then she went on.

'Dead, I said. They go to the fever sheds to die. There's not many come out. But like I said, it's better now. The fever's less than it was.' She stopped again.

'Go on, go on,' Michael said. 'You were saying about *Gort na Móna*.'

'Yes. Well, as soon as we took them in, we'd hold them in the Workhouse, but there were hundreds and hundreds of them, very little money coming in. What could we do? We couldn't feed them all, but then the fever caught them, and they died. Every day, they were taken out, thrown into the pit we had along the wall, and covered over as fast as they went in.'

Luke glanced at Pat, but Pat could no longer hold his gaze. He looked at the potatoes on his plate, but ate nothing.

'A pit?' Michael asked.

'A pit,' Sarah repeated. 'It keeps on getting longer, God knows where it's going to stop.'

Eleanor glanced at Luke. His hands were quivering. Was he thinking of Ellen Morrisroe. Or Sorcha and the old man crazy with fear.

Sarah had noticed his hands too. She remembered the last time she had seen that at the death pit in Knockanure.

'But it's getting better,' she said at last. 'At least in Knockanure, it is. Early in the year was the worst; we couldn't take in all that wanted to. But the price of corn has been dropping since then, so we're able to buy more of it, and so is everyone else. And then the Guardians started this business of sending them to America.'

'Yes,' Michael said, 'we'd heard all about that. Seen it too.'

'It was Clanowen's idea. He reckoned that with no one else paying rates, they was no point in evicting his tenants. The *Gort na Móna* people, he only had to pay for them anyhow on the rates when they reached the Workhouse. So evicting them all didn't make him any better off. Unless they died, it saved him nothing.'

'That was nothing to do with money,' Michael said. 'That was revenge. You know about his agent being shot?'

'Yes,' Sarah said, 'I'd heard of that. But that was a while back.'

'So it was,' Eleanor said, 'but we always knew that he would look for his revenge. The night of the killing they lit bonfires all across the Mountain – *Gort na Móna* and all. Dozens of them, near turned night into day. Yes, we knew he'd get his revenge, it only surprised us he took so long about it.'

'I'd never heard that,' Sarah said. She looked at Pat. 'You never told me anything of bonfires.'

'I thought the people would have told you,' Pat answered, 'or even your mother, I'm sure she knew.'

There was a silence for a few moments.

'So tell us,' Eleanor said, 'what's going to happen now.'

'It's like I told you, Clanowen will keep clearing out the Workhouse, sending them to America. By Westport, Ballina, even Sligo, it doesn't matter to him, just get rid of them.'

'It'll be a better life for them surely,' Eleanor said. 'There's more meat in America, that's for certain.'

'If they get there,' Sarah said. 'The Americans aren't letting them in, they're all going to Canada. And the stories from the ships are terrible, they die in their hundreds on the crossing, and when they get to Quebec, they die there too. Thousands of them.'

Winnie was staring at Luke. His eyes were glazed.

'I'm sorry,' Sarah said. 'I shouldn't have told you that.'

'It's as well to know,' Eleanor said.

Eleanor embraced Sarah as they left. 'Come back soon, *alanna*. Come as often as you like.'

'I will,' Sarah said. 'I promise.'

Luke helped her into the cart. 'I'll see ye all in a few years,' he said to Sarah and Pat.

See us indeed, Sarah was thinking. You'll not come back, Luke. You might think otherwise now, but you're not coming back.

Pat sat in and whisked the reins at the horse. More thin, silent people were passing by. Sarah turned and waved back at Eleanor and Michael, until the cart rounded the corner. Then she sat, watching the horse's flanks, thinking of everyone.

Winnie? Tougher than Luke? Now that she knew her better, she reckoned that Pat had been right.

Michael was a powerful man, just as she had expected. Strong in body, strong in will. But he was getting old, and a decision would have to be made, the only question was when.

What of Brigid? Decisions had already been made, and they would be followed through. She thought of the child, the open arms, the little fingers tracing lines across her face. The women's ambitions.

But Eleanor was the one who had struck her most. She had realised that all the others, even the men, looked up to Eleanor, and she could see why. Eleanor had an easy nature which masked many years of hard work and suffering, and an inner strength which gave her with the ability to bear it all.

Knockanure or Carrigard? She had told Pat that it would all depend on his mother. Now she knew the kind of woman Eleanor was. She thought again of the horror of the Workhouse. She had told Pat to wait for her. But Luke would never return.

So Pat would have to farm at Carrigard. Though he'd be a fool if he did. And damned if he didn't.

Marry him anyhow? Carrigard and the poor life of a tenant farmer's wife? Put up with the years of hunger. Pat was right. It was impossible. Yes, he could have a respectable position if he stayed working with the Union, but how many more famines would they have to face, how many more fevers? She thought of the pit. They would have to face that. Again and again and again, and for how long? Or face starving themselves. No.

Better an office in a poorhouse than a field of rotten potatoes?

A week later, Luke left Carrigard for Liverpool, Quebec and America.

He slept little the night before. He was nervous, thinking. Winnie pretended to sleep, hoping he would sleep too, but knew that he would not. She had her own fears.

'Are you still awake?' she whispered at last.

'Sorry, I just can't sleep. Can't you?'

'All those people dying going to Quebec. That frightens me.'

'I won't catch fever.'

'You'll write...'

'The minute I land in Quebec.'

'Promise me.'

'I promise. But it's you I'm thinking about. How will you get on, and me in America?'

'I'll be fine,' she said. 'I have your mother, don't I. Another few months, and we'll meet up again, and I'll have a little baby for you.'

The comment startled him. He thought of Nessa and Brigid's birth, but it was better to forget about that. Winnie was a stronger woman, it would be alright, and he knew it.

'Yes, my love,' he said. 'It won't be long now.'

At last she slept, but for a long time he lay awake, staring through the skylight at the quivering leaves of an ash tree outlined against the faint glow of the Milky Way.

They rose early next morning. It was still dark. Michael lit the rush light, as Winnie and Eleanor prepared breakfast.

'It'll be great, I know it,' Eleanor said. 'It's a fine country, from all accounts.'

'I know, Mother,' Luke said.

They sat down to a quiet breakfast. Eggs, well cured rashers and brown bread. He wondered how long it would be before he saw his mother's bread again. He put the thought out of his mind.

'You'll write as soon as you get there,' Michael said.

'Of course I will. I'll post it the moment we land.'

He finished his breakfast, and stood.

'Good luck to you now,' Michael said, grasping his arms.

'Don't worry, I'll be back.'

'I still have the right to say goodbye to my eldest son.'

Then Eleanor embraced him. 'God bless you, Luke.'

He kissed her on her forehead.

'Now ye keep yourselves well. Just look after Winnie here, and she'll look after you.'

Winnie was crying.

'Go on, Luke, go on. I don't want you seeing me like this.'

He hugged her, holding her head into his shoulder.

'I'll see you in America, *a ghrá*.'

He walked through the early dawn, all silent but for one lone dog howling on the Mountain. Images he could not forget kept haunting him. People's eyes accusing him; people he knew, people he didn't. Sorcha's eyes when he left her and her mad husband in the Workhouse, all the bewildered pain of an old woman unwanted. Ellen Morrisroe too, eyes blazing with anger and hate. Matt McGlinn, eyes watching his betrayal and the end of an old friendship. The empty eyes of men and women on the Works, not caring enough to hate him anymore. Dead frozen eyes at the old cottage in Lisnadee. The man at Lord Sligo's wall, eyes of sudden pain and shock, of blankness and death. The bodies in the pit, no eyes at all, all gnawn out.

Try to forget it. All in the past.

All an illusion?

No illusion.

What had he done to help them? What had any of them done? Built roads? Yes, they had done the impossible. Built roads with starving people. Broken stones with broken people. Put money in their pockets, but damned little. Money to feed them, but never enough to fill them. Money for clothes, but never enough against the killing snows. The Roads were built. The Kitchens were opened. Where had the money come from? Vast sums of it. The money that brought food into Westport when food was leaving. But yes, the food came. Ships lining up, waiting to feed Mayo. Corn piled in huge amounts, all along the quays and in the warehouses. Thousands of tons of food pouring in. But hundreds of thousands starving in Mayo.

The impossible done. Real ships. Real food.

But not enough.

Never enough.

All the pain, the suffering and dying. Dead bodies, dead souls. The smoke rising over Croghancoe. What had he seen there? The endless power behind the mountain. Was he mad? All an illusion? He thought of the priest and the tale of a man who came to Brockagh because he wanted to. A man who spurned comfort. A man who believed in it. Believed in what? 'Then I might see...' he had said. See what? Was it the same as he himself had sensed and feared behind Croghancoe? The power and the terror? Do I believe in it? In what?

No way to describe it. But it happened.

What happened? I don't know.

I don't believe in it anymore.

There's no way to believe now. People not able to lift a pick. Haggard faces, living skeletons. The dying screams, the stink of gangrene. The pit, the pile of half buried bodies. The rats. What kind of power did this? I did what I could though. Did I? Refusing tickets to desperate men. Bringing women to the Workhouse to die. Bringing workers to the mountains to die. Closing the Works. Closing the Kitchens. Killing a man. Guilty? Yes, guilty as charged. He was trembling. The death pit again. Rats clutching at him, dragging him in, clawing his eyes out. Stop it. Think of Winnie. Will she stick with me though? Follow me to America? She will, she promised, we both did. Till death do us part, that's what we said. Death? Why stop there? Death wins if you do. How long so? Longer than death? Much longer.

Till there's no mountains left anymore.

That's how long, Winnie.

A time beyond mountains.

Glossary of Words and Expressions

A ghrá: My love.

Alanna: Dear child or My love. From *A leanbh* (child).

Amadán: Fool.

Arra: Implies No or Don't be silly. Might be from *Aire* (care).

Boreen: A narrow road or track.

Clochán: A tiny settlement of primitive houses.

Eejit: Idiot. From the English word.

Gossoon: Boy. From *Garsún*.

Lumper: A large potato.

Molly Maguires: A 19th century Irish terrorist group, which also spread to the United States at this time.

Outshot: A bed built into an inside wall, often in the kitchen.

Poitín: An illicit spirit distilled from potatoes. Moonshine.

Rath: The remains of an ancient fort or settlement.

RIC: Royal Irish Constabulary.

Sceilp: A primitive lean-to shelter made of branches and sods.

Shebeen: A small or unlicensed bar or pub. From *Síbín*.

Sleán: A special spade for digging turf.

Spailpín: A seasonal or migrant harvest worker.

Townland: A rural sub-division of land.

Turf: In Ireland, peat dug from a peat bog for fuel.

Union: The organization for relief of poverty in a barony. Often applied to the Workhouse too.

Whisht: Silence. Be quiet.

If you enjoyed *The Killing Snows* don't miss
The Exile Breed and *Cold is the Dawn*

CPSIA information can be obtained
at www.ICGtesting.com
Printed in the USA
BVHW070901180120
569853BV00001B/34